THE SIXPENNY WINNER

Alexandra Connor was born in Oldham and still has strong connections with Lancashire. Apart from being a writer she is also a presenter on radio and television. She is a Fellow of the Royal Society of Arts.

By the same author

THE MOON IS MY WITNESS
MIDNIGHT'S SMILING
GREEN BAIZE ROAD
AN ANGEL PASSING OVER
HUNTER'S MOON

ALEXANDRA CONNOR

The Sixpenny Winner

HarperCollins*Publishers*

HarperCollins*Publishers*
77–85 Fulham Palace Road,
Hammersmith, London W6 8JB

www.fireandwater.com

Published by HarperCollins*Publishers* 2002
3 5 7 9 8 6 4 2

A catalogue record for this book
is available from the British Library

ISBN 0 00 712159 8

Set in Sabon

Printed and bound in Great Britain by
Clays Ltd, St Ives plc

This book is dedicated to all my readers.

Thanks for your loyalty; it's a pleasure to write for you.

Very grateful acknowledgements must go to the Stockport Library and *The Stockport Express* and *Advertiser*. I would also like to say a particular thank you to Michelle Kay, Collections Assistant at Hat Works, The Museum of Hatting, Stockport, without whose assistance I would never have discovered the dramatic potential of the fur former machine!

Prologue

'To hear my grandfather tell it, it were a story and a half. It were a long time ago, in the 1920s, when the Hargreaveses took over the old Royal Oak pub, down on Churchgate. It were the rough end of town – still not too hot – but then it were bordering on some of the vilest streets in Stockport.

'The pub had been renamed The Sixpenny Winner, after a local greyhound. Well, that bloody dog looked a sight – so my grandfather said – but it could run like a flaming cheetah. There's many a man who'd put the rent money on that lucky bugger, and many stood in cold, cheering it by the cinder track side. It were a local hero, that dog – so much so, that when it died it were stuffed. Not kidding, they stuffed the poor sod and gave it to the landlord of The Royal Oak, who'd apparently laid more bets than drawn straight pints. Or so my grandfather said.

'But – the dog being so lucky – the brewery decided to rename the pub and called it The Sixpenny Winner, the stuffed dog going up behind the bar. I kid you not, it's the truth. So when the Hargreaveses took over from Abe Turner, they took over The Sixpenny Winner, stuffed dog and all.

'It were a right do, my grandfather told me, but you'll have to draw your own conclusion. I'll just tell you the story and you put it into your own words. That do you? Right, then I'll begin. It all started with Ada Hargreaves . . .'

Part One

What's the use in worrying?
It never was worthwhile,
So, pack up your troubles in
   your old kit bag,
And smile, smile, smile.

George H. Powell

Chapter One

It was the most vivid memory of her childhood, Ada's father having his leg broken by the coal cart. He'd been out at work all day, as he always was – no idle Irishman – and he'd been coming home when the November fog descended. Pat Gantry knew the streets well, but it was still difficult to see, and the horse was spooked in the thick yellow smog. It was a heavy horse, an old grey shire, with feet like dinner plates, and when it came to the end of Edward Street it was just taking a breather when a boy came out of the smog, shouting.

Startled, the horse reared back, knocking Pat off his feet as he tried to hold on to its halter. Down went Pat, the fog only just allowing him a brief glimpse of the horse's back hoofs as he hit the road. Then the sound of a violent crack echoed in the smoggy night.

Only a few houses away, Ada heard it and thought that it sounded like a branch cracking. But there were no branches in Stockport, no woods; no trees in the middle of Portswood. Yet when the crack came shimmering loud on the thick air there was a long moment – a couple of heartbeats at the least – before she heard her father screaming. There had been no branch cracking, just her father's leg.

Pat Gantry walked with a limp after that, and there was no more shinning up to clean windows, or flittings, because he couldn't climb the ladders or push the barrow like he used to. He was a gimp, he said angrily, and all his good temper cracked along with his leg. They set the broken bone, but infection followed, and Pat was too bloody-minded to moan and pay the doctor another sixpence for a visit. So the leg mended slow and bent and he had to walk with a stick. Suddenly Pat Gantry was old in his forties and not going anywhere.

'You can be a hero in life, or a martyr,' Ada's mother had said darkly. 'I don't have to tell you what your father is now.'

But that wasn't fair, Ada thought, gazing out of the window at the sullen March day. He'd been a good man until the horse backed over his leg and the cart tipped up. And then the coal merchant who'd hired her father didn't hire him any longer – and said the accident was due to Pat's negligence. 'Negligence!' Pat had replied. 'I treated that bloody horse and cart better than many men treated their wives down Hillgate.'

But rage as he might, Pat was floored – not by the horse or the broken leg, but that people might think it was *his fault*. And it wasn't. It wasn't bloody fair. But then what was? Milly had been sympathetic at first, but Pat could see in her eyes what she was thinking: *He's no better than the rest, what woman can rely on an Irishman? For all his promises, we're not going to get out of Portswood now.*

Over the years that followed she repeatedly told Ada the same. Through late springs, steaming summers and hard long winters in Portswood. In the tight knot of slum streets and smells and noises. Amongst the heaving pile of people and illness and pubs – which Milly knew they would never escape.

The low, dark houses were built in squares, with a patch of ground at the rear where the earth closets were – six toilets for twenty houses and only God knew how many people. They weren't the poorest either; they had two rooms, not like the Declans who lived in the cellar next door. Two parents and four children in one dark room without heat or much light, the walls so damp in winter that you couldn't hang your clothes on them or you'd have to put them on wet the next morning. There was many a home round Portswood where the walls were hung with brown paper to soak up the wet that dribbled down from the Stockport streets and soaked up from the River Goyt nearby.

And after the freezing chill of winter, there was the smell that came in the heat of summer . . . Milly stared ahead at the earth closets, watching a man coming out and spitting on the ground. In June the earth closets were ringed with blowflies, the stench overpowering, dogs sniffing about, the doors swinging open, the closets overflowing. At night the soil men came to empty them – in the dark so no one would see what they were doing. Trouble was, sometimes there was no exit out the back and they had to carry the refuse through the houses on a board.

Pat had promised Milly something better, and he'd meant it. He'd worked like a navvy, never been drunk and put money aside religiously. They had been careful in every way, having only one child, Ada. They couldn't afford a big family, they both agreed. Better to have one child and do well by her, than have half a dozen running about with their arses hanging out of their breeches. For ten years they worked and saved and finally the Gantrys had been just inches away from moving out – when Pat had his accident.

'Stop dawdling!' Milly said, snapping at her daughter, her mouth as narrow as a buttonhole. 'Give me a hand here.'

7

Ada moved from the window, avoiding her mother's ferocious look. She would do as she said and then there wouldn't be a row. If she was very quiet, things might remain calm until her father came home. But then there would be trouble – there always was, ever since the accident. So many harsh words from her mother: sentences spat out like bitter pips.

'You can black the grate,' Milly said, passing her daughter the brush and blackening. 'Time you learned how to do it. You'll have your own home one day to look after. Might even own your own house.' She smiled bitterly as though she doubted it. 'I've blackened that grate and donkeyed those front doorsteps for years for a landlord. You see you do it for yourself, Ada, not for some rich sod who lives off the backs of the poor.'

She studied her daughter closely. Ada had inherited her dark-haired looks – well, the looks she had had *once*. Slightly too long in the face and too narrow in the body, but pretty enough to get herself out of Portswood – if she played her cards right. If she didn't fool around and give it away to the first lad who put his hand up her skirt.

'You should pull your hair back from your face more.'

Ada flushed, unused to her mother making any form of personal remark. 'I don't like to. My forehead's too big.'

'Nonsense!' Milly snapped. 'A high forehead's a sign of breeding.' She walked over to her daughter and roughly smoothed her hair back.

For a moment she felt guilty, knowing how little she had bothered with her only child over the past few years. It would serve her right if Ada turned out bad, for all the notice she took of her.

'You look after yourself, girl.'

Ada nodded obediently, surprised as her mother grasped her shoulders and looked into her face, her voice stern.

'D'you know what I'm talking about?'

'I . . . I . . .' Ada stammered, intimidated.

'I mean you don't go off with the first boy that flatters you. You keep yourself clean. There's too many sluts around here to need another adding to their number.' Milly awkwardly stroked her daughter's hair. 'You don't want this kind of life, Ada. Don't end up like me. You think I'm hard on your father, don't you? You won't admit it, but I see it in your eyes.' She paused, her hand dropping away from her daughter's hair. 'I've my reasons. Some deal with disappointment better than me. Frankly, I can't stomach it. My parents never wanted me to marry Pat Gantry; said he was a bad lot. Turns out they were right.'

'It wasn't his fault he broke his leg,' Ada said quietly, ever ready to come to her father's defence.

Exasperated, Milly turned away, viciously poking at the fire with the tip of her boot. The cheap coke sent smoke in puffs into the dingy room.

'Who cares whose fault it was – his or the horse's, or the fog's? Thing is, it happened and there's no going back. Not now. We're stuck here, your father and me, but *you* don't have to be.' She coughed, wiped her mouth with the back of her hand. Her anger came like a heat off her. 'You're fourteen now, Ada. Time to get a job. I heard there was a position going at Henessey's.'

'Henessey's?' Ada echoed, thinking of the massive hat factory on Hillgate. It was a rough area, but no worse than Portswood. But that wasn't the point. Ada had wanted to go into the mill, with her friends from school, not to some hatters, where she knew no one. 'I thought –'

'Well, you know what thought did!' Milly snapped back. 'You're not going to be some mill hand, not my girl. Henessey's want a dogsbody, if the truth be known, but you could work your way up there, learn a trade. You're not ending up in some shop or mule spinning. They're offering a wage, not much, but enough to help out.'

'Mother, I don't want –'

Milly turned to her daughter, her eyes cold. 'What you want doesn't matter. It's what *I* want for you that counts. You'll do as I say and then maybe you'll have a chance in life. Otherwise, you'll end up like all the rest. And I won't let that happen.' She paused, turned away. 'You've a good head on your shoulders, Ada. If we'd been able to afford it, I dare say you would have benefited from some more educating, but that's not possible, so I'm doing the best I can. You go and see Mr Betram at Henessey's, tell him I sent you and that you're my daughter. If he remembers the past, the job's yours.'

She stopped talking, and stared into the fire. Thomas Betram had been her first boyfriend, the lad her parents wanted her to marry. Oh, his parents hadn't wanted it at all, but Tom loved her. Trouble was, she didn't love Tom. Loved some other lad, Pat Gantry. Thought then that love was important, important enough to throw away her best chance in life. So she married the man she loved and Tom married some girl his parents had picked out for him. And if he was happy, Milly didn't know, but she knew that if she had her time over again she would marry for money. Bugger love.

'Go tomorrow, Ada,' she said at last. 'At twelve. And put on your blue dress.'

Milly had been wearing blue the evening she had met Tom. A dress as blue as her eyes had been then. Ada looked pretty in blue too, like her mother. Maybe when Tom Betram saw Ada walk through the door he might remember.

'Mum?'

Milly frowned. 'What?'

'If I don't get the job, you won't be angry, will you?'

Her mother stared into the weak fire, her voice low when she answered, 'No, I won't be angry . . . You have to understand something, Ada. I wasn't *always* angry. Circumstances changed me; *they* made me angry. Try to remember that. And try not to judge me too hard.'

Chapter Two

Down in Hillgate, on Mealhouse Brow, Clem Hargreaves was standing with his back to the kitchen door, his mother towering over him with a wooden spoon.

'I'll knock yer bloody 'ead off, you see if I don't!' she hollered, a huge woman in an old print apron. 'What the 'ell d'you mean, coming 'ome with some stupid story like that? Think I were born yesterday?'

Clem shifted his feet and wondered why it was that he was still the smallest kid in his class at the poor school. The other lads had shot up at fifteen, but not him. He was a runt, everyone said. But a happy runt. At least, usually . . .

'Hey, Mum –'

'Don't "hey Mum" me!' she shouted back, her temper dwindling, despite herself.

Her youngest was a bugger and no mistake, but he looked so damn cute with those big brown eyes and that little upturned nose. A right little elf. But he was thieving now. Oh God, not him, she thought, not like the others.

'Mum –'

'Where d'you get 'em?'

Clem looked away. He could hardly tell her that his brother had given him the slates to hide, and that they had come off the chimney of the Methodist church. Well, how could he? He'd not tell on Harry – it was more than his life was worth. Better to let his mother think it was him.

A sharp pain in his left ear made him reconsider as Evie Hargreaves yanked on Clem's lobe.

'You lie to me, you little bastard, and I'll 'ave you! Where did you get them slates?'

'I found 'em.'

'Found 'em! Aye, found 'em nailed to the bloody church roof, I'll be bound.' She jerked his ear viciously, Clem wincing. 'I thought you were different, an honest lad.'

'*Mum* –'

'Where –' she tweaked his ear again, 'did you –' and again, 'get 'em from?'

'I found 'em.'

In one movement Evie's considerable weight managed to propel her youngest son across the kitchen, his head hitting the back of the Belfast sink as he slid to the floor. At that moment he decided that his only method of defence was to play dead.

'M' head . . .' he groaned, his eyes rolling upwards in a magnificent display of semiconsciousness. 'M' 'ead . . .' Then dramatically he stopped talking, his body giving a violent shudder and then going limp.

Evie was beside him in a moment, picking him up and carrying him over to the rocking chair. Heavily she sat down and cradled her son, almost crushing the remaining life out of him in her burly arms. She was sobbing and repeating his name over and over when the door opened behind her and Harry walked in.

Her eldest son took in the scene in one glance. 'What's 'appened?'

'It were an accident. 'E'd been thieving, and I 'it 'im,' Evie sobbed, her mammoth breasts crushed against Clem's bruised ear. 'I've killed 'im! I've murdered m' own lad!' she shouted extravagantly.

Harry walked over and looked down at his brother. He could see at once that Clem was breathing, albeit with difficulty in their mother's bear hug.

'He's all right, Mum. Look, he's just taken in a breath.'

Evie looked down, then felt Clem's chest. Relief welled up in her.

'Oh, thank God! I never meant to 'urt 'im, I swear I didn't. But 'e'd been thieving the slates off the church roof.'

Behind his closed eyelids Clem waited for his brother to come to his rescue, but Harry wasn't about to own up to anything. He had had enough of Evie's clobbering over the years and was more than ready to let the youngest member of the family take a beating for him.

So instead Harry said slyly, 'D'you know what might 'elp our Clem, Mum?'

Evie's large round face was tear-streaked. 'What, lad?'

'A poultice.'

Clem heard the word and flinched. A poultice was not a treatment, it was a punishment. Round their way any bruise or injury was treated by a hot kaolin poultice, wrapped in brown paper, being tied to the affected part. The fact that it had to go on hot and remained hot for hours was considered to be the most beneficial part of the treatment. Kids turned out to school with their heads wrapped up like third-rate maharajas, the peculiar medicinal smell seething out impressively as the kaolin cooled.

'A poultice,' Evie replied, galvanised. 'Yer right, that would do the trick –'

Clem recovered in that instant and bounded out of his mother's arms like an adolescent Lazarus. As

14

Evie lurched forward to catch him, he did an eel-like manoeuvre round the table and was out the back door before she could stop him.

'The little sod!' Evie snapped, watching Clem make for the alleyway. 'And as for you,' she said, turning on her other son who was laughing behind her, and slapping him round the ear, 'that's what yer brother should 'ave 'ad.'

Fascinated, Ada paused to stare at Winter's Clock. Jacob Winter had moved up in life. From the slums in Hillgate he had strode into the town centre at Little Underbank about twenty years earlier, setting up his jewellery business in the main street. His shop was one of a row of buildings that had actually been built into the hard rock face behind. The shops were cold and they had no back doors – after all, what exit was there through solid rock? – but the real advantage was that they were said to be damn near burglar proof. Rumour even had it that originally – long before Jacob Winter came – the jewellery shop could be lowered into the basement at night for safety.

Anyway, what was certain was that Jacob Winter had done well selling jewellery and mending watches, his shop becoming a local landmark because of the clock. It was a huge, flamboyant creation, hung well above head height, its three elaborate figures coming out and striking the bells every fifteen minutes.

It had been a staple of Ada's childhood, that shop. Not that her family could ever afford to buy anything from Winter's, but her mother used to take her to look at the clock. Or Milly would suddenly stop sometimes when they were out and say: 'Hear that? That's Winter's Clock. Time's getting on.'

15

The only jewellers that Ada ever saw the inside of was the pawnbrokers up in Portswood or Hillgate, but sometimes she used to hear Winter's Clock chime and let herself dream a bit. Perhaps one day she'd be lucky enough to have her wedding band bought from there – a gold band, not like the brass ones they sold in the slums, the ones that turned your finger green after a while.

Ada breathed in and let the sound of the chimes overwhelm her. She would have to hurry now to get to Henessey's for noon. She shouldn't have dawdled; her mother would be furious if she was late.

Ada's blue dress was not really warm enough for a cold March morning, her cheap coat – a hand-me-down from her mother – patched at the elbows. As for her hat, it was out of shape, a felt thing that had long since seen better days. Ada had considered taking it off, but she was too afraid of her mother to risk being seen without it. So she hurried on, the cheap elastic cutting into the skin under her chin, her hands raw with cold.

At the gates of Henessey's she stopped, staring at the huge double entrance door and the imposing brass lettering over it: 'HENESSEY'S – HATTERS'. It seemed a forbidding place to her and she felt suddenly intimidated, uncertain of how to continue.

Then, out of the blue, someone knocked into her, almost throwing her off balance. She turned, startled, to see a straggly youth panting for breath.

'Aye, sorry, miss!' he said, looking round hurriedly.

'You nearly knocked me off my feet!' Ada replied, straightening her hat. 'You want to watch where you're going.'

He pulled a face. 'I were looking behind me, not in front,' he grinned. 'You work 'ere?'

Ada hesitated. 'Might do.'

'*Might do?*' he echoed. 'What's that mean? You're either working 'ere, or not.'

'I'm coming about a job.'

'Wot kind of job?'

'You're cheeky,' Ada replied, secretly rather taking to the boy she took to be a lot younger than herself. 'What's it got to do with you?'

'I work 'ere, that's wot it's got to do with me,' he replied confidently, 'in the factory.' He looked her up and down, making Ada blush. 'What kind of job would you be looking for?'

'I have an appointment to see Mr Betram –'

'*An appointment!*' he repeated mockingly. 'You must be very important.' He bowed in mock deference. 'Well, after you, milady.'

Embarrassed, but all too aware of the clock striking twelve, Ada walked up to the entrance, the youth trailing her footsteps. She felt very small with the building towering over her, and for a moment she was glad that she wasn't alone. At the door, Ada paused and looked at the bell. Tentatively she pushed it.

'Aye, you don't want to do that; you want to give it a right good pushing,' the boy said cheerily, pummelling the bell, the sound of it humming through the door to where they stood outside.

Ada flushed. 'What a noise!'

'The porter's deaf,' Clem replied, pleased to show his superior intelligence. 'If you don't ring fit to wake the dead, he'll never know you're there.'

The door swung open a moment later. A stout old man in a black suit stared critically at Ada.

To her amazement, the youth stepped in front of her and said: ''Lo there, Gimmons. This lady's come to see Mr Betram.'

The old man gave the lad a sour look. 'Name?'

'You know me – Clem Hargreaves.'

'I meant the young lady – what's *her* name?' the porter intoned.

Clem glanced over to Ada and jerked his head to encourage her to answer.

'My name's Ada Gantry. I've come to see Mr Betram at twelve o'clock.'

There was no response from the porter, Clem interjecting again: 'You hear her? She's got an appointment. To see Mr Betram.'

'Follow me,' the old man said. As Ada walked in, Mr Gimmons' arm came down fast to block Clem's progress. 'As for you, lad, get round the back. This isn't your entrance.'

Thomas Betram was sitting at his office desk trying to mend the handle of his middle drawer. He had tried several times to catch the screw thread, but every time he wound it on, it either slid off or jammed, the handle hanging off at a rakish angle. Small things like that irritated him much more than the big things in life. Well, why not? You could change the small things, the big things you were stuck with.

He looked up as Ada was shown in, his face white as alabaster, his eyes coolly green. He was, Ada thought at first sight, rather like a statue in the park. Yet his expression altered when he looked at her, some of his chill falling off, an unexpected warmth coming with his smile.

'Miss Gantry? Sit down, please.'

Ada did as she was bid. Nervously she crossed her chilled hands on her lap, deftly covering a darned patch.

So this was Milly's daughter, Tom thought. My God, she was like her too. Like she was at fourteen, anyway.

Not like the woman she was now. Tom glanced at the cheap blue dress and his stomach fluttered with a memory . . . a girl standing under Winter's Clock in a blue summer dress, turning as he called her name.

Oh God, Tom thought, it was all so long ago. He should have pursued Milly more, *made* her marry him, but he'd married Dottie instead – pleased everyone, except himself. And now – twenty-two years later – he was looking at Milly's daughter. And remembering.

'We've got a job here that you could do, I'm sure.'

Ada wondered how he knew that, as he didn't know her. But obviously he knew her mother. Not that she would have dared to ask Milly for any information on that matter.

'I'd do my best.'

'Don't you want to know what the job is?'

No, Ada wanted to say, no, I'm not interested. I just do what I'm told, to keep the peace and stop the arguments. Tell me to jump off the roof and no doubt I'd do it, Mr Betram.

'It's a job as a trimmer.'

All the time Tom was talking he was remembering the past. How Milly had chosen Pat Gantry over him – Pat Gantry, an immigrant Irishman with whom she fell in love. Understandably, in a way; Pat Gantry was a big, handsome man, but although he'd kept out of trouble and worked hard he'd never quite managed to pull his family out of Portswood. And there was no chance after the accident . . . Tom had heard about it, of course, had wanted to offer some support then, but how could he? He had a wife; it would look suspicious, and besides, Milly had long ago ceased to be the girl he had loved. She was slope-shouldered now, thin, almost terrifying in her bitterness, a hard

19

woman hurrying through the streets without a word for anyone.

And yet there was something of the girl in the blue dress left. Once Tom had seen her crossing at Underbank, heading for the station. It had been summer and for one infinitesimal instant the sun had shone on Milly Gantry and bleached out the lines and shadows of her face. She had turned at the sound of the tram's hooter and he had recognised her – seeing her for one instant through the tram's window before it moved on. He carried the image in his heart as another man would carry a photograph.

But he hadn't seen her since – until the previous Thursday, when he had left work. As he had locked the gates of Henessey's he had felt a touch on his arm and turned, startled, seeing her under the streetlight. Older now, sad.

'Milly?'

'Aye, Milly,' she had said, her voice brusque. 'Hard to recognise now, hey?'

'Milly,' Tom had repeated gently, 'come back inside.'

'Nah, I'm fine here.' She had wrapped her thick felt coat around her tightly, a shawl over her head. 'I won't beat about the bush, Tom Betram. You and I meant something to one another once. I'm sure I'm right there –'

'Milly, come inside.'

She had shaken her head. 'Nah, you and me inhabit different worlds, Tom. I'm better where I belong. I want to ask you a favour, though.'

'Anything.'

'Not for myself, for my girl. I've a daughter, Tom, called Ada. Fourteen now and bound for the mill unless I do something about it. You know about Pat, I suppose?

Sure you do, everyone does.' She'd glanced down the street as though checking that they weren't overheard. 'He did his best, but it weren't that good in the end. Still, I chose him so I'll stick with him. But Ada deserves something better than Portswood. She's bright – not school clever, but quick-brained, and not bad to look at either.'

'Milly . . .' Tom had said, reaching out to her.

But she had ducked back at once and the light of the streetlamp falling onto her face had aged her meanly.

'No time for sentiment, Tom. All I want to know is this – can you help her? As a favour to me, remembering what was between us.'

He had been torn between two emotions: shock, at how Milly had changed, and pity, knowing how much it would have cost her to ask for help. He had been cushioned by a comfortable income and an undemanding wife, and still looked young. By comparison, Milly had been worn thin with disappointment.

He had known at once that he would have done anything to help her.

'What d'you want me to do?'

'You're powerful. Give Ada a job at Henessey's. Give her a chance to get on. I don't want her in the mill, or in some shop. Give her a chance to learn.'

'That's not much to ask, a job at a hat factory.'

Milly had smiled wryly. 'It might not be a lot for you, Tom Betram, but it's a chance for her to learn a trade, to move up. It would be a way out for my girl. You offered *me* a way out once, didn't you?' She'd looked him full in the eyes, unexpectedly tender. 'But I were too big a fool to take it. I'm truly sorry if I hurt you, Tom, but I hope you'll take some consolation in knowing that I hurt myself more.'

He remembered the exchange all too vividly as he looked back to Milly's daughter. Tom had had no children; this was the nearest he was ever going to get to seeing how a child of his might have looked. This was the nearest he was ever going to get to help.

'As I said, Ada, you can have a job trimming the hats with the other women. Start Monday, usual starter's wage. The ladies will tell you all about it when you come. They're a good bunch, a bit raucous, but they'll look after you.' Tom stood up, Ada taking her cue and rising also. 'I'll see you on Monday then, at eight. Be on time.'

Walking out of Henessey's Ada paused on the steps and blinked in the sunlight. That was a surprise – it had been so cold when she had arrived. Perhaps it was a good omen. The sound of laughter overhead made her look up. On the first floor a window was slightly open, the sound of women talking coming loud on to the still air.

Apprehension welled up in Ada. She had always been quiet, reserved, with few friends at school. The idea of suddenly being jolted into the company of – what had Mr Betram called them? *raucous* women – was alarming. What would they think of her? Would they like her? Or think she was some stupid girl? Would they act like her mother, be critical? Bitter?

Reminded of her mother, Ada moved to the gates. Milly would be pleased. The news of her job might even prevent an argument that night when her father came home . . . Ada was so buoyed up by the thought that she was startled when someone tapped her on the shoulder.

'How d'you get on?' Clem asked, his head on one side.

She was unexpectedly pleased to see him and ready to share the good news. 'I'm going to start as a trimmer on Monday.'

He whistled, dark brown eyes mischievous. 'A trimmer? Wow!'

Flushing, she turned away.

'Hey, I wasn't knocking it!' Clem said hurriedly, dropping into step with her. 'I work in the main factory – at the fur former machine.'

Frowning, Ada stopped and looked at him. 'The *what*?'

'The fur former machine,' Clem repeated. 'Henessey's make fur felt hats and each hat has to have its own amount of rabbit fur weighed out before it goes into the machine. I work high up, on top of some steps, where I weigh the fur out and then drop it into the machine.' He made animated movements with his hands to demonstrate the process. 'The fur goes into this machine with some water and then it's swept along a conveyor belt towards a drum. You should see it.'

Ada's eyes had widened. 'It sounds terrifying.'

'Oh nah, it's easy. But they rely on me. That's the only good thing about being small: I can shinny up those steps and get around better than the bigger men.' Clem was luminous with pride. 'They couldn't do without me.'

'I can imagine,' Ada teased him, starting to walk again.

On cue, Clem walked with her, eager to have more of her company. 'Where d'you live?'

'Portswood,' Ada said quietly.

'Hillgate, me. Mealhouse Brow.'

Another slum, Ada thought, comforted.

'You got brothers and sisters?' Clem queried, his

hands deep in his darned pockets, his feet shuffling in overlarge clogs.

'No, just Mum and Dad.'

He whistled again. 'I've got four brothers. No dad, though. He upped and left m' Mam years ago, just after I were born. Said it were one too many. My Mam called me that for years – "One Too Many, come here!" She'd go to the gate and call us boys home.' Clem stopped and cupped his hands around his mouth calling: '"Harry, Arthur, Sid, Gordon and One Too Many!"' He laughed. 'Everyone thought it were m' real name for years.'

Ada stared at him, mesmerised. 'Didn't you mind?'

'Nah, I like One Too Many better than m' real name.'

'Clem, isn't it?' said Ada, remembering.

He nodded, pulling a face.

They had reached the end of the street, the sun going behind a cloud, Winter's Clock chiming out twelve thirty. She would have to get home, Ada thought, or her mother would be out looking for her and she didn't want that. She didn't want to be seen talking to Clem Hargreaves because she knew instinctively that her mother wouldn't approve and she didn't want the moment spoiling. Ada had had her first taste of freedom and was about to keep her first secret.

'It's twelve thirty,' Clem said, his head on one side as the chimes of the clock died away. 'See you Monday, eight sharp?'

'Yes,' Ada agreed happily. 'See you Monday. Eight sharp.'

Chapter Three

Within months Ada and Clem Hargreaves had become friends. Ada worked at her job at Henessey's, doing the trimmings and learning her trade, and Clem continued to work on the fur former machine in the main factory. They got on well together, Ada glad of a male friend, Clem happy with her company. She was good fun, he had realised after a while. Could be funny, and cheeky.

He liked that. And she had liked the fact that before too long the runt kid had grown six inches and expanded into a muscular young seventeen-year-old. Ada had noticed that, just as Clem had noticed that the previously whey-faced girl had become glossy and full-lipped, someone who attracted the interest of the other men in the factory.

Gradually, their friendship had altered. It was very slow, and very careful, like a continent shifts over aeons. Then one day Clem Hargreaves kissed Ada Gantry and she fell in love with him. And he with her.

It was the first time Ada had fallen in love. The women in the factory teased her, Ada blushing and hiding away whenever Clem's name was mentioned. She was so glad not to be working in the mill now, and no longer missed her old friends. After all, if she hadn't come to Henessey's she would never have met Clem. Oh God, Ada thought, what would she have missed?

Not much, some of the older women thought. Sal Fergus declared that she had never seen 'two kids so stuck on each other'. And Sal should know – hadn't she been married three times herself?

One hot morning in May, Sal paused with a hat band in her hand, a man's trilby in the other. Her sallow face was flushed with the heat, spring smouldering that year.

'She's eighteen tomorrow.'

A tiny, wizened woman next to her looked up: 'Who is?'

'Ada is. Oh, do bloody listen, Winifrid,' Sal replied patiently, starting to fix the hat band to the trilby. 'Eighteen year old. Gawd, I can't remember what I were like at her age.'

'Courting Phil Spencer,' Pearl Doyle called down the trestle table where they all worked. 'You were mad about him. And what a toerag 'e turned out.'

''E were hot in bed, though,' Sal replied, wiping the sweat off her forehead with the back of her hand. 'So good 'e had to keep running off to let others have a go!' She laughed, stared at the hat band and then twirled it round on the top of her index finger. 'Oh, 'e were a bad one, were Phil, but it's the bad ones you remember.'

The heat was building up in the workroom, the sun coming in through the high windows and baking the women underneath. You could never win at Henessey's: in the winter the windows made it cold; in the summer they let in too much heat. There were forty women in the workroom, ten to each table, a fat supervisor – Milton Clough – walking round to see that they kept working. He liked his job, did Milton, a woman hater since his wife had left him nearly fifteen years earlier.

'Hey, Sal,' he said sharply, 'stop playing about and get on with it. We've a shipment to make.'

26

'Oh, hush up!' she snapped back good-naturedly. 'Since when haven't we delivered on time?'

'Since that fiasco last summer,' he replied tartly, looking down the table. 'Where's Ada?'

'On a break,' Winifrid piped up shrilly. 'Call of nature.'

'If that call of nature happens to go anywhere near the factory, I'll have to give her a warning,' Milton said sourly, knowing only too well that Ada and Clem Hargreaves were seeing each other. It was absurd, he thought, a couple of kids like that; it was bound to end badly.

'Oh, leave 'em alone,' Sal replied, putting two pins between her lips as she tacked the hat band onto the trilby. 'You must have been young once. If you can think back that far.'

Laughing loudly, Pearl winked at Milton, knowing full well that embarrassment would make him move away. And it did.

Watching him walk off, Pearl leaned over to Sal. 'D'you think they're . . . you know?'

'What?' Sal asked, pins still in her mouth.

'You know.'

Sighing, she pinned the hat band on and turned to Pearl. 'What the 'ell are you talking about?'

'Ada and Clem, d'you think they're . . .'

'Fooling around?'

Pearl flushed. 'Well, you've no need to be so blunt!'

'It were what you were asking, weren't it?'

Sitting opposite the two women, Winifrid leaned across the table. Her heavily lined face was narrow, her nose pinched. At fifty, she looked all her years and ten more.

'She should be careful. There's many a girl got herself

in trouble and that Clem Hargreaves comes from a rum family.'

'I like Evie Hargreaves,' Sal said firmly, scrutinising the hat in her hands. 'She had a hard time bringing up five boys since her husband left her. Did a good job, I reckon.'

'Apart from the fact that they're all thieves,' Winifrid said delightedly.

'Oh, come on,' Sal replied, 'they can be a bit wild, but they're not bad lads. There's a lot worse round these parts.'

Pearl looked away and kept silent. Her only son had not been seen for several years in Stockport, rumour being that he was in prison down South. Not that Pearl would ever admit it.

'Shot up, though, didn't he?'

'Eh?' Pearl said, baffled as she glanced over to Winifrid.

'Clem Hargreaves. He were a right little runt, but now he must have grown half a foot and filled out nicely.'

'That's what love does for you,' Sal said, smacking her lips. 'I reckon Clem Hargreaves'll be seven foot by Christmas if they go on like this.'

But though the romance was common knowledge in the factory, Milly knew nothing about her daughter's admirer. She had been pleased that Milly had gone to work at Henessey's but had expected nothing less, knowing that Tom would grant her the only favour she had ever asked of him. Oh yes, Milly decided, if Ada played her cards right she might well work her way up. There was more to do at Henessey's than trim hats. They had offices there, and Ada might just land herself an office job.

Now that *would* be something: her daughter an office worker. Turning away from the stove that hot May morning, Milly cut the heads off some wilting celery and pushed the stalks into a jam jar. Not even a bloody bowl to put it in. Not one cup and saucer that matched, every plate chipped. But what else could she do, Milly thought bitterly. There was no money for pots, not a penny left over when the rent was paid. Thank God Ada was working. They'd have been hard put to manage on Pat's wage.

Milly had wanted to get a job herself, but Pat wouldn't hear about it. He was a proud man and his wife wasn't going to go out to work, he said. Even lame, he'd manage to bring in a wage . . . Well, he did, but it was precious little, and although neither he nor Ada knew, Milly went out cleaning three afternoons a week. The money she made she saved, hiding it in a pot at the back of the chimney. If Pat ever wondered how his meagre earnings managed to put food on the table every day, he never asked and Milly never told him.

As for Ada, she seemed a different girl since she'd gone out to work – lively, not like the timid little ghost who'd always crept around the house before. She was taking a lot of care over her appearance too, Milly thought. That was smart of her; the bosses always noticed a worker who was well turned out. It would set her apart from the others. Oh yes, Milly reckoned, before long her daughter might be leaving the workroom and heading for the offices of Henessey's.

And when she got there things would change. It was a pity that her address was Portswood, but a good worker could rise above her background. In time . . . Milly set out the plates on the scrubbed table, having jammed a piece of paper under the wobbly leg . . . if she was clever, Ada would never end up like this. She could marry a clerk, someone respectable, move away from Portswood and maybe – Milly stopped short. No point thinking too far ahead. She had done well to get Ada into Henessey's and away from the rough girls at the mill, away from their influence. Now she just had to take it step by step, Milly told herself, just one thing at a time.

She had a dream for her daughter and she was determined to see it become reality. There was to be no reckless behaviour, no bad marriage for Ada, no slum future for her child. Ada would have what her mother had thrown away.

Milly would let nothing prevent it.

That summer scorched the little plots of earth around Portswood, the outside toilets fetid by the end of June. In what shade there was, the dogs panted, kids too hot to run around with hoops, or even make mischief in the slum streets. At night the heat hardly faded, arguments flaring up in such confined quarters, shouting heard well into the night.

At the nearest pub, The Royal Oak, the brewery announced that they were changing its name to The Sixpenny Winner – after a local dog, a dog to which Clem Hargreaves's father had been very attached. Not once had Ivor Hargreaves put the rent money on the greyhound, not twice, but too many times to remember. It got so he used to brag that the bloody dog were better than any bank in Stockport. Then The Sixpenny Winner had retired and, soon after, Ivor had upped and left. Not that the two things were connected . . . Pat Gantry remembered the venal-looking Ivor Hargreaves and then hurriedly continued his story, Ada listening.

The Sixpenny Winner were the nearest bloody thing to a hero in these parts, Pat said drily. It were a fine dog, though, he told Ada. They had even had it stuffed and put behind the bar for everyone to see when they came in for a pint.

'A stuffed dog?' she said, aghast. 'That's horrible!'

'It's not,' Pat replied, his voice still softly Irish. 'Was a good dog, so it was. Won many a man money round here. I heard that animal saved quite a few from being turned out of their homes.'

Ada frowned. 'How?'

'By winning its race. They put money on it to win, and when it did, then they could pay the rent.'

'But what if it had lost?'

Her father tapped the side of his nose. 'But that's the point. The Sixpenny Winner never lost. That's why they're calling the pub after it. Like a monument –'

'To betting,' Milly said sourly, overhearing the last of their conversation. 'Who in their right mind would want a dead dog behind a bar?'

'People come to look at it –'

She cut him off. 'People go to drink. And if you think otherwise, you're more stupid than I thought.'

Ada glanced down at her hands. Nothing had changed at home, and even when there were moments of peace her mother would come in and stir up all the old bitterness like silt at the bottom of a sour pond. It was impossible for Ada to imagine that her parents had once loved each other. But she knew they had. Her mother had told her so once. In one of her few unguarded moments Milly had confided that Pat Gantry had been handsome and funny, and easy to love.

So where did all that love go? Ada wondered, glancing over to her mother, stiff with fatigue and failure. Beside her, her father was silent, crushed into stillness, his twisted leg stretched out in front of him. Ada knew that it hurt him and yet he never complained. Maybe he daren't. After all, Milly would have little sympathy with the injury that had kept them slum fodder. But Ada would see him sometimes surreptitiously rubbing his leg when he thought no one was looking, or pause on his stick before taking another step. She didn't want to hurt his pride by asking him if she could help, and many times Ada had wondered why her mother hadn't nursed him better. Why couldn't *she* rub his leg? Show some tenderness?

Ada couldn't imagine how all that love had vanished, yet she could never remember a time when her parents had been close. Year after year they had grown steadily further apart. They still slept together, but Ada had never seen them touch since that fateful evening.

Her thoughts shifted suddenly to Clem and she smiled, putting her head down quickly to avoid giving herself away. Ada knew that if her mother found out she would be enraged. How *could* her daughter be fond of Clem Hargreaves, she would say. A roughneck from Hillgate. Another slum kid, with slum brothers and a stout, coarse mother.

She would hate Clem, Ada knew. She would insist that Ada stopped seeing him, might even make her leave Henessey's.

'What's up?'

Ada's head lifted. 'What?'

'Don't *what* me!' her mother snapped. 'What's the matter with you, mooning about with a sick look on your face? You're not coming down with something, are you?' She crossed the kitchen and slapped her hand on Ada's forehead. 'You're hot.'

'It's a hot night.'

Milly frowned. 'Get to bed and get some sleep. You

have to be at work tomorrow, Ada. Someone has to bring regular money in.'

Up in the cramped bedroom, partitioned off from her parents' space, Ada lay down on the bed and stared at the ceiling. Outside she could hear someone whistling and a boy calling for a girl. 'Lilly, Lilly,' he called, someone else yelling out of a window, 'Get home, and stop yer yowling.' Smells of stale food and human waste sifted under the blind of Ada's room, her hand waving the stench away from her face. If the weather would just break, if it would only rain . . .

Downstairs she could hear her mother finish washing up and then go to the door.

'I'm off out,' she said suddenly. 'I need a break from this place.'

Surprised, Ada heard the door close behind Milly and then, only moments later, there was a knock on the partition wall.

'Are you asleep?'

She sat up in bed. 'No, Dad. Come in.'

He walked in, settled himself down at the end of her bed, his leg awkwardly stretched in front of him, his stick by his side. He was sweating, his face shiny, his neck flushed from the heat and the effort of climbing the stairs.

'Bloody hot.'

Ada nodded. The light was fading, but it wasn't dark. Outside there was a sudden cat fight, then silence.

'They say it'll break come the weekend.'

'Leave off about the weather,' her father said gently. 'Yer mother's out, so we can have a little chat.'

''Bout what, Dad?'

He looked at her, one side of his face in darkness, the other lit by the half-light from the window.

'You keen on someone, Ada?'

She flushed, looked down. 'Dad . . .'

He took her hand. 'Aye, it's all right with me, love, but yer mother's another matter. Well, who is he?'

'He's called Clem.'

'Clem what?'

'Clem Hargreaves.'

Pat thought of the only Hargreaveses he knew – from Hillgate, a slum family, like they were. Only worse, Evie Hargreaves was rough – had had to be. Pat knew he shouldn't criticise the woman – she had had to cope as best she could – but her sons were street kids: no father around, all of them running wild at some time or other, the talk of Hillgate.

Oh, Ada, he thought, not *that* family.

'The Hargreaveses from Hillgate?'

She bit her lip. 'Clem's nice, Dad, really nice. He works hard, has a proper job and all. He works the fur former machine at Henessey's – they couldn't do without him.'

Pat stared at his only daughter, watching her face, her eyes bright in the dim light. He knew that look; he'd had that look himself. He had seen that look on another girl's face once, a girl so like this one. Milly. When she had loved him.

Pat's eyes closed and he looked down. Ada put her arm around his shoulder.

'Oh, Dad, you're not cross with me, are you? I haven't done anything wrong.'

He tapped the back of her hand, struggling for words. He wanted to say, don't do it. It's like a repeat performance of my life, only that time I were the poor one and your mother was better off. She chose me and look what happened – what might happen to you, Ada, if you choose Clem Hargreaves. He swallowed, almost painfully. But if she loved him, if she loved him as he had loved Milly . . . Oh God, Pat thought, what a bloody mess.

'Dad, talk to me, please. Don't shut me out. I can't bear that.'

He turned and gently stroked her cheek. 'Ada, I'm not cross. Is it serious?'

'We care about each other.'

'How long's it been going on?'

Ada paused. 'We were friends for a long time, but we fell in love about six month ago.'

'But yer only a baby.'

She laughed softly. 'I'm eighteen, Dad.'

'That's no age.'

'You married Mum at eighteen.'

'That were different.'

'Why?'

'We ran away,' Pat replied, quickly turning to his daughter. 'And who's talking about marriage?'

'I'm not.'

'Thank God for that,' Pat said softly. 'Don't do anything hasty, luv. First love's always real powerful.'

'But I really care about Clem, Dad.'

'I dare say you do, but be careful,' he counselled her. 'Wait and see how you feel after a while. Wait –'

'For what?'

He clutched her hand. 'Ada, have I ever asked you to do anything for me?'

She shook her head. He never had put any burden on her, never asked for any favour before.

'Well, I ask this. Wait and see how you feel about this young man after another year's passed. Then we'll talk again.' He squeezed her hand. 'You might not feel the same by that time. You might have met someone else. People fall out of love, you know.'

'I won't, Dad,' Ada assured him. She wanted to rage against the twelve-month sentence, but couldn't deny her father the one thing he had ever asked of her. 'Why do you want us to wait?'

'Because if it's real, it'll last,' Pat replied gently. 'You know yer mother can't find out about this, Ada, or she'll stop it. If I agree to keep this a secret, you must promise to stand by what I asked. Will you do that?'

She nodded, then laid her head on his shoulder. He smelled of cheap soap and sweat. The smell of the slums.

'Do yer job well, Ada, learn what you can. Don't go giving up a chance you might live to regret later.' They both knew to what he was referring. 'If you've a hope of getting on at Henessey's, take it. If this Clem's anything about him, he'll try to get on himself. You don't want someone who'll hold you back, make you ashamed.'

Ada could feel her eyes fill for her father's humiliation. He was talking about himself, about what his wife thought of him.

'Don't get carried away with the romance of it,' Pat said, his voice falling to a whisper. 'It doesn't last. I wish it did, I wish I could tell you that the world was otherwise, but it isn't. You have to be sensible, Ada, if you want to succeed, if you want to get out of Portswood. And you do, don't you?'

Her face was still buried against his shoulder.

'Ada, I'll not be angry if you say yes. I wanted to get out, I wanted to get you and yer mother out, but it wasn't to be, not for us. But you could get out – leave the slums, leave this noise and smell.' As he paused, the sounds from outside came in to them, clear and foul.

'Have yer own home, yer own front door key. Don't settle for scrimping and saving, because love fades and bitterness is all that's left – and that's cold comfort.'

'Dad, don't –'

'You think yer mother's hard, don't you?'

Ada nodded.

'Well, she is,' Pat agreed, 'but she weren't always. Once she were sweet and funny, and such good company. You can't imagine it, Ada, but she were. When she were young. When she loved me . . . Now look at her. I do. Every day I look at her and know that I did wrong –'

'*You* did nothing wrong!' Ada said heatedly.

'Oh, yes I did,' Pat countered, his voice hard. 'I should have made her marry Thomas Betram, because then she would have been happier. But I wanted to prove something, show that I could come out on top, that I could triumph over my betters. Pride made me force yer mother's hand, not love. *Pride*. And that's why I stay with her, and take whatever she throws at me. Because I did a wicked thing once, and I'm going to pay for it for the rest of my life.'

He rose to his feet, then touched Ada on the cheek with his hand.

'You and your romance are our secret. But I don't want you fooling around and bringing shame to this doorstep.'

'Dad, you know I wouldn't do that!' Ada said firmly.

'Well, see you don't,' Pat replied. 'Don't get carried away, don't let yer heart rule yer head. Or you have a lifetime to regret it.'

Chapter Four

At the beginning of July Ada was called in to see Tom Betram. She was nervous at first, wondering if her work had not been up to standard, although she knew full well that she was the best worker on her table. The other women acknowledged that too, teased her about wanting to put them out of business, Sal merciless.

'Yer after our jobs, Ada, I know that. Yer want to put us to shame.' She winked at old Winifrid across the table. 'These youngsters, they've no heart. Their hands are more nimble than our old fingers.'

Ada was mortified. The women had been good to her over the past four years, treating her in a motherly fashion; something she was unused to at home. Aware of Milly Gantry's stern reputation, Sal had gone out of her way to cosset Ada, feeling real satisfaction as the girl gradually came out of her shell. And when Clem started courting Ada she was delighted – and well aware that the romance must be kept a secret – as all the women were. Milly Gantry was not a woman to be trifled with, and Ada had made it clear that her mother wanted something more than a factory worker for her only child.

'Oh yes,' Sal went on, 'given time I dare say Ada will take over Henessey's and then us old ones will all be out of a job.'

Ada put down the feathers she was holding and turned to Sal. 'I never meant to –'

'I were teasing you,' Sal replied, her broad face smiling. 'Yer a good girl, Ada, and a good worker. I dare say Tom Betram has something special in mind for you.'

Pearl sniggered coarsely, Sal raising her eyebrows.

'I don't mean that!' she snapped. 'I mean a new job. Promotion even.'

'My mother would like that.'

'What about you?' Sal asked, wiping her shiny forehead with the back of her hand.

The hot weather was lasting, rain showers only seeming to intensify the heat. Inside the crowded workshop the temperature was topping ninety, the women loosening their collars and rolling up their sleeves.

'I'd like it too, I suppose.'

'Just *suppose*?' Sal countered, staring hard at a hat she had just finished. 'You should know yer own mind better now.'

'It would make my mother proud –'

'There you go again,' Sal interrupted her. '"My mother, my mother" – what about you? Would *you* be happy?'

'Well, *I'd* be happy if you lot stopped talking and got on with some work,' Milton Clough said shortly, his fat body sticky in the heat, his jowls fire red. 'That's all you do all day, talk, bloody talk.'

'We can work and talk!' Winifrid said snappily. 'It keeps our spirits up.'

'Then why don't you talk about something important?' he replied, his collar cutting into his fat neck. 'Some say there's a war coming.'

'Oh, they've said that before,' Pearl replied dismissively, 'and been wrong before.'

Winifrid's wizened face took on a mean look. 'If there were a war, Mr Clough, you'd be called up.'

He flushed at the thought. 'Me?'

'Why not? They could get you to fall on the enemy. Wipe out the bloody Germans in one fell swoop.'

Smarting, Milton walked off, the women laughing.

Still curious, Sal resumed her line of questioning to Ada. 'So, yer off to see Mr Betram, are yer?'

Ada nodded, glancing at the huge round clock at the end of the workroom.

'At eleven thirty. Only a few minutes to go.' She wondered why she hadn't told her mother she had been summoned.

'Well, yer look nice enough,' Sal replied. 'Go on, get yerself off now. Don't be late.'

Having checked her reflection in the chipped mirror of the washroom, Ada walked across the courtyard of Henessey's. She could hear the men working and talking, the machines clattering, a shimmying heat haze coming off the cobbles. God, it was hot. She felt uncomfortable in her summer dress and boots, longed to take them off and her stockings with them. Even her hair felt hot against her neck as she moved into the reception of the factory.

Old Mr Gimmons let her in, the cool of the reception area as welcome as snow. A few moments later Ada was shown into Tom Betram's office. He was still the cold statue she remembered from their first meeting, but his pleasure on seeing her thawed him instantly.

'Oh, Ada, good to see you. Please, sit down.'

He had seen Ada's comings and goings over the last four years and had had her progress reported back to him regularly. Tom had even hoped that Milly might visit him to talk about her daughter, but she never did. And Tom never really expected her to. Smiling, he studied the young woman sitting in front of him. Well, she'd certainly shed her pinched look, Tom thought; grown up full-lipped and large-eyed, pretty as her mother had once been.

'I was wondering if you would like a change,' Tom began.

He knew about Ada's good work, the care she took with the trimmings. She was clever, dextrous, mastering the work within six months of starting at Henessey's. He'd wondered from time to time if she would come to see him and ask for promotion, but she never did. She seemed content, happy with the other workers, Tom thought. Maybe, if she was left to her own devices, Ada might well stay in the trimmings shed for the rest of her working life.

But Tom didn't want to see that. He wanted to promote her – some fancy he had that he would like her to achieve more from life. After all, if Ada had been his own child, he would have urged her to get on. *If* she had been his child . . .

'There's a vacancy in my office, Ada, a clerical job: filing, addressing envelopes, running errands. Nothing too fancy, but if you worked well no doubt we would think of training you on, perhaps as an accountant here. All in the fullness of time, of course.'

Ada stared at him. *An accountant* . . . God, what would her mother say to that? It was more than even Milly could have hoped. But what do I feel? Ada asked herself. What do I want to do?

'But I haven't ever worked with figures –'

'You were good at Maths at school. I read your old reports,' Tom went on, anxious for her to agree. 'And you're wasted in trimmings. That's for the ordinary women, Ada, not someone like you.'

'Like me?' she countered, remembering what her father had told her and yet, for some reason, pushing

41

the matter. 'What's so different about me?'

Didn't Ada know about the past? Tom had expected Milly to have confided in her daughter. But then again, maybe it was better to pretend. 'You're clever, you learn fast. I like to give promising youngsters an opportunity to shine. I'm one of those people who believe that a woman should have the same chances at work as a man. We all believe that at Henessey's.' He paused, trying to judge her reaction. 'So, what d'you say, Ada? Give the job a try and then, if you like it and we like you, you can take it on permanently. The money's better. Quite a lot better, in fact.'

Ada was tempted by the idea of more money. Pat hardly got any work now, and things were tighter than ever. If she brought home more cash her mother could use that money well, perhaps even cut back on the cleaning job she went to every afternoon. The one that she thought Ada didn't know about.

'There's one thing that worries me, Mr Betram,' Ada said tentatively, fully aware that she had to state her case.

'Yes?'

'What if it doesn't work out? I mean, I don't want to find myself out of a job, sir. I don't mean to sound ungrateful, but I need to work.'

He smiled, the winter face softening. 'If it doesn't work out then you can go back to the trimmings shed. You won't end up without a job, Ada, don't worry about that.'

She hesitated for one moment longer, then smiled. 'I'd like to try it, please.'

Relieved, Tom stood up and offered his hand. Unsure of what to do, Ada put forward her own and felt him clasp it firmly.

'I'm glad, Ada, really glad.' He tried to make the next words sound casual. 'Oh, and say hello to your mother for me, will you? Give her my best.'

Pat was finding walking even more difficult lately. He would move a few steps, then pause and lean against the nearest wall, or door frame. A walk of only thirty yards could take as much as an hour. He made light of it, cracking jokes with passers-by and swapping gossip, but inside he felt like an old, defeated man. An embarrassed man.

Yet the news of Ada's promotion had cheered him no end. Now there *was* something to celebrate – even if it was down to Thomas Betram. Or maybe it wasn't, Pat decided, determined not to let anything sour Ada's achievement. His daughter was a smart girl – maybe she had been promoted because of her own efforts and not simply because of help from the boss.

But in reality he thought differently and burned with humiliation that he should be little more than a passenger to his wife, a cripple without a future, bringing in hardly any money at all now; that he should be reduced to having another man put bread on his own table. Because that was what Thomas Betram was doing indirectly: promoting Ada so that a bigger wage came into the slum house in Portswood.

Pat wondered if it made Tom Betram feel like a big man. Oh, the tables were turned well and truly now, weren't they? he thought. In the past he had won over Tom Betram. It had been he, Pat Gantry, who had married Milly. But his pride was being punished now. The humiliation Tom Betram had suffered was now reversed; *he* was the benefactor; *he* was the winner; *he* was triumphant.

Leaning against a wall, Pat rubbed his leg and wondered about the gossip. Would there be a war? If there was, what good would he be crippled and unable to fight? He could imagine the further contempt on his wife's face when he was one of the men left behind. *You're useless*, her eyes would say, *a useless, penniless, broken-down gimp.*

Closing his eyes to the thought Pat then remembered Clem Hargreaves. If war did come Clem would be called up for sure. God, how will that affect Ada? he wondered, knowing that her love for Clem strengthened every day. Although he wasn't a malicious man, Pat was glad that he and his daughter shared a secret; glad that he could keep something from his wife, giving him a tiny tot of power. After all, there was little chance Milly would find out. People might live cheek by jowl, but she had always kept her distance, never giving anyone so much as the time of day. And no one called on Milly Gantry for a bit of gossip.

Pushing himself upright, Pat started to walk again. It was hot, but the evening promised a quick, refreshing shower. He would go past the allotments and chat to his friends from the old days, put off the hour of going home. To Portswood.

To Milly.

It was unbelievable! Milly thought as she looked in the fly-blown mirror in her bedroom. Ada to be an accountant! She frowned at her reflection, angered. She was looking old, washed out, peevish. Well, not for much longer. Things were looking up. At this rate she might still get out of the slums – only not with her husband's help, but her daughter's.

Milly straightened her hair, momentarily ashamed of

how she had let herself go. The cleaning job was killing her, wearing her down to the bone. And the humiliation of scrubbing other people's toilets and cleaning up their mess – it was too much. Wasn't there enough mess in Portswood? Wasn't there enough muck without adding more?

But it might all be ending soon, Milly thought wistfully. Tom had taken a liking to Ada, that was clear. Obviously he still had some feelings for Milly – why else would he promote her daughter to his own office? Thoughtfully Milly glanced back into the mirror and then rummaged through a battered cardboard box for the old dress she had had years earlier. Finding it, she held it up to her body – and then, irritated, let it drop to the floor.

Who was she kidding? She was two stones thinner and rangy with bitterness. The woman who had filled out that blue dress so long ago had nothing in common with the woman standing in front of the mirror now. It was true that Tom Betram loved me once, Milly thought, but that was a long time ago. He would think me a hag now. Who didn't? He would never fall in love with me now – but he might well *stay* in love with the memory of me. As I was once.

And that memory had to suffice, Milly thought firmly. That memory, that blue dress, that summer day, had to play on Tom Betram's mind and force him into helping Ada. There was no point thinking about what might have been if she had married him. That was past, over. Now she had to think about her daughter's future. Tom wanted to help Ada. Milly wanted to help Ada. They were together on that. She no longer had an admirer, but she did have an ally.

And, by God, she was going to make the most of him.

Chapter Five

No one would ever forget that day. It had begun hot – like many that spring – and then dipped into a cold afternoon, rain falling raw on the steaming streets. At Henessey's, Ada was filing in the small, cluttered office beside Tom Betram's. Her head was bent over the filing cabinet, her hair tied back from her face, concentration apparent.

She had thought that she would miss the women in the workshop, but she hadn't really. In fact, Ada was surprised to find herself more at home in the offices than the factory. She liked the clean surroundings, the fact that she had a little desk and chair of her own. It didn't matter to her that she was not much more than a dogsbody. She was on the first rung of a ladder which might lead anywhere. Even out of Portswood . . .

Ada might have been surprised by her ambition, but Milly wasn't. Her daughter was too much like her to be able to resist bettering herself. Milly had seen the change in Ada over the months. There was a gloss, a confidence to her which was unmistakable. She's on the way up, Milly thought. She's smelled freedom, sensed a way out and she's going to take it.

Clem noticed the change too.

'You really like this job, don't you?' he asked.

The rain had stopped. Ada turned to look at him as they sat, as they habitually did, on the back wall of Henessey's. Never at the front; her mother might pass any day and catch them. The secret took some keeping, but they had kept it for over two years and weren't likely to slip up now.

'Course I like it,' Ada replied. 'It's clean, and I can learn other skills in the office. Mr Betram's all for women getting on.'

'You'll soon have no time for me,' Clem replied, his anxiety coming off him like a scent.

She turned, put her head on his shoulder. 'Oh come on, you know how much I love you.'

'I love you too,' he replied nervously.

He had been sure of her until recently. Now she had become capable, smart, surer of herself. When she was working in the trimmings shed, Ada was his equal. But now things were different. She was no longer a manual worker, she had moved up. Office workers married other office workers and lived in up-and-coming houses. Not in Portswood or Hillgate. Not in the slums.

'Ada, you'll not run off with some clerk, will yer?'

She stared at him in amazement and then laughed. 'For God's sake, you big lout! How could I ever run away from you? It's you I want, I always have.'

'Then marry me,' Clem said suddenly, the words as much a surprise to him as they were to Ada.

'*Marry you?*' she echoed. 'You know I can't.'

'Why not?'

'I promised Dad I'd wait a year. You know that, Clem. We've talked about it before and you've never minded.'

'But it were different then.'

'How?' she asked, surprised.

'Because now you're moving away from me and I might lose you, and if I did I wouldn't want to live.' He stopped, ashamed of the outburst, his heart banging.

'Clem,' Ada said, taking his face in both hands and looking into his eyes, 'I'm not going anywhere. There's only three months to go until the year's up. I have to keep my promise to Dad, you know that. He's never asked anything of me before. I owe him this much. Besides, he's never let on to Mum about us. He's on our side, I know he is.' Suddenly she kissed Clem on the mouth. 'We have to wait a bit longer. Then I'll marry you. I promise.' Her voice was sweetly firm.

'But –'

'No buts,' she said evenly. 'We'll marry at the end of the year. After all, what can happen before then?'

That afternoon the rain started up again, falling on the windows and clattering against the glass. Freak weather, coming on after unseasonable warmth, Sal said, looking up at the rattling windows.

'God, you'd think they'd smash.'

Walking over to the table, Milton glanced upwards too.

'Get on with yer work, Sal. There's no windows falling in today. God, you'd do anything to avoid work!'

She gave him a bleak look. 'Yer call it work, what yer do? Wandering around harassing poor women? Yer want to be ashamed of yerself, Milton Clough. Yer a bully –' She broke off as a deafening crack of thunder sounded overhead. Startled, she dropped the pins she was using and cursed. 'Bloody 'ell! Blasted weather! First yer sweat yerself half to death and then yer startled to bloody death.'

Watching as she bent down to pick up the pins, Milton sighed and then glanced up at the windows again. It was a right storm and no mistake, he thought, remembering how lightning had once struck the weather vane on the top of Henessey's tower.

'If yer afraid, yer can stay with us,' Winifrid said mischievously. 'We wouldn't want a little lad like you to be on his own.'

Sal laughed from the floor, where she was kneeling down, still picking up pins. 'That bloody tower's going to fall down one day,' she said calmly. 'My man's always saying so.'

'Since when did he know anything?' Winifrid countered. 'Yer fella isn't smart enough to catch cold.'

Another crack of thunder snapped overhead, followed by a bolt of forked lightning. Milton was spooked, Winifrid laughing at his nervousness, Sal getting back in her seat at the table. Then, after the storm, there was silence. A soft, absolute silence that was somehow more alarming than the storm.

Her expression puzzled, Sal looked over to Pearl, but none of the women spoke. Neither did Milton. Some strange lassitude had come over the trimmings shed. And then they heard it. The screaming.

They heard it in the trimmings shed. Ada heard it in the office. Tom Betram heard it and put down the phone, running towards the door. A hooter sounded – an alarm – and yet all Ada could hear was screaming. She went back to her childhood in that moment, to a foggy night and the sound of a branch snapping that wasn't a branch. And screaming.

Rain was pouring down as she ran out of the main doors of Henessey's and headed for the factory. She ran in soaked, her hair dripping down her back, Tom Betram blocking her way.

'Go back, luv, go back to the office.'

Surprisingly strong, she pushed him away.

They had stopped the fur former machine. A group of men on the conveyor belt were all gathered around something immobile. Her head humming, Ada walked towards them and they looked down at her. She reached up blindly, her hand silhouetted against the light, as though she was willing one of the men to raise her up. But no one did. Instead Ada heard a soft dripping noise and glanced down.

But it wasn't oil coming from the machine. It wasn't the water they threw on to cool the fan as the rabbit fur went through. It was blood.

It was Clem's.

Chapter Six

They took Clem, barely conscious, to the infirmary, his left leg tourniqueted at the thigh, his left arm almost flayed to the elbow. There was blood all over the machine, dripping onto the floor. Blood that had splattered over Ada's boots as she followed the stretcher; blood that had smeared the front of her dress as she had held Clem to her.

Accompanied by Sal, she went to the infirmary and waited for news. Evie Hargreaves turned up soon after, her vast form pounding down the corridor, her face tear-streaked and red.

'Where's m' lad?' she asked Ada. 'Where's my little lad?'

'He's going to be OK,' Ada stammered out, still sitting because her legs wouldn't support her.

She stared up at the towering Evie Hargreaves, a vast, almost comical figure sobbing into her cheap print apron. Ada had met Evie a number of times, and was always welcomed into the ramshackle Hargreaves household. But they hadn't become close, Evie suspicious of a girl she thought too stuck up for her boy. But now she could see her son's blood on Ada's clothes and the girl's obvious distress, and clumsily tried to comfort her.

'Aye, now, Ada. 'E'll be all right. Clem were always in trouble as a lad, but 'e always came through.'

Sal stared at the incongruous pair. 'The nurse said a

doctor would come along soon and tell us how Clem were doing.'

Evie nodded, clasping Ada's hand in a ferocious grip.

'Don't worry, he'll be all right,' she repeated, trying to console herself as much as Ada. 'I always told 'im to watch out for that machine. It were all right when 'e were little, but when 'e grew it were more dangerous.' Her temper flared. 'They should 'ave put someone else on it, some sprightly lad, like Clem used to be.'

'Mr Betram's called in and said he was coming back later,' Sal offered, watching Evie's broad face redden further.

'I dare say he will be along! There never were such a good worker like our Clem. Henessey's know that. Everyone does. People thought Clem were going to turn out no good, but he proved himself. 'E's an honest lad. Right honest.' She squeezed Ada's hand vigorously. 'You did that for him. You made him settle down. Clem was a different lad after he met you, Ada.'

She nodded, unable to find words. Clem had looked so broken on the stretcher, his face white as frost, his eyes turned up, the whites showing. Jesus, she thought, please don't let him die. Please . . .

At five o'clock the doctor came to talk to them, addressing Evie, Ada listening, Sal still there. He told them that Clem would live. Thank God, Evie said, then paused, knowing there was something else.

'Well, what is it?'

'He's going to be very ill for a while.'

'I thought you said –'

The doctor cut Evie off and continued hurriedly, 'Your son will live, but he'll have handicaps for the rest of his life.'

Evie was on her feet in an instant, dragging Ada with

her. 'I don't believe it! Not my lad! Clem's always getting into scrapes. You ask anyone round our way, they'll tell you. 'E fell off the bakery wall when 'e were only five, cracked his head good and proper, but 'e were all right.' She stopped, cowed by the look on the doctor's face. 'Handicapped?'

He nodded. 'Your son should get the use of his leg back in time, but his arm will need more surgery.'

Ada could feel the corridor spinning around her and sat down to stop herself falling. Clem was seriously ill, his leg broken, his arm torn apart, needing more operations. He was suffering, he was handicapped. *He was like her father now.* And Ada knew what that meant. Knew what it meant in terms of work – and worse, knew what suffering it caused a man mentally.

'When he leaves hospital good nursing and good food will help him recover.'

'And who pays for that?' Evie countered furiously, then dug her hands into her apron pockets so that no one would see them shake. 'You don't need to worry on that account, Doctor. We're poor, but my lads never wanted for anything, and Clem'll do just fine. I'll see to it.'

The doctor sighed. 'Your son should stay in hospital for a while so we can monitor his condition. You're welcome to visit.'

'How long will 'e 'ave to stay here?'

'That depends on his progress,' the doctor explained. 'He doesn't know the full extent of his injuries and it will hit him hard when he knows. Don't be worried if he gets depressed. It happens.' He looked at Evie carefully. 'Clem needs to have something to focus on, something to look forward to. He needs to have an aim in life.'

Automatically Evie turned to Ada. She was wondering if Ada would back off, if this would be the deciding factor in the relationship. She might love Clem when he was healthy and handsome, but crippled?

'Clem's my fiancé,' Ada said suddenly. 'We plan to marry.'

Her voice sounded far away, as though she was talking in a dream, or hearing someone else through a wall. Her first reaction had been to run, to get the hell out of the hospital and hide away. Then shame set in. She loved her father and had watched him suffer, so could she really abandon Clem now? After watching the bitterness between her parents, her mother's contempt, could she really reject the man she loved? How many times had she defended her father against her mother? How many times had she made allowances, excuses, stood up for him against Milly's furious disappointment? It would not have been what she would have chosen for herself, Ada realised, but maybe she was the best person to deal with the situation. After all, it was familiar. Achingly so.

Evie's arm went around Ada's shoulder. She said nothing but at that moment she swore she would stand shoulder by shoulder with Ada Gantry. She had proved herself more than worthy of her boy.

It was after seven when Ada finally arrived back in Portswood. The rain had come down again. Listlessly her feet dragged along the pavement. Shock wearied her, made her head spin, and when Ada finally walked into her home her mother immediately sprang up from the chair by the grate.

'What time d'you call this?' Her eyes took in the

blood on Ada's clothes, her thin face blanching. 'Jesus, are you hurt?'

Hearing his daughter arrive home, Pat hobbled into the kitchen. 'Whatever's happened, luv?'

'Clem's hurt, Dad, badly hurt.'

'Who the hell is Clem?' Milly replied, looking from her husband to her daughter.

There was a long pause, then Ada moved over to the vacated chair and sat down.

'Ada! I asked you who Clem was –'

She cut her mother off, for once impatient. 'Clem is . . . Clem's the man I'm going to marry.'

Milly rocked as though struck. Grabbing Ada's arm she hauled her daughter to her feet.

'You what?' she bellowed. 'What on earth are you talking about? Clem *who*?'

'Clem Hargreaves,' Ada murmured, trying to shake off her mother's grip.

But Milly was vicious with rage. Turning to Pat she shouted, 'Did you know about this?'

He looked at her and then glanced at Ada. 'For pity's sake, Milly, not now.'

'Not now!' she snapped. 'You knew all about this, didn't you? You lying, sneaking bastard. I could do for you.' Throwing Ada away from her, Milly rounded on Pat. 'I should have known never to trust you. And now you've turned my own daughter against me.'

'Stop thinking about yourself for once. Ada's hurting. Can't you see that she loves Clem Hargreaves?'

Milly's eyes narrowed. '*Hargreaves*? Not that family in Hillgate? Tell me it's not those Hargreaveses.'

Pat said nothing.

Milly turned back to Ada, her voice frantic. 'Not those Hargreaveses. Tell me! Is it them?'

Ada's voice was breaking. 'Yes. Clem's the youngest son. There's nothing wrong with the family –'

'You've been mixing with that rubbish?' Milly shrieked. 'How long for?'

Silence fell. Milly looked from her daughter to her husband and hated him. She burned with hatred that was so intense she wanted to kill him, to beat him into the ground for ruining her life and now her daughter's. Ada had had a chance to get out of Portswood. *She* might still have had a chance to get out, riding on the back of Ada's success – but not now. Pat Gantry had made sure Milly would never leave the slums. He had known about the romance and condoned it. Kept it secret from her.

They had betrayed her.

'How long has this been going on?' Milly repeated. Ada flinched, terrified of the rage she saw in her mother's eyes.

'A while.'

'How long's a while?' Milly asked. Please say only weeks. Say it's not serious.

'Two years.'

Rocking back on her heels, Milly stared at her daughter.

'*Two years!* You've been seeing this boy for two years?' Why hadn't she heard? And then she realised why no one would have told her. No one would have *wanted* to confide in Milly Gantry. Or dared to.

'We were only friends at first. I met him at work. But now I love him, Mum –'

She slapped Ada then with all her strength, her daughter falling back against the table and slipping onto the floor. Incensed, Pat moved forward, his face transformed. Ada could see then something she had never seen before – a look of hatred in his face. Scared, she struggled to her feet as Pat raised his walking stick over his head.

'You leave that girl alone!' he bellowed, his voice travelling through the narrow walls and out to the neighbours and the street beyond. 'Leave her alone, you bitch!'

But Milly was beyond reason. All she could see was their betrayal and her last chance gone.

'You're useless, Pat Gantry, a cripple, nothing else. You're a sorry excuse for a man. It's just like you to go sneaking behind me back. You ruined my life and now you want to ruin your daughter's. You bastard!' she screamed. 'You crippled, evil bastard!'

Furiously she reached for Pat's stick, Ada getting between them just as Arnold Declan ran in from the house next door. No one had ever heard the Gantrys argue before and he was stunned by the sight that greeted him. Milly was raging, Pat shouting at the top of his voice, Ada – now with the stick in her hand – advancing on her mother.

'Stop it!' Arnold shouted, snatching the walking stick from Ada's hand, a commotion starting up outside as neighbours gathered to see what was going on. 'You'll kill each other!'

Breathing heavily, Ada stared at Arnold and then looked at her mother. Anger had temporarily blinded her, all her control evaporating as she'd heard her mother curse her father. She had hated Milly then, had wanted to hit her, to make her shut up, to close her mother's mouth once and for all. But on seeing Arnold Declan she had stopped, incredulous at her own violence. Dear God, Ada thought, slumping into the chair, what was I doing? What *could* I have done?

The crowd was growing outside, Milly, wild-eyed, shouting at the gawpers. All her careful discretion had gone: now she was a foul-mouthed, slum harpy.

'What the hell are you lot looking at? Bugger off! Go on, get away from here. There's nothing to see. Unless you want to see a cripple.' She laughed bitterly. 'Come on, come and look at the cripple!'

Shattered, Arnold stepped in front of Milly and closed the front door, the commotion continuing outside as a policeman arrived.

That was the moment that killed Milly Gantry inside. She had seen dream after dream plummet; she had lived to get old before her time, to hate her husband and resent her child. In that moment she felt Portswood squeeze the breath out of her, its smells choking her, its sights and filth sucking her down. She would never leave. There was no hope, no saviour. Her husband wasn't worth a light, and her treacherous daughter had thrown in her lot with the Hillgate scum.

And now the final indignity had come. The police were at her house. The Gantrys had reached rock bottom. They were now just one more rough-arsed, swearing slum family, to whom the coppers had to be called to break up the fights.

Confused and disorientated, Milly looked around her, trying to smooth back her hair, curious faces pressed to the window, her husband watching her with palpable loathing. She could have married Tom Betram, Milly thought. Didn't they know that? She was someone once, a pretty woman who had an eligible man dangling at the end of her string.

Bewildered, Milly looked round, then tried to gather up some semblance of dignity. Slowly she turned to the policeman.

'It's over.'

He looked round the room, took in the broken plates, the young woman crying. He knew Pat Gantry by sight, had always found him cheerful, never bitter about the bad luck in his life.

'It's fine, honest,' Pat said, his voice wavering as he struggled to control himself. 'It were just an argument that got out of hand. No damage done.'

'Well, if you're sure . . .' the officer replied, walking to the door. 'I must say, though, of all the places in Portswood, I never expected to be called to this address.'

Chapter Seven

That night Ada hardly slept. When she did doze the images intermingled. Now it was her mother injured on the fur former machine, now Clem. Later it was her father in hospital, her mother putting her arm around her and telling her that everything would be all right.

But when she woke, she knew nothing would ever be all right again. After the fight everyone had gone home, some laughing, some disappointed to see the Gantrys brought down. Everyone was talking about Ada. Had she meant to use the stick on her mother? Or had she simply been taking it off her father? Surely she couldn't have meant to hurt her mother?

'Well, the worm's turned now, and that's for sure,' Arnold Declan said to his wife. 'I knew that girl would show her true colours one day. She's been terrorised by her mother for too long.'

Others decided that Milly had been asking for it. Whether her husband had hit her, or her daughter, someone had been bound to, some day. After all, Milly Gantry was a harpy, a thin-faced shrew, always on Pat's back, riding him about his leg, never a word of compassion, sympathy. The only time Milly had been happy for years was when Ada was promoted.

So what had happened to cause such a dreadful fight, they wondered. Others presumed that it was just a one-off, something that would blow over. It was just life; people argued all the time . . . But not the Gantrys. They fought a cold battle, not boiling with heat. Words, not fists had been their weapons. And in that atmosphere Ada had grown up obedient, subservient, terrified of her mother.

It was inevitable, they said that night. When Ada went out to work she had had her first taste of freedom and begun a new life away from the strictures of home. That was the day Milly started to lose her control. Ada would have stayed with her father through anything, because she loved him. But her mother had inspired no love in her. Milly's belittling of Pat long ago souring any feeling between mother and daughter.

But would Ada have *really* hit her? they queried around Portswood that night. Would gentle, obedient Ada really have used her father's stick on her mother?

And meanwhile, as the gloomy night wound on, Ada lay in bed and heard her parents' breathing through the partition wall. They did not talk and there was no movement. Only later – around three in the morning – did Ada hear her mother get up. She knew it was Milly because of the steady footsteps going down the stairs. Tense in her bed, Ada heard the kettle being filled and the clattering of pots.

Guilt made her sit up, swing her legs over the side of the bed. She would go and make her peace with her mother. It had been a dreadful argument, but there was no reason to prolong it. And yet Ada couldn't make the trip downstairs. Instead she waited, longing for the morning, the dark night lifting on to day. In the daylight it would be easier to talk, easier to explain. She would tell her mother about Clem, include her in the romance. Maybe they could come to some kind of understanding.

When the morning came, when light came, Ada would

talk to her mother. In the meantime, she would try to sleep. She would sleep away the horror of the previous night and start clean again in the morning. That was the right thing to do: give her mother time to settle down, time to let her anger cool.

At five, Ada was woken by the first light, and crept out of bed, pulling on her dress and boots. Silently she made her way downstairs and found a half-drunk mug of tea on the kitchen table. Looking round she called softly for her mother, but there was no reply. Maybe Milly had gone back to bed, Ada thought. But knew otherwise. There had been no footfall heard through the partition wall; she would have woken at the sound. She always did.

So instead Ada walked out of the back of the house and went to the water closet. The rain had stopped in the night. Some men were up already, heading for work at the mill. Arnold Declan was swilling his neck at the outside pump. The day was going to be unusually hot, a spring mist making the houses dance hazily in the early sunshine.

'Sorry about last night,' Ada said to Arnold.

He straightened up, towelling himself down as he looked at her. 'It were a right do and no mistake. Everyone OK?'

Ada nodded. 'Everything's fine.' She glanced round, avoiding the curious glances of another neighbour. 'Have you seen my mother?'

Arnold shook his head. 'Not long been up myself,' he replied, feeling sorry for the young woman. 'She's maybe gone for a walk to cool off. I do the same m'self sometimes.'

Weary from lack of sleep, Ada moved across the shabby square and headed for the constricted alleyway

– the ginnel – beyond. It was a short cut that few people used, being narrow and lit by only one streetlamp at the far end. But in the daylight that morning it looked inviting as Ada pulled open the rickety gate and walked out.

Her head was down as she walked along, deep in thought. She would have to make peace with her mother, it was the right thing to do. Besides, she could understand some of Milly's disappointment. Her mother wouldn't want history repeating itself, wouldn't want her daughter saddled with a handicapped man. But Clem *wouldn't* be handicapped for ever, Ada thought. He was young, he would recover, she knew it. *She knew it.*

The ginnel was narrow, a few hardy weeds struggling up through the cobbles. At the bend, Ada turned and then stopped, her legs buckling as she backed away. Without wanting to, her eyes fixed on what was ahead, her brain struggling to understand what she was seeing. It wasn't real, she was still in bed, still dreaming. It wasn't real.

But it was.

At the end of the ginnel, strung from the one and only streetlamp, was the swinging figure of Milly Gantry. In the early hours before light she had made herself a mug of tea, drunk half, and then taken the clothesline down from the outside wall. She had then carried the old stool from the kitchen out to the ginnel. Alone, she had walked as far away from the houses as she could and then thrown the line over the iron arm of the lamp, tying a noose around her neck.

Then she had kicked away the stool.

It was lying on its side, only a yard away from Milly's feet. She had pulled on her boots and laced them carefully before she died.

In a trance Ada backed away from her mother, then she began to run back to the houses, shouting at the top of her voice for her father. Deep in sleep, Pat came to consciousness to hear his daughter screaming.

It was cruelly hot that day. The day that Milly Gantry died.

'Well, it's a hell of a story, like I said. I'm not going too fast for you, am I? It's just that talking about Ada Hargreaves brings it all back – all the things my grandfather told me. They say that the ginnel's haunted by Milly, but then they would, wouldn't they? Makes a good tale to scare kids with. Personally, I've never seen a ghost, but that's another story.

'I had to tell you all about the background of Ada's life – about the time before she got to The Sixpenny Winner. It's important to make sense of who she was, and why she were like she was. Why she married Clem Hargreaves and the why she were never the same after her mother's death.

'Some said – my grandfather being one of them – that Ada changed overnight after Milly committed suicide. He said she got strong after that, strong as a horse. Said it were a good thing, in a way, because the way Ada's life went she needed to be strong.

'Anyway, you ready for me to go on? Like I say, I'll tell you what I know and you put it into your own words. Where were I? Oh yes, Ada. Well, the girl's gone now, but the woman's come into her own.

'She's into the next part of her life. A married woman, with two daughters. Oh, and the landlady of The Six-penny Winner . . .'

Part Two

John Sullivan – heavyweight boxing champion in
1892 – was once challenged to a fight in a bar.
His reply: 'Listen you. If you hit me just once –
and I find out about it . . .'

The Little, Brown Book of Anecdotes

Chapter Eight

They cut down the body of Milly Gantry, and that same day Ada saw her father cry for the first time in his life. What he was crying for, she didn't ask. Later she visited Clem at the hospital, everyone staring at her and talking in whispers. It seemed to Ada that death and illness dogged her. She was quiet because she couldn't find words. Although Pat told her repeatedly that what had happened wasn't her fault, Ada – for once – did not believe him.

Her mother was dead because of her. She changed with the acceptance of that guilt, and in the months that followed the only comfort she found was in Clem. The doctor had been wrong. He never *did* suffer any depression and stayed cheerful, because he thought he owed Ada that much at least. I'll be back on my feet, you watch me, he'd say. And wink.

He was true to his word. In a much shorter time than anyone had predicted, Clem was walking, albeit with a pronounced limp. His arm healed, and although he had only limited use of his hand, he adjusted. Handicapped, his courage still made him a taller man than most, and Pat admired him for it.

So when they married Pat Gantry willingly gave his only daughter away in a small ceremony and then watched them move into a rented flat in Portswood. But they weren't going to stay there long, he knew that when he had looked into his daughter's eyes. Because the only thing which would assuage any of Ada's guilt was to prove to her dead mother that she had chosen the right man.

So they worked. Shattered by Ada's reversal of fortune, Tom Betram stepped in and gave Clem a job in the packing shed – supervising, nothing physical, but he was good with the men, and reliable. Ada kept working in the office and they both squirrelled away some savings. Their world was small: it was Ada and Clem, Clem and Ada – and Pat, of course, but he had changed.

He didn't miss his wife, and yet felt lost. But any little bit of money he made Pat popped away, and when his first granddaughter, Freda, arrived he opened a savings account at the Post Office for her. Soon after, he did the same for Victoria. And all the time, pregnant or not, Ada worked.

The winters were always hard for them, because Clem's injuries played up and the flat was bitterly cold. But no woman could have had a better partner, and Clem loved his daughters. He would change nappies, fill bottles and read stories to them when Ada was working overtime, and there was always something ready for her to eat when she came in, whatever time. They never sat down and discussed who would take on what: they didn't need to. They were so close that they worked like a hand in a glove. And so the time passed, and so their small savings grew. As did their children.

Then one evening Ada came home to find the girls settled in bed, Clem reading the evening paper. She slid onto his knee and nuzzled his neck.

''Lo there. Love me?'

'To death,' he had replied honestly.

'I was thinking . . .'

'Oh God,' he teased her.

'There's a pub they want someone to take on.'

Clem looked at her, surprised. 'A pub?'

'We could do it.'

'What pub?'

'The Sixpenny Winner.'

'Bloody hell! My father used to bet on the dog that place is named after,' Clem replied, laughing. 'It's a dump.'

'It doesn't *have* to be.' Ada's tone was firm. 'We could make something out of it. Oh Clem, we *could*. We could run it and make it our own. Our own business, think of it. You get on with people and I could do the books –'

'But we've no experience.' Clem held her at arm's length. 'Neither of us knows anything about running a pub.'

'We know as much as Abe Turner does! And he's just been fired for fiddling the books,' Ada snapped, staring hard into her husband's face. 'This is our chance, Clem. This is the break we've been looking for. We could live there with the girls and work together under the same roof. Think how much easier it'd be. And it'd be our place. *Our pub.*'

'Ada, it would be so much work –'

'It would be *ours*,' she insisted, her eyes burning with intensity. 'Trust me, Clem, this is the best chance we'll ever get.'

Clem knew at once that there was no stopping her – and besides, he didn't want to.

Within weeks Ada went to see the brewery officials and asked to take over the pub. Let me talk to them first, she told Clem. I think I can sway them better if I go in alone.

They laughed in her face.

'A woman running a pub on her own? No way.'

71

'I'm not on my own. I've a husband and two daughters,' Ada replied calmly. 'Clem's wonderful with people and a more honest man you'll never find. And it strikes me that after Abe Turner you could do with someone honest.'

Stung, George Higgins hardened his voice. 'But neither you nor your husband have any experience –'

'We can learn.'

'Oh, aye, that's what they all say,' he replied dismissively, turning away from Ada, who was sitting calmly opposite him.

'Mr Higgins,' Ada continued firmly, 'you've no call to be rude. I've come here to make you a good offer.'

He looked up at her, astonished by her cheek. She was making *him* an offer? What a nerve!

'The Sixpenny Winner's a big pub, but it's bringing in little money. It could be a gold mine. It was once, before that toerag Abe Turner let all sorts in. It's got a bad reputation –'

'Hey!'

'Oh, you know it has!' Ada replied, undaunted. 'No woman would go in that pub on her own, and no one respectable would want to drink there. It's a filthy, dingy, sleazy hellhole of a place.'

Mr Higgins's eyes grew cold. 'So why are you and your husband so keen to take it on?'

'Because we have a family and we need good steady work, an income to support us all. My husband's not fit. Clem does what he can, but he's a bit limited with manual labour. Having said that, he's got a grand way with people and they take to him fast. Customers would come *because* of Clem. There's not a man in these parts who would make a better landlord. As for me, I've a good head for figures and I dare say I can show

72

you a profit in a year.' Ada paused. Was she winning him over, or not? It was hard to tell. 'I admit I've no experience, but Abe Turner had experience and he's lost you a fortune. Strikes me that experience is no recommendation.'

To her amazement, George Higgins burst out laughing.

'I like your cheek, Mrs Hargreaves, but how can I let you run the pub when I don't know you from Adam?'

'I can give you references,' Ada interjected quickly. 'Mr Thomas Betram will vouch for me.'

George Higgins's eyebrows rose. He had known Tom Betram for years and knew he was nobody's fool. If he recommended Ada Hargreaves, it was worth thinking about.

So he leaned across the desk to her. 'I'm promising nothing, Mrs Hargreaves, but I'll talk to Mr Betram and be in touch. It's hard work running a pub. It'll cost you for a while, until – or if – you can make it a going concern. If you fail, you're out.'

At that, Ada rose to her feet, her expression almost contemptuous.

'I have no intention of failing, Mr Higgins. No intention at all.'

It wasn't easy, of course, but after two months of haggling, numerous meetings, and the recommendation from Thomas Betram, Ada and Clem finally found themselves the landlords of The Sixpenny Winner.

Who the bloody hell does she think she is? people around said, astonished by her nerve. Ada Hargreaves should remember where she came from. No one likes someone who gets above their station. Pride comes before a fall. She should remember that.

Ada knew about the gossip, but it didn't deter her. She

and Clem were going to make the best out of the opportunity Fate had dealt them, you see if they weren't. From now onwards, Ada declared, The Sixpenny Winner was going to be a family pub – and God help anyone who argued with her. So soon the whores stopped climbing the entrance steps and the drunks found other places to fall over . . .

The memories made Ada smile as she recalled the past years. Then she shook her duster out and walked back into the pub. At the entrance of The Sixpenny Winner there were two steep stone steps, the centres worn with wear, many a well-oiled customer misjudging their depth and finding himself propelled unceremoniously onto the cobbled street of Churchgate. Ada, however, negotiated them with a light step, pulling the door closed behind her and looking around.

They had done well. No one would have recognised the old place now, she thought. The engraved, frosted windows were clean, the muck of years scraped off. The toilet out the back had been a disgrace, Clem taking two days to unblock it and make it usable. These days it was spotless. And as for the beds – well, they'd been thrown out straight away, hadn't they? Too stained to keep. Too dirty for a dog to lie on.

The pub itself was built on three floors. On the ground floor was the bar itself, with the snug next to it, a makeshift kitchen and a poky living room at the back. On the first floor were three bedrooms, and a bathroom that had been put in when the Hargreaveses first arrived, much to Ada's pride. Upstairs, on the second floor, were another two bedrooms, a boxroom leading off the larger one.

It was a rum setup, Ada thought, but at least the girls had bedrooms to themselves.

Ada's thoughts turned to her husband. The injuries he had sustained that fateful day at Henessey's had been serious, but youth had been on his side then – and Ada. Determination and love had got Clem back on his feet. Ada had pushed him, and cajoled him and insisted that he do things for himself. And Clem, aware that without her he would be nothing, had forced himself back to relative health.

The doctors had been amazed by his progress, but in the years that followed, the cold and damp of Stockport had begun to settle into his limbs, his injuries becoming arthritic. Strength of temperament had got Clem well, but the Northern temperature was another matter. The easy-going, friendly man to whom customers gravitated had begun to struggle. Standing had become uncomfortable, and after a while Clem had taken to sitting longer on his stool behind the bar. He might still try to lift the beer barrels, but it was obvious that it was too much for him. The question was – how could Ada suggest getting in some extra help without humiliating her adored Clem?

'You know, luv,' she'd suggested when she'd first noticed him struggling, 'I think you could cut back your hours a bit, work part time, and we could find someone –'

Clem had flushed. 'I can hold my own!'

She had nudged him, winking. 'Oh, I don't doubt that. But you want to keep yourself fit for me, don't you?'

He had laughed at her cheek. 'I suppose I *could* just work in the evenings. I've been having some pain lately. If I rested up in the day I'd be full of beans later –'

'I was thinking that,' Ada had readily agreed, seeing

the relief in Clem's eyes. 'The girls are growing up now. They can help me. Besides, I like to keep Freda nearby, where I can watch her.'

'You're hard on that girl, Ada –'

'And you're too soft,' she had replied, kissing him briskly.

Soon afterwards, Clem had moved into the upstairs bedroom. His restless sleeping had disturbed Ada so much that he had – reluctantly – suggested the change in arrangements. It was a bitter decision to make; he hadn't wanted to lose the comfort of her arms around him in the night, and had longed for the sound of her breathing. But Clem had known how hard Ada had to work to keep the pub going when he wasn't able to pull his full weight. The least he could do was to make things easier for her. After all, hadn't she always made things easy for him?

So Clem had moved up into the top bedroom and the boxroom had been converted into another bathroom. But the closeness between them never faltered. Often Ada had sneaked up and they had made love like kids, secretly, laughing into the dark. Then Ada had crept downstairs again and looked up, reaching out her hand in the darkness as though she could push it through the ceiling and clasp Clem's hand above.

'Give us a kiss,' Clem said suddenly behind her, Ada's thoughts pulled back into the present.

'You cheeky sod!' she teased him. 'I thought you were having a nap.'

'I feel good today,' Clem replied, taking the duster from his wife's hand and wiping the top of the bar. 'D'you hear about Al Weeks?'

'There's nothing I want to hear about that man – unless he's fallen in the canal.'

Clem pulled a face as he leaned back against the bar. 'He's carrying a torch for you, Ada. He's been a widower for years and he's fancied you ever since he worked at Henessey's.'

'He was fired from Henessey's for fighting.'

'Probably over you,' Clem teased her, watching Ada's curiosity growing.

She feigned indifference but could finally stand it no longer. 'So *what* about Al Weeks?'

'He had a fall, off a roof he was tiling, and all his hair's fallen out.'

'Never!'

'I kid you not,' Clem continued. 'You'll see soon enough. When he comes in again.'

'He won't *be* coming in again if he doesn't stop picking fights. I warned him the other day – one more fight and you're banned.'

Clem pretended to be shocked. 'You couldn't ban your sweetheart?'

'Al Weeks is no sweetheart of mine!' Ada replied, then looked at her husband curiously. 'Is he *really* bald?'

'As a pane of glass.'

Blowing out her cheeks, Ada turned and then caught sight of the stuffed dog hung in a case behind the bar.

'Can you smell something, Clem?'

'Like what?'

Ada sniffed at the glass cabinet. 'Like cat pee . . . That bloody animal from Trudie Mossop's has been in here again, weeing up the case!' She snatched at the duster in Clem's hand and scrubbed The Sixpenny Winner's cabinet. 'If I catch that cat –'

The sound of a door opening made Ada turn. Knowing that her daughter was unaware of her scrutiny, Ada watched Freda curiously as she walked into the kitchen behind them. She was twenty, tall, blonde, her hair in immaculate curls around her shoulders. The flapper fashion was over; now fashionable women wore mannish suits with slim skirts and padded shoulders. Not that anything could make Freda look like a man.

Intrigued, Ada watched as Freda paused by the grate and glanced into the mirror above. She looked at herself, turned her head from one side to the other and then glanced away, a slight smile of satisfaction on her face. Oh, you're a right one, Ada thought, a flirt in your pram. She was well aware of her daughter's good looks; everyone who saw her was. It was good for the pub to have such a pretty girl around.

But was it good for Freda? She was too fond of the men, Ada thought, too easy with them by half. But where had she got it from? Ada had never been a flirt, and neither had her mother, so it wasn't from the Gantry side. As for Evie Hargreaves, well, she frightened more men than she had ever fascinated. But then Ivor Hargreaves had been a right womaniser, Ada thought. Ran after everything, Clem had told her. Couldn't keep his trousers buttoned. Or so they said.

It was funny in a man, unless you happened to be married to him. But preciousness was another matter in a woman . . . Ada kept staring at her daughter, Freda unpacking the groceries she had brought home. No one liked a flirt, a good-time girl. It was so easy to get a reputation. And a bad reputation was like a birthmark – once you had it, you were stuck with it for life.

'You got everything?' Ada asked, walking in.

Freda looked up. 'Everything you asked for,' she replied, putting some vegetables in the pantry. 'There were no sausages at the butcher. Said he'd have some in Thursday.'

Ada fingered the little brown paper bag lying next to the groceries on the table. It said Henderson's Chemist.

'What's this?'

Freda walked out, her face sullen. 'I used my own money –'

'I didn't ask if you used your own money, I asked what it was.'

'Make-up.'

Ada's eyebrows rose. 'You don't need make-up, Freda. Only fast girls wear make-up.'

'Oh, Ma,' she said patiently, 'it's 1936, things have changed. It's the fashion now.'

'Your sister doesn't bother with make-up.'

Freda sighed. 'Vicky doesn't care about her appearance. She's too busy with worthy causes, saving the world. She's never been the same since she fell in with those political harpies.' Lifting the paper bag out of her mother's hands Freda took out a lipstick. 'A woman can do more to change the world with a lipstick than she can by being a blue stocking.'

'You should be careful the way you talk, Freda,' Ada said warningly. 'One day you'll tie a knot with your tongue that you'll never undo with your teeth.'

A bell rang suddenly at the back door. It was the entrance used only by family and close friends; everyone else used the main pub entrance. Ada had never liked the back. The heavy dark door, which led out into the yard and onto the ginnel behind, made her uneasy. At night the dim electric light overhead made long, gloomy shadows on the cobbles. It reminded her of another ginnel and in all the time she had lived at the pub Ada had avoided the exit. It was a bad space, she thought, with a bad feeling to it.

'Go and see who that is, will you?'

'Ma –'

'Get on with you!' Ada snapped, walking back into the pub and checking the snug was tidy.

Everything was in order, the tables polished, ashtrays emptied, the brass work gleaming. On the far wall hung a dart board, a set of draughts in a box on the side of the main bar. At six, Ada would light the fire. The customers liked a good blaze – it made the place welcoming – and if they felt welcome, they stayed. They drank, bought more beer. And food.

Hotpot was the favourite, and meat and potato pie. Ada made them every morning in deep pot dishes in the kitchen, the oven working overtime, the window steamed up. It was a bugger in summer, she always said, boiling. I feel like a bloody steamed pudding by noon. But the customers still asked for hot pies, even if the sun was cracking the flags outside.

Ada had the sense to keep them cheap, knowing that times were hard, with the Depression, and money – never plentiful – now harder to find than ever. Many men had been laid off. It was the same all round the country, the papers said, but worse in the North. Ada hardly needed telling.

It was no good having men idle. Women could always be busy at home, with the house and kids, but men needed jobs to keep them sane. She had seen what forced idleness had done to her father, and now she was seeing it all over again. It wasn't unusual for the street to be busy at five in the morning, men setting off early to see if they could get labouring jobs on the roads or at the cotton mills. The heavy engineering works were still going, but the available jobs were halved. Men who had expected to have a job for life found themselves turned away at the factory gates at dawn, with long, empty days to fill.

Charity wasn't enough to keep body and soul together, and when the Means Test came in in 1931 people lied, or temporarily hid their few prized possessions in neighbours' houses, away from the piercing gaze of the assessors. Men who had had jobs and a place in life were reduced to ignominy and despair.

Only one thing kept them going: beer. The Stockport pubs were thriving in the Depression, beer cheap and bitter. Who cared if it made you sick up outside, it made you forget, didn't it? And where else could a man go to see his old companions and pretend that things were back to normal? He certainly couldn't stay at home, Ada thought, not getting under his wife's feet. She thought sometimes that the money they spent in The Sixpenny Winner should find its way to their houses, not into her till, but it was their choice, and if a wife came to see Ada – and many did – she helped all she could.

'Don't serve 'im,' Lettie Foreshaw had said to Ada the previous week. 'I don't want you serving Len.'

'What do I say to him, Lettie?' Ada countered.

'Say he's barred,' the woman replied. 'Tell 'im to get home and bring the money to 'is family, not pour it down 'is throat.'

'I'll tell him, Lettie,' Ada had replied, 'but it'll do no good. If he doesn't come here, he'll go elsewhere.'

It was true. At least at The Sixpenny Winner the beer was cheap and no one was allowed to get stinking drunk. Or bet. That was off limits. Times were hard enough, Ada said. If you want to bet, get down to Hillgate. It's a steep walk. It'll sober you up.

Leaning over, Ada polished the top of a table and then called out for Freda.

'Who was at the back door?'

'No one.'

Ada paused, duster in hand. 'I heard a knock.'

'Oh, that was Mr Barrowclough.'

'*And?*' Ada pressed her.

'He said the coal was late and that he'd bring it round Saturday.'

Ada sniffed. She had to keep a check on Freda, knowing all too well that young men came calling at the back when she was busy in the bar. Typical of Freda that, sneaking some assignation when she was busy.

'Go down to the cellar and get me some more beer glasses, Freda. Oh, and a bottle of port.'

Her daughter glided to the door, framed by an old velvet curtain. 'I'm not going down there, Ma. It's haunted.'

'Haunted, my foot! You don't like it because it's cold and dusty.'

'Ask Vicky to go.'

'Vicky's busy,' Ada replied shortly.

'Well, I'm not going,' Freda said, turning away and calling upstairs for her sister: 'Vicky! Ma wants something from the cellar.'

There was the sound of feet running down the stairs, then Ada's younger daughter came into the kitchen and faced her sister. Ada watched them, so dissimilar, through the doorway. Vicky was small and neat-figured, dressed in a plain blue suit, her dark hair cut short; pretty, but not obvious like Freda.

'What is it?'

Freda looked at her, her voice surly. 'Ma wants –'

'*Ma wants,*' Ada said, walking into the kitchen, 'you – *Freda* – to go down the cellar.'

'There's a ghost down there.'

'There's no such thing as ghosts!' Vicky said practically.

'Good, then you won't mind going,' Freda retorted, moving over to the table and picking up some groceries.

Resigned, Vicky looked at her mother. 'What do you want?'

'Some beer glasses and a bottle of port, luv,' Ada replied kindly. 'And watch those steps, you know how steep they are.'

Throwing a hostile look at her sister, Vicky opened the cellar door and turned on the dim light. Slowly she took the wooden stairs one at a time, hearing her mother's footsteps overhead as Ada walked back into the bar. Vicky didn't like the cellar, it was eerie, but she was damned if she was going to admit being afraid. Let Freda act silly if she wanted; she was made of sterner stuff. Kicking aside an old box with her foot, Vicky moved further into the cellar. It smelled of damp and was freezing cold, with no window to let in light from outside. Well below street level, she walked on under the vaulted ceiling to the back, hearing the sound of a cart moving overhead on the road.

Picking up several beer glasses, Vicky then reached for the port, and winced as a cobweb brushed her hand. It *was* spooky down here, she thought, suddenly wanting to get back upstairs. The old story about the ghost was ridiculous. There *were* no ghosts – but it wasn't so hard to believe in the echoing chamber below ground.

Banging her head on a low beam, Vicky cursed under her breath as she walked to the steps. Suddenly the light went out. She stiffened, her eyes trying to adjust to the darkness. Then she heard it – a low scratching noise ... Shaken, Vicky ran up the steps, dropping the bottle of port as she reached the top and tried to open the door. But it was locked. Panicked, she rattled the handle, banging frantically on the door, her voice high-pitched.

'Let me out! Let me out!'

A moment later the door was flung open, Ada looking at her daughter in astonishment.

'What the hell is going on?'

'I was ... I was startled by something,' Vicky stammered, clambering out, her dress stained with port.

Ada stared at the mess. 'That's not the port? Tell me it's not the port.'

'I was frightened, Ma. I'm sorry, but there was something making a noise down there.'

Behind her mother Freda glided into view. 'I thought you didn't believe in ghosts?'

'I tell you there *was* something making a noise!'

'Like this?' Freda asked, banging her hand rhythmically on the wooden panelling of the cellar door.

'You bitch!' Vicky shouted.

Ada moved between the two girls. 'Hey, cut it out!' she said sharply, turning to her elder daughter. 'That was a mean trick, Freda. You shouldn't do spiteful things. They have a way of rebounding on you.'

All innocence, Freda raised her eyebrows. 'It was only a joke.'

'Well let's see who's laughing now,' Ada said slyly. 'You can pay for the port out of your wages.'

Freda waited until it was busy that evening and then, when she was sure that her mother was preoccupied, she walked to the back door and opened it. Standing in the dim light was a young man, a hat shading his eyes.

Smiling, Freda posed against the doorframe, knowing that her figure would be silhouetted against the light from the kitchen behind her.

'Well, Tommy Evens. What made you come calling at this time of night?'

He leaned towards her, eyes bright with excitement. Freda was a looker and no mistake. Every man wanted her; some had already had her, if they were to be believed.

'You said I could call by –'

'I don't remember saying anything of the sort,' Freda replied, her voice mocking. 'Have you got a cigarette, Tommy?'

He fumbled in his pocket and brought out a pack of Black Cat.

'Oh, no! Not those,' she said coolly. 'Only the labourers smoke those. I thought you'd have something more upmarket.'

He flushed, embarrassed. 'I'll get some more. I just got these from a friend.'

'I like a good smoke,' Freda said, bending towards him, her lips close to his ear. 'I think men look good smoking. It makes them very . . . glamorous.'

She knew she had him. Tommy Evens would be back with good cigarettes, flattered into thinking that she thought he was someone. It was so simple, Freda laughed to herself. Men were so easy to dupe.

Suddenly Tommy moved, trying to kiss her.

'Oh no!' Freda said, feigning alarm. 'You're a naughty boy, Tommy Evens. I shall have to be very cross with you.' She turned and half closed the door on him.

'No, wait!' he said, trying to hold the door open. 'I'm sorry, I won't try it on again.'

'And me with my parents only yards away,' Freda said,

glancing over her shoulder. 'You should be ashamed of yourself.'

'Freda –'

'I didn't think you were that type of man,' she went on, knowing she had him hooked. 'Good night, Tommy.'

Then she closed the door on him, smiling and leaning against it. She could hear him call her name softly, so as not to disturb her parents. Then she heard him walk away. With his Black Cat cigarettes . . . Freda smiled. She wanted something better than that, something more challenging. Slowly she opened the door and looked out. The ginnel was empty. Good, she thought, gliding out of the door and standing on the step outside. The air was cool, damp making an aureole around the overhead lamp. She liked the semidark, the shadows, liked the way it made the ginnel look mysterious. It was her little kingdom, that back exit, a dark doorway where she stood, sometimes watched, well aware of the interest from eyes she couldn't see. She could tantalise from that stone step. It was dangerous and safe at the same time. And shocking somehow, to know that her parents were only yards away, unsuspecting, busy.

Sighing, Freda stretched, then tensed, aware of a noise from down the ginnel. Someone was watching her. Was it Tommy? Or someone else?

Smiling, she ran her tongue over her lips and then turned and walked back into the pub, turning off the back light as she did so.

'I'd like to see our Freda married,' Ada said to Clem, tucking in the blanket at the bottom of the bed and viciously plumping up the pillows. It was late; before long Clem would retire to bed. 'Like to see her settle down with a man who'd keep her from wandering.'

She was annoyed, Clem realised. Freda was playing up again. You needed a dozen pairs of eyes to keep tabs on that girl.

'You're looking well, luv,' Ada said, staring into her husband's face. Quickly she planted a smacking kiss on his lips.

'You're looking grand too,' he replied, using his good arm to pull her down onto the bed next to him.

It was cold, wintertime, and every muscle in his body had begun to ache. But it was worth the effort to tickle his wife awkwardly under the arms, her corset hard against his fingers.

'Bloody hell, Ada! I thought you'd given up that corset!'

'It gives me a good shape,' Ada replied, smacking his hand away playfully. 'I don't go for all this soft underwear. A woman should keep her bits and pieces tidy.'

He burst out laughing, feeling good again. It was worth sleeping upstairs because anticipating Ada's nocturnal visits made them all the more intense. He loved her, Clem thought, more now than he ever had. You couldn't pretend that kind of love, couldn't fake it. It was real. As real to him as the coat hanging on the back of the door.

'I love your stays, love all those buckles and belts. I bet Houdini couldn't get them untied faster than I can, bad arm an' all.'

'Cheeky bugger,' Ada teased him, jumping at the sound of a banging downstairs. 'That's Freda, slamming the door again! I tell her about it every day, but she still does it.'

'I heard her and Vicky having a right argument earlier when I was in the bar.'

Sighing, Ada lay down beside Clem on the bed, her arm across his chest. He smelled sweet, like caramel.

'They're always arguing. Vicky was talking about the hat business falling off so much. There's so many hatters setting up in Europe now, she said, and besides, we all know it's cheaper to buy a hat in the High Street than have it made by Henessey's. She was getting all worked up – you know how she does about injustice – and telling us how she'd been to a lecture in Manchester about unemployment. She cares about people, that girl.'

'Whereas Freda only cares about herself.'

Ada nodded. 'You're right. Freda's interested in Freda, nothing else. Selfish to the bone. I don't like to say that about my own, but it's true.' Ada nuzzled her face against Clem's neck. 'You ever think of Henessey's?'

'Now and again,' he lied.

In fact he thought about the hat factory every day, remembered the noise as he hit the drum on the fur forming machine. And the smell. The smell of rabbit fur and blood.

'Thomas Betram's poorly . . . I'm sorry about that. He was good to us,' Ada mused, nibbling Clem's earlobe. 'You've lovely ears, Mr Hargreaves.'

He smiled up at the ceiling. They had always been affectionate, loving. Even though, from the first, love-making had been a tentative affair. Clem's handicaps made it difficult. It should have put them off, but it did the opposite. It made them inventive, bound them closer than any normal couple.

Then when the children came they had been ecstatic. Two healthy girls, born within twenty months of each other. It was perfect, Ada said, but, if it was all the same, she'd stop there . . . Clem had known how much she wanted children, and how desperate she was to have two. There was to be no single child, no repetition of her own upbringing.

Her children would be companions for each other, confidantes. They would share, and know they had an ally through life. Well, that had been the principle, but it had turned out differently. Freda had reacted badly to the arrival of Vicky, and as Vicky reached her teens it was obvious the two girls were never going to be close. Ada had hoped that by working together with her in the pub they might find some common ground, but she was sorely mistaken.

Freda was only interested in men. She was lazy, vain, and a liar. Certainly she was also amusing, good company and quick-witted, but she had a peevish streak that worried Ada. By contrast Vicky was interested in everyone but herself. She thought the world was her responsibility. Involved in every good work, in charities, in Labour politics, she worked in the pub as a duty – never by choice.

Freda, however, loved the pub. She would have spent every moment at that bar if Ada would have let her. Trouble was, trying to keep her away, trying to stop her leaning her long body against the pumps, her blue eyes bright with interest as the men flocked round. She was laughing at them, Ada knew, but they – poor stupid mutts – didn't see it.

'I think she should stay in the back more,' Ada said, nudging Clem.

'Watch your elbow, that hurt!' he grumbled. 'I think you'll have a job keeping Freda away from the bar. Besides, she brings in trade, you know she does. I've watched the men follow her with their eyes –'

'More than their bloody eyes, if they had half the chance.'

Clem grimaced. 'I'll have a word with her.'

'Oh, and I bet she'll listen too,' Ada replied scornfully. 'Just like she listens to me. No, we just have to keep an eye on her. Rein her in, until she learns some sense, or meets a nice lad.'

'Like me, you mean?'

Ada grinned at her husband. 'She couldn't get *that* lucky.'

Sighing, he pulled her to him. 'You don't regret picking me then? Even after all the hard work?'

'Never.'

'You don't regret *anything*?' She hesitated and Clem tensed. 'What, Ada? *Is* there something you regret?'

'Well, to be frank –'

'Oh, luv, what is it?'

'Well, with your leg being bad and you finding it difficult sometimes –'

He was desperate to know. 'What is it, luv?'

'Well, I miss the ballroom dancing,' she said, giggling as he punched her playfully. 'Do I regret marrying you? Oh, for God's sake, Clem! Now, you listen to me, and listen good. You're my guardian angel.' She stroked his forehead, infinitely tender. 'You might not be the best-looking bloke, or the richest, but you do more for me, by loving me, than any man could.'

Chapter Nine

Doug Oldenshaw walked up the steps to The Sixpenny Winner and ducked his head as he walked in. The pub was noisy, full, customers leaning against the bar, the snug wreathed in tobacco smoke. Someone had told him that it was the best pub in the area. Not posh, they'd said, but a place to get a good beer and a decent hot pie. They were right that it wasn't posh, Doug thought, but clean enough.

He moved to the bar, aware that people were looking at him. After all, he was a stranger and, at six foot two and fourteen stones, hard to miss.

An old man winked as he got to the bar. 'How do?'

'Hello there,' Doug replied.

The old man frowned in concentration. 'Yer not from round 'ere, are yer?'

'No, I'm from over Yorkshire way.'

There was a sudden interest, Doug aware of the hostility around him. Lancashire was always in competition with Yorkshire.

'Can I have a beer?' Doug asked, leaning his bulk towards the bar and the neat woman behind it.

Ada looked him up and down. 'Where in Yorkshire?' she asked, pulling a pint. Bloody Yorkshiremen, tight as a duck's arse. She'd be lucky if she got two pints out of this bugger all night.

'Leeds way,' Doug replied, taking the pint and paying for it.

Behind her, Ada could sense the old velvet curtain being drawn back and knew that Freda was standing there.

Doug saw her in the same instant, and paused, his glass halfway to his lips.

'Hello there,' she said easily, gliding to the bar and ignoring one of the locals trying to get her attention. 'What brings you all the way from Leeds to Stockport? It's hardly a bustling metropolis.'

'Tommy Evens wants serving,' Ada hissed in her daughter's ear as she rinsed out some glasses.

Without looking in Tommy's direction, Freda pulled a pint and slid it along the bar. 'That'll be thrupence,' she said, still looking at the stranger as he downed his pint.

Well, well, well, Freda thought, here was a handsome one and no mistake. Big and strong-looking, not like the puny little runts around here. She stared at Doug's arms and the thick crop of sandy hair. Oh yes, she thought, things were looking up. And about time.

'Who's that?' Doug asked, glancing behind the bar.

Freda followed his gaze. 'That's The Sixpenny Winner,' she replied. 'He was a champion dog, won all his races.' She leaned towards the man. 'You like dogs?'

'Is it stuffed?'

'Well, if it isn't it's been keeping very still for years,' she replied, pleased to see the stranger laugh. 'So, how long are you going to be around these parts?'

'I'm not sure,' Doug replied, aware that Tommy Evens was watching him avidly. He leaned closer towards Freda. 'Is he your boyfriend?'

She frowned; tossed her head. 'He might like to think so, but I'm not tying myself down to anyone particular.' She looked evenly into Doug's eyes. 'I like to keep my options open, you know, just in case something better turns up.'

He was enjoying the pint and the conversation, Doug thought. As for the barmaid, she was a looker, all right. Used to females, Doug knew at once that Freda was experienced. *How* experienced, he wasn't sure, but she was very at ease with men, sure of herself. But he didn't know if he liked that part of her or not.

'Where are you staying?'

'Somewhere up in Hillgate.'

'Ma Thornton's?' Freda queried, leaning further towards him, their heads only a little way apart, Tommy watching furiously from down the bar.

'Yes, that's what it's called, Ma Thornton's. What's the place like?'

'Rough and ready.'

'Do me then.'

'You look the rough-and-ready type,' Freda went on, smiling slightly.

'You don't want to take everything on appearances,' Doug replied.

Tommy got off his seat and moved towards him. 'Hey, you!' he said, jabbing Doug in the shoulder. 'I want a word with you.'

Doug turned, taller than the other man and a couple of stone heavier. But Tommy was mad, and the few pints in him made him feel bigger than he actually was.

'What's the matter?'

'The matter is that *she's*,' Tommy paused and pointed to Freda, *'my girl.'*

A couple of men by the bar sniggered and turned back to their pints. Freda was pretty much anyone's girl, if rumour was anything to go by.

'Oh, grow up, Tommy!' Freda snapped, her eyes cold. 'There's never been anything between us.'

'Except maybe a sheet,' someone muttered from the back.

'You're my girl –' Tommy began again, but broke off when his arm was suddenly caught in a fierce grip.

'Tommy, sober up and stop it, or you're out,' Ada said firmly.

'But –'

'Stop it now, or you're out,' she repeated flatly. 'I won't have trouble here.'

'He – he started it,' Tommy stammered, pointing to Doug.

'He's just a stranger calling in for a pint. Then he'll be on his way.' She turned to Doug. 'That right, sir?'

He nodded. 'Of course. I don't want to cause any problems.'

'You're a Yorkshireman, aren't you?' someone shouted, laughing.

Ada passed Tommy his pint, soothing him like a mother.

'Now, sit down again, lad, and drink up. There's a good boy.' She shot Freda a hard look, her daughter feigning innocence at the bar. 'We don't want trouble.'

'I wasn't the one –'

'Tommy, shut it!' Ada said warningly.

But he wasn't about to stop. People were watching him now and he had a reputation to defend.

'Mrs Hargreaves, your Freda knows we have an understanding –'

'Well, I *don't* understand,' Clem said suddenly, walking between Ada and Tommy and nudging the latter towards the door. 'Go on, lad, away with you!' he said firmly. 'You can come back when you've cooled off.'

Tommy could tell that Clem meant business, and after furiously finishing his pint, he walked to the door. When he got there he turned and waggled his finger at Doug.

'You watch it. We don't want Yorkshiremen in here, and I don't want anyone sniffing around my girl.' With a dull thud the door closed behind him.

Ada steered Freda into the back room. Her face was livid.

'Can't you ever stop causing trouble?'

She was guileless. '*Me?* I like that. I was just chatting to one of the customers.'

'You were giving him the eye,' Ada replied, 'and stirring up trouble with Tommy.'

'Tommy Evens is nothing to me.'

'Then you should tell him so, not lead him on.' Ada sighed, turning to move back to the bar. 'I wish to God you were married, Freda. There's more trouble caused in this pub because of you than anything else.'

Freda bit her lip irritably. 'I can't help it if the men like me.'

'You encourage them,' Ada snapped back. 'You should hear what they say behind your back. What they whisper when they think I can't hear them. Only I've got ears like a church rat and I catch every word.' She studied her handsome daughter impatiently. 'You should be more careful, Freda. I just hope what they say's not true. If it is, my girl, you've lost your chance of marrying anyone worth having.'

'I haven't done anything to be ashamed of! I just like to have some fun. God knows, it's dull enough round here.' She moved towards the grate in the kitchen and put one foot on the fender. 'You'd be lost without me. After all, our Vicky thinks she's too good for the pub.'

'Vicky helps out as much as you do.'

'Oh yes, with a long face that damn near curdles the beer,' Freda retorted bitterly.

Ada sighed. 'I can't argue with you now. We'll have a talk later, but now I've got to get back out to the bar. Your father can't manage on his own.' She turned, then turned back. 'Meanwhile, you can make yourself useful and peel those potatoes. There's food to be made.'

Back in the pub, Ada pulled a pint and then stood watching Clem as he swapped a joke with a group of the regulars. If Freda got a job somewhere else it would be easier, but did she *really* want her daughter out of her sight? She might be an irritation in the pub, but away from it, what could she get up to? The thought was unwelcome. If only Freda was more like her sister – pliable, respectable.

'Can I have another?' Doug asked suddenly.

Ada jumped to attention. 'Can you pay for another?'

'My money's good,' he responded, not rattled by her tone. 'Almost as good as your beer.'

Raising her eyebrows, Ada pulled him another pint and took the money, leaning on the bar and looking at him intently.

'Why so far away from home?'

'I've come to seek my fortune.'

'Why leave Yorkshire?'

'Why not?' Doug replied pleasantly. 'I've seen all I want to see of Yorkshire. I fancied a change.'

'When a man says that it's usually because he's leaving behind debts, or a woman.'

Doug drank half of his pint and then laid down the glass on the bar. 'Neither.'

Ada studied him. He was good-looking certainly, a big strapping man, and nice enough. Besides, he had money in his pocket and although his clothes weren't expensive, they weren't falling off his back like some in Churchgate.

'Looking for a job?' Ada asked.

'I might be.'

'There's not much about at the moment, not round these parts. Work's getting more and more scarce. You might find it hard to get anything – especially you being a foreigner. All the employers'll be more likely to give work to a local.'

'I might have special talents.'

Ada raised her eyebrows. 'You still won't get a job, unless you're a bloody magician and you can pull one out of your hat.'

Doug took another swig from his beer. 'Is that your daughter?'

'Yes, Freda's her name. What's yours?'

'Doug. Doug Oldenshaw.'

Ada was curious and suddenly glad to talk to someone new. After all, she'd heard everyone else's story time and time again.

'She's a good-looking girl.'

Ada nodded. 'And she knows it.'

He paused before continuing. 'And that's the landlord?'

Ada nodded, glancing over to Clem with pride. 'That's the landlord, my husband.'

'He handled that lad well enough, but I saw him struggling to lift something a while ago –'

'He does his best, does Clem. There's not a more popular landlord around these parts. But he had an accident and finds the lifting and carrying difficult.'

'Must make life hard for you,' Doug replied. 'It's tough work running a pub. Every day's full from the moment you get up to the moment you go to bed. I know, I ran a pub in Leeds.'

Ada narrowed her eyes. 'So why aren't you *still* running it?'

'It was closed down,' Doug replied. 'I wasn't fired, didn't steal anything, or seduce anyone's wife.'

'Why didn't the brewery offer you another pub?'

'I wanted a change. I went to work on the docks in Liverpool first, then on the Manchester Ship Canal. That was hard work, but the pay was good. Meant I could put aside a bit of money; get some savings together.' He finished his beer, aware that Ada was listening intently.

'There's not many men with savings in the Depression,' she said cautiously. 'Not many men round here who can buy a pint and not worry about the cost.'

'My money's good.'

'Aye, you keep saying that. But it's a funny thing about men,' Ada said drily, 'they brag a lot. They start when they're lads and before long it becomes a habit. Take you, for example: here you are talking about your nest egg and for all I know it could be sixpence and a bent button.'

'You're right, it could,' he said, preparing to go. 'How far away is Ma Thornton's?'

'Go up the hill, turn right and keep on until you see a few shops. She's at number twelve. It's about three minutes' walk.'

'So close? I suppose this will be my local from now on then.'

Ada's face set hard. 'There's a pub nearer.'

'But it won't have the same charm,' Doug replied, smiling as he left.

Freda was waiting impatiently behind the curtain as

her mother walked back into the kitchen. A bowl of potatoes lay on the old table, a newspaper piled high with peelings beside it. Freda's face was flushed and she seemed oddly excited.

Ada looking at the potatoes critically. 'This has still got peel on it –'

'So, what did he say?'

'Who?'

'Doug Oldenshaw. The man you were just talking to.'

'Oh, you mean the Yorkshireman,' Ada said provocatively. 'Not much.'

'He was talking about money.'

'That's all Yorkshiremen do, *talk* about money.' Ada picked up the peelings and frowned. 'You've left a quarter of the potatoes on these.'

'He said he had money –'

'If you heard what he said, why ask me?' Ada countered. 'Look, he was bragging about his savings. He didn't look rich to me, though. And he'd been working on the docks; no rich man works there.'

'He was saving his wages,' Freda countered. Some of her fair hair had worked loose and was falling onto her cheek. She brushed it aside impatiently.

Oh God, Ada thought, her daughter was smitten with the stranger. This was a turn-up. Normally Freda was cool with men, so this could be interesting, Ada mused to herself. Doug Oldenshaw, an ex-pub landlord, with money . . .

'Why the interest, Freda?'

She flushed. 'It was just that he's someone different. A new face around.'

'A good-looking face too,' Ada admitted, 'with a nice line in chat. The kind that girls go for.'

'He said he'd had a pub.'

Ada leaned over and tweaked her daughter's ear. 'My, my, my, your hearing *has* improved. Only this morning you couldn't hear me calling you to get up.'

Freda turned away, trying to sound composed. 'I just thought that he was interesting.'

'I think he thought you were interesting too,' Ada said deftly. 'Hinted that he'd be making this place his local. But then, you heard that, didn't you?'

Freda kept her back to her mother. 'I don't know why you were so short with him. We could do with some help around the place. You've said so often enough, Ma. You've said how hard it was for us to move the beer barrels around and how we could do with a man's help in the cellars.'

Ada had already had the same thought. It *would* be a help to have Doug Oldenshaw working at The Sixpenny Winner. She liked the look of him, and his size – you needed someone big to do the heavy work. As soon as he had said he was looking for work, Ada had started thinking about offering him a job. It wasn't an instant decision; she had been thinking about getting help for months. But even the fact that Freda was smitten might well be, for once, advantage. She would be easy to keep an eye on if she was hanging around the newcomer. It might even stop her lingering at the ginnel exit talking to the local boys . . .

It would mean money, Ada thought, another wage to find. But that could be managed. She had some cash put away. Anyway, it was the Depression; everyone understood that money was tight. But if there *was* a man about the place, someone who could really work hard, things would be easier. Yes, Ada thought, it might be worth investing in Mr Oldenshaw. If only just to find out just how much money he *really* had stashed away.

She busied herself peeling some carrots hurriedly, her head bowed. There might be something in all of this. After all, she had to get Freda married soon, and Doug Oldenshaw might well make a good match. He'd been in the trade, could obviously handle himself, and was good-looking enough to keep her daughter from straying – for a while, at least . . . Ada sighed to herself and shook her head. Dear God, the man had only just arrived in Hillgate and here she was, marrying him off to her daughter! It wasn't like her to be so impulsive. But then there was something about Douglas Oldenshaw Ada had taken a liking to. And she had always been a wicked judge of character.

Looking over to Freda, Ada put one hand on her hip, the other pointing to the bowl of potatoes on the table.

'Well, what are you waiting for? Are you going to put those in water, or not?'

Chapter Ten

Victoria was sitting by her father's chair in the cramped downstairs sitting room, reading from the paper. It amused Clem how earnest she could be at times – who in his family had ever been interested in politics? He had to admit that he wasn't. In fact, his philosophy on life was simple: love many, trust few, and learn to paddle your own canoe.

But not Vicky. She was full of ideas, of dreams of travel. Things had changed so much since women got the vote, and the whole world had been turned on its head after the war. Look at the way women had stepped into men's shoes, Vicky had said repeatedly; women can do anything. She had proved it too, going to night school to learn about economics in her own time, and politics. God, how she loved politics . . .

'It says here,' Vicky paused to read the newspaper print, 'that Mussolini's announced he's running a Fascist empire now.'

'That's nice,' Clem said distantly.

Vicky laid down the paper. '*Nice!*' She saw her father's expression and grinned. 'Being boring, am I?'

'Well,' Clem admitted, 'a bit more gossip about Stockport and a bit less about Mussolini wouldn't go amiss.'

Suddenly he shifted in his chair, wincing.

'Is the pain bad today?'

'Shouldn't be,' her father replied. 'It's not cold any

more. I should be thawing out. Tell you the truth, Vicky – and not a word to your ma about this – but the bloody stairs kill me now.'

'Oh, Dad –'

Immediately he was sorry to have mentioned it. 'Don't mind me! What about you? Work, work, work –'

'Not like Freda.'

'You and your sister should get on better,' Clem rebuked her gently. 'Blood's thicker than water.'

'I'd like to spill some of hers and see.'

Clem laughed. Vicky might be overearnest at times, but she had a keen wit.

'I think your mother needs a rest, a little holiday.'

'Ma would never leave the pub, you know that. And money's too tight –' Vicky stopped, wanting to bite her tongue.

'I know, there's never enough cash. And there's many men out there who would kill for a job, never mind a holiday.' Clem paused, thinking back. 'When your mother and I were first married we saved up for near a year and then went to Blackpool for a holiday, to a place run by a woman called Gladys Hollis. She were the size of a tram, that woman, and cooked like a murderess.' He laughed at the memory. 'It were so bad – and we'd booked for the whole weekend. So I phoned my mother, and Evie sent a telegram saying "Penny's gone into labour, come home quick." Thing was, Penny was the cat! But it got us out of Blackpool and away from that bloody awful food.'

Vicky laughed, even though she'd heard the story a dozen times.

'What was she like?'

'I told you. Big as a house –'

'Not Gladys Hollis! I meant Ma. What was she like?'

'Ah, she were pretty. Very pretty,' Clem replied affectionately. 'She grew up fast, did your mum. She had to – after what her mother did.'

Vicky glanced down at her hands, thinking back. 'You know, I hardly remember my grandfather.'

'Pat died when you were still a little one,' Clem said quietly. 'He wasn't a bad man, just unlucky. Pat should have lived a lot longer than he did, but Milly's death knocked the stuffing out of him. It shouldn't have – he should have flourished when she'd gone – but somehow he couldn't live without her. Always amazed me that. Made no sense to miss a woman like her. She were a right bitch.'

Surprised by his ferocity, Vicky pressed him. 'Was she *really* that bad?'

'Milly Gantry was hard, with a vicious tongue,' Clem answered, thinking back and shivering at the memory. 'Your mother's nothing like her, thank God. Milly Gantry died of bitterness. She gave up, sick with temper. Whatever happened to your mother, she'd never do that.'

Vicky was surprised that her father was talking so much about the past. Until recently he had never spoken about it, and she had gleaned only the most rudimentary of information from her mother. Of course, as she grew up, gossip had sometimes brought up the story of Milly and Pat Gantry, but somehow Vicky had never felt she could press for details from her parents. Freda, naturally, wasn't interested. It was sordid, she said, better to forget it.

'I wonder sometimes if your mother loved me more *because* of my accident,' Clem mused. 'She'd seen her own mother ride her father into the ground about his lameness, and yet Ada never wavered. It never made a jot of difference to her. She was there for me the day it happened, and she's been there for me ever since.'

'And you've been there for her,' Vicky replied gently.

'I was more bloody help before!' Clem snapped, irritated by his disabilities. 'I can't seem to get on top of it, Vicky. It's not for want of trying, but the pain gets so bad sometimes.'

'No one runs that bar like you, Dad.'

He smiled, momentarily proud. 'That's true. I'm a good landlord, and that's a fact. But I wish I could do more of the lifting and carrying, not rely on you girls and your mother. It's not fair.'

'The regulars come because of you –'

'I know you're trying to make me feel better, Vicky, but it worries me. We need help around here, a man's help. It chokes me to say it, but we do.'

'We can manage –'

'No, you can't, and I've made my mind up,' he said firmly. 'Your mother needs some extra help – just for a while, until I'm back on my feet properly.' He paused, looking at his daughter. 'Get something for me, luv, will you?'

'What?'

'Go upstairs to my room, and feel at the bottom of the wardrobe, behind the shoes. There's a box there, with my boot polish and rags in it. Bring it here, luv, will you? And hurry.'

Moments later Vicky returned with the box.

'No one knows . . .' Clem said urgently, as he opened the box and took out the tins of boot polish, '. . . that there's anything special in here, but . . .' He pulled out a bundle of rolled-up rags and unfastened them. A wad of money, tied with string, fell onto the old sofa beside him.

'Dad!'

He smiled, tapped the side of his nose. 'Now then, young Vicky, here's my secret stash. It's not much, but it might well be a good help. Say nothing to no one – especially not your sister. I love Freda, but she's a bit wild and, well, best to keep this a secret between us. You know where the money is, and whenever your mother needs it, or you do, for something important, then help yourself.'

'I can't do that –'

'Well, what the hell do I need with it?' Clem countered. 'I've been putting that money by for years. I thought we'd all have a holiday sometime, or buy a little car.' He smiled at the thought; it seemed so trivial now. 'But times are hard again, Vicky, and before long you might be glad of a little nest egg. Your mother says nothing, but if I know her she'll have some of her own money put by.' He laughed. 'That's what makes a good marriage – a few secrets. I just want you to make sure that she gets a man in to help. If she has enough for his wage fine, but if it leaves her short, Vicky, there's always this pot you can dip into.' He turned at the sound of feet on the stairs. 'Quick, hide it!'

Vicky was leaving just as Freda walked in. Her expression was petulant.

'You want dinner yet, Dad?'

'That would be nice, luv. In a little while.'

Vicky raised her eyebrows. 'Are you cooking it?'

'Why not?'

'Well, be sure to save a bit. The hospital are bound to need it for analysis later,' Vicky replied smartly, walking out.

Watching her sister go, Freda moved over to the

window and pulled back the blind, looking down into the ginnel. The day was clouding over, rain beginning. It was always raining, she thought, and she'd hoped to get off to the park later, see if there was anyone around. Like Tommy. Oh, she'd soon have him eating out of her hand again . . .

'I don't know why Vicky's always moaning about me,' Freda said, chewing the side of her fingernail. 'I do as much as she does around here. Mind you, there's enough work to kill a horse in this place.' She was thinking of Doug Oldenshaw, trying to plant the seed in her father's mind about hiring him. She never thought for one moment that Clem was one step ahead of her. 'We could do with a hand, Dad. Someone stronger than we are. We are women, after all.'

Clem watched his first-born curiously. She was handsome and no mistake, he thought, but sly. Here she was, talking about how they were struggling. There had to be something behind it. Freda never normally thought of anyone else. Perhaps she already had someone in mind for the job.

Mischief got the better of him: 'Oh, come on, you can manage, luv. Three strapping ladies like you can handle anything.'

Her face tightened. 'We need a man's help, Dad! It was all right when you were stronger, but we need someone else – until you're well again, of course.'

'But this is *my* pub, Freda.'

She glided over to the sofa and perched on the end of it. 'No one would think of taking The Sixpenny Winner away from you, Dad. Everyone knows it's your place. Having someone in would just be temporary. We'd just hire some ordinary bloke to do the fetching and carrying.'

Clem pretended to consider it. 'But what kind of man would want to work just doing menial stuff?'

'There's enough men need a job!' Freda snapped. 'Someone could just appear out of the blue and solve our problem.'

Oh, so that was it, Clem thought. She's got her eye on someone. Some little outside flirtation she would like to carry inside to the pub, to keep an eye on her conquest. Mind you, Clem thought, at the same time Ada and he could also be keeping an eye on *them*.

'Perhaps,' he said, unable to resist taunting her, 'we should hire an older man.'

'An older man! But a young man would be strong –'

'An older man would be steady,' Clem countered, trying hard not to laugh.

'But an old man would be slow.'

'A young man might be flighty.'

'Dad! How can you talk about hiring some old fool?' Freda said, close to exasperation. 'What good would some worn-out, beaten-down idiot be to us?'

'How did he get from "older man" to "worn-out, beaten-down idiot"?' Clem asked placidly. 'Have you someone in mind, Freda? Someone not too worn out or beaten down?'

Shifting her position, Freda smoothed her hair. 'Well, someone *did* come in today –'

'That big young fella? I saw him at the bar.'

'Was he big?' Freda asked disingenuously. 'I didn't notice. Anyway, he's already had some experience –'

'At what?'

She gave her father a slow look. 'At running a pub.'

'And?'

'He's looking for work.'

'What's his name?'

'Douglas Oldenshaw.'

'That's a Yorkshire name,' Clem said shortly. 'I'll not have a Yorkshireman running my pub.'

'He wouldn't be *running* the pub, Dad, he'd just be helping us out. *You* run the pub,' Freda said slyly, then paused before adding: 'After all, haven't you been saying how tired Ma's been looking lately? She needs help. I worry about her, I really do.'

'Freda Hargreaves! You've got more brass than a colliery band,' Clem said wryly. 'I'm promising nothing, but I'll have a word with your mother later. We'll see if she's as smitten with this Oldenshaw as you are.'

At that moment Douglas Oldenshaw was descending the steep street towards Little Underbank in the centre of Stockport. There he paused, lit a cigarette, and stared at the row of steps. As he did so, Winter's Clock chimed, the huge figures coming out to strike the hour. Well, that was a hell of a thing, Doug thought, staring into the jeweller's window. He wondered then how much trade Winter's was doing. It was obvious that the town was suffering from the Depression as much as everywhere else. Maybe the pawnbrokers were the only ones left doing business.

On arrival in Stockport he had thought of going to James Seal's tobacco factory to ask for work. Standing outside the Market Street entrance, he had read the list of inviting smokes: Golden Navy Cut, Lily, Empress and Crown, and Jolly Tar. Overhead had been a sign proclaiming: 'CIGARS OF THE FINEST BRANDS', and 'ALL KINDS OF CIGARETTES KEPT IN STOCK'. He had read the words, looked up at the windows, but for some reason his heart wasn't in working there.

Because he couldn't stop thinking about The Sixpenny Winner. He had been amused by the stuffed dog behind the bar, and liked the place. Rough and ready as it was, it had also been inviting – nothing special, but not a bad place to hang your boots. Inhaling deeply on his cheap smoke, Doug watched the street ahead.

He thought of himself as a lucky man. That was his greatest talent. His old father had once said, 'Think lucky, and by God, you get lucky.' Well, his old man hadn't been that fortunate, but Doug had taken the advice and for him it had worked like a talisman. For a man with little education he had done all right for himself, ending up running a big pub in Leeds. The fact that there had been a fire and the pub no longer existed was neither here nor there. He would find something else. He was lucky, after all. But in the weeks that followed, Doug had travelled around the North and settled on nothing. Casual labour had kept money in his pocket, but he had wanted something more to work at. A challenge.

There were precious few challenges in the Depression, Doug discovered. The men with jobs were determined to keep them, and employers weren't hiring. So that was when he decided to move on from Liverpool and the canal and try his luck elsewhere – like Stockport. And he might well have picked the right place at the right time. That serendipity that had brushed Douglas Oldenshaw's life before appeared to have paid him another, welcome, visit.

Grinding out the cigarette stub underfoot, Doug made his way up the hill towards Hillgate, whistling under his breath. If he was offered work at The Sixpenny Winner he would take it. He liked Ada Hargreaves, reckoned she was smart and straight, like he was. And the place was lively enough, the daughter was pretty and he might well become indispensable. In time.

Oh yes, Doug thought, it might well work. After all, he was a lucky man. Wasn't he?

Chapter Eleven

On the corner of Churchgate Bessie Cork stood with her arms folded, Lizzie Antrim beside her. Having just closed her corner shop, Bessie was staring down the street at The Sixpenny Winner, nudging Lizzie as they watched Doug Oldenshaw lowering some beer barrels down through the trap door in the street.

'See that? Now there's a man who thinks he's on to a good number.' She nodded as a local man passed by, then turned back to Lizzie. 'Never buy a thing from me, those Hargreaveses. Think they're a cut above my shop. As for that big fella, he's not one to chat.'

Lizzie could imagine why. Bessie Cork, at a towering five feet eleven, with a voice like a loud-hailer, was hardly someone a man would gossip with.

'I heard,' Lizzie said, dropping her already low voice, 'that he'd just moved into the pub.'

Bessie nodded, her grey hair, flattened under a net, pressed into immobility. 'Last night. Moved his stuff in after the place had closed. Sneaked in.'

'Aye,' Lizzie said thoughtfully, easing the weight of her rotund little figure on her tiny, booted feet. 'Makes you think.'

'If I were Clem Hargreaves I'd be thinking all right! As for Ada Hargreaves, I'd have thought she had more sense. Well, after all, it's inviting trouble, isn't it?'

Lizzie was well aware that if the Hargreaveses had been regular customers of Bessie's they would have been judged less harshly. But, as it was, Ada had little truck with her neighbour – and had even been heard to criticise the veg.

'He's a Yorkshireman too.'

Obligingly Lizzie tut-tutted, although this was old news. 'He looks nice enough. How old d'you reckon?'

'Twenty-seven?'

'Handsome too.'

'Handsome is as handsome does,' Bessie replied enigmatically. 'I dare say that Freda Hargreaves will have noticed his looks by now. That girl's fast. If the rumours I hear in this shop are anything to go by . . . well, all I can say is, if she were my daughter I'd be ashamed.'

'People only gossip about her because she's pretty,' Lizzie offered, then seeing that the observation hadn't gone down well, changed tack. 'But you're right, she likes the men.'

'*Likes them!*' Bessie repeated, aghast. 'She's always hanging around the back entrance of the pub. My Herbert – God bless him – used to say there's many a time he'd been past at night and seen her there. Shameful, I call it.'

Fleetingly Lizzie wondered what Herbert had been doing down the ginnel anyway, but said nothing. For all the talk, she believed that Freda Hargreaves was nothing more than a flirt, a bored, pretty young woman stuck in a pub.

'Her sister's not like that,' Bessie remarked, then added disapprovingly, 'Vicky might have a good head on her shoulders, but it won't do her any good. Men don't like blue stockings.'

'I heard she were going to night school. Reading politics. Fancy,' Lizzie said, awe-struck.

Bessie sucked on her teeth. 'Politics! I ask you, what's

a woman want to know about politics? The only politics Vicky Hargreaves should worry about is politicking some man down the aisle. And she better be careful with any boyfriend she has, or her sister will scupper her chances.' Bessie kept watching Doug as he rolled another barrel towards the trap door steps. 'D'you remember when Saville Willis fell down that trap?'

'Saville Willis?'

'Oh, you know who I mean. He were that rickety little bloke from the pawn shop on Park Street. Married the redhead with a squint.' Bessie looked at her companion impatiently. 'They lived up Portswood.'

'Oh, *those* Willise's,' Lizzie replied, a memory stirring into life. 'When did he fall down the trap?'

'He were coming home one night, when it were still The Royal Oak, and he didn't see the trap were open.' She made a whooshing sound with her mouth. 'Down the bugger went, little bow legs flailing about.'

'Did you see it, Bessie?'

She pulled a face. 'Nah, but I can imagine it.'

'Was he hurt?'

'He fell thirteen feet, what the 'ell d'you think?' Bessie snapped, eyeing up Doug carefully. 'Now if that fella fell thirteen feet I doubt he'd come to much harm. Lots of meat on them bones.'

'Take some feeding,' Lizzie said wistfully.

The two women fell into silence, watching Doug move the barrels, muscles apparent under his rolled-up shirtsleeves. He was aware of them watching and suddenly turned, waving cheerfully.

Flushing, Bessie looked away. 'What flaming cheek! Who's he think he is? Well, he'll have his work cut out with Freda Hargreaves, and that's a fact. He might think he's cock of the walk now, but wait until she gets her hooks into him. There's many a man been made miserable by that little tart, and if I'm any judge Douglas Oldenshaw will be the next.'

It was nearly seven when Doug finished, closing the trap door from the inside and then washing his hands. Slowly he rolled down his sleeves and pulled on his jacket, the noise of customers sounding welcome overhead. He would go up in a minute, he thought, but first he'd have a smoke. With practised ease, Doug rolled himself a cigarette and lit it, leaning back against the wooden cellar steps to enjoy his first drag.

He had been lucky, just as he'd expected. On his third visit to The Sixpenny Winner Ada had offered him a job as cellar man and general fixer. The pay wasn't bad – enough to cover his needs and rent at Ma Thornton's. But now Doug had left there and was about to start paying Ada for the small bedroom on the second floor.

Inhaling deeply, Doug sighed to himself. The room was functional, no more: a bed in one corner, and an old wardrobe with a fly-spotted mirror by the door. Oh, and a black-leaded fireplace packed up with newspaper – Ada threatening him with bloodshed if he tried to light it.

'And that goes for throwing your butt ends into the grate too,' she had said, her hands on her hips. 'There are rules in this house. If you abide by them, we'll get along fine. If you break any of them,' she'd shrugged, 'you're out.'

He liked Ada, recognising her toughness and yet suspecting a soft core underneath. Doug breathed out some smoke and watched it curl upwards to the damp cellar ceiling. The girls would never come down, now that he was working at the pub. Freda was convinced that there was a ghost, and Vicky – well, Vicky just didn't like anything to do with pub work. She never said so, but her manner, her expressions, spoke volumes.

Never happy behind the bar, Vicky did her stint but lacked the sassy charm of her sister. Customers were polite with Vicky, but cheeked Freda. At first Doug had wondered why the two girls worked at The Sixpenny Winner. After all, Vicky was smart enough to get a job outside and bring in a good wage. Then he realised that it had more to do with Ada than the girls. Ada wanted to keep her daughters out of the factories and mills. Besides, in the pub she could keep an eye on them – especially Freda.

The girl had made it obvious from the first that she liked him, but Doug was no fool. He had wanted a job and got one, he was not about to foul his own doorstep. Besides, what exactly did Freda want from him? She had more than enough admirers already and he wasn't about to be made a fool of. Oh no, Doug thought, he was a bit too steady to let himself get carried away.

Not that it wouldn't be easy to fall in love with Freda Hargreaves. She had a way about her, a manner of talking, moving, even blinking that was somehow a fraction slower than other women. It gave her a languid air, something drowsily sexual . . . Doug closed his eyes and breathed in. He would stay in Stockport for a while and then move on. The pub was as good a place as any and, besides, he was getting fond of Clem.

At the thought, Doug stubbed out his cigarette and walked up into the bar. A couple of regulars nodded to him, Freda turning and giving her slow smile. He smiled back, then moved away.

Ada was just coming out of the kitchen, wiping her hands on a tea towel.

'You get the beer in?'

'All sorted.'

'Thanks.' She jerked her head towards the kitchen. 'There's a meat pie in there for you –'

'Hey, thanks. I look forward to that.'

'You haven't eaten it yet,' she replied wryly. 'When you're done, Doug, pop upstairs and have a chat with Clem, will you? I said I'd go, but I've too much on down here for a while and, besides, I know he likes your company.'

Surrounded by the smell of cooking, Doug sat at the kitchen table and then pulled the pie towards him. For a moment he savoured the aroma before cutting into it, the steam rising like a feather from the brim of the crust. A memory stirred him, for a moment so painful that it made him rest his hand against his heart. In another kitchen, there had been a table not unlike this one. Another pie, not unlike this one. Another chair with a rickety leg . . . Mortified to feel his eyes fill, Doug picked up his knife and savagely cut into the pastry, the gravy gushing out over the edge of the brown enamel dish.

Up in the top bedroom, Clem was listening to the radio. But the reception was so bad and there was so much crackling that he turned it off. The autumn night was coming down, shadows beginning to dance on the ceiling, the streetlamp lit outside. He was getting worse and he knew it. It was a comfort to know that Doug was working in the pub, but, God, Clem thought, he was so jealous of him.

The thought was shaming and made Clem move, as though by shifting his posture he could throw off his unease. It was somehow worse because he liked Doug. On the few occasions they had talked, Clem realised he had found himself an ally, discovering how much he had missed close male company. He had always chatted easily enough to his customers, but having grown up surrounded by brothers he felt it was good to have a man in the house again. It was a relief to talk about football, about work, the days before the Depression.

'How do?' Doug said, walking in and breaking into Clem's thoughts. 'Thought you might like a bit of a chat.'

Clem smiled, sitting up as straight as he could.

'How's business?'

'Good,' Clem said.

Doug pulled a chair over and sat down. He rolled a cigarette for himself and one for Clem, passing it over to him after he had lit it.

'Nice bacci,' Clem murmured, taking a long drag.

'What's up, Clem?'

He shrugged his shoulders. 'Nothing.'

'What's up?' Doug repeated patiently.

'Dark thoughts,' Clem admitted, clearly embarrassed. 'I get them now and again. Nothing to worry about.'

'Get them myself, sometimes.'

Clem let the smoke out of his mouth languidly. 'You?' he asked surprised. 'I thought you told me you were lucky.'

'I am,' Doug replied, 'but I still get down sometimes. You know, when you think about the past; when you remember something . . .'

Clem understood. He had done a lot of remembering that afternoon when his leg had been playing him up.

'Funny how the bad times come back to haunt you when you're down.'

'That's why,' Doug replied, 'because when you're up you don't let them in.'

Clem frowned, then asked, 'How old are you?'

'Twenty-seven.'

'I thought you were older.'

'It's my mature way. I fool everyone.'

Laughing, Clem relaxed. He always found that Doug soothed him, let his luck – or was it good humour – rub off?

'You like working here?'

'Sure.'

'What about your room, is it OK?'

'Do fine for me, and your wife's a smashing cook.'

'Aye, she can cook like an angel and no mistake. Vicky's like her, but Freda . . .' Clem laughed. 'Freda is a moody cook. Some days it's good, other days you'd swear she'd put acid in the gravy.'

Doug nodded. Something in the gesture alerted Clem. 'You like our Freda?'

'She's very pretty, amusing.'

'You know what I mean, Doug.'

He looked Clem in the eyes. 'Yes, I like her, but I wouldn't do anything wrong. It wouldn't be fair, what with me living under your roof and taking your money.' He paused, trying to find words to continue. It was difficult to talk about private matters after so long hiding things. 'I don't want a girlfriend at the moment.'

Clem nodded, but didn't really understand. 'Someone else? Back home?'

'In a way.'

'A wife?'

'In a way.'

The light was fading, throwing shadows against the wall.

'Did she leave you?'

'In a way.'

'Bloody hell, Doug!' Clem said, not unkindly. 'Whatever d'you mean?'

Doug looked at his hands – big hands with long fingers. Workman's hands. 'Would it be rude to say I didn't want to talk about it?'

'Nah, just honest.'

'I'll tell you something, though,' Doug went on, looking up, 'when I finished work she'd have a meal ready. Sometimes a pie – in a brown enamel dish.'

Rain started outside, tapping against the windowpane and dribbling into the water barrel below. The sound echoed eerily in the still evening.

'I failed her . . . That's why I don't want a girlfriend, and why I don't fool around. When – if – I ever fall in love again, I want it to matter. And I want to make sure we look after each other. For life.'

'That makes sense. But you mustn't worry, Doug, bad things happen to everyone.'

'They do that,' Doug replied, smiling faintly.

'Remember how lucky you are!'

'I am,' Doug said emphatically. 'I don't think of losing my wife, I think I was lucky to have her for a while.' He sat up, suddenly shaking off the gloom. 'Right! I brought some cards up here, Clem. You ready to get a right good thrashing, or not?'

Chapter Twelve

Laying down half a pint on the top of the bar, Freda looked at the woman in front of her. Lizzie Antrim was sipping at the beer delicately, her eyes magnified by the thick glasses she was wearing. To look at her no one would have suspected that she had a drink problem, but she had. Being a widow, Lizzie had time on her hands and her late husband's few savings kept her in beer, fortified wine, and port at the weekends. No one ever saw Lizzie drunk, only merry, and only the bin men knew for sure exactly how many empty bottles came out of the back door of Lizzie Antrim's terraced house.

Freda knew that she was a close friend of the dreaded Bessie Cork, and had watched as Lizzie came in, looking around anxiously as she passed through the door to check that Bessie hadn't caught sight of her. It would be unlikely that she had, as Lizzie visited the pub only at night, long after she knew Bessie had shut up shop. She would be up in her flat now, reading books that the Jehovah's Witnesses had lent her. Lizzie knew that Bessie would hardly approve of her drinking – let alone drinking in the despised Sixpenny Winner.

'Quenches the thirst a treat,' Lizzie said, laying down her glass.

'I saw you talking to Mrs Cork,' Freda said mischievously. 'You two are great pals, aren't you?'

Lizzie's eyes looked startled behind glasses. 'Oh no, Mrs Cork and I just pass the time now and again.'

'You should bring her in for a drink,' Freda persisted, 'after all, we all live nearby.'

Lizzie smiled woodenly. 'Mrs Cork's not one for drinking.'

'Odd you're friends then,' Freda replied, turning to the man beside Lizzie. ''Lo there, Mr Potter. What's your poison?'

'I've been coming here for three year, what d'you think?' he snarled, leaning on the bar, one thin arm poking out of his jacket at the elbow. 'I've been walking this town since five this morning and there's not a job to be had.'

Freda had heard it all before. There was no work, so the men came in and made half a pint last for three hours rather than go home and face their wives.

'I heard there were jobs at Henessey's,' Lizzie offered.

Mr Potter looked at her with contempt. 'Nah, that's just gossip, nothing more.' He pushed a penny over the counter towards Freda and then picked up his half-pint. 'I heard Arnold Declan's died.'

Overhearing the name, Ada turned. 'Arnold Declan dead? When did that happen?'

'Last night. Heart attack, someone said.'

She thought back, remembering Arnold coming to the house in Portswood the fateful night of the argument. He had been kind to her. As though it was yesterday Ada could see him washing himself under the outside pump that spring morning. The morning her mother died.

'I'm sorry about that,' Ada said sincerely. 'How's his wife doing?'

'Packed up and gone off, before the bailiffs came,' Mr Potter replied. 'Someone said she'd gone back to Ireland, to her folks. Kids are all grown up now, so she's probably better off.'

Of the people around the bar, only Freda wasn't listening. She was watching Doug instead, wondering why he was ignoring her. Mistakenly she had thought that once he moved into the pub, he would seek out her company, but the opposite was true. He was avoiding her. Wiping out a glass, Freda stared at Doug's back as he moved into the kitchen.

He had soon made himself at home, becoming friends with her father and spending a lot of time with him. He should spend time with her instead, Freda thought bitterly. How often had she lain awake at night longing for his footsteps on the stairs? She had almost *willed* him to knock on her door in the early hours – but he never had. He had been polite with her, just as he was with Vicky, but shown no obvious interest.

It was infuriating, she thought, wanting him all the more because of his indifference. After all, how many *other* men wanted her? How many others waited at the back entrance to see if she would come out and chat when it was dark? God knows how many little presents she had had; men like Tommy Evens begging her to go out with them . . . But not Doug.

He had obviously told the truth when he'd said that he had run a pub before. All the petty, tiring jobs that had to be done daily he did without asking. There was always beer on tap, clean bar tops and polished glasses. He seemed to anticipate what would need doing almost by a sixth sense – much to Ada's delight.

Her mother might tease Doug about his being a Yorkshireman, but she was impressed by him. Freda knew her mother too well not to notice how Ada looked Doug up and down, measuring him like a tailor measures a suit. He might well do, Ada's look said after

Doug had been at the pub for a month. Oh yes, he might well do for a son-in-law.

Unfortunately Doug appeared disinterested in his potential elevation. Instead, he got on with his job. He rose first, laying the fire in the grate in the kitchen and then later checking out the cellar with Clem. When Freda and Vicky came down they always found two plates and mugs in the sink, testimony to the men's early breakfast. But although their father ate with them at other times, Doug never did. Even at night, he would have a drink with the customers, but then take his food to his room and eat there. The weekends varied: Doug would work at the pub when needed, otherwise he would go out. Alone. But no one knew where.

All Freda's flirting had been useless, she thought irritably, watching as Doug moved out into the back.

Her sister tapped her on the shoulder. 'OK, it's my turn now.'

'For what?' Freda snapped.

Vicky raised her eyebrows. 'At the bar. You're normally chaffing at the bit to get off, Freda. What's up?'

'Nothing.'

Vicky pulled a wry face. 'Mr Oldenshaw still not falling for your charms?'

'Oh, shut up!' Freda snapped, throwing down the drying towel and rounding on her sister. 'I don't give a damn for Doug Oldenshaw.'

'That's good, because he's obviously not interested in you.'

'I think I'll have another,' Lizzie said suddenly, breaking into the sisters' spat. 'Just a nip of brandy, to keep out the cold.'

'It's only September, Lizzie. You'll be downing a bottle a night by the time it gets to Christmas,' Freda said churlishly, pushing the brandy over to the old woman.

'Maybe he's got someone else.'

Freda stared at her blankly: '*What?*'

'Douglas Oldenshaw – maybe he's got someone else.'

'I don't know what everyone's going on about! I don't give a damn about Douglas Oldenshaw,' Freda replied heatedly, mortified that other people had noticed her interest. And his disinterest. 'Mr Oldenshaw works here, that's all. He's an employee – Hardly a man *I'd* be interested in.'

Her heart pumping, Freda left the bar and walked into the kitchen. There she stood for a while trying to control her fury. How dare he ignore her? How dare he? He was no one and she was the daughter of the landlord. He should be glad to have a job. God knows, there were few enough around. If he thought she was interested in him, he was wrong. Oh yes, he was very mistaken.

Her temper rising, Freda moved over to the cellar and wrenched open the door. She would put Douglas Oldenshaw in his place, make him realise he was an employee, nothing else. He had had his chance and ruined it . . . Slowly she took the steep steps one at a time.

The light was on below. Doug was in the cellar.

Clem had done his stint serving and had gone upstairs, Ada now alone at the bar as Vicky was making them some tea. After checking that everyone was served, Ada had just moved some dirty glasses when a familiar voice bellowed loudly from the snug.

'Yer bugger!'

Al Weeks! Ada thought, her eyes blazing. She'd been waiting for him to show himself again. She moved hurriedly from the main bar into the snug, then stopped dead. Clem had been telling the truth, *Al Weeks was bald*. Totally bald. And red in the face with drink. Weaving on his feet, Al had already rolled up his shirt-sleeves and was towering over another man, a known troublemaker.

Exasperated, Ada stared at him. When Al was sober he was a reliable man, honest, hard-working, polite, but when he had had too much beer inside him he would have fought with a wardrobe.

'Al! Stop it!' Ada snapped from behind the bar. 'I've warned you.'

'You'll not stop him, missus,' someone called out. 'He's too drunk to hear you.'

'He'll hear the back of my hand, if he doesn't watch out,' Ada snapped back, lifting the slat between the bar counters and walking out.

'You big bald sod!' his cowering victim taunted him, Al flinging aside chairs to get at him. 'You want to paint that head of yours yellow and we could save on the streetlighting.'

Ada winced, knowing the effect such an insult was bound to have on Al Weeks. He had had a fine head of hair until his accident and now he looked – well, *odd*. But not odd enough for her to have pity on him.

'Al! Al Weeks!' she shouted, tugging at his elbow.

He swung round, his eyes fierce until he saw it was Ada. His voice softened at once.

'Oh, 'ello there, Ada, how you doing?'

Seeing his chance, Al's tormentor leaped to his feet and threw a sly punch whilst Al's attention was diverted.

The fist cracked into the side of Al's chest, a whooshing sound coming from his lips as his lungs emptied. Astonished, Ada watched, expecting Al to fold like a burst paper bag.

But Al Weeks was made of sterner stuff. Flinging himself round with all the energy his bulk – and the beer – had given him, Al swung his left arm as high as he could and then brought it crashing down on the other man's head. The effect was spectacular. The man's teeth crashed together. His knees buckled. Then he threw up. All over the snug floor.

'Right! That does it!' Ada hollered, pushing Al Weeks to the door. 'Out you go! And out you bloody stay!'

The fight had gone out of Al all at once. 'But it wasn't my fault, Ada –'

'The name is *Mrs Hargreaves* to you. Not that you'll be needing to use it. You're barred, Al Weeks. Don't ever cross this doorstep again.'

Crushed, Al stumbled out into the street, then turned, his bald head glowing in the moonlight.

'I'll be back. I'll be back –'

'If you are,' Ada replied, her tone steely, 'you'll be leaving with fewer teeth than you've got hairs on your head.'

When Freda reached the bottom of the cellar steps she stopped and looked around her. It was clammily cold. She shivered.

'Oh, hello there,' Doug said cheerfully. 'Something I can do for you?'

His casual tone irritated her even further. 'Have you cleaned the cellar out?'

'No, does Mrs Hargreaves want me to?'

'*I* want you to,' Freda replied imperiously. 'You don't

just work for my mother, but for the whole family.'

Doug's face was all passive calm. 'I see. So *you* want me to clean out the cellar?'

Nodding, Freda walked further into the cellar and looked about her. 'Sweep the floor and then wash it down. There are cobwebs everywhere.'

'It's a cellar, what d'you expect?' Doug replied evenly.

He had been dreading some kind of outburst from Freda, anticipating it for several weeks. Anxious to avoid any involvement with her, he had kept his distance, but apparently that had not worked. She was taking his reserve as rejection. Bugger it, Doug thought, now what should he do?

'All right, I'll clean out the cellar –'

'And when you've done that, you can clean out the yard,' Freda went on, pushing him, desperate to provoke him. 'You have to earn your wages, you know.'

'I've always earned my wages, Miss Hargreaves,' he replied, his tone cooling.

She was standing only a yard away from him, her beautiful hair carefully arranged, her face white with fury. He thought at that moment that he had never seen anyone so angry, and so sensual at the same time.

'Oh, and there's no need for you to spend so much time with my father,' Freda said cruelly. 'I think that's more a family duty.'

'Funny, I didn't look on it as a duty,' Doug replied, putting down the crate he had just moved and facing her. 'Anything else, Miss Hargreaves?'

She flushed at the formal use of her name. God, she wanted him. And every man wanted her. So what was the matter with him?

'Your manner is too familiar,' she said finally.

He burst out laughing. 'Isn't the problem that my manner isn't familiar *enough*?'

The slap rocked him, Freda lunging out without thinking. Then she turned away and moved hurriedly towards the steps.

He was there before she reached the third stair, grabbing hold of her and lifting her off the steps. Struggling, she found her feet again and tried to push him out of the way, but Doug blocked her exit. He had lost control and was angry. The slap had humiliated him. Who did she think she was? Some pretty flirt who had to have every man fawn on her? Well, not him, Doug thought, *not him*.

'Apologise,' he said, gripping her arm.

'*Apologise*? Are you mad?' she snapped, her head thrown back, her eyes hard as stone.

And then he kissed her. She felt his lips on hers and was surprised by the ferocity of the embrace, then found herself wrapping her arms around his neck, her body pressed against his. Lowering himself onto the steps, with Freda lying on top of him, Doug kissed her repeatedly, the attraction he had felt for so long overwhelming him.

Above their heads customers moved around, Ada's boots clicking on the bar floor. The pub door opened and closed, the sound echoing in the vaulted cellars, ringing around the bottles and the beer crates in their sorted rows. And on the steps Doug held Freda to him. They had stopped kissing, and were holding each other as though they would break if parted.

Contented, Freda leaned her head against Doug's shoulders and sighed to herself. And as she did so, Doug stared straight ahead. He had tried to resist, tried to tell himself that he didn't want Freda, that he didn't want an involvement with any woman. But he'd been lying to himself. And he had been lonely too long. So finally the inevitable had happened.

He would act honourably, because he was an honourable man. But somewhere – beyond the passion – there were troubled echoes of the past. Of another place, another woman. A past as cold and unwelcoming as the cellar where they lay.

Chapter Thirteen

1939

As Vicky would tell anyone who would listen, there was a war coming. Chamberlain would not manage to avoid it, whatever people hoped. She wasn't the only one who was worried, hope fading as the months passed. It was obvious what was going to happen, Stockport people said. Look at Germany. Look at the way Hitler's behaved. There's going to be bloodshed. Again.

Earnestly Vicky had talked with her father about what was in the papers, telling Clem about the political rallies she had attended. She was intense, scared; so was he. But he wasn't about to show it.

'There might *not* be a war, luv, not after the last one,' Clem assured her.

He had lost weight and was now bedridden. Pain was a constant, but he had grown used to it; grown used to his strange existence in the top bedroom, away from the rest of the world. His active role in life was over and he lived by proxy – in the talks he had with his wife and his son-in-law. Clem smiled to himself. He liked Doug, had been pleased to see him marry Freda, Clem insisting that he was brought downstairs for the service at the registry office. They should have a proper do, he had said, otherwise people will think Freda's pregnant. But neither Freda nor Doug would hear of it. The marriage was the important thing, not the service.

Afterwards, Freda had seemed to settle down, and Doug had effectively taken over the running of The Sixpenny Winner. Another man might have resented being usurped, but Clem was relieved to know that Doug Oldenshaw was not only looking after the pub, but his family. He was a safe pair of hands, a steady influence. Oh yes, Clem thought, it had been a lucky day for them when Doug Oldenshaw had walked into The Sixpenny Winner.

But if there was a war Doug would be called up. He would have to leave his home and his family. He would have to fight, risk his life . . . Dear God, Clem thought helplessly, don't let it happen. Please, not again.

'Are you listening, Dad?' Vicky said, interrupting her father's reflection. 'The ultimatum expires at eleven o'clock today. If there *is* a war –'

'You should find yourself a nice young man.'

She blinked. 'And see him killed in action?'

'Oh, our Vicky, you always look on the dark side,' Clem chastised her. 'You'll get old before your time if you go on this way.' He smiled at her, taking her hand. 'You're young – get out and enjoy yourself whilst you can. All this book reading, talking, listening to these politicians, it's all right, but it's heavy. Look at Freda – she's settled down and happier now than she's ever been.'

Vicky persisted: 'If there's a war, Dad, Doug will have to go off and fight. Then what will happen?'

'And if there's no war, no one will have to go away and life will go on the way it always does.' Clem sighed, leaning back on his pillows. 'Aren't you interested in anyone, Vicky?'

Flopping down in the chair next to her father's bed, Vicky ran her hands through her thick dark hair. He didn't understand, didn't seem to know what was about to happen . . . Nervously, she glanced at the clock on the dressing table. Ten o'clock.

'Vicky!' her father repeated. 'Aren't you interested in anyone?'

'I see a couple of men –'

'Anyone special?'

She thought of Sydney Hope and Charlie Forbes and shook her head. There was time for romance, time to think about frivolous things – but not now.

'Chamberlain thinks that he can –'

'Tell me about your boyfriends,' Clem interrupted her.

He didn't want to hear about the war for a little while. Ada and he had talked about it that morning as she lay on the bed next to him, her arm thrown across his chest. Always strong, she had pretended to pooh-pooh the idea of warfare, but when he mentioned Doug her hand had closed tightly over his.

Vicky sighed. 'Sydney's forty-one –'

Clem shook his head. 'Too old for you.'

'– and Charlie's a Communist.'

'Never!'

'I'm joking,' Vicky said, winking. 'They're not important to me, Dad. I've never met a man I really liked.'

'Maybe you're looking in the wrong places,' Clem said tactfully. 'You know how it is, Vicky, men don't take to clever women.'

'Times change, Dad. The world's changed. Women have the vote; we're involved in areas we never had a say in before. Life doesn't begin and end in the home. There are other things besides being a wife and mother.'

'Like what?' Clem said, moving his legs and wincing with pain.

'Like travel, seeing the world.'

His eyebrows shot up. 'You want to travel?'

'I might,' Vicky replied, 'I might not. But I want to have the choice.'

A silence fell between them. Vicky wondered if her dreams of travel might soon be over for good. If war broke out, no one would be travelling for pleasure, only to fight. She shivered.

'Freda's never been happier since she married.'

'That's Freda,' Vicky answered, laying her head back against the chair.

It was true, Freda *had* settled down, even seemed besotted with Doug. Uncharitably, at first Vicky had wondered how long the honeymoon period would last, how many months would pass before her sister could no longer resist creeping out to the back entrance at night. But Freda seemed glossy with contentment, her beauty warmed, mellowed.

Incredible what a man could do, Vicky thought, wondering briefly if she would ever find someone who would have that effect on her. And if she wanted it. Did she *really* want to settle down to family life? To live in some house in Stockport? To settle for so little when there was so much? She had always disliked the pub, had worked there because she was needed, but had never enjoyed it.

She was the outcast, the one unit of the family which didn't gel with the others. Clem was the kind old confidant, Ada was the matriarch, Freda was married and settled, and Doug was the driving force behind The Sixpenny Winner – but where did she fit in?

'Who am I like?' she asked suddenly.

Clem frowned. 'Hey?'

'Who am I like in the family?'

'Well, you look like your grandfather, Pat Gantry. But your character's not like any of us really.'

She mulled over the words. 'What about Ma?'

'Your mother's never been interested in politics, or travel.'

'What about *your* mother?'

He laughed until he coughed, Vicky patting him on the back. Finally, tears streaming down his face, Clem spluttered, 'My mother wasn't what you might call an intellectual.' He laughed again. 'She were from poor stock, never learned how to read or write. When she were older she were too busy raising me and my brothers to have time to think.' He shook his head. 'Poor Evie, when she gave you a hug you could hear your ribs cracking.'

'Don't you ever wonder about him?'

'Who?'

'Your father.'

Clem thought for a moment before answering. 'Things were different then, Vicky. Like you say, times have changed, but then we were all so poor. Surviving was what you did. That was what kept your mind occupied. I never remember my father. Heard some gossip, but that was about it. And Evie never said anything about him – even at the end. All she wanted was for her boys not to be thieves and to get a good job and a good wife. That was the height of her ambition. When I married your mother she was made up. Thought I'd hit the jackpot.' He smiled to himself, remembering. 'The world was harder then, but simpler. Evie thought I was a toff when we took over this pub; thought we'd really gone up in the world. Which we had. But now you want more –'

'I'm not saying –'

'Hush!' Clem said kindly. 'I'm not criticising you.

Parents should want their children to do better than they did. The world's opening up, Vicky, but remember this: in the end there's only one thing that matters in life. *Is there someone who loves you?* Someone who would die for you? Without that you could have all the money and power in the world – and have nothing.'

Ada was thinking about Doug. He had always said he was a lucky man, but she considered herself pretty damn lucky to have him fetch up on her doorstep all that time ago. Now there was no more worrying about Freda, no more anxiety about running the pub. It was heaven, that's what it was. Besides, no one messed with Doug. He was quietly tough – nothing brash about him, nothing coarse, but there was a look in his eye which warned people, 'I'm not to be pushed about.'

It was a good thing, Ada thought, otherwise Freda would have run rings around him. If she'd married any other man she would have crushed him within months, but not Doug. Oh no, Ada thought, this one has the upper hand. And he's keeping it.

She looked at the row of hot pies on the kitchen table and counted them. Enough for opening time, Ada thought, and any left over were eaten up quick enough. Stretching, she thought longingly of bed, knowing that a full day's work lay ahead before she could sleep again. But to curl up and close her eyes. Alone . . . She should feel guilty, but Clem slept better in his own bed and she needed those few dark, dead hours when her mind stopped whirling. In fact, she longed for them as someone else would long for a lover. Sleep was – and always had been – her anaesthetic against the world.

But there was a day to get through before she could sleep again. And who knew if anyone would be sleeping soundly come night-time? Glancing at the clock, Ada read the time – ten fifty-one. Getting nearer to the ultimatum minute by minute. Hurriedly she touched her stomach as it lurched, a coldness settling around her heart. War would be hard . . . Jesus, it would be hard.

She could turn on the radio in the kitchen to get the news – or go and listen up with Clem, who seemed to be hoping that war could be avoided. Or maybe he was just trying to reassure her, hoping against hope that peace *could* be maintained. It was obvious why. In the last war Clem had been too ill to fight. This time would be no different. For him. Except that this time he had a son-in-law to lose.

Oh, don't think about it! Ada told herself. Keep busy. Quickly she turned and counted the glasses. If there *was* a war the Germans would try to wipe out the industry in Manchester, and that was nearby. Very near. Count the glasses, Ada, she told herself, twelve, thirteen, fourteen . . .

Straightening up, she looked at the clock again and then suddenly hurried up the stairs to Clem's room. Once there she nodded briefly to Vicky and turned on the radio.

'Hey –'

'Listen!' Ada said sharply to her husband, sitting on the bed beside him and taking his hand.

The radio crackled, the reception bad. Vicky leaned forward, her face strained. The words were not clear, the static increasing, a low whistling starting up. Infuriated, Ada leaped to her feet and banged the top of the wireless. But there was no improvement, only a shrill whirring.

'Bloody hell!' she snapped, glancing at the clock. 'And it's eleven o'clock.'

She hurried out of the bedroom, and paused at the head of the stairs, listening. Far down below, on Churchgate, she could hear the paperboy calling out: 'War is declared. The country is at war with Germany. England is at War!'

Feeling her legs weaken, Ada leaned against the banister rail. A moment later Vicky came out and slid her arm round her mother, resting her head on her shoulder.

'Oh, Ma –'

She could feel Ada's whole body shake. Then, after a moment, the shaking ceased. Drawing herself up to her full height, Ada patted Vicky on the back.

'We'll be all right,' she said firmly, moving on into her husband's room.

Then, for the first time in years, she closed the door behind her.

Chapter Fourteen

A week later Doug was cleaning out the fire grate when he heard a soft knocking on the back door. Wiping his hands he frowned. Who would come knocking past twelve at night? The rest of the family had gone up to bed, Freda anxious about the coming war, begging him over and over again not to go off and fight. I'll have no choice, Doug told her. Don't you love me? she had replied. God, don't you love me at all?

'Who is it?' Doug said as he moved over to the door.

'Me.'

'Me who?'

'Oh, for God's sake, Doug, it's me, Duncan.'

Opening the door, Doug flicked on the dim outside lamp and stared at his younger brother. The years had been luminously kind to Duncan. He seemed to have cheated time and looked untouched by age. His dark hair was wavy and black, his eyes deep-set and amused.

'Well, aren't you going to show me in?'

'What for?' Doug asked, his voice low. 'The only reason you've fetched up after so long is because you want something. Last I heard you were still in Dartmoor.'

Duncan leaned against the door frame. 'I've learned my lesson –'

'I doubt it. Once a thief, always a thief.'

Surprised at the hostility of his brother's tone, Duncan changed tack.

'Look, I've nowhere to stay, nowhere to go. There's a war on. I needed to look out the only family I had.'

'You needed a bed more like,' Doug replied sourly, his bulk blocking the doorway. 'Anyway, how did you track me down?'

'You have friends in Yorkshire, people you kept in touch with when you married.' Duncan smiled. 'I can hardly imagine it, my brother married. *Again.*'

Doug flinched at the word. He wanted nothing to do with Duncan. Everything about his brother reminded him of the past, of his old life, his dead wife. Looking at Duncan all he could see was the pub in Leeds and the way it had burned that night. The night his wife died.

The memory snapped at him, suppressed too long. Duncan had been there that night. He had been one of the men who had held Doug back when he wanted to try to get Emma out. Doug had never forgiven his brother for that. He had told him as much – 'You should have let me go, let me try to get her out. I failed her because of you. I should have died in there with her, not stayed alive without her.'

He blamed Duncan for it all. Even though he knew it was wrong, unfair, he blamed his younger brother for not letting him save Emma. Or maybe he blamed him more for letting him live. Either way, Duncan was too much a reminder of a past Doug thought he had buried. And wanted to *keep* buried.

'You're not welcome here, Duncan.'

The younger man flinched under the cold light. 'I thought we could let bygones be bygones. I never did you any harm.'

But there was something about his brother Doug dreaded. If he thought himself a lucky man, he thought that Duncan was unlucky, tainted by some nasty trick of nature which might well attract violence and chaos. He didn't want his brother here tonight, or any night.

And yet, as he thought it, Doug felt guilty. He wasn't naturally cruel, and besides, he was settled now and should be ready to forgive. Fate had been kind again. He had a home, a wife, a place in life. Maybe he had been too hard on Duncan. War had been declared, God knew who would survive and who wouldn't. Perhaps it *was* time to make amends.

But as he thought it, some shadow moved over his heart and made him cold to the bone.

'I need a job,' Duncan began. 'I'm honest now, really I am, Doug. I swear I wouldn't steal from you.' He paused, implausibly handsome on that dingy back step. 'I can work hard, I can help you out. You'll need me – if you're called up.'

'What about you being called up?'

'I can't be. I had rheumatic fever. Don't you remember?' Duncan asked, watching Doug's eyes flicker. Was he angry at the thought of Duncan avoiding service? Or guilty at having so obliterated that memory of their childhood?

'I don't want to say this, but I can't trust you, Duncan –'

'You can! You can now,' Duncan assured him. 'I was stupid, but that was a one-off. I'm sorted out now. Honest.'

A moment swung between them. Doug was fearful that if he let his brother in, some of his bad fortune would come with him. And yet, at the same time, he was aware of his filial responsibility. He had loved Duncan when they were children. Throughout a cruel childhood they had been firm allies; throughout the violence and random viciousness of their parents' tyranny they had clung to each other. Could he really forget that now? Refuse his brother refuge when he was in need? *Could he?*

'Don't let me down, Duncan,' he said at last. 'You mustn't let me down.'

'Why would I? I can help you – be another pair of hands.'

'Times are hard. I can't pay you much more than tobacco money – and give you a place to stay,' Doug replied shortly. 'My mother-in-law, Ada, is a rum one. Don't ever let it slip that you've been in jail, or she'll give you your marching orders.'

'I never thought my brother would be scared of a woman,' Duncan said smiling.

The remark stung. 'We're respectable here. If you want to be a part of this life, you behave right. If I see you act, look, or say the wrong thing, I'll come down on you like a ton of bricks. And if I ever – *ever* – catch you with your hand in the till you'll find yourself wiping your arse with a hook.'

Stunned, Duncan raised his hands in submission. 'I've told you, I went wrong, but I'm sorted out now.'

'You better be,' Doug said warningly, 'or God help you. Because I won't.'

Another moment passed, Doug unable to move. Then finally he stepped aside to let his brother enter The Sixpenny Winner.

Far in the distance an owl hooted. It seemed, to Doug's ears, like a ghost laughing.

'And who the hell might you be?' Ada said, coming down in the morning to find Duncan making tea.

The day was starting bright, sun coming in at the windows of the kitchen, Trudie Mossop's cat sunning itself on the yard wall outside.

'I'm Doug's brother. M' name's Duncan. Pleased to meet you.'

'I dare say you are, but I'm not so sure I'm pleased to meet you,' Ada replied smartly, pulling on an apron and looking round. 'Where's Douglas?'

'In the cellar. He said he'd only be a few minutes.'

Ada snorted, then moved towards the oven, lit it then blew out the match. All the time she was staring at Duncan. Well, who would have thought that this was Douglas Oldenshaw's brother? He was a good-looker, all right. Not like Douglas – smoother. Almost Latin-looking. And fancy him turning up like this, out of the blue. Her son-in-law had mentioned a brother, but they hadn't seemed close. And now to find him here – well, it *was* a turn-up for the book, and no mistake.

'D'you cook?'

'Hey?'

'I said – do you cook?' Ada repeated, turning as Doug walked in.

'Oh, you two have met.'

'I found him making tea in my kitchen,' Ada replied tartly. 'That had to serve as an introduction.'

'He's my brother, Duncan.'

'I gathered that,' Ada retorted, her hands on her hips. *'And?'*

'He's out of work.'

'There's many on street corners round here who can say the same.'

Doug held Ada's hostile gaze, without backing down.

'He needs a job, and somewhere to stay. I've made it clear that there's little money for him, but we can put him up. Until he gets something else. Or . . .'

'Or?' she asked, her eyes like frost.

'If I'm called up, you'll be glad of the help. Duncan's my brother, so it's family.'

'And why, pray, would Duncan *not* be called up?'

'Because he was very ill when he was a child.'

She looked away. 'Well, I still say we could manage alone.'

'Clem's poorly, you know that,' Doug said gently. 'How much time d'you spend nursing him now, Ada? And when I'm called up, how can the girls manage the pub without you watching over them? They aren't like you. Vicky's a fish out of water and Freda doesn't have your way with money –'

'You can say that again!'

'So you admit you'll need help?'

'I've told you! I can manage –'

'You can't!' he said firmly.

'But you might not be called up.'

'You know I will. It's just a question of time,' Doug replied, dropping his voice so that Duncan couldn't hear what he said. 'My brother knows about pub work. He used to help out now and then when I were in Leeds.'

Ada glanced over her shoulder at Duncan and then turned back to her son-in-law.

'I don't know . . . He doesn't look the reliable type.'

'He's my brother. He's promised not to let me down.'

Something didn't feel right about it to Ada. She knew that Doug was no liar, but something about Duncan Oldenshaw made the hairs on the back of her neck rise. For all his good looks, he worried her. He was too out of place, glowing in that shabby kitchen, his sleek darkness at odds with the grim surroundings.

'Where's he been and what's he been doing?'

Doug had anticipated the question and breathed in, steadying himself for the lie.

'He's been down London way for the last two years.'

'Doing what?'

'Bar work.' Doug almost winced at the unintentional pun.

'Is he married?'

'No. Never has been.'

'Good-looking man like that, he *should* be married,' Ada replied, watching him. 'Make yourself at home, Duncan. Don't stand on ceremony,' she said sarcastically.

'I was just making tea,' Duncan replied, watching as Ada pulled her son-in-law out into the pub beyond.

Closing the door behind her, Ada turned to Doug. 'No.'

'What?'

'I said no. I'm sorry, I know he's your brother, but there's something about him that worries me.'

'Please, help him out.'

'Why should I?' she snapped. 'I know that type, one hand in a man's pocket and the other up a girl's skirt. Oh, don't look at me that way, Douglas! You know what I mean, and I guess you might well think the same of him yourself.'

'I used to. But he's changed.'

'How d'you know?' Ada countered. 'Because *he* said so? That's hardly written in stone, is it?'

'He's my brother.'

'You keep saying that,' Ada replied, 'but it changes nothing. Your brother or not, I still don't want him around.'

'I owe him,' Doug said, his tone curt.

Surprised, Ada looked at him carefully. 'You owe him *what* exactly?'

Sighing, Doug moved over to one of the pub tables

and sat down, resting his head in his hands. Having never seen any sign of weakness before, Ada found herself momentarily wrong-footed. Doug was always cheerful, reliable; never really worried. Until now.

Sitting down in the seat next to him, Ada looked about her, uncertain of what to say. The sunlight hadn't moved round the terrace yet and the bar of The Sixpenny Winner was in shade, the overhead lights unlit. On the other side of the double entry doors she could hear feet passing, the stained-glass above the etched windows gloomy before the sun warmed the colours out of them. And behind the bar, as always, was the stuffed dog in its case. She would have to have a word with next door, Ada thought. Trudie Mossop's bloody cat had been creeping in and spraying up the side of the glass case again.

It wasn't much of a pub, but it was hers. She ran it and she said who came into it. Through the front door – or the back.

'What d'you owe your brother?' she repeated finally.

Doug mumbled something under his breath.

'Oh, speak up!'

'When we were children, we were very close,' Doug began uncertainly. 'We stuck together like glue. Later we went our own ways. Had a falling out.'

'What about?'

'The way he was.'

'Like what?'

'Duncan could get into scrapes –'

'Oh God, that's all we need in a pub.'

'Not now. He's settled down.'

Doug thought back. His brother *had* settled down, toed the line. Even found himself a job he loved in Leeds. On the market, wheeling and dealing. Then Doug had got the pub and Duncan had followed. And then the rest . . .

'When Emma died –'

'I wondered how long I'd have to wait to hear about your wife,' Ada said, not unkindly.

'There was a fire at the pub in Leeds . . .'

Ada stared at him, unblinking.

'. . . Duncan stopped me going back into the pub to try to save Emma.'

'God, Douglas!' Ada said, aghast. 'She died in the fire?'

He nodded, hardly able to force himself to remember that night. 'I hated Duncan for stopping me –'

'He's your brother; he wanted to save you.'

Doug nodded impatiently. 'I know! I know! But I hated him so much . . . We had a fight.'

'Go on,' Ada urged him.

'I hit him hard, real hard.'

At first Ada couldn't imagine it. And then she realised that of all people Douglas Oldenshaw was probably the one who would be the most dangerous if roused.

'You hit him. Then what?'

'I *kept* hitting him, over and over,' Doug said, his voice plummeting. 'Then I stopped – kind of came to, like I'd been in a trance. I swore from then on I'd keep my temper. And I have done. But Duncan bolted. I tried to find him, to make amends, but he'd done a runner.'

Ada frowned. 'But he's found you now.'

Doug nodded. 'Yeah, he's found me now, and now he's asking me for help. And I can't refuse. Because I owe him. It weren't his fault Emma died. It weren't his fault that I couldn't save her. *But he saved my life . . .* Trouble was, I didn't see it that way. I wanted to die, you see, and he'd stopped me. So I hated him for that. I hated him for everything – for Emma's death, my survival, everything.' He looked at his mother-in-law, shame-faced. 'I'm not the nice guy you thought I was.'

'I never liked you anyway,' Ada joked, nudging him with her elbow. 'But why's Duncan come back now?'

'He says it's because of war being declared. He wanted to find what was left of his family –'

'Who just happens to be doing quite nicely for himself.'

Doug held Ada's gaze unflinchingly. 'I know what you think. Maybe part of me thinks it too. But he's not all bad. Duncan's not a bad man. He might be on the make, but he's still my brother and he deserves a chance.'

'Not at The Sixpenny Winner, he doesn't!'

Wearily, Doug shook his head. 'Have I ever asked anything of you?'

'No.'

'Have I proved myself?'

'Well, you married Freda, you deserve the VC for that.'

'And have I run the pub well?'

'Only because I showed you how,' Ada replied, then added more seriously, 'You've been the best thing that's happened here for a long while. You've been a good husband for Freda, a friend for Clem, and my right hand. Without you I don't think we could have coped. You've been a godsend, Douglas.'

'Then let me ask you a favour. Please.'

She hesitated, not wanting to refuse and yet fighting against her own instincts.

'I don't trust your brother,' she said at last.

'Give him a chance,' Doug pleaded. 'I've given him the gypsy's warning and Duncan's no fool. He won't let you down. He won't dare to . . . Think about it, Ada, he'll help you when I'm away. You'll still have a man around the place to do the donkey-work. And besides, Duncan's family – not some stranger off the street.'

Sighing, Ada looked down at her hands and then began to twirl her wedding ring around her finger.

'There's only the little room you used to have empty, off Clem's,' she said at last. 'He'll have to make do up there.'

'Thanks.'

'Oh, don't thank me!' Ada said shortly. 'Brother or no brother, Douglas, I warn you now, if Duncan Oldenshaw causes any trouble, he's out.'

Chapter Fifteen

'Who died?'

'Our business, by the look of it,' Vicky replied, glancing over to her mother.

The Sixpenny Winner was deserted; a full hour after opening time. Since the war the trade had dropped off, only old men and wide boys coming in to drink. Oh, and Lizzie Antrim. She would sit at the bar, hugging her half-pint, and talk about her late husband. If she got really tipsy, she would talk *to* her late husband. Sometimes Mac Potter would come in too, avoiding his wife. He was still out of work, too old to be called up and, in desperation, had volunteered as a blackout watchman. All his frustrations had come out with his little peck of power, and he was violently, abusively, efficient.

Ada looked round the pub, sighing. 'I can hardly believe this is same place it was a year ago. God, if Doug could see it now.'

As he had predicted, Doug had been called up and was now in France, fighting with the army. He would look like the perfect soldier, Ada thought, big and tough. A man no one would mess with. She wondered if he would manage to keep his temper with the war. Or the Germans. She wondered how long it would be before he came home permanently. And she wondered how long Freda would keep whining. Ada sighed again. She missed him.

Mind you, they had his brother for company . . .

'Where is the toerag?' Ada asked Vicky.

She knew immediately who her mother meant. 'Said he had to go out.'

'Where, this time?'

'Who knows? Let's just pray for a bombing raid.'

Ada sighed again. 'He'd find shelter.'

'Not if he was out in the open, somewhere away from a place to hide.'

'Mind you, if he was next to a high building it might fall on him,' Ada suggested hopefully.

Vicky shook her head. 'You know it would miss him, don't you?'

'I think that if we staked Duncan out in an open field, with a bull's-eye painted on his chest and a flashlight trained on him, he would *still* survive.' Ada picked up a duster and began to polish the already shiny bar top.

'I'm on duty tonight. At the hospital.'

It was inevitable that Vicky would volunteer to help as soon as war was declared. They needed workers in the munitions factories, but she didn't want that, wanted to be amongst people. So she became an auxiliary nurse, dressed in her white uniform, leaving the pub in the evening and returning at all hours. Why can't you work days? Ada had asked her. Because they need extra people at night, Vicky had replied, as though it should be obvious.

Ada considered her younger daughter. If she got lucky she might meet someone at the hospital. A doctor, perhaps. Or an injured soldier. Hopefully one with all his limbs.

'When's Doug coming home on leave again?'

'Said Christmas-time,' Ada replied, alerted by the sound of footsteps behind them.

'I'm hungry,' Freda said, her expression sullen as usual.

'Then feed yourself, you're not a baby,' Ada replied.

'It's not exactly busy in here, is it?' Freda went on, moving into the pub and standing squarely in the middle of the empty space. 'We're not making any money like this.'

Ada glanced at Vicky in mock surprise. 'Did you know that? *We're not making any money.*'

'Hey, I thought all we had to do was to open up the pub and that was it. I didn't realise we had to *sell* drinks as well.'

Freda pulled a face. 'Oh, keep it up! You two should be on the stage.'

'We might end up there if things don't improve,' Vicky replied, leaning on the bar top.

She had let her hair grow longer and now wore it tied away from her face. A little extra weight had softened her features and filled out her small frame. By contrast, Freda had lost weight, but her pungent sexuality was still apparent in every restless movement.

'I miss Doug.'

'We all miss him,' Ada replied.

'Not like I do!' Freda snapped. 'He's my husband.' She managed to put into the simple sentence an inference that made both Vicky and Ada uncomfortable. If she had said she missed sex, it could not have been more obvious.

'He'll be home soon.'

'*Christmas!* That's hardly soon,' Freda moaned.

'Why don't you get a job?' Vicky suggested. 'Do something. Ma can manage the pub.'

Astonished, Freda turned on her sister. '*Get a job?* What the hell d'you think I do here? *This* is my job. Besides, I'm a married woman.'

'So being married makes it impossible for you to take on any extra work, does it?' Vicky countered, putting her hands on her hips. 'Well, maybe I should get married and then I can retire.'

'You have to have an offer first. And from where I'm standing, it doesn't look like you're fighting the men off.'

Vicky flushed, Ada throwing down the duster in exasperation. They had been at each other's throats, on and off, for weeks. You should never have two women in a kitchen, Ada had said to Clem, but try putting three women in a pub. It's bloody impossible. They were all different, all stubborn and strong-willed. None of them liked backing down.

'I'm going up to see your father,' Ada said simply, walking out to the stairs and standing for a moment on the bottom step.

The light was dim, rain threatened, the building was quiet. Her eyes moved up to the large window on the stairs, crisscrossed with tape in case of bomb blast. And above it the blackout curtain hung, waiting to be let down, like the lid on a weary eye.

Slowly Ada mounted the first flight of stairs and then paused on the landing. Her room was on the right, Vicky's next door, the largest room the furthest away: Freda and Doug's room, when he was home. Shadows grew with the lengthening day, the sounds of shrill voices coming from the pub below. So they were still arguing, Ada thought, making for the second flight of stairs.

When she reached the top she was slightly out of breath. The door of Duncan's room was closed. Curiosity made Ada want to go in, but she resisted, creeping into Clem's room instead. He was dozing, his chest rising as he breathed, his hair still thick round the emaciated face. Dear God, Ada thought, he's so ill. She had known it for a long time, and yet she *hoped*. Always walking in on him and praying, wishing, that he was not as bad as she had thought.

He turned at the sound of her footsteps, putting out his hand.

''Lo there, luv.'

Gently she slid onto the bed beside him, lying on her side, one arm across his chest as though protecting him.

'You're warm, Clem,' she said, nuzzling his neck. 'I wish I was as warm.'

With a massive effort, his slid his arm around her and hugged her. 'Soon will be, old girl. Soon be warm as toast.'

Deftly she wriggled off her shoes and slid her feet under the blanket, tickling his. Clem laughed, the sound low in the dim room.

'Want to fool around a bit?' he asked, although both of them knew it was impossible.

'I always want to fool around with you,' Ada replied, her left leg crossing over his body, her hair brushing his cheek.

There was no sexuality in the action, rather a profound loving which went beyond the physical. It was as though she said with her body, 'I love you.' With intimacy, without desire. When first married they had spent many snatched hours in bed, the curtains drawn in the afternoon. Even up on the high land behind the town they had made hurried love. They'd gloried in it. And as Clem became more and more ill and sex became impossible, their closeness never wavered. They no longer had sex, but they *remembered* it together.

'Duncan called in to see me earlier.'

'What did he want?' Ada replied shortly.

'To have a chat.'

'About what?'

'Just passing the time of day.'

She blew out her cheeks. 'He does a lot of that – passing time. In fact, time passes Duncan more readily than it passes anyone else.'

'I don't think he's a bad lad.'

'He's a creep, Clem, and you know it.'

'Well, he's not his brother, and that's a fact. I miss Douglas.'

Ada nodded. 'Me too. But what could I do, Clem? I could hardly refuse to take his brother on, could I? It made sense at the time – having Duncan to help out. But now we don't really need him. The pub's not doing much trade, and if Lizzie Antrim goes teetotal we're sunk.'

'But you can't fire Duncan, can you?'

'I'd like to fire him from a bloody cannon!' Ada replied sharply. 'Mind you, the thing I was most worried about never happened. I thought that Duncan – being such a masher – might turn Vicky's head. Or, God forbid, Freda's. Oh, I know what you think, Clem – she's married – but you know our Freda, and Douglas *is* away.'

Clem shook his head. 'Hey now, Duncan is his brother –'

'And a brother hasn't betrayed a brother before?' Ada queried, her eyebrows raised. 'Anyway, it's all right. Apparently Duncan isn't to Freda's taste. She thinks he's common.'

Clem looked at his wife and then smiled as Ada burst out laughing.

'*Common?*'

'That's what she said,' Ada replied, 'that he was "rough as a bear's arse".'

She hooted with laughter again, Clem staring at her in amazement. 'Freda said that? I don't believe it!'

'Oh, she did. And Vicky said that Duncan was shifty.'

'Shifty.' He considered the word. 'Yeah, that's about the measure of it.'

'She thinks he's a bit of a villain.'

'Never!' Clem replied. 'Not Douglas's brother.'

'Why not? Because *he's* so honest, it doesn't follow that Duncan is. Think about your brothers, Clem. They're all lying toerags, but you turned out all right.'

'I had you. And besides, I wanted to live.'

She laughed again, lying against him on the bed. 'I was thinking about that dog you used to have, Clem. The one with the wall eye.'

'I never had a dog with a wall eye,' he said, thoughtfully. 'But I once had a girlfriend with a wall eye.'

'You never told me that before,' she said, biting him lightly on the chin. 'Why didn't you marry her?'

'Some quiet little thing came along and bowled me over.'

'I was never quiet!'

He laughed again, his chest rising and falling. 'You were; you were a little mouse once, always so timid, like you were afraid to draw attention to yourself.'

'I was,' Ada admitted; remembering her mother and father. And the arguments. 'That was a long time ago.'

'A long time ago,' he agreed, thinking. 'Before Freda and Vicky were born.'

Ada snorted. 'They fight like dogs, those two! I can't think why, but they do. Always getting at each other. They should be friends. I used to long for a sister when I was growing up.'

'I used to long for peace,' Clem replied. 'There were always so many of us in the bloody house. Never anything of your own. Not your own clothes, or shoes. God help you if you were the last to get up in the morning – because you were left with the rubbish. All the best stuff had already gone.' He thought back. 'But Evie was a good mother really. Everyone thought she was a rough old bird, common as muck, and she was, I suppose. But she was kind, always kind. Mind you, she could be handy with her fists!'

'Remember that dress she wore to our wedding?' Ada said, trying not to burst out laughing.

It had been made out of some kind of floral-patterned material, bought on the cheap, because Evie couldn't afford anything else. But she was so unused to wearing anything reasonable that she didn't know it was curtain material. She'd had the dress made up and thought she was everybody at the wedding. What she didn't know was, from the back, she looked like a moving allotment. And when she stood against the sunlight the material was transparent, her heavy legs, with their long drawers, visible for everyone to see.

No one said anything. But Ada had noticed, and so had Clem, and both of them had avoided looking at each other, terrified they would break out laughing.

'She never knew about that bloody material, did she?'

Clem laughed, shaking his head. 'She thought people were staring because she looked so nice. Afterwards she said to me – "No one thought Evie Hargreaves could look like a lady. But I showed them, didn't I? And they called *me* a rubbing rag."'

Ada laughed again. 'She was great, your mother.'

'Yours weren't so good, though.'

Ada shuddered at the mention of Milly, Clem's arm automatically tightening around her.

'I sometimes think . . .'

'Go on, luv,' he urged her.

'It sounds so daft, but when they talk about life after death – you know, how you're supposed to meet up with the people you knew before – well, I wonder . . .'

He frowned. 'Wonder *what*, Ada?'

'I wonder if she'll be there. Waiting for me. Waiting to tell me how it was all my fault. How I killed her.'

'You didn't kill her! She killed herself.'

Ada pushed her face against her husband's neck, her voice muffled. 'I still see her sometimes, swinging at the end of that ginnel . . .' She shuddered again. 'She was so angry. I could never say the right thing, or do the right thing, and she was always on at my father. Day and night, on and on at him.' Suddenly Ada rolled over onto her back, staring up at the ceiling. 'I don't want to see her again. *Ever*.'

'When you die you only see the people you loved, and those who loved you,' Clem replied softly, clinging to her hand. 'Don't you worry, luv. I'll come and meet you. I'll be there waiting for you.'

The words seemed poignant, as though he was making a promise; as though he had thought about it for a long time and was finally voicing it. Had he? Ada wondered. In pain, alone for much of the day, had her beloved Clem lain in his bed and thought about death? And was he afraid of it? She was. She didn't want this death, this bruised, dim thing to steal him, to take him away from her. Being alone would be damnation, but what was the choice? She might want to die before Clem, but she knew with bitter acceptance that he would go first.

And then what? Her husband had been the centre of her life. The one constant was the fact that he loved her. Clem had always been there, always faithful, always grateful that she had chosen him.

'Hey!' Clem said suddenly, nudging her. 'It's getting dark.'

She didn't understand for a moment what he meant, and then leaned over and flicked on the light. The room came back into itself, and her bleak mood shifted. How could she be so selfish when it was Clem who was suffering?

Smiling, Ada got off the bed. Then carefully she interlocked her fingers in front of the lamp and began to make shadows on the opposite wall. Her hands were nimble, quick, making the shape of a bird, its wings flying upwards in the cramped Northern bedroom.

'What's that?'

'A bird!' Ada said shortly. 'What about this?'

Her fingers made the shape of a fox. Years earlier, Pat Gantry had taught her, when they had been alone, at peace, making shadow animals on the wall – when Milly wasn't around.

'Hey!' Clem said excitedly. 'That's good! I didn't know you could do a church!'

'That's a fox!' she snapped, knowing that he was teasing her.

Her hands moved again, making the head of a cocka-too, her fingers rising up suddenly into a shadow crest. It was magical, Clem watching, Ada intent on the game, her face animated. He loved her so much, he thought suddenly, his heart shifting. This tough little lady was his life. God, Ada, he thought, I don't want to leave you. I don't want to miss a day of your life. Not one word, or action. I shall be such a jealous ghost.

'An elephant!' he shouted delightedly, Ada making a trumpeting sound and then falling back onto the bed, laughing. 'Is there anything you *can't* do?'

'Whistle,' she replied seriously. 'I can't whistle in tune.'

Pursing his lips, Clem whistled softly – a band tune, low and sweet.

'Try. Copy me,' he urged her.

She did so, but the notes were flat. Grimacing, Ada shrugged her shoulders.

'See, I told you. I never could whistle.'

'Then I'll whistle for you,' Clem replied. Then suddenly he took her hand and looked into her eyes. 'Ada, we both know I'm none too well. When I go – no, don't interrupt me! – when I go, you listen out. Sometimes, just stop what you're doing and listen. You never know, if you concentrate real hard, you might just hear me whistling for you.'

Chapter Sixteen

1942

Walking down Lower Hillgate, Vicky paused underneath Winter's Clock. It was silent, the figures encased in their hideaway behind, idle for the duration of the war.

Three years had passed, Vicky thought incredulously and another Christmas just gone. Whoever thought the war would last so long? Wasn't it supposed to be sorted out years ago? Wasn't that what the politicians said? Thank God for Churchill, she thought. The country needed someone who looked as though he knew what he was doing.

Bleak news was coming from abroad, from Germany. She shivered. Surely it couldn't be true what the rumours said about the Jews and the concentration camps? It was unbelievable. But then again, *was it*?

For years Vicky and her political friends had been talking about Hitler. At first their discussions had centred around the gossip smuggled out from Germany and Poland. Then, as time progressed, the news became widespread, reported everywhere. Only that September there had been an outrage: the SS slaughter of the Jews in the Warsaw ghetto. Jesus, Vicky thought, it was bleak, and it was going to get worse. Through working at the hospital she had come into contact with a Jewish family who had fled Germany and now lived over a shop in Lower Hillgate. The father was a skilled diamond merchant and they had had a prosperous life before the war. But now the family – mother, father and three children – all lived cramped in two rooms above a derelict butcher's shop.

Vicky had seen them occasionally, hurrying down the street, or queuing for treatment at the hospital. One child was seriously ill. The father – too old to fight – had taken on work in the munitions factory, his wife selling or pawning whatever jewellery she had left to pay the rent and buy food. A striking woman, she stood out, her skin sallow, her eyes dark and wary. She seldom spoke and when she did so, kept her head down, her voice hardly audible.

And that was only one family, Vicky thought. How many others *hadn't* got out of Germany? She looked up at the clock and remembered its chiming from her childhood. When exasperated, Ada would take her and Freda to see the clock and show them the rotating figures. If she was angry with their squabbling, she would tell them that at night they would be stolen away and kept prisoner behind the clock, sentenced to be forever coming in and out, in all weathers, telling the time, but never able to come home.

It should have frightened them, but Ada couldn't keep a straight face and so, for years afterwards, when anyone was at the end of their tether they threatened to leave home and take up residence in Winter's Clock.

Vicky smiled. Just like her mother that was . . . Rain started, wetting her hair and the shoulders of her coat. Ducking quickly into a doorway, Vicky decided she would wait until the shower had finished before moving on. There was plenty of time to get to the hospital. Her thoughts wandered as she looked up the steep street. It was so quiet, now that most of the men had gone off to fight. So quiet, so empty. Like The Sixpenny Winner.

Where had the glory days gone, the days when it was hard to get into the pub by the front door because it was so crowded? She had never liked the place, but it had been comforting – the sounds of clinking glasses, of conversation, laughter, all seeping into the backdrop of her childhood. So many times she had done homework to the accompaniment of the old piano being thumped into submission downstairs. Music-hall tunes and jazz melodies had pounded through the floorboards, in later years each one censored by the lack of an upper C.

Ada had said repeatedly that they would get the piano tuned and repaired, but it hadn't happened. The war had happened instead, and now no one played any tunes, even jingoistic ones. It was sad, because Ada had taught herself to play quite well . . . Vicky sighed and looked up into the heavy rain cloud overhead. A memory came back sharply. Her mother playing 'Daisy Bell', her father leaning on the top of the old piano and tapping his fingers in time to the music. When it came to the chorus, they had both sung together, Clem winking flirtatiously at his wife. He had been fit then, young, his hair still brown, in the days when they had just taken over the pub.

It was to have been their big achievement, their climb out of the worst of the slums. A real income, steady work, something of their own. And now what? Vicky thought. Now her adored father was dying and her mother was walking about an often empty pub like a lost spirit, her hands clasping and unclasping endlessly.

Of course Freda could do more to help, but that wasn't her way. If someone was suffering badly, Freda was always suffering worse. She missed Doug, she said repeatedly; longed for his leaves, then when he came home she monopolised him with a litany of what life was like for her, never giving a thought to ask what war was like for *him*, how *he* managed away from home, how *he* coped with fear and the loss of his friends.

Vicky stared at the street growing more water-marked by the moment. Or maybe her sister *did* talk to her husband, in bed. In the early hours did she hold him and comfort him and bolster his confidence? Tell him that they could cope, that the war would be over soon and he would be back with them? That things would return to how they used to be?

Vicky doubted it. Freda's interest extended first and foremost to herself. Others always came second. She loved Doug, Vicky was sure of that, but she whined about missing him and when he came home, nagged him about leaving her. As though the war was some kind of personal attack on her home life.

If *she* was married, it would be different . . . Oh, stop bloody raining! Vicky thought, pulling up the collar of her coat and shivering. It wasn't likely she would get married; there were no men around that she liked the look of. Oh yes, there was Milton Brown, Fred Heathcote and Bobby Driver, but they were talkers, too puny to fight. And, over time, talking politics hadn't been enough to make Vicky fall in love with any of them.

And at the hospital the only young men she came across were the injured. Most of the younger doctors had been called up, and as for Dr Riley, it wasn't likely Vicky would fall madly in love with a short, pot-bellied Irishman with a stammer. Hurriedly she ducked her head out from under cover and then ducked back. The rain was setting in. She would wait a little longer, and then make a run for it.

A long run, but there was no alternative . . . Vicky sighed. She was mystified by men. Wasn't she attractive? She thought she was. She had eyes, she could see other women, and she didn't seem any less attractive than they were. So why hadn't she fallen in love? It wasn't fair. Freda could have had any man she wanted before she married, and as for Doug, she had run him to ground within weeks. Shuddering in the cold, Vicky thought back to the time when her sister had been single, to the many occasions when she had come across Freda at the back entrance of the pub, standing under the lamp, talking to some man, or *men*. Always so confident, so arrogantly sure of her appeal.

Had she never been intimidated by this other race? Vicky wondered. Had she never worried what they would say about her, or do to her? Or maybe she had *wanted* them to make passes at her, to dream about her. To make love to her . . . Vicky flushed. That was what was the matter with her: she was a prude. Damn it, she was! That was why men didn't flock around her; she was too shy, too awkward.

If they had been friends, she would have asked Freda for tips. But she would have died rather than enlist her sister's help. Then, miraculously, Freda got married and it was all over. The competition had been put safely to bed. Vicky smiled to herself at the apt analogy.

Uncharitably she had thought that Freda might stray when Doug went off to fight, but she hadn't. And it wasn't as though there was any lack of temptation . . . Vicky flushed to her hair roots, so mortified that she stared hard at her feet, trying to control herself. Her boots wanted polishing – she should have done that before she set off . . . But then her mind wandered back to where it had stalled. *Temptation*. It came in a six-foot package, with blue eyes and dark hair and a smile that should have been censored.

Duncan. Mortified, Vicky could feel her temperature rising. Thank God she managed to cover it up at home. No one had any inkling – except Duncan. She was sure he knew that she liked him. It was a mercy Freda hadn't noticed; she would have been a bitch about it. It was also a mercy that Freda hadn't collared Duncan for herself . . . Oh, grow up! Vicky thought angrily. He's no good, that's obvious. A right handful, the kind of man even Freda would have trouble managing.

But nevertheless, it was surprising that she didn't like him. Why was that? Vicky wondered for the thousandth time. Duncan would have been so obviously her type in the old days – charming, flirty, easy with women, and very attractive. Clem had said that Duncan looked like a young Victor Mature. Or Victor *Manure*, as he called him. From then on they secretly referred to him as *Duncan Shit*.

It was so hard not to think about him, Vicky mused, amazed that, for once, she hadn't confided in her father. But he would have been so disappointed in her. And surprised.

'You're interested in Duncan Oldenshaw? Aye, luv, you could do better with your brains. He's not your type.'

Her father would be right, but what had brains to do with it? Vicky might know all about the political history of England from 1800 to 1900, but so what? What did her night-school classes matter now? She had no burning desire to teach and certainly no ambition to run for Parliament. Education was necessary, Vicky had told herself repeatedly over the years. But in reality her forays into knowledge had often been her only means of escape from the pub.

But now people thought of her as a blue stocking, a swot, a clever clogs – just the kind the boys avoided. Well, what could she expect? She had earned her reputation – as had Freda. As had Duncan . . . The cold rain pelted down on the doorway over Vicky's head, splashing up from the cobbles and drenching her boots.

Vicky's mind wandered again. Just what *was* Duncan really like? He had never been married, had no children, and yet he spent a lot of time away from the pub on his days off. So did he have a girlfriend? Or was he up to something? Vicky had heard about the black market and wouldn't have put it beyond Duncan to do some shady trading. Besides, the eggs that materialised every other week, and the nylons he had found Freda were hardly readily available.

And her sister had been so ungrateful, Vicky remembered with some feeling. Duncan had given Freda the stockings and she had looked at them critically, then mumbled a sullen thanks. Ada had been delighted with the eggs, but had warned Duncan that she didn't do prison visits. And what had Duncan brought for her? For Vicky? A book on history!

What the hell did she want with a book, she thought disgustedly. When he gave it to her she could cheerfully have crammed *The Wars of the Roses* down his grinning throat. It had come from the library, anyway. She had seen them try to flog some old books for a few pennies – and no doubt Duncan had helped himself. It was a poor worn thing too, ragged-edged, probably teeming with old spittle and greasy fingermarks.

A book! The memory made Vicky wince with fury.

No stockings for her. Even the bloody eggs would have been better, made her look like a home body, the kind of woman a man marries. You wanted a woman who knew what to do with an egg. But a history book, what did that say about the way he thought of her? Dried up, boring, dull, and well worn.

Annoyed by her own temper, Vicky decided to move. The rain was still coming down hard but anything was better than standing in a doorway brooding over a toerag like Duncan Oldenshaw. In the hospital she would be busy, with no time to think. She would talk politics with the soldier with the burned leg and read the newspaper to the blind sergeant. They would like her and think she was smart.

But they wouldn't dream about her – and that was a bloody shame.

Ada stamped her foot loudly twice.

'Oi, Duncan!'

Summoned, he popped his head up through the trap door behind the bar.

'Yeah?'

'Don't bring anything else up. It's so quiet at the moment. Leave it a while and hope we get some more customers tonight.'

Drumming her fingers on the bar top, Ada then looked around. She would have to find something to do. All this mooning about was bad for her. Of course she could go back up to sit with Clem, but he was sleeping now and it wasn't fair to disturb him. Sleeping, and dying. Oh God, not yet, Ada willed, please let me have him a little while longer.

It was doubly hard because Douglas was away. The thought of Clem dying whilst the women were alone was almost unbearable. They had Duncan, but honestly, what good was he? Until he'd gone, Ada hadn't realised just how solid and calming a presence her son-in-law was. In the years since the war had started, the atmosphere had changed in the pub. Ada knew only too well that she wasn't getting on with her daughters, and the trade that came was poor fodder. As for Duncan, Ada had hoped that when things took a turn for the worst she could somehow elbow him out, but he was too wily for that. Black market treats materialised with enough frequency to make sure Duncan's feet stayed firmly under the Hargreaveses' table.

And she felt she'd heard enough about Monty and Rommel, and any of those black-and-white men whose images she watched at the Roxy cinema on the Pathé news, flickering shapes in the dark. Ada watched the pictures and tried to understand the politics. Churchill had given a speech after the victory of El Alamein: 'It is not the end. It is not even the beginning of the end. But it is, perhaps, the end of the beginning.'

But what does that mean exactly? Ada had thought then. Things changed from day to day. England was winning, losing, winning again. The troops were in Germany, France, the Far East. And just where *was* the Far East? Ada had tried to concentrate, but her thoughts had kept drifting back to Clem. There might be a war on, but she had her own personal battle – how to keep her man alive.

Rubbing her eyes, Ada made up her mind. She would give him a surprise. Yes, that was what she'd do.

Ada called up the stairs for Freda in her room above. 'Get down here, luv! I want some help.'

Yawning, Freda walked down.

'Were you asleep?'

'Why not? There's nothing to do.'

Ada gave her daughter a slow look. 'Well, *I've* got something for you to do.'

'Aw, Ma –'

'You're doing nothing else, Freda! You can help me, for once.'

Dragging her reluctant daughter back upstairs, Ada went into her bedroom and closed the door firmly behind her. On the bed was an old suit she had refashioned, her best shoes highly polished, next to her bag. And by the window, on the shabby dressing table, was a jam jar full of clear liquid.

'Right, I want you to do my hair.'

Freda stared blankly at her mother. 'What?'

'Would you like me to give it to you in sign language?'

'OK, I heard,' Freda replied sulkily. 'Why d'you want your hair doing?'

'For a change. I want to surprise your father and I want it doing like Ingrid Bergman's –'

'You don't look like Ingrid Bergman.'

'I want a hairdo, Freda, not surgery.'

Sighing, Freda lifted up the comb and brush her mother had laid out and began to brush Ada's hair.

'Careful! I bet you don't tug your own hair like that.'

'You're hair sore.'

'I wasn't before you started,' Ada replied smartly, pulling a towel round her neck. 'Now make sure you do a good job, Freda. I know you're clever with this kind of thing. I mean, look at your own hair. I want it like that. You know, professional.' She jerked her head towards the dressing table. 'I've got some sugar and water ready. It'll have to do to set it.'

'It'll make it sticky.'

'Not if you don't put too much on. Oh come on, get going.'

'What's the surprise *for*?' Freda asked, parting her mother's hair on the right side.

'I told you. Your father.'

'Why?'

'Because he's not well.' Ada paused. 'He's very sick, Freda, very sick indeed.'

Freda said nothing, just kept brushing her mother's hair, but the action altered from abrupt tugging to a gentle, rhythmic movement.

'How ill is he?'

Ada took in a breath. This was the time to tell her. Vicky knew, now Freda had to be told.

'He's dying, luv.'

She stopped brushing her mother's hair, then – after several seconds – slowly began again.

'I thought . . . I thought he wasn't so bad.'

'Well, he is,' Ada replied, feeling unexpectedly close to her daughter as she rhythmically brushed her hair.

'What will you do?'

'Huh?'

'When Dad dies, what will you do?'

The question caught Ada off guard and for a moment she floundered. There was no sympathy in the question, but no malice either – just detachment, as though Freda had other things to think about.

'I'll carry on the same as usual, what else? We'll sit out the war and wait for Douglas to come home.'

'What if he doesn't?'

Ada stiffened, but Freda seemed not to notice and kept up the brushing. Of course Douglas was coming back! Ada thought furiously. How could anyone think differently? Douglas *had* to come back.

'My son-in-law knows how to keep out of trouble. He'll come back safe and sound.' Suddenly Ada turned in her chair and looked up at her daughter. 'Freda, are you fretting that he might be hurt?'

'He might be killed.'

Ada flinched. 'You've coped so well, why are you so worried now?'

'Things have changed,' she said quietly.

'How?' Ada paused, trying to read her daughter's face. 'Oh, Freda, you're not! *Are you?*'

She paused before answering, her voice low. 'Yes, I'm pregnant.'

Jumping out of her seat, Ada hugged Freda to her.

Freda dropped the brush and drew back. 'Hey!'

'I'm so pleased,' Ada said genuinely. 'Oh God, a baby! It's such good news, luv, such good news. Wait till I tell your father.'

'It's only a few months –'

'How many?' Ada asked, throwing aside the towel and trying to tidy her hair.

Freda paused before replying. 'Four and a half months . . . Ma, sit down, I haven't finished your hair –'

'Oh, bugger the hair! This is more important. You should have spoken up sooner. Four and a half months gone – what a thing to keep a secret, you sly one! This is the best news for years. You, a *mother*! God, Freda, you're going to be a mother. Nothing will be the same now. It's a whole new life for you, a whole new life.'

Chapter Seventeen

She would remember that night for as long as she lived, Ada told anyone who would listen. Trying in vain to comb the sticky sugar water out of her hair, she gave up and wrapped a headscarf around her head. Then she rushed upstairs, propped Clem up in bed and put hot-water bottles around him to keep out the freezing winter night. Finally Duncan materialised with a rickety electric fire that Ada was convinced would burn them all to cinders.

Sitting on the end of the bed, Vicky opposite her, and Ada in the chair next to Clem, Freda finally made her announcement.

Each of them reacted differently to the news: Vicky with shock, Ada with pride, and Clem with laughter. He threw back his head, laughing fit to burst, then called a quiet Freda to him and kissed her on her cheek.

She was still reserved when Vicky turned to her.

'So you're having a baby?'

'No actually, a rabbit.'

'It'll have your ears then,' Vicky replied curtly.

'Oi, that'll do! I don't want arguing any more,' Ada interrupted. 'Freda has to be calm and think good thoughts.'

Vicky raised her eyebrows, Clem pulling a face at her.

'It's wonderful, luv,' he said again, 'a baby. My grandson. What are you going to call it?'

Freda shrugged. She hadn't thought about calling it anything. Hadn't really thought about having it. Oh Lord, if only they knew ... It was careless of her, Freda thought, stupid and careless to have left it until it was too late. When she'd gone to see the woman in Oldham she had been convinced that it could be sorted out. But she'd told her – you're too far gone. If you'd only come a couple of weeks ago we might have been able to do something ... But you *have* to do something. My husband's away fighting and I don't want this child when he's not home ... Hard luck, the woman replied. I can't do anything for you, luv. You should have taken precautions.

Well, it was all right saying that, but how could she have stopped him when he was eager as a rabbit? She had wanted it too. But now here she was, a mother-to-be ... The thought made Freda queasy. How would she look pregnant? Children had never really come into her view of life. She was only young; plenty of time to think about kids later.

Or maybe not. Time to think about it now, because now she was having this baby and by the look of things her family were delighted, even if she wasn't. Freda smiled wanly, then realised that actually it could turn out to be an advantage. She would be fussed, petted, spoiled, and when Doug came home he would treat her like a queen. After all, she was having his son, wasn't she? Because it was going to be a boy. She knew that.

'You remember, years ago, when we went to Blackpool and I saw that gypsy?'

Ada nodded. 'What about it, Freda?'

'She said I'd have a boy.'

'Well, she had a fifty per cent chance of being right,' Vicky chipped in.

Freda ignored her. 'If it is a boy, I want to call him William. Billy for short.'

'William,' Clem repeated, 'that's a good name.'

'See if Doug likes it when you tell him –'

Freda cut her mother off. 'If I want the baby to be called William, it will be.'

Oh God, Ada thought, I can see the way this is going. No calming effect of pregnancy on Freda. No, she was going to milk this for everything she could. Oh well, Ada thought smiling to herself, who cared? It was worth her daughter being a pain in the neck if it brought a new life into the family. *A baby*. God, would it bring Clem round? Would it give him the will to live a bit longer? She would have to take extra special care of Freda now she was pregnant. Nothing must happen to this baby – it was too important to them all.

If she wanted to call it Billy, fine.

Exhausted, Clem leaned back against his pillows, Ada trying to make him comfortable. Maybe they had exhausted him, she thought guiltily, got him too excited. He would have to sleep now and get his strength back. Gently she stroked his head and then kissed his mouth. Breath, sweet and smelling of bread, came from his lips.

'Rest for a while, luv, and I'll come back up.'

'Send Vicky in, will you?'

'Later.'

'No, Ada, send her now.'

Ushered in by her mother, Vicky moved over to the bed and sat down, waiting for the door to close. When she was sure Ada had gone, she leaned towards her father.

'Did you want me, Dad?'

'My special girl,' he said, opening his eyes and trying

to squeeze her hand. 'It's good news about the baby, isn't it?'

She nodded. 'It is that. I tease Freda, but it's great news.'

He fixed his eyes on hers. 'My first grandson – if it is a boy and that gypsy's right. I like the sound of that.'

'I'll be an aunt for the first time.'

'But not a spinster one.'

She rested her head on her father's hand. 'You know me so well, don't you?'

'Know you well enough to realise that you'd be feeling a bit left out. Don't be, Vicky. I know you'll marry and have your own kids. It's just not your time. But you know you're my favourite, don't you? You're the one I love the best. I shouldn't say it, but it's true.' He winked, the action strained. 'Remember about the money?'

She nodded.

'Any left?'

Vicky laughed. 'Plenty.'

'Good. Add to it yourself when you've got any spare cash. You're the sensible one, Vicky, the one with her head screwed on.'

'Ma's got her head screwed on.'

He pulled a face. 'That silly, flighty thing?' Laughing, he squeezed Vicky's hand again. 'I know, she's grand. But she might need some help and I want to know that you'll always look out for her.'

'You know I will.'

'Freda's not reliable.'

'She has her own family to think about now.'

'Like I said, Vicky, you will too. But not yet. Not just yet.' He sighed. 'I think I'd like a little sleep now, luv. It's been quite an evening, and that's a fact.'

*   *   *

On the first landing Ada was waiting. She had drawn the blackout curtains and there was only one lamp burning. It made a huge shadow out of her, her figure looming up against the blank, distempered wall behind.

'What did he want?' she asked Vicky, her voice low as she guided her daughter downstairs. 'What was it all about?'

'He told me about his past –'

'*His past?*' Ada's eyes widened. 'What about it?'

'Well, you know his mother wasn't his real mother, don't you?'

'Evie wasn't his mother!' Ada repeated aghast. 'Who was?'

Vicky paused for dramatic effect. 'Promise you won't tell anyone? You must promise.'

'I promise! I promise!'

'Jean Harlow.'

The name went into Ada's head, rattled around a bit, and was then tipped out.

'Very funny,' she said at last, folding her arms. 'Am I to take it that you won't tell me?'

'He just wanted to say that he loved me. He thought I might feel left out, because of Freda being pregnant.'

Ada's expression softened. 'What a man, hey? Did you ever know such a kind man?' She moved towards the stairs and then turned back to her daughter. 'I tell you, Vicky, you find a man like your father and you'll do well for yourself. Don't go for looks, or money, go for the bit in here.' She jabbed at her chest with her hand. 'That's where it matters. Pick a man who can feel for you, and with you – that's what makes a marriage work.'

Closing up shop at the end of Churchgate, Bessie Cork

put up the Closed sign on the door and flicked the bolt to. It was raining again. She was lonely, if the truth be known. Lizzie had said she would pop round, but Bessie didn't really feel like talking, so she'd ignored the knock, pretended she was out. Kicking off her shoes, Bessie lowered her bulk into the wicker chair by the grate and then rolled up a cigarette. Her husband had taught her how to do it, years ago, and although she'd never admit to anyone that she smoked, Bessie enjoyed her secret vice. Sighing, she put the rolled cigarette in her mouth and lit a match. Then, luxuriously, she inhaled.

There was a sound behind her, Bessie snatching the cigarette out of her mouth and automatically stuffing it under a cushion.

'Oh, hello there, Bessie,' Lizzie said, walking in. 'I were knocking and knocking at the front, but I couldn't make you hear me. Lucky you'd left the back door open.'

Bessie stared at her, wondering if she could smell the smoke.

'Something burning in here, Bessie?'

'I was just trying to light the fire,' she stammered, then jerked her head. 'Sit down, why don't you, now you're here?'

'Good news, innit?'

'*What's* good news?' Bessie answered, wondering if, when she got up, the cigarette would have been put out by her bulk, or remain smouldering, ready to leap into life.

'The baby.'

Oh bugger! Bessie thought. She could feel the warmth growing under her left buttock.

'I said, it's good about the baby, isn't it?' Lizzie repeated.

'Your nephew Ken's wife having a baby? That's five kids now. I wonder they can afford it,' Bessie said, her thoughts mangled by the increasing heat.

'Not Ken, *Freda*.'

'Freda? Freda who?'

The cigarette was burning more rapidly. It would go through the bloody cushion and burn her arse, Bessie thought. But she couldn't move. How could she – churchgoer and moral crusader – be caught smoking?

'Freda Oldenshaw – Ada's girl.'

'What about her?' Bessie asked, her voice rising as her left buttock began to heat up.

'She's pregnant.'

Jesus, she was going to burn to death in front of Lizzie Antrim's eyes. She could imagine the headline of the *Stockport News* – 'WOMAN INCINERATED IN FRONT OF FRIEND'.

'Good to hear about a birth in these times. Cheers you up good and proper,' Lizzie went on. 'Are you all right, Bessie?'

Her friend's eyes had begun to water with the pain.

Seeing a means of escape, Bessie shook her head and feigned emotion.

'Aye, Lizzie, you'll have to excuse me, luv. I always get sentimental about babies.' She waved her hand towards the door. 'Go, luv, please, I don't want to show myself up.'

Touched, Lizzie hurried out. Well, who would have thought it about Bessie Cork? And people imagined she was such a hard old cow. Just goes to show, you never really know people at all.

Back in the kitchen Bessie heard the door close and then leapt to her feet, the cushion bursting into flames as she did so. Cursing and holding her buttocks, she then ran to the sink and hoisted herself up, putting her backside under the cold-water tap and turning it on full.

Chapter Eighteen

Mac Potter was sitting next to Lizzie Antrim, both huddled over their halves of bitter. He looked unusually animated, his eyes never leaving his companion. Vicky watched the unlikely couple, Ada serving a couple of workmen who had just come home from the munitions factory.

Seeing Vicky's interest, Ada walked over. 'What you watching?'

'Those two,' Vicky replied, her voice low. 'D'you think there's something going on?'

'Mac Potter and Lizzie Antrim?' Ada snorted. 'You're joking.'

'They look cosy.'

'They're both three sheets to the wind, that's why,' Ada replied, looking more attentively. 'See what you mean, though. They *are* a bit wrapped up in each other.'

'Bad for business,' Vicky said ruefully.

'How d'you make that out?'

'Well, Mac comes in to avoid his wife and tell everyone how badly the war is going, and Lizzie comes in to talk about how lonely she is. Being miserable makes them drink. Now, if they get together, they won't be miserable any more and might find other things to do.'

'Not if I know Mac's wife, they won't,' Ada replied, suddenly spotting next-door's cat as it sidled through the kitchen door. Hurriedly, she flicked a tea towel at the animal, making it bolt under the nearest table. There it regarded her with malevolent patience.

'If I turn my back for one instant that bloody cat will pee up the side of our lad's case.' She turned and fondly tapped the cabinet of The Sixpenny Winner. 'I hate cats, dirty things.'

'It's because he's a tom that he sprays.'

'If I catch him he won't be a tom for much longer,' Ada said darkly. 'There's no difference between cats and men; the males always go around putting their mark on everything.'

They stopped talking, eavesdropping on the conversation going on at the table on the other side of the bar. Mac was well into his stride.

'Now in my time, a war was a war,' he said, his voice rising slightly as he got merrier. 'I could tell you stories, Lizzie, that would make your hair curl. I was brave. I shouldn't say it, but I was. There's many a man alive now that wouldn't be if it weren't for me.'

'There would be more alive if he gave up driving,' Ada whispered to Vicky.

'. . . It brought out the best in me, fighting.'

'Oh,' Lizzie said admiringly, 'were you decorated?'

'Yeah, with a yellow streak down his back,' Ada said quietly, Vicky turning away to laugh.

Since Freda's pregnancy things had become easier in the pub. Complaining of morning, afternoon and evening sickness, Freda dodged working in The Sixpenny Winner as much as she could, and stayed upstairs in her room, reading romantic novels and eating. She had decided that if she was going to get fat, she would keep away from people. Well, men actually, and then re-emerge as a glossy new mother later.

What she didn't realise was that she was now regarded

in a different light. As a mother-to-be. Not as a wife or a young woman, but a mother-in-waiting. It rankled on Freda, made her uncomfortable. Everyone was always talking about the baby: when it came, how it would look, what they would do. It would be christened here and taken there, and what did Doug think about it?

Ada had been astonished when her daughter told her – matter-of-factly – that Doug didn't know she was pregnant. She was waiting to tell him on his next leave, she'd explained. It would be better to tell him in person.

'But surely it would be good for him to know now?' Ada had remonstrated. 'Give him something to think about, to look forward to?'

'Whose baby is this?' Freda had snapped. 'I'll do it my way.'

Well, there had never been any doubt about that, had there, Ada thought, reckoning that it would be a while until Doug came home on leave again. And how big would Freda be then? She was getting some weight on her already – God knows what size she'd be by the time Doug saw her, or by the time she gave birth.

Fully aware that her vain daughter would not want people to see her in a less-than-glamorous light, Ada was secretly delighted when Freda spent more and more time on her own. It meant that Ada ran the pub with Vicky – and Duncan. The latter was his usual helpful self, all eyes and ears, all charm. He seemed to be an open book – but, in reality, no one knew that much about Duncan Oldenshaw.

Like where he went on his days off . . . He must have a girlfriend, Ada thought. Good thing too. She had been worried about Prince Charming being around her two girls, but Duncan seemed immune to their charms. He was, Ada mused, the perfect help: around when he was needed, a good strong back and easy with the customers, and when he wasn't needed he was off. For once her instincts had been wrong, she thought, surprised. Duncan Oldenshaw had never given her a moment's worry.

'I meant to tell you, Ma,' Vicky began nonchalantly, 'I'm driving an ambulance now.'

'You're what?'

'They needed drivers –'

'That's men's work.'

'So is working in the munitions factory and all the other jobs women are doing now. We can do men's work. Times change; we're capable.'

'Be that as it may, the men won't like it when they come home,' Ada replied. 'They'll want their jobs back. And the women will have to get back to the house-work.'

Vicky raised her eyebrows. 'For a woman who's always had a career, you have very old-fashioned ideas.'

'Look, I had a career because I had to have one, not because I wanted one.'

'Liar!' Vicky teased her. 'You love running this place, you know you do. What would you have done all day just looking after Dad and us?'

'I would have taken afternoon naps and kept my looks longer,' Ada replied, adding quietly, 'And I would have been bored out of my mind.'

Silence fell between them. Mac's voice was getting louder, and the two workmen were having a spirited discussion about Hitler – about how someone should bump him off and do the world a favour. Sleepily, Vicky cupped her chin in her hand and leaned on the bar. The windows were blacked out, the pub getting muggy with cigarette smoke. She was glad she didn't have to go out that night. Tomorrow she was on duty, but tonight she would help her mother out and then have a bath.

She thought about the signs going up all over town: 'MAKE-DO AND MEND', imploring women to repair their clothes rather than buy new. And her favourite, a blonde with men hovering around her, the message stamped out underneath: 'Keep Mum, she's not so dumb.' Why were they always blondes, Vicky wondered, these femme fatales, these irresistible spies?

'Getting a bit busier,' Duncan said suddenly, breaking into her thoughts.

Surprised, Vicky straightened up and then found herself blushing. Oh God, she thought, not *blushing*.

'A couple of new customers,' she said, indicating the workmen. 'We need them.'

He seemed about to move away but then paused, looking at her.

'You working tonight?'

What did that mean? Vicky wondered. Was it just an idle question, or did he want to ask her out?

'Well, no. No, I'm not.'

Did she sound eager? Oh, God, she hoped she didn't sound eager.

'I was wondering . . .' Duncan began.

'Yes?' Vicky prompted him.

'You don't have to –'

'Have to *what*?' she asked, her breath fixed in her chest.

'Well, if you wouldn't mind . . .'

'*What*, Duncan?' she asked, exasperated.

'I was wondering if you'd cover for me tomorrow lunch time? I've got to be somewhere else.'

Her face fell, but pride made her smile and cover her feelings.

'Be somewhere else?' she repeated stupidly.

'Only for a couple of hours.'

Somewhere else, for a couple of hours. With someone, some woman? Some blonde? He wasn't asking her out, he didn't even realise that she was female. He just wanted someone to stand in for him.

She was so annoyed she could have spat.

'Fine, Duncan,' Vicky replied when she found her voice again. 'But don't make a habit of it.'

He would have liked to hold on, but Clem realised that there was no way he was going to see the birth of his first grandson. The knowledge saddened him. He had wanted to see the child, and certainly hadn't wanted to add sorrow to the occasion. But there it was – and couldn't be avoided. His time had come.

And he couldn't tell Ada. He had to keep it a secret, because she would want to fight, to put up her fists, to hang on to him through the sheer strength of her personality. And for what? For another day, another hour? He would have to go, and it was better he went clean. Easy.

Not that it made it any the easier. He had seen a lot in his life, and in the last years he had lived another kind of existence that few had ever experienced – by proxy, news coming with family and visitors to the upstairs room. He hadn't minded, because the pain had hobbled him. He had even *liked* his vicarious existence, his days chock-full of visits, gossips, cuddles from Ada when she stole upstairs. They were almost a courting couple again, without the boredom of marriage. Odd, but sweet. In the way life can be when you least expect it.

And besides, now he wasn't so worried. Duncan had proved to be reliable – a dark horse, for all his easy manner, but a constant presence. For the past three years Clem had listened to the sounds of Duncan's coming and going from his little room next door. He had heard him singing and his radio going on. Sometimes he had woken to the sound of Duncan coming in, and smiled to himself in the dark. Now where had he been? To see some woman? Or up to some funny business?

Clem would never know as Duncan wasn't exactly the forthcoming type. He had secrets, and he hugged them lovingly to himself. Doug would have chatted and confided – at least sometimes – but Duncan had never confided *anything* – except the name of a horse or the dog which was 'a sure-fire bet'. At times Clem had looked at Duncan and realised that, for all the open, glossy features, he was a hard man. Others would have thought that Doug was the tough nut, but they would have been wrong. Duncan Oldenshaw was the formidable one.

But *how* formidable was he? Not in a fight, Clem thought, but perhaps he was hard with people. He could imagine Duncan being emotionally cold, controlled, and in all their conversations Duncan had never once spoken of his brother, or his family, or a girlfriend with affection. The responsibilities and guilt that drove Douglas eluded his brother completely.

Ah well, Clem thought, be that as it may, Duncan will do until Doug gets home. And then there will be the baby and a whole new family in The Sixpenny Winner. And his adored Vicky, grown up capable and clever . . . He closed his eyes, surprised at his own calm. Was he dying now, he wondered. Could it possibly be so easy?

Then suddenly Clem heard the sound of Winter's

Clock chiming . . . That was odd: it was wartime, the clock had been stopped . . . And now he was *on his feet*, walking again, turning to the sound of Ada calling him. It was summer and she was standing under the clock, beckoning to him.

The image changed. Now Henessey's, now Evie, with her poultice and the line of washing flapping in the ginnel between the dark sentinel rows of houses. Ada, he called out, Ada, and she was there. But no longer under Winter's Clock. Now she was standing, reaching her hand up to be lifted on the day he fell, the day at Henessey's when he was crippled. The day he knew how much she loved him.

I love you, she said suddenly, her voice coming from nowhere. I love you, she was telling him again. In love, in bed. Times gone. Times back . . . Clem smiled, his eyes still closed, his mind reliving and reloving . . . Come on, Ada called him, come on, Clem. I'll never leave you, never . . . And she never had. Never. He'd been so lucky. And there was Evie again, hands on hips, Ada beside her, laughing, the fabric of his mother's print dress transparent in the sunlight. At their wedding. On their wedding day.

Sssh, someone said, ssh, let your father sleep . . . Clem wanted to call out then, to grab hold of Ada and ask her to hold on to him. No! This time don't let me sleep, let me stay with you. But the voice faded, and now all that Clem could see was Ada's face – when she was eighteen – and the sound of Winter's Clock chiming out the closing day.

Chapter Nineteen

'It's changed her, and that's a fact,' Lizzie told Bessie anxiously. 'Ada Hargreaves is not the woman she was. You should see her –'

'I don't hold with drinking.'

Lizzie smiled wanly. 'She's lost so much weight since Clem died. I thought she'd get over it, but you hardly see her in the p –' Lizzie checked herself, 'in the town.'

Bessie shifted around the tins on the shop shelves. There was so little she had to make it look more than it was. Rationing, always rationing. And no sign of the war ending.

'Even now that the baby's born, Ada's not herself.'

'She should be glad she's got her family around her,' Bessie said piteously. 'Some of us don't have that much.'

'But still . . .'

'Hand me that tin of biscuits, will you?' Bessie said, climbing awkwardly up the small stepladder and putting them on the top shelf. 'How does that look?'

'Are those the same biscuits you've had since the war started?' Lizzie asked ingenuously.

Heavy-footed, Bessie got off the steps and then towered over Lizzie.

'You have to make the most of what you've got.'

'But they must be fusty now,' Lizzie persisted gamely.

'Like I say, you have to make the most of what you've got. And that goes for Ada Hargreaves as well.'

*　　*　　*

Watching her sister, Vicky felt a nip of envy and then guilt. How could she be jealous of her sister? She had the right to a family. Vicky's eyes rested on the top of Billy's head. He was a strong baby, a lot like Freda, and he cried. God, how he cried. Freda hadn't taken too well to being a mother, and when Vicky showed interest in looking after Billy, she found herself lumbered.

If Freda could have turned her son over to her sister entirely, she would have done. But that was out of the question. She was a mother now and Doug worshipped her for giving him a family. So when Doug was around Freda did everything for Billy, and then, when Doug went away, she called on Vicky again.

It was a situation that suited them both. Freda – her figure almost fully restored – was back working in the pub. Her exile had sharpened her appetite for attention, and Ada was more than willing to let her daughter serve the customers. All the condolences after Clem's death had not soothed but salted the wound. Every time someone mentioned his name her stomach ached with loss. Ada had thought that the grief would fade after time, but it didn't. She missed him. She missed her confidant, her ally, her man.

Freda was settled, Vicky was capable, she was what? A widow, her time over. It was madness, as she was still relatively young, but Clem had been Ada's anchor. He had been the only one who had known everything about her past, her insecurities. With him she could show her weakness. But those days were over. She was alone now and would have to learn to cope in a different way.

She did it by changing her personality. Within weeks Ada had toughened up; within months she had hardened a shell around her that no one was able to penetrate.

Kindness she abhorred, because it unlocked feelings in her. Work was the only thing Ada trusted, because counting money and wiping bar tops required no emotional input.

So from the day Clem died Ada took the first step back to her childhood. She would never be the downtrodden child again, but the reserve that had marked her early life returned in force. As a landlady, she was exemplary; as a mother and grandmother, she was a martinet.

And so the years moved on and when 1944 came in it was celebrated in the pub with as much enthusiasm as a tired, beaten-down town could muster. Bombing raids had hit Manchester and the industrial areas, gas leaks had caused havoc, and the water mains had burst and flooded some of the worst-affected areas. Stockport took no direct hits, but there were indirect affects of bombing, houses damaged and windows blown in.

Victory was coming, the people of Stockport insisted, but when? When? Ada had managed to keep the pub afloat, but only just. Her savings, and Vicky's wages, had kept them going, and Duncan's 'presents' of food and the occasional treat had been a lifeline. But it was hard. Clothes were darned, patched, Billy wearing Vicky and Freda's old baby clothes, altered to fit. Ada wanted better for him, but it was impossible, so they made do.

And they kept making do. And all the time Ada thought about Clem and the way *they* had struggled to make ends meet. Then the pride they had felt at becoming landlords of The Sixpenny Winner. A long way from the greasy slums of Portswood, Ada thought, and now what was there left for her to do? She was a pub landlady, and would die in The Sixpenny Winner. That was all there was to it.

'What is it?' Ada asked, suddenly aware she was being watched.

'I was . . . nothing.'

'Where's Billy?'

'With Freda, but I'm going to put him to bed.'

'Freda should be down here now. We open up soon,' Ada replied, her voice even.

No warmth in it – where did it all go? Vicky wondered. Was it only your husband you loved? Not us? She wanted to talk to her mother but didn't dare, afraid of being rejected or dismissed. Ada was now an almost frightening figure, her expression fierce, fighting the world alone, though she had no need to.

'Ma?'

'What? I'm busy,' Ada replied.

'I just wanted to say . . .'

'Vicky, what is it? Spit it out.'

But she couldn't. So instead Vicky walked over to the clothes rack and began to fold Billy's nappies. She felt alone too; missed her father and their talks. Freda had a husband, a child, but she had no one. It was pointless, she thought angrily, she and her mother should be friends. Not like this, not this uneasy coldness.

'Here you go,' Freda said, walking in with Billy and putting him on the rocking chair. 'He's ready for bed.'

She paused by the grate and then checked her reflection in the mirror. Pleased, she then stepped back and glanced at her legs.

'Check my seams, will you, Vicky?' she asked.

The seams of the nylons Duncan had given her were in perfect symmetry.

'You're fine. Are you expecting any giants in tonight?'

Freda frowned. 'Huh?'

'Well, unless your customers are ten feet tall and can see over the bar, no one will know if your seams are straight or not.'

Irritated, Ada looked up. 'I can't work if you two are gossiping. Go on, get out of here and let me alone.'

Raising her eyebrows, Freda moved into the pub, Vicky following.

'I want to have a word with you.'

'Oh, not now,' Freda moaned. 'Later.'

'No, now,' Vicky persisted. 'Do you think Billy's putting on enough weight?'

Freda shrugged. 'He looks fine. They said he was coming on at the clinic. You worry too much.'

For a moment Vicky wondered why it was *her* who was worrying. Just who was Billy's mother? Sometimes it seemed she was, not Freda.

'Look, I have to get into the bar –'

'You think more about the pub than you do about your son!' Vicky snapped, the words out of her mouth before she could check them.

'Oh, grow up!' Freda retorted sharply. 'You're so bloody serious about everything.'

'There's not much *to* laugh about at the moment. There's a war on, in case you hadn't noticed.'

'My husband's away fighting – of course I've noticed!' Freda replied heatedly. Honestly, she thought, Vicky was such a prig. 'I don't know what you're going on about. You seem happy enough to look after Billy –'

'I love him, of course I like looking after him! But I have a job to go to at night.'

'So what d'you want, a medal? I can't get a job, Vicky, I have a child to look after.'

Vicky was incredulous: 'You have help with your child!'

'And you enjoy looking after him,' Freda repeated, 'so don't try and make yourself into some kind of martyr.'

'You really are a bitch!' Vicky snapped. 'Can't you think about anyone but yourself?'

'I have my own life to lead and my own problems,' Freda replied coolly. 'God knows, I worry about Doug all the time –'

'Oh, yes!' Vicky retorted. 'I've seen how much you worry. Seen the strain it is for you to keep chatting up the customers.'

'The customers are mostly old men,' Freda replied coldly, leaning towards her sister. 'What's the matter, Vicky? You bitter because you haven't managed to get yourself a man? Not even a wounded one? I thought even *you* could pull that off. After all, they can't run away when they're in hospital, can they?'

With all her might, Vicky lunged out at her sister, Freda stepping back to avoid the blow.

'Watch it!' she snapped. 'Where's your sense of humour?'

'I lost it – like you lost your sense of responsibility,' Vicky replied. 'I just wanted to warn you that I'm not here for your convenience.'

Still annoyed, her sister merely shrugged. 'You should be grateful to me –'

'*Grateful!*'

'Yes, grateful,' Freda repeated, her tone steely. 'Grateful that I'm letting you share my baby, Vicky. And one day when – *if* – you have your own child, you might come to realise just how generous I've been.'

Lying on the bed, Nora stretched her arms over her head

and reached out for Duncan. He watched her, keeping his distance. Then he leaned forward, caught hold of her wrists and jerked her upright until she was sitting on the edge of the bed. Her face was upturned, looking into his.

Slowly he ran his finger over her lips, her eyes closing momentarily, then he allowed his hand to run down her neck and along her shoulder. Finally he slowly, languorously, stroked her breasts. She sighed longingly, just as he knew she would.

Not bad for her age, he thought. But, like so many women when they passed forty, mad for any attention she could get. And he was willing to give her attention – in his own way, and when it suited him . . . Duncan was feeling a little peevish, a little out of sorts. He didn't actually want to make love. He had lost some money on a fight and was bored out of his mind at the pub. But he wanted a diversion, something to amuse him.

'Take your blouse off,' he said suddenly.

Nora looked at him, her expression quizzical. 'What?'

'I said, take your blouse off.'

She looked down, embarrassed. 'You do it.'

'No. You take it off,' Duncan said firmly.

'Turn out the light then.'

'I want the light *on*,' he replied, knowing that he was humiliating her and that she liked to make love in the dark.

'I can't.'

'Then I'm off –'

She clung to him greedily, bewildered. 'Why? Duncan, why are you being like this?'

'I want to look at you,' he said, smiling glossily. 'Come on, Nora, let me look at you.'

Blushing, she hesitated. Then reluctantly she unfastened the buttons on her blouse and took it off. She was wearing a pink-coloured bra underneath, her midriff soft, fleshy.

'Now take off your bra.'

She shook her head, mutely ashamed.

'Nora, do what I say,' Duncan repeated.

He knew that she would, in time. He would make her. The power he felt suddenly lifted his spirits. He had control over her, like all women, really. They just asked to be pushed around. She'd do it. In time.

'Take off your bra!'

'I can't . . . Unless you turn out the light.'

'Why?'

She was close to tears, a forty-two-year-old woman reduced to begging.

'It . . . it doesn't feel right.'

'But I want you to do it.'

'Don't make me, Duncan. Please.'

'Nora, take off your bra,' he repeated. God, what a performance. What were a pair of breasts anyway?

'I can't . . .'

He turned again, as though to go, Nora letting out a small cry and feeling behind her to unclasp her bra. Slowly she let the straps fall down whilst she held the bra over her breasts to cover them.

At last, her face flushed, she looked up at him.

'Good,' Duncan said simply, 'now let go of the bra.'

Crying noiselessly, Nora let the bra slip, Duncan staring at her bare breasts for a long moment.

Then he sighed, handed the bra back to her, and said: 'I think we'll have a cup of tea now, shall we?'

The war was going to end, Doug thought. This time they

would be right, it *would* end. He shook his head. God, he longed to get home to Freda and Billy. *His son.* His child. Doug took out the photograph from his wallet and looked at it. Didn't he know every fleck, every speck, every tiny dot of the print? Of course he did, but it never stopped him looking. And showing everyone: 'This is my son, my boy.'

God, he would spoil him when he got home – take him everywhere, look after him, teach him things. It was a blessing, a real blessing. Doug paused, stared ahead of him. Just let me get through the war, he prayed, please God, let me get through it. I have a family now, and I've always been a lucky man. Let me *stay* lucky.

Memory came back sudden and sharp: Emma, his first love, the woman he had married and wanted so much to start a family with. They had talked about it constantly, but it never happened. Weird as it sounded, maybe he had been lucky there too. He could never have lived with himself if a child had died in the fire with Emma . . . Doug blinked, as though clearing the image from his sight. This was no time to think of the past. Life was good again. He was lucky again. He had his adored Freda, and his wonderful son.

He would miss Clem, because he had loved the man, but Doug longed to return to The Sixpenny Winner, longed to touch the optics and go down into the cellar and remember the first time he had kissed Freda there . . . Oh God, life could be so good, so very good. He just had to get home, that was all; keep himself safe for the good times to come.

Billy Oldenshaw, William Oldenshaw – would he grow up to be a publican like his dad? Or better? A doctor? A lawyer? No, Doug thought, no good being fanciful. Anything the boy wanted to do was all right by him. He just wanted him happy and strong, like his dad. Oh, and *lucky*.

Lucky Billy. Like lucky Doug. Lucky, lucky, lucky.

Chapter Twenty

Freda was staring at Doug thoughtfully as he polished glasses, ready for opening time. He was home now. The war was over. It was tremendous, everyone said. So why didn't she feel good? All the time Doug had been away she had longed for him, but now he was back it was different. Sex had been good, welcome at first, but within weeks Freda was getting irritated by the presence of her husband. The bedroom wasn't hers any more, and it was crowded with Billy and Doug.

He didn't see her irritation and could only revel in being home, and realise just how much he had grown to love the pub. On his return he had walked round The Sixpenny Winner and touched everything – the optics, the beer barrels, checking the cellar and the books, which Ada had kept so meticulously. He was at home, he thought, as much in love with the pub as Clem had been.

Ada watched him with pleasure and then resentment. She should be pleased, she thought, delighted that her son-in-law was back to help them. But in reality it felt as though she was being usurped, thrown out of the last remaining power-hold she had. She could see it all so clearly: she was going to be shunted off, Doug and Freda taking over The Sixpenny Winner. And where would that leave her? Pushed aside, maybe relegated upstairs to the role of mother-in-law, ex-publican? The hell she was! It had been the pub Clem and she had shared. Now he might have gone, but she was still in charge. Doug had better remember that.

Guilt made her withdrawn. How could she think about Doug like that? But she was too young to take second place, and too lonely to be parted from her territory, the place that held so many memories of good times.

Watching Doug whilst she polished the bar top, Ada wondered how Duncan would take to the shift in power. He seemed thrilled to have his brother back, but who really knew what Duncan was thinking? Was he wondering if he would have to move on now? Or trying to work out a way to stay? Because he wanted to, Ada could see that.

It had been a house of women for so long, Ada realised. Oh, Duncan had been there, but not around much. Most of the time it had been her, Freda and Vicky. And then Billy. But he was only a child. Now, to hear Doug's voice again and his heavy footfall on the stairs were reminders of Clem, and poignant in the extreme.

Although Duncan had spent little time with the women during the war, when Doug came back the brothers quickly became close. Ada wondered if that was Duncan's way of securing his future, or if he was genuinely glad of male company. As for Doug, he was glad to be alive.

'We could decorate,' Doug said suddenly, breaking into her thoughts, 'cheer the place up a bit.'

The idea rankled. 'I did the best I could with it! Times were hard during the war.'

He looked at his mother-in-law, surprised. She had changed, closed in with grief. Who would have thought it of Ada? She of all people. But although she was still relatively young she seemed remote. Freda hadn't mentioned the change in her mother, and on Doug's leaves he had seen so little of Ada that he hadn't noticed it himself. But now he found himself saddened and missing the woman he had come to respect.

'You tell me what colour you want, Ada, and I'll get it.'

'Huh!' she said shortly. 'As if you'd listen. Your generation are all the same. Freda would never take a word of advice about Billy. She knew everything about having a baby and bringing one up. Never wanted to heed a word from me.' She folded her arms across her breasts, almost in a protective gesture. 'I suppose everything will change now?'

'I was only thinking about painting the bar –'

'You know what I mean!' Ada said darkly. 'This is my pub, Doug. I would like you to remember that. You were a good help before the war and I want you to help me now, but The Sixpenny Winner's not yours. Not yet, anyway.'

Watching his mother-in-law walk off, Doug jumped as Duncan tapped him on the shoulder.

'Good to be back?'

Doug turned and grinned. '*Great* to be back.'

'I bet you got a nice welcome from Freda,' Duncan said, winking.

'Mind your own business!' Doug teased his brother. 'Time you found a wife and had some kids.'

'Me!' Duncan exclaimed, genuinely taken aback. 'Oh, no, not me.'

'You'll fall in love one day. The ones who play the field the most always fall the hardest,' Doug replied, leaning towards his brother, his expression quizzical. 'Don't tell me you've been lonely all the time I was fighting for King and Country?'

Duncan looked shocked. 'You know me –'

'That's exactly what I mean!' Doug responded, nudging his brother out of the way. 'It's a good thing I'm back. We'll get some real work done now.'

Later that night Doug was lying in bed with Freda, talking – about the war, about the pub, about being home. And all the time she was listening she kept staring up at the ceiling, irritated. Why was he talking on and on when he should be fussing her? Honestly, Freda mused, it was downright rude of him. She was his wife and the mother of his son, surely she deserved some consideration?

'. . . and I was thinking that we could redecorate the bar. Something a bit brighter –'

'God Almighty!' Freda finally exploded.

Doug rolled over onto his side and looked at her. 'What's the matter?'

'Why bother coming home if all you can do is *talk*?'

Stunned, Doug looked at his wife and then stroked the length of her back. Freda was beautiful, desirable, and he wanted her so much. But she was still self-absorbed – that much hadn't changed.

'I just wanted to get things clear in my head. We all have to settle back gradually, darling. After all, now your dad's dead Ada probably feels left out –'

'What about Vicky?' Freda snapped nastily. 'What about how she feels? And don't forget Duncan, or Billy. You must think about everyone first and then – when you've time – perhaps you'd ask how I am.'

Smiling, Doug began to play with her hair. Annoyed, Freda jerked her head away, but he persisted, making her smile, then roll over. Then finally she hugged him to her, and all thought of Ada or anyone else disappeared.

* * *

What an anticlimax, Vicky thought, wandering over the Vernon Bridge and heading towards Prince's Street. She shouldn't think it, but now that the war was over, so was the excitement. Oh, there had been plenty of hardship and God knows how much worry, but she had been so busy, so needed in the hospital, then driving the ambulance. It had hardly been life-threatening, but it had made her feel involved.

And now it was over, and after the initial relief that Doug was home and they had all survived – apart from Clem, that is – after that there was a sense of resentment at having to give back the jobs to the men; hand over the power again, the responsibility. And Vicky knew only too well that things would never go back to the way they were.

Of course, there was Billy to brighten up her life. She had loved helping Freda with the little one, but ever since Doug's return her time with Billy had been limited. It was natural for a father to want to be with his son, especially as he had missed much of his first years, but Vicky missed the child. Missed waking up to find that Freda had put the little one in bed with her sometime during the night, when she was on day shifts. 'Because he cries,' Freda had told her pettishly. 'Billy *never* cries with you.' Other times she would come in from work at night and immediately have a sleepy child thrust into her arms. Billy, still damp from his bath, wrapped in a towel.

If the truth be known, she grew to be glad of Freda's casual attitude to her son, because it meant that she had more time with him. The envy Vicky had first felt at Freda being a mother soon lifted when the mother became bored. He likes you, Freda would say in her best wheedling tone. Take him for me, Vicky, please . . .

At first she had thought that she was getting one over on her sister, but in fact it was *Vicky* who benefited the most.

And so, for all this time, they had shared Billy. Ada had been interested at first, but since the death of Clem, she had become withdrawn from everyone. She would pet the child, and talk to him, but she never sought him out. The baby she had hoped would keep her husband alive had failed her.

As for Duncan, there had never been any competition from that quarter. Duncan wasn't exactly sure how to talk to children, and it was obvious that he was in no hurry to learn. The sight of soiled nappies and bottles of warmed milk had repelled him and Billy was almost two years old before Duncan ventured any conversation.

'How do?' he'd said one morning, Billy looking up at him from his high chair, a spoon raised high in one mucky fist.

'Aargh!'

Duncan had blinked and turned to Vicky. 'Is that it?'

'What d'you expect, Latin?' she answered wryly. 'He's only a baby.'

'Big baby.'

'Yeah,' she had agreed, looking at the sturdy child.

'Lot like our Douglas.'

'I think he looks like Freda more,' Vicky had replied, watching as Billy had blown a milky bubble.

'I was never very good with kids.'

'You surprise me,' Vicky had said, spooning some food into Billy's mouth.

'Find them a bit . . . you know, a bit . . .'

'Too much like hard work?'

He had grimaced, the baby grimacing back. 'You

know, I'm right,' he said again thoughtfully, 'he's a lot like our Douglas. Same table manners.'

Vicky smiled at the memory. But it had been just one more pointer to the fact that Duncan Oldenshaw wasn't a family man. So why hadn't she stopped carrying a torch for him? God knows, he had given her no encouragement, no hint of any interest, and he had had plenty of opportunity, living under the same roof for so long.

Ruefully, Vicky sighed and then stopped and looked through a gap in the railway bridge. Far away she could make out the impressive bulk of the Stockport viaduct and wondered fleetingly how far it went. If she got on a train now she could go anywhere. She had no husband, no children to consider, she was an intelligent woman. One of the new breed, who could do anything they wanted: educate themselves, take on men's jobs, drive cars, see the world.

So why were her sights stuck firmly on a man in a backstreet pub in Stockport? Irritated, Vicky tapped her foot and then started walking again. It was going to stop, and stop now, she told herself. Time to move on. The world had changed and so would she. No more thinking about Duncan Oldenshaw; she would find herself another man. A new man. She had changed jobs several times, and had now applied for a clerical post at the hospital, working with two other girls and a young man called Bernard.

You never knew, Vicky thought, Bernard looked OK, seemed quite lively. She would have to regard him in a different light, open up her world a bit more. Go out with the girls, enjoy herself. The war had been over for a year, it was more than time to move on.

Besides, she mused, Duncan might not be at The

Sixpenny Winner for ever. He was happy now, working side by side with his brother, but he wasn't the kind to settle down anywhere permanently. One day he might just up and leave, walk out without even looking back.

After all, she thought with a sinking heart, he had no reason to stay.

'If you ask me it's only a matter of time.'

'For what, Bessie?'

'For *trouble*.' She looked at her friend darkly. 'I've been expecting it ever since Douglas Oldenshaw got home last year. Thought something might already have happened. But it's quiet – *too quiet*.'

Lizzie sucked her teeth thoughtfully. 'What kind of trouble are you expecting?'

'Big trouble. You can't have two men running a pub.'

'It's Ada's pub –'

'Well now, that's a matter of opinion.'

A customer walked in on their conversation, looking to be served. Annoyed by the interruption, Bessie stared at the woman defiantly.

'How do, Mrs Rimmer?'

'How do, Mrs Cook? Got any greens?'

'What d'you call those?' Bessie replied, pointing to several wilting cabbages.

'My husband's partial to some veg now and again.'

That's not all he's partial too, Bessie thought, tapping her foot impatiently.

'How many d'you want?'

'Are they cabbages?'

'No, they're unexploded bombs,' Bessie retorted sourly. 'What do they look like?'

'Because Gordon won't eat anything green unless it's a cabbage.'

Losing patience fast, Bessie picked one up and held it in front of her customer's face.

'Your Gordon would have to go a long way to find a cabbage like that.'

Too right, Lizzie thought to herself. Mrs Rimmer wasn't impressed either. Slowly she inspected the cabbage from all angles, then took in a breath.

'I'm not sure. You see, if it's not fresh, it'll make him windy –'

'Do you want the cabbage or not?' Bessie snapped.

Mrs Rimmer pulled a face. 'I'll have a think about it.'

'It's a cabbage, not a bloody Rolls-Royce!' Bessie said, exasperated.

'But if it makes him windy –'

'Your Gordon works at the gasworks, who'll notice?' Bessie replied, wrapping the cabbage in some newspaper and taking the money out of Mrs Rimmer's hand. Hurriedly she then ushered her out and finally turned the 'Open' sign to 'Closed'.

'As if my cabbages would make anyone gassy!' she said to Lizzie, offended. 'It's the bloody way she cooks, that one. Couldn't keep a lodger because of her cooking. And you know lodgers, normally eat anything on a plate. *As well as* the bloody plate.'

Lizzie waited for the storm to abate and then nudged Bessie's memory.

'What were you saying about The Sixpenny Winner?'

Relaxing, Bessie returned to her theme. 'I said, wait and see, Ada Hargreaves will get pushed to the back before long. Douglas Oldenshaw's just taking his time, that's all. Lulling her into a false feeling of security.'

'Douglas Oldenshaw's a nice man,' Lizzie said earnestly. 'I don't think he'd do something like that.'

'He might not, but Freda would. She makes the bullets and gets him to fire them. Anyway, you only have to look at the great soft a'p'orth, still gooey-eyed over that son of his. Douglas Oldenshaw would knife anyone through the throat if they harmed a hair of Freda or Billy's heads.' She slammed down a packet of tea. 'Knife them, slash their necks open.'

'Oh dear,' Lizzie said, appalled. 'I don't think he's the type –'

'You never know the type,' Bessie went on. 'You only know when they're standing over your bed with an axe in their hands.'

Lizzie's eyes were bulging uncomfortably. 'You've been reading those American detective books again, haven't you? You shouldn't do it, it's bad for you, Bessie. Give you nightmares reading about all those murders.'

'I've told you once and I'll tell you again, you never know,' Bessie insisted, leaning over her counter, 'what a person is. Or what they would do, when the chips are down.'

'The what?'

'The chips are down,' Bessie repeated. 'It's an American expression. It means don't get fooled by appearances. Not that I'm a person to judge anyone – as you know only too well, Lizzie – but there's something about Douglas Oldenshaw that makes you think.'

'You said that about his brother when he first came here.'

Bessie blinked, wrong-footed, then recovered herself.

'Yes, well. It's obviously something in the family. Both of them. You mind my words, Lizzie, there's more to those two than meets the eye.'

Chapter Twenty-One

'You like it here, don't you, Duncan?'

Duncan tensed. Was his brother about to tell him something? To hint that he no longer needed his help? He had been expecting the conversation for a long time, then relaxed when it didn't come. Together they had run the pub – side by side, as brothers. Something Duncan didn't want changing.

'I like it here, Doug.'

'I do too. It's everything I could have dreamed of. My own home, my own family. You don't know what it's like to have a son, Duncan, a lad of your own. It makes things different, makes you see the world in a new light. I used to dream about him when I was away during the war. Freda sent me his first little bootie and I kept ... I kept it with me all the time.' He blushed at the sentimental memory. What a dope his brother would think he was. And yet Doug didn't care. He was happy, and he wanted everyone to know it.

'About the pub –'

'I can't believe how good the world feels,' Doug went on, still glowing about his family. 'Haven't you got a girlfriend *yet*, Duncan?'

'I've a friend –'

'Close friend?' Doug said hopefully. What could be better than his brother settling down too? They could enjoy each other's families then.

'It's not that kind of thing,' Duncan replied, a mite shortly.

'So no wedding bells?'

'Jesus, Doug! I'm not the type. You should know that. I've said it often enough.'

'I know. I just thought that now you're older . . .' Doug said seriously, '. . . people *do* change. Besides, you've settled down here well enough –'

'I wanted to talk to you about that.'

'– and you've kept your nose clean ever since you came to The Sixpenny Winner.'

Exasperated, Duncan caught hold of his brother's sleeve. 'What are you trying to say? D'you want me to stay on here?'

Doug stared at his brother, his bewilderment obvious.

'Why? D'you want to leave?'

'Christ!' Duncan replied, his hands running through his hair.

'Whatever it is, just spit it out!' Doug snapped.

'*I* want to stay around. Do *you* want me to stay around?'

'Of course, I do! Why would I want you to go? We work well as a team, don't we?'

Duncan sighed, relief obvious. 'I just wondered, that was all. I mean, you weren't that pleased to see me when I first arrived.'

'That was a long time ago, Duncan. But you've proved your worth now,' Doug replied gratefully. 'You're family, my brother – and from now on I want *all* my family around me.' He slung one muscular arm around Duncan. 'We weren't close for a long time, but we're close now. Want you to leave? Never! The Sixpenny Winner's your home and mine. You're going nowhere.'

* * *

Ada had thought that her depression might lift. She had waited for it, but time had passed and she *still* felt like an outsider. The war had been over a year now, and the pub was busy again. Life had gone on. Freda and Doug seemed happy, Duncan more than established at The Sixpenny Winner, and Vicky had a new job.

It was summer. The sky was clear, bright with sun, the windows of the terraced houses blinking in the happy light. People had recovered – most of them. They had forgotten the past – most of them.

But not Ada. Her depression was so absolute and overwhelming that it seemed to drag on her like weights on her ankles. She had tried to rally, tried to join in, but all she could think about was the little empty room at the top of the pub. And the empty bed. She had expected to miss Clem, but had also expected the grief to lessen over time, not increase. And the return of Doug had meant an unwelcome shift in the house. He had left when Ada was the matriarch, but he returned to find her a bitter widow.

She had tried to control herself, but she hadn't been able to. Her sense of humour had long ago left her and she had little interest in her family. There was no one left to worry about, or nurse. There was no place for her.

But to get so bitter, so resentful – God, how *could* she? Hadn't she seen what bitterness did? Hadn't she seen the worst example in Milly? Life was so cruel, Ada decided. She might have sworn she would never get like her mother, but events, or blood, had dictated otherwise. She was angry. She was lonely. She was a bitch.

Sighing, Ada left the street and walked across town, pausing momentarily under Winter's Clock. Then she moved on, without thinking of where she was going, just walking blindly. Street after street she passed, full of people, radios turned on, the voices of Gracie Fields and Vera Lynn echoing down the sunny ginnels. Why was it only she that felt this deadness inside? Why couldn't she be normal, full of joy?

Slowly Ada walked. The evening lengthened, her mood overwhelming her. She felt as though she would never be at home again, or feel safe. As though some wicked germ inside had finally poisoned her. And there was no cure. Walking on, as the sky darkened and the streetlamps went on, Ada was surprised to find herself in Portswood.

Startled, she looked around her. Some of the buildings were damaged, others derelict, her parents' house boarded up. God, it was sour, decayed, Ada thought, pausing by the basement where the Declans had lived. The night came down on her, taking away the sunshine, the laughter and music long faded away from the streets beyond.

A devil walked with her . . . Slowly she moved on, taking off her jacket, the night close and humid around her. Her eyes fixed on the street ahead, and then she entered – as she knew she would – the ginnel where her mother had died.

The streetlamp was still there, lit, the passageway deserted. Had her mother felt like this, Ada wondered. Had *she* fought against it and lost? Were they – the thought was paralysing – alike after all? Mother and daughter. Milly and Ada. Two harpies? Two bitches? Two women drawn under by the dark?

Solemnly, Ada walked towards the lamp, looking up at the iron bar where her mother had hanged herself. Her hand went up to her throat immediately. Did it hurt? Or was the pain less than the pain of being alone?

She touched the black iron lamp and let her fingers rest against it. The memory came back like an electric shock – her mother's body hanging there, the laces of her shoes so neatly tied. And the stool lying on its side, where she had kicked it away.

The iron seemed to warm under her touch, not frightening, almost welcoming. Perhaps death wasn't so bad, after all, Ada thought. She would be with Clem again. All the pain would be over; she would be at peace. Hanging her head she rested her cheek against the lamp, weariness overwhelming her.

And then she heard it. A whistle. A low whistle. Someone was coming, Ada thought, too tired to care. Someone was coming towards the ginnel, whistling as though they hadn't a care in the world.

'Hey, what you doing?'

Ada's eyes snapped open to find a young lad standing in front of her. He was filthy, his hands in his pockets, his hair matted.

'Who wants to know?'

'I do,' he said defiantly. 'You drunk?'

'No!'

'I just wondered, what with you leaning on that lamppost.'

Ada straightened up. 'Why aren't you at home? Your mother will be looking for you.'

He shrugged. 'I'm on m' way. In a while . . . Anyway, what you doing here?'

'I used to live here.'

'Get away!'

'That's just what I did,' Ada said, finding her spirits shifting. Pushing herself from the streetlamp, she walked over to a low wall and sat down, her jacket on her lap. 'I was a kid here.'

He stood in front of her, weighing her up. 'You don't look that poor.'

'I got married and left,' Ada explained. 'I married a good man. He was called Clem. Clem Hargreaves.'

'Were 'e poor?'

'We both were. Poor as beggars. But we worked hard and saved and,' she turned to look at the boy with pride, 'and then we got a pub together.'

'You never!'

She nodded, happy with the memory. 'Oh yes, we got The Sixpenny Winner –'

'I've heard of that!'

'Everyone knows The Sixpenny Winner.'

She was right, everyone *did*. Everyone round those parts knew the pub, just as they had known Clem, and knew her. Ada Hargreaves. Oh, she'd done well for herself. Got above herself, some thought. But suddenly Ada felt good; felt like she used to in the old days. Felt that there was something left to live for. She wasn't sure *what* exactly, but her fight was coming back.

'Why were it called that?' the lad asked, curious.

'The pub's named after a dog which ran so fast it won everyone money that bet on it. You ask your dad, he'll tell you about it.'

The boy was transfixed by the story, Ada studying him and remembering. *She* had been that poor once, clothes falling off her back sometimes. Sleeping in the heat and the smells from the water closet . . . So why had she gone soft now, Ada wondered suddenly, now that life was easier? Now her children were sorted? What had happened to her nerve? She should be ashamed of herself.

'What 'appened to it?'

Ada blinked. 'What?'

'What 'appened to it?' the lad repeated.

'I still have the pub.'

'No, the dog! What 'appened to the dog?'

'He was stuffed a long time ago,' Ada said, bursting out laughing, because it *was* funny, stuffing a dog. 'We've got him behind the bar, in a big glass case for everyone to see.'

The boy was impressed. 'Don't it smell?'

'Nah! He's grand, that dog is. Looks like he's still alive. Like he could jump out of that case and win a race – just like that!' She clicked her fingers.

'So why aren't you there now?' he asked, his head on one side.

A silence fell between them, a long moment passing before Ada spoke again.

'What's your name?'

'Gerry.'

'D'you believe in ghosts, Gerry?'

'Nah!'

'Me neither,' Ada replied firmly, looking towards the streetlamp. 'I came here tonight because I had a choice to make – whether to live and be happy, or give in.'

Far away, she could hear the whistling again, but the boy was nudging her to continue.

'What you going to do?'

'D'you hear that?' Ada asked, turning her head to the sound of the whistling.

'What?'

'That whistling?'

'Nah, there's no one whistling,' the boy replied. 'I can't hear a thing.'

'That's because it's not for you.' Ada smiled and pulled on her jacket. 'It's a special whistle, one only I can hear.'

He looked puzzled. 'But what about the ghost? You said there were a ghost 'ere.'

Ada hesitated. 'I was wrong,' she replied finally, hearing the whistling again. 'I thought there was, but there wasn't after all.'

'Bloody hell!' the boy said curtly. 'That's not much of a story, missus.'

'Maybe not,' Ada replied, laughing as she walked off. 'But it'll do me.'

Chapter Twenty-Two

At Stockport Infirmary, Vicky was typing up some notes when there was a knock at the door. She looked up, beckoning for a young, bespectacled man to come in.

'Hello there,' Bernard Young said, beaming from ear to ear. 'How you doing, Vicky?'

She smiled automatically. Well, you couldn't help but like Bernard, there was nothing about him to dislike. He was clean and tidy, and doing well – highly thought of by his superiors. A reliable clerk, destined for higher things. Might even get his own office one day, his own secretary. And there were a few of the typists and clerical workers after him. A catch, no less.

But not exciting, Vicky thought. They had gone out a few times, and the previous night they had been to the flicks and watched *Brief Encounter*. He had squeezed her hand and she hadn't complained . . .

'I'll walk you home,' he said later, breaking into her thoughts.

Why not? Vicky reasoned. It was time he saw The Sixpenny Winner. He knew where she came from, but he had been reluctant to mention it. Perhaps he was a little disapproving. She wondered about that, how judgemental Bernard could be.

She was soon to find out. They walked through town talking easily, but as they entered Churchgate, Bernard was less forthcoming, and by the time they reached The Sixpenny Winner he was quiet. It was obvious that Bernard was no pubgoer.

Looking round, his expression was strained as Vicky unlocked the back door.

'D'you want to come in?'

'Sure he does,' Ada replied, materialising suddenly and hauling them both into the busy kitchen. By the fire Freda was reading one of her romantic novels, her hair in rags.

Immediately, she leaped up. 'How could you?' she snapped, wrenching out the makeshift curlers. 'I didn't know we were having company.' She rushed out, and they all heard her feet hammering up the stairs, and the slam of the bedroom door above.

Rolling her eyes, Ada ushered Bernard to a chair beside the kitchen table. Only a few yards away the sounds of the busy pub came through loud and clear: glasses clinking together, a man shouting with triumph as he scored at darts, and then someone began to play the piano.

'Stan Foreshaw, Lettie's eldest,' Ada said, wincing. 'If he was wearing boxing gloves, he couldn't play worse.'

She turned back to their visitor. A boyfriend for Vicky! This was good news. And he seemed a likely lad. A bit nervous, mind you, but that wasn't a bad thing. Better than being a wide boy any day.

'You work with our Vicky, I hear?'

Bernard nodded, accepting the cup of tea that was pushed towards him. 'Yes. Yes, I do.'

'Nice that.'

'Yes,' he agreed, wincing as Stan murdered a Gershwin number.

'Take no notice,' Ada advised him. 'You should hear him play when he's drunk!'

Bernard wasn't that sure that he wanted to. He liked Vicky a lot, but he hadn't been prepared for her background. A pub! Bernard had thought when he first found out. What kind of a girl grew up in a pub?

And now his worst fears were being realised as he sat in the smoky kitchen and listened to the bar noises beyond. Obviously her mother was a bit of an eccentric ... His eyes wandered round the kitchen, taking in a row of newly made pies, cooling on the windowsill, a cat eyeing them hungrily.

'Who's this then?'

Bernard jumped, Ada smiling at Doug, who had just walked in. 'This is Bernard ...'

'Young.'

'... Bernard Young,' Ada agreed. 'He's Vicky's friend.'

'How do, lad?' Doug replied, shaking hands with the visitor.

'Fine, fine ...'

Flinching at the pressure of the handshake, Bernard smiled distantly. 'Well, I must be off –'

'What about something to eat?'

Bernard didn't like the look of the pies, or the fact that the cat seemed to have nibbled the crust of one.

'No, no, I've to go now ... Work tomorrow.'

Relieved, Vicky walked him to the door. Flicking on the outside light, she stood on the top step and looked at Bernard Young curiously.

'You don't go to pubs much, do you?'

He shifted his feet. 'Well ... not much.' Then he added, 'But it looks fine. Fine ...'

She wanted to laugh, but stopped herself. Poor Bernard, he was quite shocked.

'See you tomorrow at work?'

She nodded. 'Unless I'm murdered in my sleep.'

He looked – for a moment – as though he thought it was a possibility. Then he smiled.

'You and your jokes, Vicky. You're a one-off and no mistake.' Turning his hat in his hands, he then moved towards her and kissed her lightly on the cheek.

'Oh,' she said simply.

'You don't mind, do you?' he replied, his tone anxious. 'I've been waiting to do that for a long time.'

'No, I don't mind, Bernard,' Vicky said honestly. Then she turned and closed the door behind her.

For a moment she listened to the sound of his footsteps dying away, and then sighed. She had wondered what it would feel like, standing at that back door where Freda had enthralled so many men. Would she have a sense of excitement? A thrill? The same thrill which had made Freda glisten with triumph and sensuality? Hardly.

Doug was eating a sandwich when she returned to the kitchen. Ada looked up from her seat.

'That lad wants a dose of liver salts. He's a bit nervy, isn't he?'

'A bit,' Vicky agreed, slumping down in the rocking chair in front of the grate. 'I don't think he approves of pubs.'

'Poor bugger,' Doug said drily, 'he doesn't look like a man who does a lot of laughing.'

Glancing over her shoulder, Vicky changed the subject. 'What's up with Freda? She off colour?'

He shrugged. 'Just moody.'

'Oh,' Ada said, mocking. 'Just moody, hey?'

'You reckon it's a bad sign, Ma?'

She looked at Vicky and nodded. 'Aye, it starts with

the moods, then comes the twitches, then the tick in the eye.' She winked, started laughing, Vicky grinning back at her.

'What did you really think of Bernard?'

'I thought,' Ada replied, 'that it was lucky he wasn't one of twins.'

When Vicky finally went upstairs she headed for her own room and then doubled back, stopping on the landing outside Freda and Doug's door. She couldn't hear any noise from inside and thought maybe that her sister, and her nephew, were asleep. But just as she was about to walk away, Freda came out.

'What the hell are you doing here?'

'Waiting for a bus,' Vicky replied drily. 'I was just wondering if you were still awake.'

'Can't sleep,' Freda said, brushing her hair, the blonde waves crackling with electricity. She was edgy, her actions tight. 'Billy's dead to the world.'

Vicky peeked over her shoulder. Her nephew was in the centre of the bed, curled in the foetal position.

'He looks tired out.'

'We went to the park,' Freda volunteered, unusually communicative. 'You want to come in for a minute?'

Surprised, Vicky followed her. There had been a change in Freda during the past year. At first she'd seemed pleased to have Doug home, but then she'd got restless. He didn't want her in the bar as much; said Ada and he could manage. She was a mother now, after all. Surely she wanted to spend more time with their son? We can run this place, Doug assured her, you've worked hard long enough.

Trouble was, these days Freda didn't think pub work was hard. She thought motherhood was exhausting. Soon she began to see Doug's kindness as a banishment, and got prickly with him, although he never seemed to notice. The only one who did was Vicky.

'What's up?'

'Men.'

Vicky nodded, for once feeling on equal ground with her sister in that department. 'Bernard Young, that fella who came back from work with me . . .'

'Yes?'

'He kissed me.' God, Vicky thought, why had she confided that in Freda?

'Did you like it?' her sister asked, suddenly less sullen, even interested, as she sat down at the foot of the bed, the hairbrush still in her hand.

'Nah, not really,' Vicky admitted. 'He's not very . . . you know.'

'Exciting?'

Vicky nodded. She felt grown up, included – suddenly not the blue stocking her sister had laughed at for so long.

'Some men are like that. Boring,' Freda replied fretfully. 'I miss the old days.'

'But you're married!'

'So?' Freda challenged her. 'Doug's a good man, but you get bored after a while with the same person.'

Vicky couldn't understand what her sister was saying. How could she be bored with her husband? She had everything – a home, a son, a man who worshipped her.

'But he loves you.'

'I know,' Freda replied, unimpressed. 'That's what makes it so boring. Takes the challenge away.' She stared into Vicky's shocked face. 'Oh, come on, you're not as innocent as you make out! No one could be. You know what I mean. Some men are exciting, others are just . . . husbands.'

Vicky wasn't sure that she wanted to hear any more, and yet her curiosity made her stay. Was this the way women felt? Was this something she would experience? It was an unwelcome thought, but she couldn't leave. She wanted to be a part of her sister suddenly, to see if some of Freda's sexual gloss would rub off on her – some of her experience, her unashamed discontent.

'I thought you were happy with Doug.'

'I am – in a way. And I love him – in a way,' Freda agreed, picking at the nail on her forefinger. 'But this can't be all there is to life, can it?'

'You've got a husband and a son –'

'So have millions of women.'

'But some men didn't make it back from the war –'

'Is that my fault?' Freda asked belligerently. 'I'm glad Doug's home, but things are so different now. I feel pushed out, like some good little wife all tucked away.'

'He thinks you want to spend time with Billy.'

'I do!' Freda snapped, then dropped her voice. 'I just want other things too.'

Suddenly she sighed and threw the brush onto the floor. Billy shifted in his sleep, but didn't wake. At that moment Vicky could see that her sister was disturbed by something – not just restless, but on edge.

'Are you two getting on?'

'We have sex, if that's what you're asking.'

Vicky flushed, out of her depth. Sex was in a different league from one peck on the cheek from Bernard Young.

But Freda seemed compelled to talk. 'All the men used to want me,' she went on, 'I could have had anyone I set my cap at.'

'You wanted Doug.'

'I know! And I got him. But after I got him I didn't

realise things would turn out so dull.' Her mouth set in a hard line, as though she was struggling to keep her temper. 'You don't like this pub, Vicky. You have a life outside. So why should it be enough for me?'

Stunned by the remark, Vicky took a moment to answer.

'You love The Sixpenny Winner –'

'I used to! When I was a part of it. But now I'm Doug's wife and Billy's mother. I'm not Freda any more.'

'That's crazy –'

'I tell you what's crazy!' Freda exclaimed. 'Being stuck with a husband and child when I'm still young. It's all right for Doug, a family is what he wants. But how am I supposed to settle down? It's not me, not me at all. I miss my old life.' She leaned towards her unsettled sister. 'I don't feel alive any more.' Savagely she pinched her own arm, and a red mark darkened her skin. 'I'm surprised I can feel that. I thought maybe I'd died.'

Shaking her head, Vicky stared at her. 'You're talking like a mad woman –'

'Maybe I *am* going mad. Look at me, Freda Hargreaves –'

'Freda *Oldenshaw*.'

Freda nodded reluctantly. 'Yeah, Freda Oldenshaw. Well, whatever . . . just look at me. I take Billy out to the park and play with him. I talk toddler talk and then feed him and bathe him and then sit and listen to my big strong husband tell me all about his day.'

Her bitterness was corrosive. Vicky glanced over to Billy, but thankfully he was still asleep.

'You should be grateful –'

'*Grateful!* Doug wanted me, he got me and I gave him a son. I think he did well enough out of the bargain.'

'It's not a bargain –'

'Oh, what would you know about it!' Freda hurled back. 'You're not even courting. You think marriage is all love and kisses. Well, you wait, Vicky, wait till you get married and then tell me how exciting it is.' She stared at her sister, her expression hostile. 'You fall out of love with them, you know. You lay there whilst they paw you and then they roll over and grunt in their sleep. And you think, surely I don't have to live like this for the rest of my life?'

'Freda, don't –'

'Freda, don't,' she mimicked back. 'Why not? It's the truth. I thought Doug would be different when he got back from the war. I thought we might move on, get our own pub, but he wasn't for going anywhere. He *likes it here*. Likes Ma telling him what to do, likes the customers, the town. Likes every bloody thing I don't!' Her voice wavered, temper on the tip of her tongue. 'It's all right for him – he was out in the world young, really young. He's been places in his life, even had another wife – but what about me? I've done nothing and now it looks as though I never will.'

Vicky was finding it hard to think of anything to say to help matters. She was aware that Freda was on the verge of losing her temper and wanted to avoid that at all costs. But she was also angry. Her sister was ungrateful, uncaring, selfish. She had what most women dreamed of – and it still wasn't enough.

'What *do* you want, Freda?'

'Excitement,' she answered, her eyes burning. 'Danger – like I used to have, sneaking to the back and waiting to meet someone. Wondering who would be there. Wondering if anyone would catch me –'

'Jesus! You sound like a tart.'

Freda's temper ignited at the word. 'A tart! Yeah, well

225

maybe I am, Vicky. Maybe I'm not cut out for being a wife and mother. Maybe it doesn't satisfy me as much as some other things.'

Vicky flushed at the intimation. 'That's enough!'

'No, it isn't!'

'Keep your voice down!' Vicky warned her. 'You don't want to wake Billy.'

'Wake Billy! Nothing wakes Billy. It's always Billy, Billy, Billy, isn't it, ever since he was born?' Freda's face was ashen with rage. 'Billy this, Billy that, everyone talks and pets Billy –'

'You should be glad everyone loves him.'

'Why?'

'Because he's wanted. Because he's yours.'

Freda banged her hand on the bedstead. 'Billy can do no wrong.'

'Of course he can't! He's a child,' Vicky countered, her voice low with contempt. 'Billy isn't to blame for how you're feeling.'

Bitterness was making Freda reckless. 'Oh, you're wrong there, Vicky. Very wrong.'

'What are you talking about?'

'Your little Billy, darling little Billy, isn't quite what he seems.'

'What?'

'It doesn't matter,' Freda said, turning away, but the words stung her mouth and it was all she could do to keep them in.

'Freda,' Vicky snapped, taking her sister's arm and jerking her round to face her. '*What* about Billy?'

'Nothing.'

'Spit it out! You want to say something, so say it.'

'He's not Doug's child.'

As though struck, Vicky flinched, her hand gripping

226

her sister's arm tightly. Freda was flushed with anger and something else. *Triumph* . . . At that moment Vicky hated her so much that she could have struck her and kept striking her until she stopped talking. Until she never spoke again. Her sister had cheated on her husband – on Doug. Whilst he was away fighting she had betrayed him and then, worse, she had passed off her bastard child as his.

'Christ,' Vicky said, her hand dropping away from her sister's arm. 'How could you?'

'It was an accident,' Freda said, her tone softening. She suddenly wanted sympathy, understanding. 'Doug was away, I missed him –'

'You missed him! So you slept with another man?' Vicky countered incredulously.

'It didn't mean anything –'

Hurriedly Vicky caught hold of her sister's arm again and marched her to the door. For once compliant, Freda went with her to Vicky's room. Once inside, she shut the door and turned on her sister.

'What if Billy had heard you?'

'He's asleep –'

'He could have woken.'

'But he didn't,' Freda replied, rubbing her arm. 'No one knows about this – apart from me and you.'

'And I'm supposed to keep quiet?'

'What's the alternative?' Freda came back. 'To tell anyone would be a disaster. Doug worships Billy –'

'Who's the father?'

Freda looked at her sister and then glanced away.

'Don't tell me you don't know!'

'I know, I know!' Freda snapped. 'But it's not import-ant.'

'Oh, I think it is.'

'Well, I don't.'

'Freda, you have to tell me. I need to know everything. If you expect me to keep this secret – which I will, not for your sake, for Billy and Doug's – then I want to know the whole truth.'

'It won't help,' Freda said, almost crying with self-pity. 'It won't help.'

'Who is Billy's real father?'

'Guess.'

'How the hell can I guess? Tell me.'

'Billy's father is Duncan.'

For an instant Vicky only *thought* she heard her sister say Duncan. Then she realised that she really *had*.

'Duncan?' Vicky repeated, sitting down heavily on the bed, all energy gone out of her legs. 'You slept with Duncan?'

Aware that she had said too much, Freda began to panic. Dear God, would her sister tell Doug? Or Ada? Would they make Duncan go away? She couldn't live with that – not that. Not having Duncan leave her. Her head down, Freda feigned shame, but in reality she was plotting. How could she repair the damage and protect herself? Even more importantly, how could she keep her lover?

'You slept with Duncan Oldenshaw under this roof, whilst your husband was away fighting?' Vicky said, her voice little more than a whisper.

For years she had been besotted with Duncan, always wondering why he never noticed her. But now it was so obvious. He didn't want her *because he was sleeping with her sister*. How many times had they crept to each other's bed at night? Whilst her father was dying, did they make love only yards from where he lay? Oh God,

Vicky thought, bile in her throat. How could they? How could they?

'Get out of my sight, Freda!' she snapped, pushing her sister away.

'Vicky,' Freda pleaded, catching her sister's hand, 'listen to me, listen.'

'I don't want to listen to you! I never want to hear another word. You are incredible. I always knew you were out for yourself, but this . . . Duncan, *your husband's brother*, who came here asking for a handout, you slept with him. No, you can't have done! No one could be that cruel.'

Panic set in, Freda thinking rapidly. 'Vicky, you're wrong –'

'How am I wrong, Freda? You've told me that Doug isn't Billy's father and I haven't seen a star rising in the east lately to explain it any other way.'

'All right, all right. I did sleep with Duncan. And he *is* Billy's father,' Freda said, her thoughts running on, planning as she spoke. 'But it was bound to happen –'

'No, it wasn't bound to happen! Duncan should never have let it happen. He was allowed here on trust, and he betrayed our parents and his own brother. And you let him –'

'It wasn't like that!' Freda blustered, suddenly seeing a way out, if she was sly enough. 'Duncan never wanted me. I was just a fling. It meant nothing. He wanted someone else.'

'Is that supposed to make any of this better?'

'He wanted you.'

Vicky took in a breath, her hand moving to her diaphragm as though to remind herself to keep breathing. Freda saw the action and realised that she had hit her mark. She knew only too well that Vicky had been in love with Duncan for years, but it had never bothered her – after all, she was twice the woman her sister was. How could Duncan even look at Vicky when Freda herself was around? It had even been a kind of triumph for her: seeing Vicky moon over her lover and knowing – *knowing* – that she had Duncan under her complete control. It made her feel more powerful – and it made Duncan more desirable.

And now Vicky's infatuation might prove even more fortuitous.

Slyly she regarded her sister. 'Didn't you know, Vicky?'

She shook her head. 'No . . . I thought . . . I don't believe it!'

'You must,' Freda said, coaxing her into believing the lie. 'Duncan wanted you from the start, from when he first came here. But he was scared of you, you being so smart.' Her voice was convincing, lulling. 'And I was so jealous of you, I wanted to get him for myself. So I seduced him.'

Looking into Freda's eyes, Vicky totally misread the expression. And because she wanted to believe the words, fatally she ignored her own instincts.

'Duncan loves me?'

'Yes, yes! He always has.' Freda stroked her sister's arm, savagely gentle. 'Forgive me, Vicky? You don't know how hard it's been for me to carry this alone for so long. But I couldn't get rid of Billy, could I? I couldn't abort him. And when I saw how much Billy loved you, it was poetic justice.'

She was warming to her theme, relaxing now she was safe again. She had neutralised the threat of exposure, and now there was only one other thing left to secure – Duncan remaining at The Sixpenny Winner.

'Is it true?' Vicky asked, hope making her dizzy. 'Does he really love me?'

'Always has,' Freda replied, sitting down beside her sister and talking softly into her ear. 'This must be our secret – about Billy. But as for Duncan . . . Vicky, you have to talk to him, let him tell you how he feels, how much he loves you.' Her voice caught, as though the emotion was too much for her. 'I don't mind, honestly. It was wrong what I did and now this is my punishment. And I deserve it. Duncan wants you, you must let him know that you want him too.'

The room seemed to hum around Vicky, her ears full of the sounds of promises. The shabby wallpaper she had studied inch by inch was transformed, its colour lightened, the vast old gaslamp outside the window as lyrical as a tree. Duncan Oldenshaw loved her. *Her* . . .

'Remember,' Freda urged her, 'you and I are sisters. We never got on well before, but now we must stick together and help each other.' She kissed Vicky lightly on the cheek. 'Talk to Duncan in the morning. When Doug and Ma are busy in the pub, I'll bring him to you and then leave you both alone.'

'What will I say?'

Gently, Freda stroked a hair away from Vicky's cheek. 'Tell him what you've wanted to tell him for years, dear. Tell him the truth.'

Chapter Twenty-Three

Freda ran downstairs and hurried into the pub, Doug turning to look at her. Further down the bar Ada was pulling a pint, a white blouse tucked into her straight black skirt, her hair newly permed. Good to see that someone was blooming, Freda thought bitterly. Doug walked over to her, smiling.

'Billy in bed?'

'What?'

He frowned. 'I asked if Billy was in bed.'

'Yeah, yeah.' Freda glanced around the bar. Where the hell was Duncan?

'Well, 'lo there, Freda,' Mac Potter said, Lizzie simpering next to him. 'We don't see you so much these days.'

'She's a busy mother,' Doug replied, Freda taking in a breath. Jesus, he was talking for her now.

'And how *is* Billy?'

Billy, Billy, Billy . . .

'He's well, Mr Potter, thanks for asking,' Freda replied, smoothing her hair automatically.

'You need something?' Doug asked, obviously wondering why she seemed so jumpy.

'I was just . . . just . . .' Impetuously, Freda took his arm and then kissed him lightly on the cheek.

Lizzie sighed.

'What was that for, Freda?' Doug asked, touched.

'I just wanted to do it, that was all. I was lonely upstairs.' She paused, surreptitiously glancing round the

232

crowded pub for any sight of Duncan. 'Billy's asleep and it's quiet now.'

'Talk to Vicky.'

'We were having a chat earlier.'

'Good to see you two girls getting on. Life's short, you want to keep on good terms with your family,' Lizzie said thoughtfully. 'I never speak to my sisters.'

Freda frowned. 'I didn't know you had any sisters.'

'Five.'

'Five!' Mac Potter exclaimed. 'All as bonny as you?'

Lizzie flushed coyly. 'Well, I was considered the beauty.'

The rest must have been modelling for coffin handles, Freda thought bitterly, letting go of Doug's arm and asking him: 'Where's Duncan?'

He was surprised by the question. Freda never sought his brother out. In fact, they had never really got on.

'Why d'you want him?'

'I don't. But Vicky wants to talk to him,' Freda said, in a calm voice.

This was news. Vicky hadn't seemed to take to Duncan either.

'Vicky wants to talk to Duncan?'

'Yes. Why it that so surprising!' Freda snapped, then softened her tone and turned her back on Lizzie and Mac. 'Things have taken a right turn, Doug. You wouldn't believe what she just told me.'

'Half a pint, luv, please,' a voice said. Ada hurried over to serve the customer, throwing quizzical glances at her son-in-law and daughter.

'Why? What's going on?' Doug replied.

'Half of mild, Douglas. When you're ready.'

Nodding to the man who was tapping his money on the bar top, Doug pulled a draught.

Ada hurried over. 'Look, if you two want to talk, wait till later. Unless you've not noticed, we've customers.' She glanced at Freda anxiously. 'Where's Billy?'

'In the canal,' Freda said impatiently. 'He's asleep upstairs. Honest to God, you two don't think I can leave him for a moment.'

Annoyed, Ada moved away. Doug nudged Freda and pointed across the pub.

'If you want him, Duncan's over there.'

Hurriedly Freda moved between the crowd of people, some stopping her to talk, others asking after Billy. Of course, she thought, who else? In her light blue dress she stood out among the pool of dark work clothes, her blonde hair catching the overhead light. As though he knew he was being watched, Duncan turned and saw her. His first instinct was to turn away, but she waved to him.

A moment later she was by his side.

'I need a word with you, Duncan.'

His expression was calm, but his eyes were questioning. Dear God, she was risking it, wasn't she? They had hardly exchanged a sentence in all the time Doug had been back, and before that they had been very careful to give the impression that they could hardly stand each other.

'Can't it wait, Freda?'

'No,' she said firmly, walking off. Duncan followed her.

They moved behind the bar. Ada looking up curiously, and then they passed into the kitchen beyond. Finally Freda opened the back door and gestured for Duncan to come out with her. He paused, then followed, closing the door behind him. It was a warm night, unexpectedly mild for April, the outside light shining on Freda's hair and shoulders.

'What the hell –'

'Shut it and listen!' she barked.

He paused; lit a cigarette.

'Vicky knows about us.'

'You *what*?' His good-looking face was ashen suddenly, his eyes wary. 'How the hell did she find out?'

'Does that matter?'

'Of course it does!'

'I told her,' Freda admitted at last.

'*You told her?*' he repeated, obviously aghast. 'Why? Why would you do that?'

Freda leaned towards him. The scent she was wearing was heady, lulling, her breath against his cheek.

'Do you love me?'

'What the –'

'Do you love me, Duncan?'

'You know I do,' he said, his lips moving over hers, Freda's arms going around him tightly. He was dazzled by her, as he always was, seduced by the touch of her skin, her fierceness.

Slowly she murmured: 'I couldn't live without you.'

'Nor I you.'

'What if you were sent away?'

Duncan swallowed, holding on to her. *Sent away!* Bloody hell, he didn't want to leave The Sixpenny Winner. He had his life worked out; he was cosy. Nice home, nice job, nice woman . . .

Another thought struck him sharply: 'Does Doug know?'

'Would I be here if he did?' Freda countered. 'No, he knows nothing. And if we play our cards right, he never will.'

'But Vicky will tell him –'

'No, no, she won't,' Freda said, kissing him again, her

tongue finding his, her body pressed against him. When she pulled away, she fixed him with her cool blue eyes. 'I've thought of a way to keep her quiet – and keep you here.'

'How?' he asked, impressed. Jesus, just how could Freda pull this one off?

'Vicky's in love with you.'

'Nah!'

'She is,' Freda assured him. 'I thought you knew.'

'Well, I had a bit of a notion – when I first came here. But she never seemed to encourage me.'

'Good thing,' Freda said sharply. 'I wouldn't have liked that, Duncan.' Her hand touched his chest, toyed with the buttons on his shirt. 'Like I said, Vicky's in love with you. And she's pretty, Duncan, isn't she?'

This was a dynamite question. Did she want him to say yes or no? Duncan knew how jealous Freda was and tried to field the question.

'She's not a patch on you.'

'But she's good-looking, don't you think?' Freda persisted.

'She's OK. Yeah, she's OK.'

He was taut with tension. What the hell was she up to?

'And you want to stay here very much, don't you, Duncan? You want to stay here, so we can still see each other?'

'Sure I do.'

'There's a way.'

'What way?'

'If Vicky tells Doug, you'll be out on your ear. No cushy job, no Freda.' She paused, let him think about it for a moment. 'You wouldn't like that, would you? I mean, who else would give you a job with your background?'

'I thought you didn't know about that!'

Freda smiled, then ran her tongue over her lips. 'Oh, come on, Doug tells me everything – all about his wayward brother who'd been thieving. *But now Duncan's good, turned over a new leaf* . . . Of course I know about you! Doug and I talk, like couples do, in bed.'

She had the satisfaction of seeing Duncan wince, his jealousy apparent. Oh yes, Freda thought, she could pull this off.

'So in order to keep Doug in the dark, we have to keep Vicky quiet.'

'How?'

'You have to marry her.'

'You what?' he snapped, pulling away from Freda, his eyes burning.

Freda sighed, folded her arms and leaned against the door surround. Why was he being so stupid?

'OK, then we let her tell Doug about us. About Billy.'

About Billy . . .

Duncan flinched at the name, just as she knew he would. There was the faintest possibility that Doug might forgive an affair, although he would banish Duncan for ever. But to know that his beloved Billy wasn't his child, to find out that Duncan was Billy's father – no, he would *never* forgive that. And then Duncan remembered his brother's temper. Jesus, he thought, Doug would kill him.

'Duncan, about Billy –'

'Keep your voice down!' he snapped, looking about him. The ginnel was empty, only one streetlamp burning at the end. It was a sordid place.

'I could throw myself on his mercy,' Freda went on, provoking him, 'but as for you, Duncan, he'd hunt you down, you know he would. Everyone thinks that Doug's a kind man, but we know different, don't we? He's very jealous and he loves Billy so much.'

Duncan was panicking, running his hands through his hair.

'What are we going to do?'

'I've told you. You're going to marry Vicky,' she replied calmly. 'That way you get to stay here. When I've finished with her, she'll think you wanted her all along, that you never wanted me. That I was your second choice.' She smiled as though the thought was ridiculous. 'She'll never think we still want each other. It's the perfect cover, Duncan. You'll be my brother-in-law, living here, all under the same roof. Who would suspect anything? As for Billy, he's Doug's son, isn't he? Everyone knows that.'

Shaken, Duncan stared at the woman standing so calmly in front of him. He had always known that Freda was dangerous – that was what had drawn him to her – but this was playing with dynamite. In that same moment he also realised that she had him over a barrel. If he didn't agree, she would tell Doug everything. The besotted Doug wouldn't throw *her* out, but he would banish Duncan. Or worse.

But if he played ball, if he married Vicky, he would stay at the pub – and have Freda too. He hesitated, hating the fact that she was blackmailing him and yet too cowardly to resist.

'Vicky cares about me?'

Freda nodded. It was so easy; men were so pliable. 'She's been crazy about you for years.'

'I thought she was seeing someone.'

'Oh, that! He's just some toerag clerk at the hospital. You've no competition there.' Freda leaned towards

Duncan and then ran her tongue over his lips, hearing him sigh and reach for her. But as he did so, she stepped back. 'Hey! Not here. You know how careful we have to be.'

'I thought –'

'No, Duncan, *I* do the thinking,' she replied gently. 'I told Vicky that I would arrange for you two to have a talk in the morning. At eleven o'clock. So that you could tell her how you feel –'

'How *I* feel?'

'You have to tell her that you love her, that you've *always* loved her.' Freda paused, then: 'Oh, come on, Duncan, you can lie! You've been lying to women all your life. Vicky wants to hear that you love her. Tell her, and you're safe. *We're safe.* You have to convince her. If she has any doubts, she'll reject you – and then she'll tell Doug everything. I know my sister, she has principles. The only way Vicky can square this with her conscience is if she believes that she's doing it for love.'

Disturbed, Duncan stepped back from her. For a moment he was afraid of the blonde woman who stood in the doorway under the lamplight, her face so perfectly composed, her words so effortlessly cruel. If he agreed, he could keep her. The thought enticed him. No woman had ever aroused him so much and the danger made it all the more exciting. But if they were discovered . . . And besides, if he agreed, Freda would have control over him for as long as she wanted.

But then, she already did. Duncan puffed on his cigarette, Freda watching him calmly. What was the option? Dear God, if Doug found out . . . *But if he made a run for it . . .* If he stole away tonight he would avoid everything. And Freda would hardly follow. She couldn't if she didn't know where he had gone.

Dropping the cigarette stub, Duncan ground it out with the toe of his shoe. He knew he was walking into trouble, but he had always liked trouble. Half of the thrill of his relationship with Freda had been knowing that they could be discovered. But they hadn't. For years they had played their parts to perfection; fooled everyone. All the stolen hours, making love on the quiet, exchanged looks – oh, it had been sweet and bitter at the same time.

Could he live without that? If he left he could find another woman easily, but she wouldn't be Freda. And yet, was he *really* prepared to marry Vicky for her? To marry her sister, to lie and cheat for the rest of their lives? To bed Freda whilst he wed Vicky? It was a hell of a suggestion, a hell of a way to live. Dangerous. Underhand.

Exciting.

'So?' Freda said, at last.

Duncan looked at her, and then smiled slowly. 'What if she won't marry me?'

Freda tossed her head. 'Oh, Duncan, that's the least of our worries.'

Chapter Twenty-Four

All night Vicky drifted in and out of sleep. Finally she got up at three and went down to the kitchen to make herself some tea. It was cold, the previous warm day having given way to a chilling night. Shivering, she wrapped her dressing gown around her, and set the kettle to boil.

It was all so incredible, so unbelievable. Billy was Duncan's son. Freda and Duncan. *Freda and Duncan.* Her sister and Doug's brother, carrying on under this roof. And she had never suspected. And how long had they been sleeping together? Had their affair gone on for a while? Or had they just made love once? After all, they had never got on, never spent time together, never seemed to have anything in common. Apart from sensuality. They both had that.

Vicky thought back. Duncan had gone out a lot, Freda had also gone out. Did they meet up on his days off? Or sneak out through the back door to the ginnel exit, squalid scene of so many of Freda's triumphs? The kettle started to whistle and she made herself some tea. Sitting down in the rocking chair in front of the grate, Vicky then riddled the ashes, a few cold flames coming into life.

Duncan loved her. *Duncan loved her.* Not Freda, *her.* So why wasn't she euphoric? Wasn't that what she had always wanted? Wasn't that what she had dreamed of for so long? And yet, there was something that didn't ring true. Duncan had never cast any sly looks in her direction, watched her, or even offered a lame innuendo. In fact, Duncan Oldenshaw had never shown any interest in her at all.

Maybe Freda was wrong. But then Freda was never wrong about men, was she? Vicky sipped her scalding tea, staring blankly ahead. She should tell Doug the truth, make them confess, expose Freda and Duncan and force them to own up to their actions.

But what good would that do? Doug adored Billy; it would break him to learn that he was not his son. Doug had lost a wife before – how could he manage to cope with the knowledge of Freda's adultery and with his own brother? Could any man come to terms with that? Besides, he loved Freda. She was everything to him. Hadn't he said so, over and over again? *It's so good to have a family, a wife, a son. I'm so lucky. Lucky . . .*

Vicky put down the mug and stood up. Then sat down again. She couldn't tell Ada – that was madness. Her mother would have Duncan thrown out. Vicky flushed. That was the last thing she wanted. He had to stay. It was imperative that Duncan stayed, that she got her man. But was it worth all the lies and deceit? God, *was it*?

Could she live with the knowledge of what Duncan was? Could she love a man who had behaved so dishonourably? And could she ever look Doug in the face again if she threw in her lot with Duncan? Could she hide so much? Forgive so much? Lie so much? Could she be that much of a hypocrite?

Freda was adept at deception, but Vicky wasn't. She had lived her life being open, straight with people. She had principles and had always wanted to do the right thing . . . Vicky sighed. Why hadn't she fallen in love with Bernard – with any of the other decent men around? She was an intelligent woman, why was she being such a fool about Duncan Oldenshaw?

It was no good, Vicky told herself firmly. She couldn't go against her own nature. She wanted to be happy, but she wanted peace of mind too. Irritably, she shook her head. Who was she fooling? If she was honest – not being the good little Vicky – she wanted excitement, love, sex. She wanted what she had envied in Freda. And she wanted – *longed for* – Duncan.

But would she do anything to get him? Would she lie and kid herself for a man? *Any man?* God, Vicky thought helplessly, I have to think clearly. I have to do the right thing.

But suddenly doing the right thing wasn't enough.

'Move over!' Freda barked, jabbing Doug in the ribs. He snored once, then woke up, turning to her.

'What is it?'

'I can't sleep.'

Immediately he took her in his arms, her head resting on his chest. In the half-light her eyes were open, wary.

'I love you, Freda.'

'I love you too,' she replied distantly.

'Is that Billy?'

'What?'

'Is that Billy moving around?' Doug repeated, sitting up in bed and listening. They had partitioned off a portion of their bedroom, Billy, now four, was old enough to sleep alone. So Freda had said.

'He's asleep,' she assured him. 'Come on, lie down.'

'Maybe I should check on him.'

'No!' she snapped, then murmured, 'Why don't you check on me?'

Her hand slid into the opening of his pyjama trousers, Doug moaning and leaning back on the bed. She had to keep him sweet, had to make him think that she never even noticed another man, that she longed for him. Undoing his trousers, she then unfastened his pyjama jacket and ran her tongue down his chest.

She had heard the movements outside too, but had known at once that it wasn't Billy, but Vicky, walking about, thinking. Wondering what? What she would say to Duncan? What he would say to her in the morning?

Doug sighed, caught hold of Freda's hair and pulled her to him, his mouth searching for hers hungrily . . . It had to work, Freda decided, her thoughts elsewhere, *it had to*. She had to keep Duncan at The Sixpenny Winner, or she would go mad. Just think of living with Doug for the rest of her life, the good little wife and mother . . . Her tongue found Doug's and she rolled on top of him, pulling her nightdress over her head. She knew that he could see her body in the half-light, loving her, wanting her.

But was Duncan up to it, Freda wondered as she made love to Doug. Could he work it out with Vicky? Could he pretend to love her sister? Could he make love to Vicky? . . . The thought disturbed her, Freda beginning rhythmically to move, Doug under her, gripping her thighs, then reaching up for her breasts.

Then he climaxed and Freda rolled off him, turning over in the bed and closing her eyes. But all she could think of was Duncan. And Vicky. Her man. And her sister. Making love.

By morning Freda had cooled down and was in control again. After all, she was duping her sister, forcing Duncan to marry Vicky. He didn't want to, but he was going to – just to stay around her, Freda. That was proof of her hold over Duncan, surely – proof of his obsession with her.

Hurriedly Freda explained to Vicky that everything was set. She would get Duncan into the kitchen for their talk just as soon as Ada and Doug were busy in the bar. At eleven o'clock. Relax, she urged her sister, just talk from the heart.

Minutes later she visited Duncan, kissed him avidly and then told him that she had every faith in him. Besides, it wasn't wicked, it was for them. For their love. For their child . . . The last remark would dance in his head uneasily, Freda knew all too well. It would remind Duncan – just in case he was thinking of bottling out – that he had a lot to lose.

At ten to eleven, Vicky came down into the kitchen. She was wearing a blue suit and navy shoes, her hair brushed neatly.

'I phoned work, told them I had a dentist appoint-ment,' she explained to Freda. It was the first lie, Vicky had thought when she did it. The first of how many? 'I said I'd be in later.'

'You will, you will,' Freda assured her, listening for the sound of footsteps. 'Duncan said he'd be along any minute.'

But when ten minutes had passed, Freda was impa-tient. Vicky was staring at her feet. He hadn't come, she thought. Her sister had been wrong. Duncan Oldenshaw never loved her . . . Shame made her wince. She had gone along with Freda, denied every principle she had ever held dear, and for what? He didn't want her after all.

Freda was annoyed too, but she was thinking along different lines. Duncan had done a bunk. He had upped and left her. The bastard! The craven, lying bastard!

She'd have him, get Doug on to him, make sure no woman fell for his good looks again. Her face flushed, Freda drummed her fingernails on the table top. He had bested her, tricked her – pretended he was going along with the plan when all the time he was just stringing her along and making his getaway. You bastard. You bastard, Freda thought repeatedly.

'He's not coming –'

'Shut up!' Freda snapped, then apologised. 'Sorry, Vicky, I was miles away. Sure Duncan's coming. How could he not?'

'Did you tell him I wanted to talk to him?'

Freda turned to her sister. Christ, what was she wearing? She looked like she was going to church, not about to seduce the man she had been mooning over for years.

'He was thrilled,' Freda lied. 'Said he never hoped that you loved him.'

Vicky nodded, but her eyes were filling. 'So why isn't he here?'

'Maybe he's been held up.'

'Where?'

'I don't know. Doug sent him out on an errand first thing – maybe he's running late.'

'Maybe he's running away.'

Freda wanted to jump up and slap her sister, to scream: I want him too, you silly cow. He's my man. If I hadn't confessed to you, none of this would ever have happened. We would have carried on as we had done for years. But I blabbed, I bloody blabbed, and now he's gone.

'Maybe I should get to work –'

'No, stay,' Freda told her, looking up at the clock. 'It's only twenty past eleven.'

'But if he was keen, he would have been on time. Or early.'

'Since when did you know so much about men?' Freda countered. 'Look, Duncan's not your usual kind of man, he's more complicated. Maybe he's trying to pluck up courage somewhere.'

'Do you love him?'

The words were out of Vicky's mouth before she had time to check them, but she had to know. If she was going to go along with this – if she had the chance – she had to know how Freda felt.

'What did you say?'

'I asked you if you loved Duncan,' Vicky repeated patiently.

'No,' Freda replied, because at that moment she didn't.

She wasn't really sure if she'd ever loved him. Sex was what held them together. Making love with Duncan was unlike anything she had ever known. He was firm, almost rough, inventive, sexy. He made her feel good, satisfied, whole. She could catch a glimpse of Duncan and feel sexually excited ... But did she love him? No, she was drawn to him – like a drunk to a bottle of port.

'Are you sure?'

'Oh, for God's sake, Vicky, I don't love Duncan,' Freda replied heatedly.

'It's just that you seem upset.'

Freda paused, thinking, regaining her composure. 'I'm worried for you,' she said at last. 'Look, I feel responsible. I want this to work out for you two. Duncan and I were – well, it wasn't to be – but you could be happy together. You love each other.'

Vicky softened at the words. Love made it all right.

'So you think he'll come?'

'He'll come,' Freda assured her. Oh Jesus, she thought, please come.

'Looks like a bloody wake in here,' Ada said, walking in on the two girls. 'Why aren't you at work, Vicky?'

'They said I could go in later today.'

'Where's Billy?'

'Playing upstairs,' Freda replied, willing her mother to leave. She couldn't cope with Ada when Duncan came. Or if he didn't come . . .

'Had a quarrel?'

'No,' Vicky replied, 'we were chatting, that's all.'

''Bout time you got on better, you two,' Ada said, walking over to the windowsill and staring at the pies laid out there. Half were already cooked, the others due to go into the oven. 'Smashing pies, those. You know, your father used to say that I made the best meat pie in Lancashire . . .'

'He never ate them, though,' Freda said quietly.

'. . . he said I could achieve things with pastry that should be impossible . . .'

Vicky exchanged a look with Freda, both of them trying not to laugh. The moment tingled between them, a closeness. Maybe it *could* all work out, Vicky thought, if Duncan would just come.

'When we were first married he used to eat like a bloody shire horse. I always reckoned that Evie couldn't feed him enough. Hollow legs, poor little beggar.' Ada didn't notice that her daughters were willing her to leave. 'He was a runt when I married him after the accident, but I soon got him well, on his feet again. Down to my cooking, that was . . .'

'Ma –'

'. . . he used to say that I fed him like a king . . .'

'Ma –'

'. . . always so grateful.'

'Ma, Doug's calling you,' Freda said, stemming the flow of reminiscence.

At once, Ada hurried away, back to the bar.

'*Was* he calling?' Vicky asked her sister.

'Nah, but she'll get caught up now, give us some peace.'

A silence fell between them. Vicky studied the clock.

'You did say eleven?'

'Yeah.'

'And he seemed pleased? You know, he seemed to want to talk to me?'

Freda sighed. 'Yeah. He wanted to talk to you.'

'She loved him very much, didn't she?'

Baffled, Freda looked at her sister. 'What?'

'Ma loved Dad very much.' Vicky thought of her father, then flushed.

He wouldn't have approved of what she was doing. He would have wanted Duncan out, everything clean and above board. No room for lies in Clem's life. Besides, he would have told her, how can you think of going with a man who'd cheat on his own brother?

God, Dad, she thought helplessly, forgive me.

'He's very late.'

The clock wound round another series of minutes, Freda cupping her chin in her hand, trying to disguise her fury.

Vicky watched the clock. 'I have to go. I have to get to work.'

'Stay a bit longer.'

'But –'

'Just a bit longer.'

Vicky was touched, deceived into thinking that her

sister was anxious for her, for things to work out. Whereas Freda was dying inside, craving the man she wanted and terrified that she had lost him.

In the distance they both heard Winter's Clock chiming. Twelve. Noon.

In one quick movement, Freda pushed back her chair and stood up. 'I'm going upstairs to check on Billy,' she said, her voice strained.

Numbed, Vicky watched her go, then picked up her handbag and walked to the back door. She wouldn't cry, she told herself. She had to get a grip. It would have been no good, no good at all. She had been spared, really, from something that could never have worked. Freda must have got it all wrong. Duncan Oldenshaw had cheated them both.

For a moment Vicky hesitated, then opened the back door, locking it after her as the rain pelted down.

A touch on her shoulder made her turn. Duncan, smiling, was holding an umbrella over her.

'I thought Freda would never go,' he said simply. 'I've been watching through the kitchen window, wondering how long she'd hang around. Did you think I wasn't coming, Vicky?'

She smiled, her lips dry. He had been there all along. He hadn't let her down. He had wanted her and come for her. He didn't want Freda, just her.

'I –'

He moved quickly, kissing her on the lips, Vicky immediately putting her arms around his neck and pulling him to her. She was greedy for him, all the years of waiting and frustration coming together in that moment. Her mouth moved against his, Duncan's right arm struggling to keep the umbrella over them as his left hand reached inside Vicky's coat and stroked her back.

God, he thought, he had dropped lucky. She adored him, he could tell that, and she was quite something. Not at all the little bookworm he had thought she was. Marrying Vicky Hargreaves wasn't going to be much of a punishment, after all. Thank you, Freda, he thought to himself, thank you very much.

When they finally pulled away from each other, Duncan was smiling.

'I didn't think you'd even noticed me.'

'I thought the same,' Vicky replied, rain hitting the umbrella over her head and making drip, drop, drip, drop sounds. Rhythmic, soothing. 'Freda said –'

'Forget what Freda said,' Duncan told her. 'I want you, Vicky, want to marry you.'

'But –'

'Ssh!' he ordered her. 'Not another word. Will you have me?'

Will you have me? The sentence echoed in Vicky's head, along with the sound of the raindrops hitting the umbrella over their heads. *Will you have me?* She looked into Duncan's eyes and felt a rush of pleasure. He was handsome, exciting, and he wanted her.

Would she have him? She'd send anyone to hell who tried to stop her.

'Vicky, answer me.'

'Yes,' she replied, laughing, 'I'll marry you, Duncan. Of course I will.'

Chapter Twenty-Five

The news was all over town in hours. *Vicky Hargreaves was marrying Duncan Oldenshaw*. Now if that wasn't a turn-up for the books! He'd dropped lucky and that was a fact. No one ever knew where the bugger had come from and now he was all settled, with his feet under the Hargreaveses' table. And soon under one of the Hargreaveses' beds.

They weren't the only ones who were surprised. Ada was downright stunned when a luminous Vicky told her the news.

'But . . . but . . . you hardly know him.'

'How can you say that?' Vicky replied. 'Duncan's been living here for years.'

'But you two never got on. And now you're telling me you're going to marry him! You're mad,' Ada decided, as she trimmed the pastry around a meat pie she had just made. 'Duncan Oldenshaw's not your type. You've hardly talked to him, let alone gone out with him. Anyway, what makes you so interested in him all of a sudden?'

'I've had my eye on him for years –'

'It looks like he can say the same,' Ada answered.

Vicky took the pie out of her hand, then led her mother over to the kitchen table. 'Sit down, Ma, please. Let's talk this out.'

Reluctantly Ada took a seat, her arms folded.

'I've been in love with Duncan for ages.'

'You never said! My God, I know Freda's deep, but I thought you and I didn't have secrets.'

'It wasn't a secret! I was embarrassed, thought I had a crush on him which would pass. But it didn't. Oh, Ma, how could I say anything? You would all have laughed at me. I didn't think Duncan had even noticed I was alive; always thought I was carrying a torch for someone who didn't care.'

'Hah!' Ada replied shortly. 'He knows a good thing when he sees one. Got himself set up nicely.'

'Why do you hate him so much?' Vicky countered, a little more heatedly than she had meant. 'You seemed glad enough to have him here when Doug was away. Duncan helped us out during the war, didn't he? Got us things, looked after the place?'

'Looked after himself too,' Ada retorted, 'and now he's making sure he won't have to move on. Oh, I can see the way that bugger's mind's working. He wants to stay where he's comfortable.'

Vicky flushed. 'So it has nothing to do with me? He's lying when he says he loves me?'

It was Ada's turn to bluster. 'I didn't say that. I just wonder about Duncan Oldenshaw, that's all. He's too much of a dark horse for my liking.'

'He's Doug's brother –'

'Oh, that doesn't count for much. Remember Cain and Abel.'

Vicky pressed on. She knew she had to defend Duncan to her mother; get Ada to like and accept him. Or was she really trying to convince herself that this sudden declaration of love was genuine?

'Why is it so impossible to believe that he loves me?'

'It's not,' Ada said flatly. 'I bet many a man could love

you, Vicky. But why pick Duncan Oldenshaw? I thought you were keen on Bernard Young.'

'Oh, Bernard's just a friend.'

'And what about those other lads you used to see? You got on with them, and they had the same interests as you – politics, world affairs. And then there's the hospital – there must be some nice young men there.' Ada looked into her daughter's unexpectedly hostile face and faltered. 'Vicky, you know what I mean. Duncan's not exactly educated and you always put such stock in that before.'

'It's not everything.'

'He's turned your bloody head!' Ada snapped. 'Learning used to be everything to you. You were always trying to understand things, take an interest in the world. You marry Duncan Oldenshaw and the only thing you'll take an interest in is *him*.'

'You don't know that!'

'Oh yes, I do!' Ada retorted firmly. 'I know more about men than you think. And as for Duncan Oldenshaw, I can't see anything to recommend him.' She paused then, realisation dawning. 'Oh, I see. It's his looks, isn't it? Well, let me tell you something, Vicky, looks fade. It's character that matters.'

'I know. I know –'

'He might seem glamorous and exciting, but that charm of his could end up just a bit too exciting. He doesn't look the faithful type, Vicky, I'll be honest. And you're not the kind of woman who could take betrayal.'

'I haven't married him yet!' Vicky retorted, stung. 'What are you talking about betrayal for?'

God, she was so near the mark, Vicky realised. Her mother might know nothing of Freda and Duncan's affair, but she had sensed trouble and knew by instinct the kind of man Duncan Oldenshaw was. Or the kind of man she *thought* he was. And she was right . . .

Jesus, Vicky thought, I must be mad to think of marrying him. But she couldn't think of *not* marrying him. Duncan had fascinated her and all the long years of waiting and longing had finally materialised into reality. And – going against every instinct she had – Vicky was damned if she was going to lose her chance.

'I thought you had more sense!' Ada said finally. 'I tell you, no good will come of this. No good at all.'

Women, Duncan thought bitterly, they were all the same. He had been embarrassed by Nora, by her hysterical outburst when he'd told her it was over. What could she expect? he thought incredulously. She was married, it was an affair – nothing that was going to lead to anything. Oh, but she hadn't seen it like that. She'd clung to him and cried – he hated women crying – and then looked red-faced and blotchy. As if that would sway him.

He had been glad to get away. Out on the street he looked up at her window and then moved off as soon as he realised she was watching him. Well, it was time for it to end. Things would be too complicated otherwise, what with Freda and Vicky . . . He paused at the end of Bridge Street, then moved suddenly into the Warren Bulkeley Arms Hotel, his eyes blinking in the dimness inside.

Ordering a pint, Duncan stood at the bar and looked round. The pub seemed depressed, quiet, its only customers silent old men. The Sixpenny Winner had recovered from the war much quicker, trade picking up steadily. Jobs weren't plentiful yet, but the men wanted to drink. And they knew where to come and spend their money. In fact, there was enough money coming in to pay his wages easily. And when he was married to Vicky he would have more of a say in running the business. Oh, Doug did well enough, but he wasn't ambitious, never had been. But he was, Duncan thought. People misread him, took him to be a bit happy-go-lucky, but he was canny enough when he saw an opportunity. And he had seen one now. There was money in pubs, and if you owned more than one . . .

Steady, Duncan told himself, one step at a time. First marry Vicky and then make yourself invaluable to the business – then see how the land lies. There was Freda to think of, naturally, but when Duncan was married his first thought would have to be for his wife, wouldn't it? The stranglehold Freda thought she had on him might turn out to be only a slipknot after all.

Down in the pub cellar Doug was whistling to himself, his spirits high. Duncan was going to marry Vicky! God, what a turn-up. It was wonderful – his little brother had finally found a woman to settle down with and that woman was Freda's sister. Doug leaned against a barrel and smiled to himself.

If the truth be known he had missed his brother when they were estranged. Then when he heard that Duncan had been imprisoned for theft he had wanted to wash his hands of him for ever. But guilt stopped him. Duncan might have turned out bad, but he was family, after all. His one and only brother, his only kin. So when Duncan re-emerged that night so long ago and asked for help, Doug had secretly been delighted.

And now this! His brother, Duncan, was marrying Freda's sister and they would all live together at The

Sixpenny Winner. He was thrilled by the thought of his family increasing year by year, seeing himself as the patriarch, guarding over and guiding his brood.

He would train Duncan up. The days of him jobbing around and doing the menial work were numbered. He would still have to pull his weight, Doug thought – just as he did – but maybe Duncan might be considered more seriously. After all, hadn't he proved he was straight now? Hadn't he kept his nose clean for years, never taken a penny from the pub, or done anything dishonourable? He had been a help, a reliable support – just what Doug needed most.

It was wonderful to know that Vicky was getting married, but to know that there wasn't a stranger coming into their lives, that the man she had picked was Duncan, that there would be no awkwardness, no clash of personalities – the thought was bliss.

The terrible time of Emma's death, the loss and pain, had passed. Doug had found – against all the odds – a new wife and family. And now there was more. Once again, his luck hadn't failed him. His brother was back, and he was staying for good.

Chapter Twenty-Six

'So where is he?' Ada hissed to Freda in the front pew of the church. 'Where the hell is that toerag?'

She had wanted to stay with Vicky at the back, but Freda had shooed her out. You fuss too much, she had said, joining her mother later in the pew. After all, Freda had agreed with her sister, she didn't feel right being a bridesmaid.

She should have insisted on staying with Vicky, Ada thought. Oh God, don't let the bastard stand her up. And God help him if he does.

'Will you stop worrying?' Freda said, trying to cover her own nerves. 'Duncan will be here.'

'You'd think he could get up in time for his own wedding.'

'You know Duncan's always late for everything,' Freda replied, lapsing into silence again.

Ada sighed. Then fiddled with her leather gloves. An arm and a leg they'd cost her, but she'd wanted to look her best. Had a hat made too, and got a navy suit from Barry's in the town centre, even though it was a wicked price. It was important she looked smart, Ada thought, knowing how the busybodies would turn out to stare. As for Vicky, God, the girl was a beauty. She'd never seen it before, Ada thought, but love had transformed her. She glowed.

Mind you, glowing or not, Ada had made sure that the wedding dress was fitted around the waist. No rumours, thank you, no hints about shotgun weddings. They *could* have waited, Ada mused. What was the rush, after all? But apparently this secret love, once admitted, was now dragging all behind it like a runaway horse.

But where was the bridegroom? Ada turned and caught sight of Bessie Cork. What the bloody hell was she wearing? With that fur collar round her neck, she looked like she was being swallowed by a moose.

A jab in her back made Ada turn again. Lizzie was smiling, grinning from ear to ear. Beside her was Mac Potter. His wife had only just died – was barely cold – and here he was escorting Lizzie.

'How do, Ada?'

'Hello there, Lizzie.'

'Duncan's a bit late, isn't he?'

Ada winced, turning round in her seat and looking Lizzie full in the eyes.

'Your watch is fast.'

'Oh, no, I don't think so,' Lizzie said, holding it up to her ear. 'I set it by the radio this morning.'

Sitting beside her, Mac nudged her sharply in the ribs. 'I think Ada's right, Lizzie –'

'But I set my watch this morning,' Lizzie went on, Ada making a mental note to give her the meat pie with all the gristle next time she was in the pub.

'He's here!' Freda hissed suddenly in her mother's ear.

Ada beamed as she got to her feet. 'See, your watch *was* fast, Lizzie,' she said, watching Duncan hurry to his seat.

He was a good-looking one, she thought reluctantly, handsome in that hired suit. All black hair and white teeth . . . Then her eyes moved down the aisle as the Wedding March started up and Vicky, arm in arm with Douglas, headed for the altar.

'Oh Lord . . .' Ada said simply, turning to Freda.

Freda's expression was unreadable.

'Bet you're sorry you're not a bridesmaid now, hey?'

'This is Vicky's day,' Freda replied blankly, looking across the aisle and catching Duncan's eye.

A look passed between them, a look of complete understanding and blistering deceit.

Later they had a do at The Sixpenny Winner, Doug getting tipsy for once, Ada finally pressed into playing the piano, friends and customers all gathered round and singing together. Only Freda was silent, watchful at the bar as she studied her sister and her lover. Together.

He was making a good show of being in love, she thought, but then that was Duncan all over – a hypocrite through and through. He would never come to love Vicky, she assured herself. She wasn't his type. Sipping her brandy, Freda continued to study them. How long before Duncan and she could risk meeting up? And where?

The thought soothed her, made her less resentful of Vicky's time in the spotlight. You enjoy your day, she thought. Remember it, because it won't last. Duncan is mine – always will be . . . Sighing, Freda leaned her head against the bar prop and closed her eyes. She thought of Duncan and her making love, of his hands over her skin, moving over her breasts . . .

'Are you sickening for something?' Ada asked suddenly.

Freda snapped to attention. 'Hey?'

'I said – are you sickening for something?' She put her hand on Freda's forehead. 'You look hot.'

'I'm fine.'

'Maybe you've got a temperature.'

'No, I'm fine,' Freda repeated, holding on to her patience. 'It's stuffy in here.'

'Well, I have to say I'm surprised, but those two lovebirds look like they were made for each other,' Ada said, watching the newlyweds. 'They'll enjoy their weekend in Blackpool, away from all of us.'

Freda's expression was metallic.

'Douglas did a good job, didn't he?' Ada went on proudly. 'I was glad to see him give Vicky away. Clem always had a soft spot for Douglas.'

She peered over the bar, looking down at Billy, fast asleep in a low chair. 'Little lad's tired out.'

He had been good in the church, no trouble. But then Billy seldom was trouble: a very composed little boy, almost too composed. Not for the first time he reminded Ada of herself, a shy child afraid of drawing attention to itself.

'Four years old,' Ada went on, looking lovingly at her grandson. 'He gets more like you every day, Freda.'

Good thing, her daughter thought wryly.

'Be going to nursery school soon. He could start this September.'

Freda was still watching Duncan and Vicky, her jealousy bile in her throat.

'I said, Billy could start school this autumn.'

'Yes, yes!' Freda snapped, then put her hand to her forehead. 'Sorry, Ma, I think I *am* feeling a bit under the weather.' She turned, no longer able to bear watching the newlyweds and think of what they would be doing later that night. 'I'll take Billy up.'

'You want a hand?'

'No, I can manage,' Freda replied, lifting her son and feeling the child stir against her.

Duncan's child, Duncan's son. God, what would her

mother say if she knew, if Freda stood up now and told everyone in the pub what the truth was? If she said – Duncan is my lover, the father of my child. We arranged this wedding. Vicky means nothing to him. It's me he wants?

She could imagine the pandemonium, Doug's expression, Duncan's, Ada's and Vicky. Don't forget Vicky. Oh, they all thought everything was so sweet, but they didn't know the truth. No one did except her and Duncan. Automatically, Freda held Billy more tightly, suddenly protective. This is my child, she thought, staring at the newlyweds again. This is the son I had with Duncan, and no one can take him away from me.

Enjoy your day in the sun, Vicky, she thought. Enjoy your white dress and white veil, your fairy-tale wedding. Because that's what it is. A fairy tale. Nothing more.

Chapter Twenty-Seven

The living quarters of The Sixpenny Winner were reorganised whilst Duncan and Vicky were on honeymoon. Doug and Freda kept their room on the first floor, Billy was given his own, and Ada moved up to Clem's top space, giving her bedroom over to Duncan and Vicky. So the two sisters would sleep – with their respective husbands – on the same floor, across the hall from each other. They would share the same bathroom and toilet. It would be cosy. Very cosy.

'I'll be happy upstairs,' Ada insisted to Freda, who was not keen on the adjustments. She had presumed that Duncan and Vicky would be upstairs, not merely yards away.

'It's cramped, Ma.'

'No, it's not. We could take down the partition wall so it'll be a fair-sized room, Freda.' She looked round at the old iron bedstead and mattress where Clem had died.

'It's morbid.'

'Rubbish! It's where your dad lived for years,' Ada replied, sitting down on the bed and touching the mattress. 'I've got happy, as well as sad, memories up here.'

'You should keep your old room.'

'And have Vicky and Duncan all cramped up? Never.' Ada turned as she heard footsteps, Billy coming in and running to her. 'Hey, little lad, how are you doing?' She looked over to Freda. 'He grows by the day. He'll be as tall as his dad soon. How tall *is* Doug? Six one, six two?'

'Six two,' Freda replied, wiping a smudge off Billy's face. 'You must be careful coming upstairs, Billy. Always hold on to the banister rail.'

'Yes, Mum,' he said solemnly.

'And never run.'

'Yes, Mum,' he agreed, Ada laughing and hugging him to her.

'Oh, this is great. Three generations – two married couples, a little one, and a widow – all under one roof. I like that, Freda. It feels good. Clem would have liked it too. We're all one big family now, no arguments, no bad feelings, just all of us pulling together.' She sighed contentedly, her grandson on her lap. 'I'm a happy woman, Freda. A very happy woman indeed.'

It seemed that Duncan was avoiding her, Freda thought, waiting for a sign from him. Which didn't come. Instead he seemed to fuss over Vicky, who was glossy with triumph. I know why you're smiling, Freda thought, I know that look.

Her impatience increased in the weeks that followed, and the long summer set in. He was just being careful, Freda told herself. Just being cunning, making it look as though he was in love with Vicky. But it was very convincing. Fooled everyone.

But it doesn't fool me, Freda thought, I know you're lying, pretending. I know *you*, Duncan . . . But *did* she? It would have been easier if she could have talked to him, touched him, but he avoided her. How was that possible? Freda thought angrily. Their rooms were on the same damn floor, they used the same bathroom. How was it possible? Because he was clever, very clever.

Didn't avoid her in public, just private. In public, when there were people around, Duncan talked to Freda like a friend, a sister-in-law.

And so the summer dragged on, Freda walking Billy to the park or Sunday school, taking him out as much as she could to avoid her sister and brother-in-law. At first she found her child a nuisance, but soon Billy became a comfort to her. He was her only contact with Duncan; he carried Duncan's blood.

By the time August had arrived people were commenting on what a wonderful mother Freda had become.

'You never see her without her little one,' Lizzie said, surprised, 'and he's growing, is Billy. Getting to be quite a big boy. And active, running and climbing everywhere. And he talks so much! Oh, she's got her work cut out with that little lad, has Freda.'

It was true, Billy was a handful. And he was also devoted to his mother. After all, Freda was beautiful, almost exotic. When they were out people stared at her. Even a child as young as Billy could see that, and it made him feel proud. This was *his mother*, his wonderful mother. Slowly he came out of himself, and equally slowly Freda relaxed with him. At times she could be with Billy and even manage to forget Duncan. And Vicky. For whole half-hours she could play with Billy and never give them a thought.

But when her steps turned from the park and she walked her son home, Freda began to fret. She would grow tense, Billy holding tighter and tighter on to her hand, because he didn't understand, but he knew something was wrong.

'Mum, are you sad?'

She looked down at him, surprised. 'Sad? No, why?'

'You look sad.'

At once Freda stopped and sat down on a bench, Billy sitting beside her. Slowly she slid her arm around him and pointed to the ducks on the pond.

'See those?'

He nodded.

'Every one of those ducks isn't a duck really.'

Billy looked at her curiously. 'What are they?'

'Wishes,' Freda said. 'Every duck is really a wish. You can pick one, Billy, and wish for anything you want.'

'Yeah?'

She nodded in agreement. 'Yeah.'

Transfixed, Billy looked at the ducks and picked the whitest one. Then he closed his eyes and wished. Freda did the same, picked a duck and wished with all her might.

'What did you wish?' she asked Billy when he finally opened his eyes.

'I wished you'd be with me for ever and ever.'

Touched, Freda glanced down, shame balling up in her throat. She had wished that Duncan would make love to her, that he would grow distant from Vicky and love her again. It was selfish, but she couldn't help it. And what had her son wanted? To be with her for ever. Jesus, Freda thought, why couldn't Duncan wish for the same?

'Will it come true?'

'What?' Freda asked, turning back to her son.

'Will my wish come true?'

'Yes, Billy. I'll always be with you.'

'What did you wish, Mum?'

'Nothing today,' she replied briskly, standing up and taking her son's hand. 'There wasn't a duck I liked the look of.'

*   *   *

266

Standing at the back entrance of the pub, Freda lit a cigarette and watched a couple pass. The whole world was in couples now, she thought, no single men around, no lovers come whispering in the night-time, jostling for her attention. What has happened? she asked herself, almost panicking. Had her star faded so soon? And if so, what was left? A marriage to Doug, Duncan cheating her. Oh God, Freda thought, poker-faced with disappointment, if she didn't have Billy she would go mad.

Since September came in, Freda had stopped waiting for Duncan to make a move. Instead she had come to like being with her son, keeping away from the pub as much as she could. But then, as summer limped out, Billy started to spend more time with the friends he had made at nursery school. He was starting to grow up, grow away. The thought winded Freda. Suddenly all the hours she had shared with him were ranged before her like a million empty boxes – hers to fill, but with what?

She had no hobbies, and The Sixpenny Winner was run by Duncan and Doug. Besides, Ada could never keep away from the business and still did the accounts. There was only one person left to talk to, and that was Vicky. Luckily she was at work all day, Freda thought, and when she came home she was eager to spend time with her husband. *Her husband.*

It was incredible, Freda mused to herself that night, lying in bed. She had thought she had worked it out so nicely, and she had – for them. Not for herself. Sometimes, in the early hours, as Doug snored next to her, Freda thought of blowing the whistle, exposing everything. But what good would it do? She would achieve nothing, only Doug's distrust, her mother's hatred and, God forbid, such a confession might make them curtail her influence on Billy. Or Duncan and Vicky might try to take Billy over themselves.

Oh, God, *what* was she thinking? Freda turned over irritably. It was no good worrying at night: in the early hours everything seemed so wicked – out of proportion. But it had been three months since the wedding, three months without Duncan.

Almost weeping with frustration, Freda got out of bed and padded down the corridor. The corridor was dark and empty, only the half-moon giving some reluctant light as she used the toilet and then went into the bathroom. Running the water over her hands, Freda suddenly felt someone catch hold of her.

'Stay there. Don't move,' Duncan ordered. Freda was facing the window, and he stood behind her, his mouth moving over her neck, her upper back, his hands lifting her nightdress and moving between her legs.

'Duncan,' she murmured, 'Duncan . . .' then she stopped, tried to turn round. 'What are you doing? You've ignored me for months –'

His hands kept working her body, her breasts, moving rhythmically between her thighs. She could feel his breath on her cheek and reached her arms back to grasp his hair. Then suddenly Duncan turned her round and, pushing her back against the basin, entered her.

It was over in a minute, Freda leaning her head on his shoulder, Duncan breathing heavily. The moon came suddenly out from behind clouds, the enamel of the bath and basin white as a corpse.

'I missed you, Freda,' he murmured finally.

'You didn't show it.'

'You know how careful we have to be,' he muttered. 'We can't do anything rash.'

'I think of you all the time.'

'I think of you too,' he replied. 'I lie in bed and think of you sleeping only yards away from me, with Doug.'

'And you with Vicky.'

'Yes,' he whispered. 'Me with Vicky.'

'Do you love her?'

'Nah, I'm fond of her, but she's not you. Never will be.'

Freda leaned against him, feeling his bare legs against hers. 'Can we meet up more often now?'

'Sure. It will be easier soon.'

She looked into his shadowed face. 'Why's that?'

'She's pregnant.'

'*What?*' Freda stammered, her voice barely audible. 'What did you say?'

'Vicky's pregnant. Keep your voice down,' Duncan cautioned her. 'You'll hear about it soon enough. She's so excited, she's going to tell everyone later today.'

Freda's head was swimming. *Vicky was pregnant, having Duncan's child.*

'How could you?'

He looked amazed. 'How could I what?'

'Make her pregnant!'

'For God's sake, Freda, she's my wife.'

'And what am I? Your whore?' Freda asked, getting off the basin and pulling down her nightdress. 'You always were a bastard.'

Annoyed, Duncan caught hold of her arm. 'Now, listen to me, Freda. I got Vicky pregnant to keep her sweet. She'll get so wound up in the baby coming that she'll relax her grip on me.' He kissed Freda hard on the mouth. 'You know I only want you – you're the one I've always wanted, not Vicky. She's sweet, but not like you. Not like my Freda.' He moved to the door, half naked, wearing only his pyjama bottoms. 'Remember what I said. It's you and me, Freda, always has been, always will be.'

'Can I believe that?'

'Believe it,' he assured her. 'Soon we'll be able to spend more time together. Soon. Very soon.'

Then he left. Freda could hear his bare feet pad on the floor and the squeak of his bedroom door as he walked in.

For a long moment she stood motionless, the words drilling into her head. Vicky was pregnant. Vicky was having Duncan's child, a child Duncan could call his own. Not like Billy. Not like the bastard child they had lied about for so long.

Seething, Freda tried to get her breath. She would choke, she thought, trying to calm her breathing. Exhausted, she rested her head against the cold windowpane. The moon peered at her, white and round – a huge full womb, grinning at her from the black night sky.

Chapter Twenty-Eight

It irked Freda to see how Vicky enjoyed her pregnancy, how she was petted over, fussed by Ada and Duncan. By the time she was six months gone, Vicky was huge, her swollen belly straining at the seams of her skirt.

'Oh, I don't know how to let your clothes out any more,' Ada said, anxiously. 'I'll have a look and see if there's anything you can use of mine.' She glanced over to Freda, who was cuddling Billy on her knee. 'Shame you're so much slimmer, you could have lent Vicky some of your things.'

'She could try them,' Freda said distantly. She knew that nothing would fit, but she would like to see her sister struggle to put them on.

'Oh, come on, Freda!' Vicky said, laughing. 'We all know I couldn't get near your clothes. Even the ones you used when you were pregnant.'

She shrugged. 'How's the morning sickness?'

'OK now, thanks for asking,' Vicky replied, putting her feet up on a stool in front of the fire.

'Giving up working at the hospital helped,' Ada said firmly, tucking a blanket round her daughter's legs. 'Freda got as much rest as she could when she was carrying Billy.'

Vicky turned to look at her sister. She felt closer to Freda than she had ever done, sharing the same experience of being a wife – and soon a mother. How things change, Vicky thought to herself. Only months ago I felt left out, ready to make do with Bernard Young, and now I've got the man I always wanted, and his baby's on the way.

She sighed happily. 'If it's a girl, I think I'll call her Stella. It means star.'

Freda watched her closely. 'What does Duncan think?'

'Oh, he doesn't mind. He just wants me to be happy.' Vicky leaned towards her sister, her tone confidential. 'You know, I think Ma's surprised about how he's turned out. She was against it at the first, but Duncan's winning her over.'

It was all Freda could do not to slap her complacent face.

'Has the doctor given you a date?'

Vicky nodded. 'He says April the twenty-third.' She touched her stomach with the tips of her fingers. 'God, what a size I'll be then . . . Did you ever wonder about that? About whether Doug would go off you when you were pregnant?'

'He was away fighting,' Freda reminded her. 'Doug never saw much of me when I was carrying.'

'I sometimes wonder if Duncan still thinks I'm pretty . . . Oh, you know what I mean – if he's still attracted to me –'

'Modern women!' Ada interrupted shortly. 'What a thing to worry about. You're having his child, don't fill your head with things that don't matter. If a man loves his woman he loves her fat, thin, sick or pregnant.' She paused, sitting down at the kitchen table with her two daughters. 'Your dad told me I was beautiful every day. And God knows some days I looked like the hag of the dribble. But he never saw it. Always saw me like he'd first laid eyes on me – that morning when I went for a job at Henessey's.'

Vicky patted the back of her mother's hand. 'I miss him too.'

'It's just that you two having babies and your own husbands, it makes me think back.'

'You could marry again,' Freda said suddenly. 'You're still young.'

'Marry again! To who?'

'There's a couple of men who wouldn't say no,' Freda continued. 'You know who I mean. Mac Potter for one.'

'Lizzie's collared him!' Ada said laughing. 'And besides, he's no catch after your father.'

'There's Al Weeks.'

'Put drink inside that man and he'd fight his own shadow!'

'What about Frank Billings?'

Ada stared at her daughter in amazement. '*Frank Billings!*'

'He told me once he thought you were a wonderful woman.'

'I wish I could say the same about him,' Ada replied tartly. 'Frank Billings couldn't hold a candle to your dad.'

'No one could, the way you tell it,' Freda said, passing Billy over to her mother, and then standing up to look at her reflection in the mirror over the mantel.

A young woman looked back at her, blonde hair loose around her shoulders, her mouth sensually full. A looker, all right. Glossy again, now that she felt like a woman once more. And who was responsible for that? Freda thought, applying some lipstick carefully. Duncan. Her Duncan. She glanced over her shoulder, watching her mother talk to Vicky. My poor sister,

Freda thought, little do you know just how much your husband cares for you.

They were seeing each other regularly again, snatching meetings. Sometimes in the bathroom in the early hours, sometimes in the cellar. Once at the door leading to the ginnel, making love quickly against the brick wall outside. He made Freda feel wanted again, took her back to her glory days, and the very fact that they could be caught at any time only added to the excitement. He was no good, she knew that, but he was like her – restless, immoral. Sly.

No one had any suspicions. Once Freda had even bumped into a sleepy Doug as she made her way back to bed after one late night meeting. He had watched her coming up the stairs from the kitchen and tapped her on the shoulder.

'Jesus!' Freda had said, startled.

'What are you doing?'

'I . . . I wanted something to eat,' Freda had replied, praying that Duncan would hear their voices and be tipped off downstairs.

'You look flushed,' Doug had gone on, touching Freda's face and then yawning. 'Go back to bed, I'll be with you in a minute.'

Scurrying off, Freda had glanced over the banister rail and just caught the shadow of a figure moving downstairs. God, if Doug had found them . . . It didn't bear thinking about. But who would have expected him to wake up? He normally slept through the night, flat out, like an old horse.

'You coming back to bed?' Doug said, coming out of the toilet and yawning again.

Freda watched him stretch his arms above his head, the sleeves of his pyjamas flapping around his face.

Duncan never wore pyjama tops; he had too good a body to cover. Not that Doug's was bad, but he was paler, his chest hairy. When they first married she had asked him to sleep without his pyjama top, but he had laughed at her, saying he'd get cold. *In this bloody weather? Are you joking?*

Duncan didn't seem to feel the cold.

'What you waiting for?' Doug asked, standing at the door of their bedroom. 'You seem strange tonight, Freda. In fact you've seemed strange for a while.'

God, she thought, is he suspicious?

Frowning, Doug took his wife's hand and then led her back into their bedroom. Once there, he looked into her face carefully.

'Is there something you want to tell me?'

'What are you talking about?' she blustered.

He studied her, Freda paling under the scrutiny.

'Is there something you want to tell me?' he repeated. 'Something important?'

'Like what?' she asked, her voice hoarse.

'I've seen you looking at Vicky lately. And I've watched the way you care for Billy: like you'd kill anyone who even looked at him wrong. You're a great mother, Freda, no one could deny that.' He paused, touched her stomach tenderly. 'I know money's tight, but it always is. But if you want another baby, we'll manage.'

She could have laughed with relief. *Another baby!* That was the last thing she wanted.

'Oh, Doug,' she replied, laying her head on his shoulder, 'I have thought about it.' Outside she could hear Duncan returning to his room. Then the safe click of his lock turning. 'Another baby would be wonderful, but I think we should wait a bit.' Tenderly she stroked her husband's face. 'You're so clever, you know everything that goes on in my mind.'

'You're my darling,' he replied lovingly. 'What you feel, I feel.'

At the end of Churchgate Bessie was standing in her shop, wondering whether or not to wash the windows. It hadn't been long since she'd done them, but the winter smog had made them filthy again within days. It was a hard job, something no woman should have to do, but she did it. After all, there was no man in her life to help her out.

Not like Ada Hargreaves. She had two sons-in-law now, two to fetch and carry for her. No cleaning bloody windows for Ada. And then there was Lizzie. Bessie didn't see that much of Lizzie now, not since she had set her cap at Mac Potter. If Lizzie played her cards right, there was another woman who wouldn't be cleaning her own windows for much longer.

The bell rang over the door as Duncan walked in.

''Lo there, Mrs Cork. I'll have twenty Capstan, please, luv.'

'Don't call me luv!' Bessie snapped, slamming the cigarettes on the counter top. 'I know your sort.'

Duncan grinned. 'What sort's that?'

'The wrong sort,' she replied tartly.

He turned, nearly falling over the bucket of water she had brought from outside.

'Hey! Mind where you put that. I could have broken my neck.'

'Hope springs eternal, Duncan,' Bessie snorted. 'When's that baby of yours due?'

'Eight weeks' time.' He jerked his head towards the bucket. 'You cleaning your windows, Mrs Cork?'

'I was going to. Why? What business is it of yours?'

'I'll do them for you.'

Bessie blinked. Maybe she had been wrong about Duncan Oldenshaw, after all.

'You would?'

'Give me half a crown, and I'll have them done before dinnertime.'

'Half a bloody crown!' she exclaimed, pushing Duncan to the door. 'For half a crown I could get the mayor to clean 'em! Now, take your fags and go. I've work to do.'

Thoughtfully she watched him leave and then turned back to the bucket of water. Half a bloody crown! Did she look like such a soft touch? Oh, Duncan Oldenshaw might fool some, but not her. Pouring in some white vinegar, Bessie then wrung out the old leather and began, grudgingly, to wash the windows.

Chapter Twenty-Nine

The sound of screaming woke Ada on the morning of 23 March. Startled, she threw on her dressing gown and ran downstairs. Duncan was on the landing, panicking, Doug just coming out of his room with Freda.

'It's Vicky,' Duncan stammered. 'I think she's having the baby.'

Without a word, Ada pushed past him, calling out: 'Get some hot water and some towels and go for Dr Chappell!'

Vicky was lying on the bed, crying and frightened, the lamplight shining on her scared face. Her waters had broken. Seeing her mother, she caught at Ada's hand and gripped it fiercely.

'Ma –'

'It's all right, luv,' Ada said soothingly, 'it's just the baby coming a bit early. Obviously frightened to miss anything.'

'But it's too soon –'

'They come when they come,' Ada reassured her. 'There's no setting watches by babies.' She looked at the bed, and at Vicky's drenched nightdress. 'Here, luv, take that off or you'll get cold.'

'The pains started slow and then got so fast!'

Ada nodded, pulling off the nightdress and handing Vicky a clean one. 'Come on, put this on and get warm again. How long is it since you last had a pain?'

'Ten minutes.'

Ada snorted. 'Why didn't Duncan call me earlier?'

'He was asleep.'

'Asleep!' Ada snapped. 'Bloody hell, how could he sleep?'

'Oh, Ma,' Vicky moaned, 'don't go on now, please.'

Hurriedly Ada walked to the door and called downstairs, 'Has someone gone for Dr Chappell?'

'Doug's gone for him,' Freda called back from below.

'Good. Where's Duncan?'

'Down here.'

Useless bugger, Ada thought. Men were hopeless when it came to birth.

'You bring that water and towels up, Freda, and leave Duncan downstairs. I don't want to be tripping over him.'

She then moved back to the bed and took Vicky's hand.

'Will the baby be all right, Ma?'

'Babies are tough, luv. Mrs Clements's fourth fell from the roof when he was two and lived to be a right little bastard.'

'I don't believe you,' Vicky said, trying to smile.

'It's true. She said that was because he didn't fall on anything important, just his head.'

Freda walked in carrying the water and towels. She saw her mother and then looked at Vicky. Guilt welled up in her so suddenly she felt faint.

Seeing her pale face, Ada rolled her eyes. 'Oh God, not another one! *Do* get yourself sorted, Freda, luv. I need your help.'

Putting down the things she was carrying, Freda moved over to the bed.

'The baby's early,' Vicky whispered.

Freda nodded, struggling to find her voice. 'It's OK. Billy was early.'

'Not this early.'

The light was dim, Vicky's face deeply shadowed, her eyes huge and frightened as she gripped her sister's hand.

'It hurts.'

'I know.'

'But it hurts so much.'

Freda nodded. 'Soon be over.' Quickly she glanced over to Ada. 'How soon before the doctor comes?'

'Search me. But the sooner, the better.'

Three hours and fifteen minutes later Vicky gave birth to her daughter, Stella, Dr Chappell in attendance. The baby was underweight, but perfect in every other way, and dark-haired like her parents. Picking up the newly born baby, Ada laid her in her mother's arms. Exhausted, Vicky stared at her child and then looked up – at Freda.

A moment passed between them, a bonding. It left Vicky comforted, and Freda sick with shame.

There was no shortage of people wanting to wet the baby's head, Duncan taking the congratulations in the pub, Doug looking on, as proud as if it had been the birth of his own child. Upstairs Ada sat with Vicky and the baby, groaning as she heard someone begin to play the piano.

'Oh God, not that.'

Vicky smiled, Stella lying in her arms. 'She'll have to get used to noise, living here.'

'Noise, but not torture,' Ada replied, looking round. 'Nice cards and flowers you got. A woman always gets spoiled when she's had a baby. Mind you, Duncan's in his element.'

'He gave me this,' Vicky said, showing her mother the gold chain round her neck.

'Watch your skin doesn't turn green.'

'Oh, Ma!' Vicky chastised her. 'How could you?'

Leaning towards the baby, Ada looked at her second grandchild. Oh, this was a strange little one all right, she thought. She's been here before.

'She looks like you, Vicky.'

'She does, you're right. I wouldn't say it to Duncan, but she doesn't seem to favour him a bit.'

'Lucky kid.'

Vicky gave her mother a warning look, then smiled. This was bliss, she thought; this was what she had wanted without ever knowing it. All her good works, her interests in world affairs, politics, were nothing to this. This was reality, not something read in books. This baby was real, in her arms, part of her. No learning could ever match this. God, Vicky thought, she'd been lucky. It could have been so different if Freda hadn't confessed that day.

In fact she owed all her good fortune to her sister. And she had been suspicious of Freda for so long. The thought was an uncomfortable one. She had been so unfair to Freda. Who had helped her? Guided her? Led her to Duncan? Who was responsible for her marriage and her being a mother? Freda.

She would make up for their past differences, Vicky decided. They would become even closer now. After all, they had children in common, and Billy could be a good friend to Stella. They would grow up together – perhaps with more children to come for both her and Freda. It was the start of a new time, and, by God, they would make the most of it. Sleepily, Vicky closed her eyes, holding her baby to her. She had never been sure of a heaven before – but she was now.

It was here. And all due to her sister.

Chapter Thirty

Winter's Clock was just striking twelve when Vicky pushed Stella past the jeweller's in her pram. A number of people had stopped to look at the baby, complimenting her, Vicky shiny with achievement. Just wait until she got home and told Duncan about it.

Crossing over, she turned towards the High Street and stopped at the chemist for some baby milk. Mr Thomas came out from behind and had a chat, looking at Stella and asking after Ada. It took a long time to do the shopping these days, Vicky thought. When she had been single, she could nip out and get anything in minutes, but now she was always stopping to chat with someone or to let them look at Stella.

Still, it was a good thing to keep to a routine, Vicky mused. She hadn't changed *that* much from her old, careful ways. Every morning she would get up, feed the baby and Duncan, then herself. Finally she would get Stella in the pram and be out by ten thirty, whatever the weather.

'Your baby will shrink,' Ada said warningly that morning. 'I've never known anyone push a pram so much.'

'Fresh air is good for babies,' Vicky had replied, 'I read it in that book I got.'

'Books, books, books! How to do this, and that. And don't tell me, it was written by a man. And what's a man know about babies?' Ada had teased her. 'Seems to me the only thing they know is how to make one.'

Smiling to herself at the memory, Vicky pushed the pram up the steep street, pausing to look into a greengrocer's window. Rationing was still on, but more food was becoming available, and more material. Only yesterday Ada had been up to the market and come back with some glazed cotton for the sitting room. She would make the curtains herself, she'd said. You wait and see Bessie Cork's face when she sees a yard or so of glazed cotton staring her in the face.

Of course when the weather got worse in the winter, Vicky wouldn't take the baby out. No point risking a cold for fresh air. But for now it was ideal – coming into summer, the days lengthening, even birds singing as they perched on the town hall windowledges. That was odd, Vicky thought; during the war she had never seemed to hear birds singing.

She would stop at the butcher's and see if there was anything halfway decent for dinner. It was time she made a meal for everyone. Ada and Freda had done plenty for her over the last few weeks. And how close they had become: having long chats in the evening, Billy put to bed, Stella in her cot. Ada would talk about when her kids were little and they would swap stories about which child did what, when. A gleam had come over the house, Vicky thought, the sounds from the pub below now soothing, irritating no longer.

As for Duncan – what woman could have a better husband? He had been so sweet with her, so tender. And thought enough about her not to rush her into making love again. It'll wait, he had said, until you're ready. How considerate he was, Vicky thought, almost wanting to share it with her sister. But then again, maybe it was *too* private, something to keep between husband and wife.

''Lo there, Mrs Oldenshaw,' the butcher said cheerfully. 'Nice day.'

'It is that. What have you got today? Any meat?'

He pulled a face. 'Nothing special. Got some liver, though.'

'Liver,' Vicky replied. 'I'll have some of that. I'm going to make a special meal for my sister and Ma.'

'How is your mother?'

'She's well.'

'Don't see so much of her now, not with you doing all the shopping.'

Vicky glowed. 'She still checks everything when I get back. Just in case.'

Weighing the liver, he smiled at her over the scales. 'A right tartar, your mother. Every time I weigh anything for her she says, "Mind you don't put your thumb on the scales, George. I'm not paying extra."'

Taking the parcel, Vicky paused. 'You know, I thought I'd walk a bit further, but it's quite warm now. Maybe I should pop home with the liver and then go out again.'

Fifteen minutes later she was back on Churchgate. The Sixpenny Winner hadn't opened yet. The doors were still locked, and Doug was swilling down the ginnel outside. Vicky could hear him whistling as she walked through the gate, opened the back door and walked in. It was cool inside, and quiet. Ada had gone to have her hair done, a luxury she treated herself to once a month.

Hurriedly Vicky unpacked the food and put it away, placing the liver on a plate and putting it in the meat locker. Then she turned back to Stella, moving the pram towards the back door again. It was bright sunshine outside and she didn't want to miss a moment of it.

A noise above made her pause. Freda was home, of course! Maybe, Vicky thought, she would pop upstairs and have a chat. After all, usually she wasn't home until much later and Freda would not be expecting her. Kissing Stella on the cheek, Vicky moved to the stairs. She was deep in thought, wondering how to cook the liver, when she reached Freda's bedroom.

Lifting her hand to knock, Vicky paused. No, she would just walk in, surprise her. Turning the handle, she opened the door. Then stopped. Her eyes took in a scene – but she couldn't accept it. Because it wasn't happening. It wasn't Duncan on top of her sister, moving rhythmically in that way she knew so well. It wasn't Freda, her eyes closed, moaning under him, with her legs wrapped around his back.

Transfixed, Vicky watched them. But they hadn't seen her and before they had chance to she backed away, pulling the door closed silently. Outside, in the corridor, Vicky leaned against the wall. She could hear her heart beating loudly in her ears, Duncan's voice saying: *I don't want to rush you, darling. We'll make love when you're good and ready. I can wait. I can wait for my sweetheart.*

Vicky could hear the ticking of the old grandfather clock downstairs, and the far-off sound of Doug whistling in the ginnel outside.

Her legs seemed hardly able to hold her up as she moved to the stairs and began to walk down. One step at a time. One, two, three, four . . . Rage filled up in her suddenly. It choked her, stung behind her eyes and under her fingernails. *She would kill him. She would kill her sister.*

No, no, she wouldn't, Vicky told herself. She would have to think. *To think . . .* Sitting down heavily on the stairs, Vicky covered her ears and rocked herself. Oh, how clever they'd been. How bloody clever. No wonder he didn't want sex with her, when he was sleeping with her sister. And for how long? Her own stupidity stunned her. If she had only listened to her instincts, admitted to herself from the first that Duncan was no good. Freda and he had been lovers before, had had a child together – had she really thought it was over? Had she been that stupid?

Yes, yes, she had! She had been so blind, so trusting, so much in love with him that she would have believed *anything* to get him. And what about Freda? The lying bitch. The conniving, lying, scheming, hypocritical bitch. Making a friend of her, confiding in her, betraying her. And laughing at her. Oh yes, Vicky thought, I bet you've both had a good laugh at my expense.

Running her tongue over her dry lips, she stood up. They had thought they were clever, but she was smarter. How easy it would be to confront them now, but for what? And what about Doug? About Billy? It would all come out. And for what? she asked herself again. How much more satisfying to rid herself of her husband by sleight of hand. Get him banished, out of her life – and Freda's. If she exposed them now, Duncan might leave with her sister – and what revenge would there be in that? Oh, no, Vicky thought. Your days are numbered, Duncan. And as for you, Freda, I'm going to pay you back in full.

Steadily moving downstairs Vicky could see the sunlight coming in through the top half of the windows of The Sixpenny Winner, the stained glass throwing splashes of lurid colour on the floorboards. Suddenly the most important thing to her was revenge. She had to rid herself of her husband, punish Freda, *and* ensure her own future and that of her child.

Think, she willed herself, think. You're smart, smarter than they are. You've a good brain, Vicky, use it now . . . Her feet moved silently across the floor to the pram. Stella was asleep. Taking off the brake, Vicky turned the pram towards the back door and headed outside.

The sunlight blinded her, made white specks in her eyes and bleached out the street for an instant. But inside her head – as clear as an engraving in stone – was the sight of her sister and husband making love.

Vicky walked past Doug, still whistling, past the ginnel, the street, the shop on the corner. On and on she walked, her baby with her, her teeth biting deep into her lip to stop the tears coming.

'I told you when we started that it was a story and a half.

'Now the last bit no one knew at the time. It all came out later, when . . . Oh, no, I'm running on too fast. Best to stick to telling you events in order. As they happened, so to speak.

'You see that Ada's back to her old self. That were a good thing, my grandfather said. I know he carried a bit of a torch for her, but he never let on. But you can tell, can't you? Even as a lad I'd see how he used to light up when he talked about Ada.

'I'm not going too fast, am I? Good. I want you to get it all down.

'Poor silly Vicky, the last woman anyone would have thought a man could fool. But there you are, women go daft sometimes when they're in love. And good, honest Douglas – he was duped by his brother too. Anyone else he would have sussed out straight away, but not Duncan. You see, it's always difficult when you want a dream so much you can't see the truth staring you right in the face.

'I remember asking my grandfather if anyone suspected anything. He said no. The Sixpenny Winner was doing well again, the family all seemed to be getting on fine under one roof. You have to remember that it was like that in those days. Families did all muck in, live in the same house, share the business. It was normal, a cheap way to live, each helping the other out when needed.

'You expected trouble to come from the outside. Never thought that you'd taken it in, harboured it, fed it and made it welcome.

'So when you found out . . .'

Part Three

The women take so little stock
In what I do or say
They'd sooner leave their cosseting
To hear a jackass bray;
My arms are like the twisted thorn
And yet there beauty lay.

W. B. Yeats

Chapter Thirty-One

It was a very sober Vicky who came down into the bar later that night, nodding to Ada and then walking over to Doug. It had taken every ounce of her courage to act normally, when in reality she wanted to scream with frustration and hurt. Injured as she was, when she looked at Doug she felt an overwhelming protective instinct. He didn't deserve it, Vicky thought. If he found out, it would kill him to know what his brother and wife had done. And as for Billy . . .

Taking in a deep breath, Vicky tapped him on the arm.

He turned and smiled at her. ''Lo there, luv. What's up?'

'Is Mac in tonight?'

Doug looked round the bar, then pointed to a far corner where Mac Potter was sitting, thankfully alone.

'He needs some cheering up. Lizzie's ill.'

As Vicky approached his table, Mac looked up. 'Lizzie's poorly.'

'I heard. Sorry about that, Mac. It's not serious, is it?'

He shook his head. 'Nah, just a cold. But you know what summer colds are like. Mind you, they're not so bad as they were when I were a lad. Those days you could get a cold and before you knew it, pneumonia.'

As she sat down in the seat next to Mac, Stan Foreshaw started to play the piano.

'Oh, bloody hell!' Mac said. 'He plays like a deaf man.'

'Mac, I was wondering,' Vicky began carefully, 'you know Al Weeks, don't you?'

His eyes widened. 'I do that. I used to see him here regular – before your mother banned him. I mean, it were only a fight, and what man doesn't get in a fight now and then?'

'Al Weeks got in a fight every week,' Vicky replied, then leaned further towards Mac. 'Do you still see him?'

'Sure I do. He's my best mate.'

'Is he still . . . you know, does he still know about everything that's going on?'

Mac eyed Vicky carefully. Now what would a young wife and mother want with an old rake like Al Weeks?

'He still helps people out,' Mac said carefully.

It was common knowledge that Al Weeks could find anyone. His methods were dubious, but there was many a woman in Stockport who had got Al on to her man's tail. Businesses relied on him too. When a debt wasn't paid, Al went in and before long the money materialised. Well over six foot, he was quietly spoken and cheated his fifty-odd years by being fit. But he could be violent when needed.

'I want to see him.'

Mac's eyebrows rose. '*You* want to see Al?'

'When could you set up a meeting? In confidence, Mac. It must be in confidence.'

'I could talk to him. What's it about?'

'That's between me and Al,' Vicky replied. 'Sorry, Mac, but this is private.'

'Money trouble?'

'Private trouble,' she replied firmly. 'Can you set up a meeting?'

'Al does nothing for nothing, luv. It'll cost you.'

'Oh, everything does,' Vicky said bitterly, 'everything does.'

The following evening Al Weeks was waiting in the ginnel at the back of The Sixpenny Winner. His bald head was uncovered, and the light summer jacket he was wearing did nothing to disguise his size.

'Well, hello there, Vicky,' he said, his voice a quiet Northern bass. 'How's your ma?'

'Same as ever,' Vicky replied evenly. 'Sorry you're still banned from the pub.'

Al shrugged. 'There's others . . . I heard you wanted to talk to me.'

'I do, Al,' she replied, looking around her.

The ginnel was empty, night come down, the shadows threatening. A sudden, bitter wind cut them both to the bone. So much for summer, Vicky thought bitterly.

'I need some help, Al.'

'It'll cost you.'

'I've got money,' Vicky replied, thinking of her father's nest egg. What better use could she put it to? But then again, would Clem have approved?

'If there's any rough stuff, it'll cost you more.'

'No rough stuff, Al. I want you to find out about someone, about their history.'

He nodded, pushed his hands deep into his pockets. The streetlamp lit his face evenly, his eyes alert.

'Who?'

'My husband, Duncan Oldenshaw.'

Al knew too much about people to ask why a wife would be asking about her husband. Besides, it wasn't his place to ask why, only to do the job.

'You mean, before he came here?'

She nodded. 'I know he was in Yorkshire, but that's

all. I want to know what he did, who he mixed with, what his job was. He used to help his brother out at another pub – in Leeds, I think. But that's all I know. And I need to know *everything*.'

Al sniffed, tucked his head down further into the collar of his jacket as the wind caught at him.

'We talking about work, or women?'

'Both.'

'How much money have you got?'

'How much money will it cost, Al?'

'A fair bit. It'll take time too.'

'Not with your contacts. Oh, come on, Al, I know about you! You could find out everything really quick if you put your mind to it.'

'Maybe I could, and maybe I couldn't.'

She sighed, reached into her pocket and passed him a note.

'This should start you off. But don't try to spin it out, Al. I'm not in the mood to be cheated.'

'Why would I cheat you?'

She ignored the question. 'And this is in confidence. No one needs to know what I've asked you to do.'

'Sure.'

'I mean it, Al! No one needs to know what I asked you to do, or what you find out.' She paused, looking him straight in the eyes. 'I need help – and you're the only person who can help me. I need to know I can trust you.'

He glanced away, down the dismal ginnel, thinking back.

'I remember you when you were small, Vicky. You were a cute little thing, but always so serious. Surprised me a lot when you married Duncan Oldenshaw. He didn't seem your type. I had you down for a teacher, something like that.' He looked back to her, embarrassed to see tears in her eyes. 'Hey, come on, luv! Buck up. There's nothing so bad it can't be sorted one way or other.'

Vicky's voice dropped to a whisper. 'You can't change the past, though, can you?'

'Nah, but you can take care of the future,' Al replied, making to go and then turning back. 'He's not hitting you, is he? I won't stand for a man hitting a woman.'

'No, Al, he's not hitting me.'

'Cheating on you?'

'I want to know about Duncan's past,' she replied, dodging the question. 'Don't spare me anything, Al.'

'It might not be to your liking, luv.'

'Oh, I already know that.'

Hearing Stella crying, Ada had hurried into the kitchen from the bar. Surprised that Vicky wasn't around, she picked up the baby and rocked her until she was quiet again. Then she laid her back down in her pram and walked to the window, looking out. She still seldom used the back door, still disliked the atmosphere, but as Ada looked through the window she could see the outside light was lit.

Now who was out there? She was surprised to see Vicky pass through the gate and bolt it behind her. For a moment her daughter leaned against it, her face composed, but bloodless.

'Vicky?' Ada called out to her.

She jumped, then walked in. ''Lo, Ma.'

'What are you doing out there? Stella was crying.'

'I went for a breath of air,' Vicky replied, straining to keep her voice natural.

If her mother found out she would only tell her that

it had been what she expected all along. *If you would marry Duncan Oldenshaw . . .* Oh, the humiliation of it, Vicky thought resentfully.

'But it's got cold out there, and it was so warm earlier on.'

'I had a bit of a headache, Ma.'

'Sounded like Stella had one too, the way she was crying.'

Anxiously Vicky moved over to the pram and looked down at her daughter.

'She's OK.'

'She is now. She wasn't when I came in,' Ada retorted. 'And where's Duncan? Doug's been calling for him repeatedly.'

'I don't know.'

'Is he upstairs?'

'I don't know.'

'With Freda?'

'Ma, I don't know!' Vicky snapped.

'Dear God, you're so bloody ratty today! And as for Freda, she's walking around in a daze. I can't think what's got into the girl.'

She has my man, Vicky wanted to say. She's happy because she's made love with my husband.

'When I was young, a mother never let her baby out of her sight –'

'I was only gone a minute!' Vicky hissed. 'What harm can come to a baby in a minute? You think I can't look after Stella? I can, better than anyone else. *She's my child.*'

Stunned by the outburst, Ada walked over to the grate and set the kettle to boil. This wasn't like Vicky. She had never been the temperamental one. Perhaps she was sickening for something – a summer cold perhaps. After all, the weather had been up and down for days. And hadn't Lizzie been hanging around the pub, dripping her germs everywhere? Ada hoped it wasn't that. It would be bad for the baby.

'You need a rest, luv,' she said at last.

Vicky nodded, close to tears. 'I've just a headache, Ma, I'm OK. But you're right, I think I *will* go upstairs and lie down.'

'D'you want me to send Duncan up when he comes in?'

'No!' she snapped, then softened her tone. 'No, men never understand women's headaches.'

Ada nodded. 'All right, luv, you go up with Stella. Have a good sleep. Things always look brighter in the morning.'

Well, well, well, Al Weeks thought as he leaned against the wall outside The George Arms. He had travelled about a bit, following the trail of Duncan Oldenshaw, and heard plenty that no wife would like to hear. He was a right bastard, some said. Men, that was, not women. Duncan seemed to like women and they liked him. Apart from Nora Barton, and she'd had plenty to say about what a sod he was.

It was at times like this that Al hated his job. It was all right chasing down money and rogues. He never minded breaking a man's nose if he'd been smacking his wife around. But this was so shoddy. Duncan Oldenshaw had been in prison for theft. Now I bet Ada Hargreaves doesn't know that, Al thought, wondering if Doug did. Never – Douglas Oldenshaw was as straight as a die. He'd put money on that.

But then again, Duncan was Doug's brother and you give a brother a chance that you'd never give a stranger. Perhaps Doug thought Duncan had gone straight. Maybe he had – now. But he'd been a bad boy in the past and no mistake. Not the kind of man anyone would want within ten yards of a till. Or his wife.

Al knew instinctively that Vicky was ignorant of her husband's criminal past. She was not that kind of girl, he thought. Now, Freda was another matter. Al could imagine that she might find it exciting to have a rogue in her life. But Vicky? Never. But did she *suspect*, Al wondered. Was that why she had hired him to find out about Duncan? But why now?

Women, he knew, could be blind as statues. When they loved a man they saw only the good. Al had lost count of the mothers who refused to hear a bad word about their sons – *But he's a good lad. Don't I know my own son?* No, he wanted to reply, you've no bloody idea what he's like. One case he'd had was finding a man who had later been charged with killing his wife. When Al spoke to the mother, she said: 'I don't believe it. And if it's true, she drove him to it.' Drove him to jamming a crowbar through her brain. Like hell she drove him to it.

Well, at least Duncan Oldenshaw wasn't a murderer. A thief, an adulterer, a liar, a cheat. But not a killer. But then again, what comfort would that be to Vicky? Who wanted a villain for a husband, for the father of their child? And then there was that other rumour he'd uncovered. About Douglas Oldenshaw's old pub . . . Was it true? If it was, God, it was damning. But then people could be malicious. He knew that only too well. And Duncan Oldenshaw was good-looking and charming, the type some liked to knock.

Vicky would have to be told what he'd uncovered, because that was what she had hired him for. But he wasn't going to tell her the rumour he'd heard. That was too much. He might ask around a bit more before passing that one on.

Curious, Mac Potter had tried to wheedle information out of Al, but he'd blocked him. One thing his clients could rely on was that Alfred Weeks could keep his mouth shut. Other people couldn't though. He sighed, then headed for his old car. He would get back to Stockport and tell Vicky Oldenshaw the news.

His old beef with Ada didn't sting so much any more. How could he bear her a grudge when he knew what he did about her son-in-law? Besides, he had always had a soft spot for Ada. Clem had known, even teased him about it. Not that Al would have tried anything on. A man's wife was just that – *his* wife. No one else's. But when Clem died Al had hoped – stupidly – that he might somehow wheedle himself into Ada's affections.

The trouble was that Al couldn't wheedle. He could be formidable, kind and tough, but he couldn't wheedle to save his life. His idea of courtship was not designed to have women dropping in their tracks. He had even – Al still blushed at the thought – given a girlfriend a brace of kippers as a present once.

'But she likes kippers!' Al had said, mortified when the story got round. 'Not for her bloody birthday, she didn't!' Mac Potter had replied . . . Al sighed. He was too old to bother now. Anyway, a woman wouldn't get on with the way he lived or the hours he kept now. Better to be alone. And besides, he might be widowed, but he wasn't lonely. There was always too much to do, too many rogues to keep him busy.

But Al still glanced in at the windows of The Sixpenny Winner when he passed, still admiring Ada Hargreaves.

Life was funny, Al thought. Ada Hargreaves had thrown him out of her pub because she didn't like his type. If she knew about Duncan Oldenshaw's past, her son-in-law would never have got over the threshold.

Chapter Thirty-Two

'You look nice,' Freda said, assessing her sister. 'Going out?'

'Just taking Stella for her walk,' Vicky replied, fighting to keep her voice steady. You hypocrite, she thought, you smiling hypocrite.

'Be gone long?'

Why was she asking? Vicky wondered. Oh, don't worry, Freda, I won't be coming back early. You can have Duncan as long as you like. In fact, make the most of him, because he won't be around for much longer.

'I'm going to the park, Freda. It's a lovely morning.' She took the brake off Stella's pram. 'And it's good for the baby.'

'D'you want to take Billy too?' Freda asked, smiling. 'It's Saturday and he gets bored if he's not at school.'

Vicky smiled. Why not? Better to have little Billy with her than risk the child walking in on something he shouldn't see.

'OK. Go and get him, I'll wait here,' she replied, tucking Stella's blanket around her.

A minute later Billy was ushered off by his mother, Freda waving from the entrance of The Sixpenny Winner. It was only when they reached the park that Vicky breathed easily again. The sun was shining and Billy stood by the park lake, feeding the ducks. In her pram, Stella watched her cousin and gurgled happily, Vicky silent as she sat on the park bench.

'Auntie Vicky?'

She shaded her eyes from the sun. 'What, luv?'

'There's a swan.'

'It's a goose,' Vicky corrected him.

'But it looks like a swan. Like the one in my school book.' He stared at the goose, gliding by on the still water.

Duncan's child, Vicky thought, studying him. Yes, he *was* like him in a way – not in appearance, but in manner. She was surprised that no one had noticed it before, but then they would only see that his colouring was Freda's and that he was big built, like his dad. Or the dad they took to be his – Douglas, not Duncan.

Frowning, Vicky turned to look at her daughter. By contrast, Stella was very like Duncan; there was no doubt whose child she was. If the circumstances had been different, Vicky could never have passed Stella off as Doug's child. Freda had been lucky there, but then Freda had been lucky for a long time. She made her luck, by using other people, by being deceitful.

'Auntie!' Billy shouted suddenly, pointing across the water. 'Look!'

Standing up, Vicky moved over to him, watching a boat float on the water of the park lake. It was a model boat that some father had made for his child, the sails high and white, the blue stern bobbing on the glassy water.

'Can we have a boat?'

'Yes, Billy, we'll have a boat. Ask your father to make one for you.'

'Dad's busy.'

'He'll make you one, if you ask,' Vicky replied, knowing full well that Doug would do anything for Billy. Would he do so much if he knew the child wasn't his?

'Look!' Billy shouted again, his excitement contagious. 'It's stuck.'

The little boat had grounded itself on the small ornamental island in the middle of the lake. Its blue stern was now tipped up, its white sail lying limply in the water.

'Dad'll make one that won't break,' Billy said with certainty. 'A big one, big as you like.'

Without answering Vicky looked at the boat – beached, its moment of heady confidence overturned in an instant.

''Lo there, Vicky.'

Startled, she looked up, shielding her eyes from the sun.

'Hello, Al. How did you know I'd be here?'

He stood beside her, his arms folded. 'My business to know . . . Nice baby you've got there.' She smiled, looking over to Stella. Al continued, 'I've got some news.'

'I thought you might have.'

'It's not too nice –'

'Just tell me, Al.'

'Your husband's been in jail. For theft.'

Vicky took in her breath. Al waited, then when she said nothing he carried on. 'It were in Yorkshire. He got three years, but they let him out early for good behaviour.'

She laughed bitterly. 'What did he steal?'

'Some woman's jewellery. They had him marked for nicking a car too, but they couldn't prove it.'

'God, Ma would go mad if she knew about this!' Vicky said, her voice hard. 'Go on.'

'What?'

'There's more. I know there is.'

Al leaned forward, looking over the water. 'Duncan's fooled around a lot. With other men's wives.'

That was no surprise.

'So he's a liar, an adulterer *and* a thief?' Her voice was flat. 'What else?'

Oh no, Al thought, he wasn't about to tell her the rumours. Fact was one thing, but you didn't want to go wrecking a person's life on a rumour.

'Nothing else.'

'You sure?'

'You doubt me?'

'No.' Vicky stared at Stella for a long time and then looked at Billy. Dear God, what a father you children have.

'Are you OK?' Al asked anxiously.

'What do you think?'

'So he never told you about being in jail?'

'No, he never told me.'

Her husband was a thief. That she – Vicky Hargreaves, the upholder of justice and integrity – could have married a *thief* . . . But was she really surprised? Hadn't she known from the start the kind of man Duncan Oldenshaw was? Known it, but ignored it. Wanted him too much to admit just how worthless he really was.

Vicky's mind cleared slowly. Her first reaction had been shame – but then she wondered if Duncan's dishonesty could be used to her advantage.

'Keep digging, Al. I'll pay you.'

'It's not the money, Vicky. You sure you want to know any more?'

'I want to know everything,' she replied, her tone chilling. 'Everything that man has ever done.'

'You look wonderful, sweetheart,' Duncan murmured, putting his hands behind his head as he lay on the bed watching his wife undress. 'What a lucky guy I am.'

Vicky smiled, treacherous to a fault. It was much easier than she had thought, playing the hypocrite. It wasn't really that difficult to say one thing and be thinking the opposite. Not if you were blistering with anger and famished for revenge.

She had avoided Duncan's attentions for a week, pleading tiredness, then finally succumbed on Saturday night. Vicky liked to imagine how Duncan's mind was working, how conceited he was, how greedy for sex. Any sex, with any sister. So whilst he huffed and puffed on top of her, Vicky watched him – detached – and she hated him.

When he had climaxed, he rolled onto the bed beside her.

'I love you, Vicky.'

I love you, Vicky.

She wanted to punch him in the face, split his lip, go for his eyes with her fingernails, but she didn't. Instead, to her amazement, Vicky cuddled up to him. Give him something to remember, on those long lonely nights without her. A condemned man's final fling.

After all, Vicky thought icily, it was going to be the last time he ever touched her.

'Oh, hurry up!' Freda snapped, edging past her sister as she hurried to serve someone. 'What you standing there for, like a statue?'

Without responding, Vicky watched her. Oh, her sister was making it easy. If she had been kind – even pretend kind – Vicky might have had second thoughts. But Freda was being a bitch, and making it simpler with every sharp word she uttered.

The pub was busy that Saturday night, the takings good – so good that Vicky and Freda had been pressed into service beside the two brothers. It should have been just Duncan on duty, with Doug. Duncan taking the orders – and taking the money. But maybe it was better this way, Vicky thought. Now she was in amongst everything. She could watch her plotting unfold, watch everyone's face, everyone's reaction.

Her mouth was dry with bitterness. Repeatedly she could hear the till registering, the clink of the drawer opening and closing. Her heart was dead. It was the only way, she told herself. What other way was there? To tell Doug everything? And then he would ask her why she hadn't told him before. And – more importantly – why she had married Duncan knowing what he had done.

No, there was only one way out of the mess, and she would have to take it. Besides, she wanted to. Hurt had scarred her inside, drilling into her brain. Sleeping next to Duncan she had tensed every time he moved, waiting for him to steal out of bed. But he hadn't that week. Or maybe he and Freda had met up somewhere else.

It was a miracle no one had caught them before, Vicky thought as she served another customer. But then Ada lived on the top floor now, far away from the others, and as for Doug, it would never have occurred to him to mistrust his brother or his wife. He was a lucky man, wasn't he? Bad things didn't happen to lucky men.

'Go and get a break,' Doug said suddenly to her. 'Take twenty minutes. But no more. Put your feet up whilst you've got the chance.'

Reluctantly Vicky went upstairs to her bedroom. The sounds of the pub below grew louder as she lay down in the darkness, her hands clutching the edges of the sheet. Above her head she could see the lamplight and the shadows flickering, hear the door of The Sixpenny Winner opening and closing, and then the sound of the piano starting up. Not Stan Foreshaw this time, Vicky thought, it was Ada playing.

Rolling over onto her side, Vicky listened. She was playing well, a tune Vicky knew from her childhood. Tears filled her eyes suddenly. Where had that childhood gone? That safe time, when she could talk to her father? Oh Dad, she thought, if you were alive now, you'd help me. You'd tell me what to do.

You'd tell me not to do what I've planned, I know you would . . . Vicky closed her eyes, the music-hall tune coming sweet and sad from below. I loved Duncan so much, she thought desperately. Had he *ever* loved me? Or was the whole marriage a sham, a cover for his affair with Freda? Had he made love to me, thinking of Freda? Had we conceived Stella whilst he was still hot from her? Had every touch, kiss, shared glance, been a lie?

She couldn't bear it, she thought suddenly, covering her face with her hands. She couldn't bear it! Then the moment passed, and Vicky calmed herself. She *would* bear it. She wasn't her mother's child for nothing. Duncan was going to pay for what he had done, and so was Freda. She just had to wait a little longer and it would all be over.

So that Saturday evening spun on. Vicky heard Freda come up to check on Billy, Duncan and Doug working in the pub downstairs. Ada had finished at the piano, was probably back labouring at the books, Stella asleep beside her on the couch.

With heavy legs Vicky roused herself after twenty minutes and returned to the bar. No one had even seemed to notice she had been missing. Freda was flirting with Mac Potter, Duncan laughing, Doug piling some coal onto the snug fire. The night drove itself on. People came and went, drinks were poured, money exchanged, the piano being played by different hands as the evening lengthened into night.

Then finally the pub closed. Ada called out good night to Vicky before she went up to bed.

'I'm off now, luv. Stella's in her cot, fast asleep.' A long yawn. 'See you in the morning.'

Vicky nodded at the foot of the stairs. 'See you in the morning, Ma. Thanks.'

Tense, she waited at the foot of the stairs. After a while Freda passed her, irritable with tiredness. And still Vicky waited there. For a while she could hear Doug and his brother clean up and then, and only then, did she move up to the bedroom. Slowly she undressed and then slid between the cool sheets.

Thirty long minutes passed before Duncan came in.

'You awake?'

She didn't answer. Didn't move.

'Vicky, you awake?'

Again, she stayed silent. He sighed, undressed in the darkness and slid under the covers next to her. His body was warm, the heat curling around her. For an instant she wanted to turn to him, to beg him to leave Freda alone, to love *her*. She would forgive him, forgive him anything.

But how could she do that? She had been a fool too long; it was time to grow up. The innocent Vicky, the young woman who had no experience with men, had had her crash course in deceit. They had relied on her gullibility, her naïvety, but now that was over. Gone, as the old version of Vicky had gone. Washed up, like the little boat on the island.

But not beaten . . . Bitterness and hatred welled up in her as Vicky continued to feign sleep. Soon Duncan's breathing regulated. She waited. Another half-hour passed before the sounds of her sister and brother-in-law moving about ceased. Then the pub was in silence.

Slowly Vicky pulled back the blanket and slipped out of bed. Duncan stirred, then turned over and fell back to sleep. Silently she passed Stella, asleep in her cot, opened the door and moved downstairs. The pub was dark and silent, eerily so, as she walked to the till and opened it.

The money looked up at her, a lot of it, surprisingly so. Vicky knew that her mother would already have totted up the takings, but left the money in the till until the morning. Then she would put it away upstairs until Monday, banking it together with the takings from Sunday's trade.

Her heart pounding so loudly that she could hardly think, Vicky picked up the notes and peeled off three from the top. *Three pounds*. Her mother would notice that for sure. With the money in her hand, Vicky hesitated. Where could she hide it? She looked round, then made for the door that led down to the cellar.

No one would look for it there, and, besides, no one would think *she* would go down there. Wasn't silly Vicky afraid of ghosts? Well, wasn't she? Nervously, Vicky opened the door, flicked on the light, and walked down the steps. The cellar was dank, smelling of damp, the walls freezing to the touch.

Vicky walked further in, paused, then made for the furthermost corner. There she tucked the money behind an old barrel – an old, empty barrel, which had stood there for years. As she felt the money fall from her fingers Vicky almost panicked, but stopped herself.

It was no time to be soft. Or kind. She had been kind all her life – been fair, compassionate. And where had it got her? Nowhere. A different Vicky dropped that money behind the barrel; a different Vicky walked out of the cellar and locked the door behind her. And a different Vicky moved up the dark stairs without conscience for what she would do when morning came.

Chapter Thirty-Three

'Jesus!'

Doug looked over to Ada, frowning. 'Nice language for a Sunday.'

'Bugger Sunday, we're short!' Ada replied, waving the money in front of her son-in-law's face. 'Three pounds short.'

'Never,' Doug said, taking it from her and counting the pile of notes. 'Are you sure you counted it right last night?'

'Of course I am! I can count. I'm not a moron.'

'But it was late, and it'd been busy –'

'I don't lose my senses when the sun goes down, Douglas.'

'But . . .' He trailed off, counting the notes again. She was right, there were three pounds missing. 'Did you lend anyone money, Ada?'

She gave him a withering look. 'Did you?'

'Nah.'

'What about Duncan?'

She could see Doug tense, and frowned. 'What about Duncan? Did he borrow some money?'

'I didn't lend him any.'

'Did he help himself then?'

'He wouldn't do that!' Doug protested, his overreaction making Ada suspicious.

'Douglas, do you know something I don't?'

'About what?'

'About the money! About Duncan!'

'*What* about Duncan?' a voice said behind them.

He walked into the bar smiling, his shirtsleeves rolled up. A good night's sleep had made his skin glow, his good looks more out of place than ever.

'Have you borrowed any money?'

He stared at Ada, for once honestly surprised. 'No, course not.'

Standing beside him, Doug was scrutinising his brother carefully. Surely Duncan hadn't gone back to his old ways? Why would he? He had a home, security, a wage. He wouldn't be stupid enough to jeopardise that, would he?

'Duncan, think carefully, did you lend anyone money last night?'

'No, course not!'

'Did Vicky ask for a loan?'

'Don't make me laugh!' Duncan replied, genuinely amused by the idea. 'What about asking your Freda?'

'I gave her some extra money yesterday, she had no reason to borrow any more,' Doug replied, his tone cold. 'Duncan, I want a word with you –'

'Hey, you can stop that now!' Ada interrupted them fiercely. 'Anything you have to say to Duncan, I want to hear. This is my pub, and it's my money gone missing. I want to get to the bottom of it, and I don't want to be shut out.'

Doug knew he was caught. He had hoped to be able to talk to Duncan alone. If he had taken the money, he could have returned it then, without Ada being any the wiser. But now there was no way he could protect his brother. If Duncan had taken the money, Ada was going to find out.

'Well, go on! What did you want to say to your brother?' Ada pushed him.

'I wanted to have a private word –'

'About what? The money?' Ada's eyes narrowed. 'D'you think he took it? Well? Answer me! Why would he, Douglas? Is there something I should know?'

Duncan's face had coloured with indignation. 'I've told you, I've never taken any money!'

'But your brother doesn't seem too sure,' Ada countered, hands on hips as she faced them. 'Look, I don't like being taken for a fool. Do you know anything about this missing money, Duncan?'

He was about to protest again when Vicky joined them. Her face was pale and she was still in her dressing gown.

'Admit it, Duncan –'

'What!' he bellowed.

She looked hurt, confused. 'I didn't want to say anything, but I've just overheard you talking. Duncan's been taking money from me for months, Ma. He's always asking me for money and when I don't give it to him, he takes it out of my purse.'

Duncan was momentarily shocked into speechlessness. Then suddenly he found his voice again. 'WHAT ARE YOU TALKING ABOUT?'

Ada's expression was glacial. A thief in her house. Her own son-in-law taking money from her own daughter, and now from her own pub takings. She had always known Duncan Oldenshaw was a wrong 'un, and she was right.

Turning to Douglas, she asked: 'Do you know anything about this?'

'I'VE NOT TAKEN ANY BLOODY MONEY!' Duncan shouted.

'Keep your voice down!' Doug hurled back. 'You want to wake the kids?'

'But it's a lie!' Duncan insisted, his blue eyes baffled. 'Vicky, you know I never took a penny from you.' But she wouldn't look at him. 'Vicky! Tell them you're lying,' he pleaded.

'Why would I lie, Duncan?' she replied, finally looking straight at him, her expression steely. I didn't *want* to admit it. I wanted to cover up for you, but I can't any longer.'

He was glassy-eyed, disbelieving. Why was she doing this? Then realisation dawned. She knew about him and Freda, and now she wanted to get her own back – to get him banished. Jesus, Duncan thought blindly, what a dangerous bitch she had turned out to be.

'I never took any money –'

Vicky cut across his protestations and turned to her mother. 'If you go into the cellar you'll find the three pounds there, behind the old barrel in the far corner. I saw Duncan take the money out of the till, then followed him last night and saw him hide it there.'

White-hot with fury, Ada hurried to the cellar.

Doug turned on his brother. 'I warned you! What kind of a stupid bastard would do something like this? I thought even *you* would have more sense than to shit on your own doorstep.'

Befuddled, Duncan headed towards the cellar, Doug and Vicky following. Ada was just stretching down behind the old barrel when they reached her. They watched as she felt around, then paused, then brought out the three pound notes.

Her voice was thick with contempt. 'You bastard, Duncan –'

'I never took it.'

'Vicky saw you!' Ada hissed.

'She's lying –'

'So how did she know where you put it?'

'Because *she* put it there!'

That was too much for Ada. 'How *dare* you call my daughter a liar and a thief! You piece of dirt.' Blazing, she turned on Doug. 'I warned you – brother or not, if he turned out bad, he was out.'

Unable to find words, Doug stood there whilst Ada moved back upstairs, Vicky close behind her.

Slowly he turned to his brother. 'You bastard –'

Without waiting to hear another word, Duncan took the steps two at a time and ran back into the pub where Ada was talking to Vicky.

Catching hold of his wife's arm, he pulled her round to face him. 'Tell them you're lying!'

'You can't get out of this one, Duncan,' Vicky replied, her tone icy. 'You're a thief –'

'I'm no thief!' Duncan pleaded, looking from his brother to his mother-in-law. 'I've been straight for years.'

'"Been straight for years",' Ada repeated, her voice lethal. 'You bugger! You've thieved before.'

'All right . . . all right. I was in jail in Dartmoor,' Duncan admitted, trying vainly to stem the avalanche of disaster. Maybe, for once, the truth would save him.

'Jail!' Ada snapped, turning to Doug. 'You knew about this?'

He nodded, leaning against the bar, his head bowed. 'I knew.'

This was getting too much for Ada. '*You knew* – and you let him in here? You let him into my family and my business?' She was terrifying in her coldness. 'You let a *thief* in? You let a *thief* marry my child?'

'I thought Duncan had changed! He swore he had, said he needed to make a fresh start,' Doug said lamely.

It all seemed so stupid to him now. How could he have been taken in? 'Duncan's my brother, I had to help him.'

'Well, I don't!' Ada snapped, turning to Duncan. 'Get out of here.'

'You can't do that!' he shouted back at her. 'Your daughter's lying, I tell you. I never took the money.'

'Why would she lie?' Ada shouted, beside herself. 'What reason would she have?'

'Because she's jealous,' a voice said from behind them. Everyone turned to see Freda standing in the doorway. Her hair was ruffled from sleep, the drowsy sensuality apparent. 'Go on, tell them, Vicky. Tell them why you're lying.'

It was Vicky's turn to falter. How could she tell everyone the truth? It would hurt too many people. Her mind swam with confusion as the four faces turned to look at her. God, it was all going so horribly wrong. She had just wanted to get rid of Duncan and punish Freda. But if the truth came out the whole family would be shattered.

So she didn't answer Freda. She couldn't do it.

And Freda knew it. 'Tell them why you lied.'

'I – I didn't lie . . .' Vicky stammered.

'Why in God's name would Vicky be jealous of you, Freda?' Ada snapped, exasperated.

The truth tingled between the two sisters, Freda smiling slowly.

'She –'

'Shut up!' Vicky snapped violently.

Jesus, Freda *couldn't* expose the truth. How could she even consider it? Unless she wanted them to banish Duncan – *so she could go with him*. Leave the pub, leave Stockport, find the excitement she had always craved. Dear God, Vicky thought, would she risk so much misery to protect her own interests? Of course she would.

But Vicky wasn't going to let her. There was too much at stake.

'Keep your mouth shut, Freda,' she said warningly. 'You'll go too far.'

'I want answers, and I want them now!' Ada snapped. 'Why are you jealous of Freda?'

What could she say, Vicky thought. What was there to say? Her revenge was turning its teeth on her.

It was Freda who finally answered. 'She's jealous because Duncan loves me.'

'Oh Christ!' Duncan said, slumping against the wall.

The words punched the air, made thudding sounds in the silence. Douglas didn't move, but his whole body tensed, like someone about to take a blow – or strike one. Seeing his reaction, Ada automatically moved closer to Doug's side. So close she could feel him tremble with rage as he turned to his wife.

'Duncan loves you?'

Her nerve didn't desert her as Freda stood her ground. 'Yes, he does.'

'Do you love him?'

'Yes,' she said again. Simply, cruelly.

It was for the best, Freda thought; time to let the cat out of the bag. She had had enough of hiding and creeping around. Now Duncan would be thrown out and she would go with him. Away from her boring husband and her boring life. It wasn't the way she had planned it, but it was going to work out in her favour. She would get her man once and for all.

Something terrible had been set in motion, Ada realised, something too huge to stop. She didn't know what it was, but from the way Vicky was panicking it was damning. Her mouth dry, Ada watched her younger daughter plead.

'Freda, don't say any more. Don't . . .'

But Freda was past stopping. She didn't seem to notice that Duncan was moving further and further away from her and that Doug was blank-faced with rage. She was like a stupid child who keeps repeatedly taunting a caged animal. Only Doug wasn't caged. And he was only a foot away from her.

'Why shouldn't I go on, Vicky? You set a pretty trap, but you're not that smart. You wanted to get rid of your husband, did you? Have him thrown out as a thief? Well, that's fine by me –'

'What are you both talking about!' Doug said, his tone threatening.

His world had been ripped open. *His wife loved his brother*. So had they been lovers? Of course they had, Doug realised, looking from one to the other. They had betrayed him. His family, the people he loved so much – his beloved wife and brother – were nothing but sordid liars. They had cheated him, duped him. The happy family he had wanted so much was nothing but a joke.

Temper almost throttled Doug in that moment, the violent temper he had fought to control all his life. Startled, Duncan saw the expression in his brother's eyes and panicked, remembering the beating he had taken so many years before.

'They're both lying, Doug! Listen to me, believe me!' he shouted, looking from Freda to Vicky in despair. 'Doug, listen to me, there's no truth in any of this. Would I do that to my own brother?'

But Doug wasn't listening. He moved and cornered

Duncan. Freda flushed with shame and humiliation. Her lover was calling her a liar! He was going to say *anything* to save his own skin. She had exposed their affair – and for what? She would be disgraced and get nothing out of it. Oh, no, Freda thought, looking at Duncan. You're going to suffer, you bastard. You don't play around with me and get away with it.

'How could you do it?' Doug said, his voice deadly as he towered over his brother. 'How could you sleep with my wife?'

'I wasn't my fault,' Duncan blathered. 'I tried to stop it, but she was always after me –'

Freda was across the room in a second, lunging out at Duncan, her voice hysterical.

'*I* was after *you*! You couldn't leave me alone, you pig. Tell them, Duncan – tell them how we crept into the bathroom at night and made love. Tell them how we had sex in your brother's bed.' She was screaming, her face distorted with anger, Vicky white-faced at the chaos she had unleashed. 'TELL THEM WHAT WE DID UNDER THEIR NOSES!'

'Christ!' Duncan pleaded. 'Shut up, you stupid cow!'

The words slapped Freda full in the face. He was calling her names, treating her like a common whore! How dare he? They had been lovers for years, laughed together, the two of them cocking a snook at every-one behind their backs. And now her brave lover was cowering in fear and trying to blame her.

By now beyond reason, Freda was willing to damn herself in order to get her own back on Duncan.

'Don't tell me to shut up!' she hissed. 'I haven't even started.'

Sensing impending disaster, Vicky caught hold of her sister's arm and tried to pull her away. 'Let it go –'

'Let *me* go!' Freda snapped, turning on her husband and punching Doug on the arm. 'Go on, hit him! Hit your brother! Knock the bastard out. He's a lying, cheating pig.'

Angrily, Doug caught hold of Freda's arm and bent down, looking into her face, his voice lethal. 'You had sex in *our* bed?'

Incredibly, she still stood up to him: 'Yes.'

'You made love in *our* room? Amongst *our* things –' He stopped short. 'No, you couldn't have! Just tell me, Freda, tell me that you never did it in front of our son. Tell me you never made love in front of our son.'

No, Vicky thought blindly, no! Stop now. Stop everything now. This is not how it was supposed to be. This is not what was supposed to happen. She wanted to break up the scalding little knot of people, push them back into their rooms and slam the doors on them. Tell them to start the day again, living normally.

But she couldn't. She had started it. But it was to be her sister who would strike the fatal blow.

Vainly she tried once more to stem disaster: 'Shut up, Freda!'

But Freda was past reason. Her face bitter, she looked up at her husband.

'*Our son*?' she parroted. 'You stupid sod! He's not your child, Doug. Billy is Duncan's son.'

No one knew how Doug managed to move so fast, but straight away he caught hold of his brother and threw him against the pub wall, Duncan striking out and punching Doug in the ribs. They fell crashing to the floor, Ada trying to separate them, her two daughters looking on, frozen into immobility.

'I'll kill you!' Doug swore, his hands going round

Duncan's throat. 'I'll bloody kill you!'

No one doubted it, Ada least of all. She had never seen her son-in-law like this. He was transformed, the easy-going man turned into a vicious thug. Betrayal and disappointment had made Doug Oldenshaw into a monster, his muscular hands squeezing hard around Duncan's throat.

'Stop it! STOP IT!' Ada screamed, pulling at Doug's arms. 'He's not worth it.'

Sensing a momentary lapse in Doug's grip, Duncan quickly brought his knee up into his brother's diaphragm. Doug was winded and gasped for breath as Duncan scurried to his feet. But he didn't even reach the door before his brother was on him again, Doug's left arm around his throat, pulling back Duncan's head.

And then Vicky saw the child.

Apparently Billy had woken from sleep and come downstairs to see what the noise was all about. Everyone had been so preoccupied that they hadn't noticed him. So, unseen, Billy had watched the adults, panicking, his child's mind distressed. He had seen his father and uncle fighting and all he had wanted to do was to stop it.

No one had noticed him climb up onto the bar. No one saw him until Duncan threw a punch at his brother. And missed.

His arm swung round into the cold air. Until it stopped, hitting Billy. The force knocked the child off the bar and into the pub beyond. He was propelled like a shuttlecock, almost weightless, Ada screaming as her grandson fell, his head slamming violently onto the bare floor when he landed.

He was still when they reached him. He was still when Doug picked him up and cried and screamed and rocked him. He was still when Ada touched his face and felt the blood stick to her fingers. He was still. He was dead.

Duncan Oldenshaw had killed his own son.

Chapter Thirty-Four

'Have you heard what's happened?' Bessie Cork said, coming out onto the street and stopping Lizzie that morning. 'It's Billy Oldenshaw, he's dead.'

'Billy? Don't be daft, he's only a lad.'

'He were killed. Some kind of accident in the pub,' Bessie went on dramatically, pulling Lizzie into the shop and closing the door behind her. 'There's more – Duncan Oldenshaw's gone.'

'He killed him?'

'He were having a fight with his brother,' Bessie hurried on, 'threw a punch, missed Doug, and hit the little one. It weren't deliberate.'

'Oh God,' Lizzie said, putting her hand over her mouth and scurrying out. Immediately she told three women she knew on the street and then crossed over to stop Mac Potter in his tracks.

'Oh, Mac, Billy's dead.'

'Billy who?'

'Billy, Freda's lad.'

'Dead! How?'

'It were an accident. Duncan hit him when he were having a fight with his brother –'

'Why were they fighting?'

Lizzie looked around furtively, then lowered her voice. 'Someone said they were fighting over Vicky –'

'Freda more like.'

'I don't know which one it were!' Lizzie replied

impatiently, 'but that little lad dying . . . God, it's awful.'

The news was passed from mouth to mouth, incredulous people hearing it and then telling the next person they met. Ada Hargreaves's grandson was dead. It wasn't possible. And then, of course, the rumours started. It was Freda's fault. The fight had been between the two brothers, hadn't it? Well, anyone could guess why. Besides, Duncan had buggered off. Not a sight of him.

But it was an accident, someone else said. Duncan wasn't really responsible . . . He should have stayed around, though; comforted his brother . . . More like he comforted his sister-in-law, another replied . . .

The doors of The Sixpenny Winner stayed locked – no sign of life. No one moved at a window and no one came out, only the undertaker going in later. The street held its breath.

As the day wore on, people came to stare at the pub, trying to look through the windows, though all the curtains and blinds were drawn. And still no one came out. Then, around six o'clock, the rain started, the summer evening dark and unkindly cold.

People continued to knock on the pub door, but no one answered. But there's lights on inside, they said. God, what are they doing? What can you do? Is the little lad in there? Where else? Someone said, of course he's there. And will be until he's buried. Offers of help and condolences were pushed under the door, but no one came out. And the street went on holding its breath.

'Eat something,' Ada said quietly, putting down a plate of cold ham and some bread in front of her two daughters. 'Go on, eat.'

Freda shook her head. Vicky also. 'I can't.'

'You have to. Starving yourselves won't bring Billy back.'

Uttering a strained exclamation, Freda left the kitchen and went into the sitting room. On a table was the open coffin, Billy clearly visible. Nervously Freda walked over to it and looked at her dead son. She longed for comfort, but found none inside herself – and none offered from anyone else in the house.

In their room upstairs Doug lay on the bed and stared at the ceiling. He felt nothing. Heard nothing. Could smell or sense nothing. All he knew was that his Billy was dead. And it wasn't even *his Billy*. The child had been his nephew, not his son. But that didn't stop Doug loving him, didn't stop him wanting to bang his fists into the walls until they bled, the same fists that had struck out at Duncan, and indirectly caused the death of his child.

He replayed the scene over and over – not in slow motion, but quicker and quicker so that it was always impossible for him to catch the boy and break his fall. He could see Billy on the bar top, see him struck accidentally by Duncan, hear the sickening thud as he landed on the floor. He had been trying to stop them fighting, a child frightened and wanting desperately to help.

It was no good hating Duncan. That was too easy. Better to hate himself, Doug thought, to hate his temper, his loss of control. If he had just talked to his brother, kept everything calm, it could all have been avoided. Billy would never have woken, would never have come down.

He would be alive now, lying in his own bed, Doug able to hear him breathing. For years he had woken and listened to Billy in the night, his child, his family. But that was all an illusion. Billy had been Duncan's child.

Freda had been Duncan's mistress. Douglas Oldenshaw had had nothing. He had been so blind and stupid. So happily ignorant.

And he would have stayed that way – but for Vicky. Her accusation had set in motion the whole horror. If she hadn't tried to incriminate Duncan, Billy would still be alive . . . No, Doug thought, it wasn't her fault. It was Freda's fault for sleeping with Duncan, for passing off Billy as her husband's child.

It was also his fault for being stupid. It was his fault for being trusting. And it was his fault for losing control . . . His head throbbed with pain. Would the day never end? But why did he welcome night? He wouldn't sleep, and he couldn't bear the thought of Freda lying next to him.

Not on this bed, Doug thought, screaming inside. Not in this bed, *my* bed. The bed I loved my wife in, held my child in, dreamed my dreams in. The bed I longed for all the years of the war. The bed I fell into at night after a hard day's work. The bed I thought was safe. The bed I thought was mine.

The bed they stole from me. And soiled. And maybe even conceived Billy in. Did they laugh at me here? Doug thought, his hands tightening on the covers. Did they cling on to each other and laugh at how big a fool I was? How easy I was to dupe?

And all the time they were laughing at me there I was thinking myself a lucky man.

Across the hall Vicky was staring at her own bed. Taking off her clothes she pulled her nightdress on and sat in the chair by the window. She was past crying, but not past thinking.

Her husband had gone. His clothes, razor, comb and

shoes were still there, but he had gone. In the end, it had been Ada who had thrown Duncan out. He had panicked when he saw that Billy was dead. His mother-in-law had gripped his arm and marched him to the back door.

'Get out!'

'I can't, Billy –'

'It was an accident. I'll vouch for that. A terrible accident. But I want you away. I want you away. And if you know what's good for you, you'll go now, before I change my mind.' She snatched her hand away from his arm. 'I can't look at you! I can't look at you and think of what you've done. A boy lies dead because of what you and my daughter did. Get out!' she shouted again, pushing him violently.

'I've got nothing with me.'

'You'll take nothing from here!' Ada snapped. 'You've taken enough. You go in what you're wearing and thank God I've let you off so lightly.'

'But –'

'Get away, Duncan!' she shrieked. 'Or, by God, I kill you myself.'

He backed away. 'I never meant to hit him! I never meant to kill Billy. He was my son. I never meant to hurt him!'

'And that's the only reason I'm letting you get away,' Ada answered, her voice terrifying. 'You clear off, go somewhere else, Duncan Oldenshaw. Take your bad luck and bad morals to another door. But remember what it cost you to cheat your own.'

'Ada, wait. I have to talk to you, to Freda –'

'What about *Vicky*?' she snapped. 'What about your wife? The wife you duped, the wife you made a fool of –'

'She tried to frame me.'

'To get rid of you! I see it all now,' Ada replied. 'Poor silly cow, if she'd come to me and confided in me I'd have given you your marching orders long enough since.'

'It's her fault –'

'It's everyone's fault,' Ada answered him, her voice dull. 'It's my fault, for taking you in when my instincts told me to slam the door in your face. It's Douglas's fault for not telling me what you were like, for trusting you. It's Vicky's fault for being so in love with you she lost her reason. And as for Freda – it's Freda's fault for sleeping with you, for cheating on Doug, for giving birth to a child she passed off as his when all the time she knew Billy was yours. It's her fault for being so selfish that she let the cat out of the bag.' Ada paused, winded with anger and grief. 'You go now, Oldenshaw. Go now, without her. Because that's the worst punishment I can inflict on my daughter. When you leave without Freda, she'll be stuck here with no escape. Stuck to live with the husband she betrayed and the sister she cheated. Stuck to live – every day – with what she's done.'

He blanched. He didn't want Freda with him, but was shaken by the ferocity of Ada's fury.

'You can't do that to her, it's too cruel –'

'Who are you to tell me about cruelty?' Ada shouted. 'Get away! And leave by the back door, where you came in. And if I ever – *ever* – see you again, Duncan Oldenshaw, I'll make your life hell. God help me, but I'll make you wish you'd never been born.'

Slamming the door closed, Ada went back into the kitchen and sat down in front of the unlit fire. She was cold, but didn't want to warm herself. What was the point? Billy was cold, in the other room. He'd never be warm again. She could stand the cold, if he could. An hour passed, then another, Ada still sitting there when Freda walked timidly into the kitchen.

Ada gave her a look of such loathing that she rocked on her feet.

'Ma –'

'Don't talk to me!'

'I have to –'

'Don't talk to me!' Ada repeated. 'There's nothing you can say, Freda. But I'll tell you this, I'm ashamed that you're my child, ashamed that I gave birth to you. And I thank God that your father's not alive to see this.'

'Vicky started it –'

Ada moved across the kitchen in an instant, Freda stepping back, intimidated.

'*You* started it! And *you'll* finish it. You've had your fun, now I'll tell you what you're going to do with the rest of your life, Freda. You're going to try to make it up to every one of us. You're going to struggle to make me stop wanting to hit you every time I see your face. You're going to have to lie with a husband who despises you and sit opposite a sister who wishes you dead.' Ada's face was frightening in its implacability. 'You're going to know what pain is, Freda, because I know you, and losing Billy wasn't the worst thing that's happened to you –'

Ashen, Freda faced her mother. 'What d'you mean?'

'He's gone.'

'Who?'

'Duncan Oldenshaw. Your lover, he's gone.'

'No!' she screamed, moving to the back door.

Ada snatched her arm and pulled her back. 'He went hours ago. He left you. He didn't give a damn about you, Freda. He used you.' Ada paused. 'Now, sit down and think about what you've done –'

'I can't stay here!'

'SIT DOWN!' Ada shouted, dragging the sobbing Freda to a seat and then sitting down opposite her. 'Now you think, Freda. Think about what you are, and what you did. And I'll sit with you. I'll keep an eye on you, remember that. From now on, wherever you are and whatever you do, I'll see it. You think it's over? Jesus, girl, it's just begun.'

Chapter Thirty-Five

The police came round to The Sixpenny Winner that night, after Douglas called them. He tried to explain what had happened, but it was beyond him, and in the end the explanation fell to Ada. The officer knew Ada Hargreaves well, had been in for a drink at the pub often enough.

'Duncan Oldenshaw killed Billy,' Ada said firmly.

Doug was slumped in a chair, Vicky white-faced at the kitchen table, Freda blank, wiped of all expression.

'But it was an accident.' Ada paused: she would keep a hold of her emotions, she had to now. 'I might add that I wish I could say it *hadn't* been. Wish I could damn Duncan Oldenshaw to hell – but I tell you here and now, he never meant to hurt the child.'

The officer was shaken. 'I'll have to talk to him, Mrs Hargreaves.'

'That'll be difficult,' Ada replied, looking the policeman directly in the eyes. 'I threw him out after Billy . . . after it happened. Duncan Oldenshaw's gone. And there's no way he'll be back. You know me, officer, you know I don't lie, and I've told you the truth – it was an accident. Duncan and Douglas were fighting and the little lad got in the way. *It was an accident.*'

Ada stuck to the story, as did everyone else in the family. Because it was the truth. But the gossips put their own twists and turns on it and when the inquest took place there was a queue for seats. Another scandal at The Sixpenny Winner, the locals said, feigning sympathy. It were awful. And Duncan Oldenshaw gone off like the louse he was. Police couldn't find hide nor hair of him. But with the family all saying Billy's death was an accident, the inquest ruled that it was.

Whatever the law or the locals said, who cared really? Ada remarked bitterly. After all, whatever *anyone* said, nothing could bring Billy back.

Over a hundred people lined Churchgate on the day of Billy Oldenshaw's funeral. Flowers covered the small coffin in the hearse, and on the roof was a wreath with the inscription 'To My Billy, from Mum'. Ada hadn't sent flowers, but she followed the hearse in the next car, her hands folded on her lap, her eyes staring straight ahead. Beside her sat Freda, Douglas riding in the front. Vicky was supposed to stay home, but in the end she pushed Stella in the pram all the way to the cemetery.

Once there, she made her way over to the graveside, keeping her distance. Freda had lost weight, her eyes pouchy with crying. Beside her stood Doug, his expression unreadable. Only Ada seemed alert, accepting condolences and exchanging a few words with the mourners who approached her, but always, always, keeping her eye on Freda.

Touching Stella's hand, Vicky felt her eyes fill. Her actions had indirectly caused the death of her sister's child. Whatever Freda had done, no one deserved so severe a punishment. As for Duncan, her husband and Freda's lover, he had gone – left them both in the end.

It all seemed so pointless, Vicky thought. How had the two of them been so besotted with such a worthless man? The future looked so bleak, so empty suddenly.

She was alone, but at least she had her child. Duncan had never even said goodbye to Stella . . . Suddenly she realised that she might never see him again, and was ashamed of the pain the thought gave her. How *could* she still have feelings for him?

Her gaze moved back to Freda, who was standing woodenly beside Ada, her head bowed. Rumours had spread, Freda's old reputation remembered. People might not know the whole story, but they had already decided where the blame lay. They might be sorry for a woman who had lost her child, but their real sympathy lay with the cheated wife.

But that was wrong! Vicky thought fiercely. They should hate *her*, despise *her*, see her for what she was – a manipulative, jealous schemer. She wasn't a good person; she had been wicked. Cruel, vicious, plotting her attack. And where had all her planning got her? To a graveside – with a lifetime of guilt to follow.

Moving away, Vicky took the other route out of the cemetery and made her way back to The Sixpenny Winner before the service ended. She would get back before them and no one would know she had ever been at the funeral. She would put the kettle on. Make something to eat that no one would touch, and wait for their return.

Only this time there would be one less.

Standing at the corner of Churchgate, Al Weeks lit a cigarette and inhaled, blowing the smoke out from between his lips. What a bloody shame, he thought, little Billy Oldenshaw dying like that. He thought of Ada suddenly and wondered if the scrawled note of condolence he had pushed under the pub door had been appropriate. Banned from the pub, maybe he should have kept his distance.

The death of Billy had come as a shock to Al, but Duncan's sudden departure intrigued him. Inhaling again, he thought of what he had found out about Duncan Oldenshaw, and then pondered on the rumours he had heard.

Good thing the bastard was out of the way, he thought. No good would come of having a man like that under your roof. But he felt sorry for Vicky. And as for Doug – what an eye-opener. He was a changed man. It had happened so quickly too, Al seeing Doug in town collecting some supplies, his large frame stooped, his expression blank. God Almighty, Al thought, he looks like a hulking corpse.

Someone else told him that Doug seldom came into the bar any more. The Sixpenny Winner had reopened within the week, but Ada was now serving, with Vicky. And bloody uncomfortable it is there, they said. The women are strained with each other, and there's no sign of Freda. Mind you, the place was busy. There's nothing like a scandal for helping trade. Al would have liked to see for himself, but that wasn't likely.

It wasn't just morbid curiosity, but a genuine interest. Surely they wouldn't keep running the pub, he thought. How could they, with such bloody awful memories? But then again, what else could they do? It was their business, their livelihood. And as for Freda, how was she going to cope? People were talking about her, but no one was on her side; no one came to her defence. And how glad they were to know that Duncan had gone. Deserted her.

Serves the bitch right, they said, she was always so sure of herself. Always so selfish. Sleeping with her own sister's husband, and if the rumour's right, Billy was Duncan's kid, not Doug's . . . How the rumour started, Al didn't know, but once it was on one pair of lips, it seemed to be all over Stockport. Freda had committed adultery with her sister's husband and passed off Duncan's child as Doug's.

Oh, how they loved the story, loved to chew over the gossip, and tear Freda into pieces. She was immoral, a tart, a bitch. From then on – as Al was told by a regular of the pub – everything Freda did was watched. If she walked into the bar, people nudged each other, moved away. If she came down the street, women turned their backs on her, and men stared – at her and at her companion, the ever-present Ada.

This is a messy bloody business, Al thought, stubbing out his cigarette and moving away. Perhaps if he had never told Vicky about her husband's past life none of this tragedy would have happened. But then again, maybe it would . . . Al sighed to himself. The previous day Vicky had sent him a note, telling him that their arrangement was over. Thank you, but it's finished with now. Did she owe him anything? she had asked.

Did she owe him anything? The words seemed so poignant to Al, like those of a little girl trying to be grown up and brave in the face of disaster. Well, Vicky might want to try to block her husband out of her mind, but he would keep his eyes and ears open for her. She didn't have to know. Neither did Ada. It was just something Al wanted to do. He might even ask around for any titbits of gossip. It was easy for him.

He had a nose for trouble, Al did. He could feel it like another man feels the sun on his skin. And there was trouble at The Sixpenny Winner. Oh, not the trouble they'd experienced already, but something else. Something in the air which hung about the pub, waiting for its chance to strike.

Al knew trouble. And he also knew that there was more to come.

Chapter Thirty-Six

'Sorry to hear about your trouble,' the butcher said when Ada walked into his shop. 'It were terrible about Billy.'

She nodded brusquely. Freda was hanging behind her, almost a ghost. George tried to catch her eye and offer his condolences to her, but she kept her head down. God, she was changed. Nothing flashy about her now – no sly, sidelong glances at the men.

'Thanks for your kind thoughts, George,' Ada replied, looking over his produce. 'We just get by day to day.'

That much was true. They *did* exist hour by hour, day by day, week by week. And soon the first hideous week crawled into the second, and before long months had gone by. The New Year of 1949 had come, people celebrating the new start – but not the family who lived in The Sixpenny Winner.

They lived knowing that every one of them was always observed, talked about. It was a great story of deception and tragedy, one which no one was prepared to forget in a hurry. The fact that the family was on show, running a pub, did nothing to help their grief. Each word and gesture was public – and they all reacted differently to the scrutiny.

Ada, although shattered by her daughter's behaviour under her own roof, was not prepared to throw Freda to the wolves. Her punishment was to be slower. After all the freedom Freda had enjoyed before, she was now a prisoner. There were no chains, no locked doors, only the expression in her mother, her sister and her husband's eyes.

Ada knew that at first Freda had thought of running away, but to where? Duncan had left her high and dry; there was nowhere she *could* go. Besides, the death of Billy and the abandonment of Duncan had crushed Freda. All her confidence, her arrogance, was being slowly dissolved in the acid of criticism she faced every day. Not in the spoken word – that would be too obvious – but in expressions and silences.

Doug's silence was the worst. Ada knew that Freda was convinced he would finally forgive her. But not this time. When – several months after Billy's death – she finally tried to hold him, he shook her off with such revulsion that she flinched. Ada had seen the exchange and it had shaken her. Her son-in-law hated her daughter, she thought. God, how could Freda stay married to a man who loathed her? Stay under the same roof with him, in the same room, in the same bed?

And why did Douglas stay? Ada wondered. That question was much easier to answer. *Because Douglas Oldenshaw was a broken man*. The big, sturdy, lucky man who had come to The Sixpenny Winner all those years before was dead. In his place was a depressed semblance of a man. Douglas wouldn't leave because he couldn't. There was nowhere he wanted to go, nothing he wanted to do. He had no ambitions, no aims, no hope left.

He might hate his wife and the pub that held so many memories, but in a way it was the only place Douglas could find comfort. In The Sixpenny Winner he could remember Billy and the days when he had been so happy.

There was another reason Douglas stayed. Guilt. *He* had brought Duncan into the pub. *He* had hidden his brother's background from everyone. *He* – even though it had been done with the best intentions – had hatched the snake that had poisoned them all. How could a man like Douglas Oldenshaw run away from that?

Ada sighed to herself, her thoughts turning back to her daughter. She knew that Freda missed Billy more than anyone expected her to. But no one asked Freda how she felt. They presumed that an adulteress who had stooped so low would somehow cope with the tragedy. But she couldn't. And she couldn't find words to tell Doug either. The atmosphere wasn't one in which sharing was possible.

As for Vicky, she had tried over and over again to approach Freda, but had been rebuffed. She didn't know if it was because her sister hated her, or because she was too ashamed to face her. Either way, communication between the women was over.

'I hope things get better for you this year,' George said pleasantly, passing Ada some wrapped corned beef. 'And for you, Freda.'

Surprised that he had spoken to her directly, tears pricked behind Freda's eyes. It was the first time anyone had said a kind word to her in months. But she still didn't look up and a moment later silently walked out of the shop behind her mother.

'Aye, that's a bloody awful do,' George said, moving into the back room where his wife was darning a sock. 'I've just had Ada Hargreaves in here, with Freda.'

'Well, she got what she deserved,' Enid replied. 'Do wrong and it comes back on you.' She bit the cotton with her teeth and admired her handiwork. 'Those should see you right for a while longer, George.'

But his mind was still on Ada and her strange, withdrawn daughter.

'Freda Hargreaves were a beauty once –'

'She were a bitch too,' Enid said shortly. 'All you men were silly over Freda Hargreaves and look where it got her. I'm amazed that husband of hers didn't throw her out.'

'Steady on –'

'Don't tell me to steady on, George! You know as well as I do, if Duncan had asked her, Freda would have gone off with him like a shot.' She waved a reel of cotton at him. 'Half her trouble isn't conscience, but hurt pride.'

Unconvinced, George watched the two figures grow smaller and smaller in the distance as they climbed the steep street and headed for Churchgate. He had heard his wife's argument a thousand times in his shop, women gossiping amongst themselves about the tragedy, always damning Freda and often defending Vicky. However, some weren't so charitable. They said that a wife should keep her husband on a shorter lead, or that Vicky must have known what her sister and husband were up to. Or even, that Vicky couldn't keep her man from straying.

But in the end Freda was always to blame. The sexy, pretty blonde who had turned their men's heads was now downtrodden, and the women were loving it. Not so clever now, is she? they said. Not now her lover's buggered off – and it looks like Douglas Oldenshaw can hardly give her the time of day.

Ada knew what they said. So did Freda. And no one ever suggested that she didn't deserve it.

It was a freezing early morning when Vicky woke and, shivering, got out of bed. For a moment she glanced at the empty half where Duncan had used to sleep and then turned away. Softly she crept over to Stella and looked at her child. A peaceful child, the only peaceful person in the building.

It was not the first time Vicky had woken early and wanted to go to her sister. But how could she? By waking Freda she would wake Doug, and then what? But if Freda had been on her own she would have gone in and talked to her. Told her that she was sorry. Yes, *sorry*, because whatever Freda had done, it hadn't warranted Billy's death. And besides, Vicky had played a major part in this tragedy.

Duncan had been a weak man, over which two women had fought, but Billy had been a child with all his life to live. And she had, indirectly, curtailed that life. It had not been Vicky's intention, but that didn't absolve her of guilt. The child was dead because of what she had set in motion. It was something Vicky would never forgive herself for.

The sound of a movement outside made Vicky turn. Carefully she unlocked her door and looked out, to see Doug – dressed and ready for work – descend the stairs. Waiting until she heard him move into the kitchen, Vicky crossed the landing and knocked on Freda's door. There was no answer. Remembering the last time she had arrived uninvited, Vicky nevertheless walked in. Freda was awake, sitting by the window in her nightdress, a scattering of Billy's clothes and toys around her feet. The temperature was bitterly cold and yet she didn't seem to notice it. Just as she didn't notice her sister walking in.

'Freda?'

She turned from the window, blank-eyed.

'Freda, are you all right?'

Without answering, she turned back to look out at the street beyond.

Timidly Vicky moved over to her, bending down and starting to tidy up Billy's things.

'Leave them!'

'Freda –'

She turned to her sister, her eyes bright with hate. 'Haven't you done enough?'

Stung, Vicky tried to remonstrate. 'You don't know how sorry –'

'*How sorry you are?*'

She nodded.

'I don't care how sorry you are.'

'Freda, neither of us is innocent in this. I don't hate you for sleeping with my husband, for lying to me –'

'Your child is still alive!' Freda snapped, her old vigour momentarily returning. 'What have I got left? Duncan's gone and my child is dead. Look, Vicky, look at what I have left. Some clothes, some toys.' She snatched one up and waved it under her sister's nose. 'Smell it. It still has his scent on it.'

'I never meant for anything to happen to Billy –'

'But it did,' Freda replied, lapsing back into a monotone. 'Billy died. My son died. My son – and Duncan's.'

'Freda, I lost my husband –'

'You still have Stella!' Freda retorted. 'And you never had to pretend that *she* wasn't Duncan's child.'

'I never slept with another man and passed her off as someone else's baby –'

'How noble,' Freda said bitterly. 'But you always were the caring one, weren't you, Vicky? Always so careful of people's feelings. The nice daughter that everyone liked. Poor Vicky, whose wicked sister committed adultery with her husband.'

'You did!'

'Yes,' Freda said coldly. 'I did.'

For an instant Vicky wanted to walk out, to leave her sister. But she couldn't. Whatever Freda said – whether fair or unfair – was nothing to the pain she was feeling.

'I never thought it would get out of hand. I just wanted to get rid of Duncan.'

'You succeeded.'

'You *can't* still love him!' Vicky said heatedly. 'Not after what he did. He killed your child –'

'It was an accident!'

'But he didn't stay around to explain, did he?' Vicky countered. 'Dear God, Freda, we have to work this out between us. We can't live like this.'

'I can,' her sister replied flatly. 'I'm not going to make it easy for you, Vicky. I'm not going to say it's all right, you don't have to feel guilty. I'm not nice, you see, not like you. Although you're not really such a good person, after all, are you? You plotted a sordid little plan which backfired. Now neither of us has Duncan. And none of us has Billy. You didn't just rob me, you robbed our mother and Doug too.'

'And what about you?' Vicky said, close to tears. 'You started it all. You were sleeping with Duncan.'

'But no one knew, did they? No one was hurt – until you stuck your oar in.'

'That doesn't make it right!' Vicky blustered. 'Someone would have found out sooner or later.'

'They did. *You* did. Pity it wasn't Doug. I could have made things right with him after a while, I know I could. He would have forgiven me because he loved me. But not now. Not now his beloved Billy's dead.' She stared into her sister's face. 'You sleep alone. Hard luck. Well,

I sleep with a man who won't touch me, look at me, or talk to me. I sleep with a corpse.'

Vicky was shaking with emotion. 'That's not my fault.'

Unmoved, Freda held her sister's gaze for a long moment before replying, 'It's both our faults, Vicky. I'm guilty, you're guilty. The difference is, I can live with it, and you can't. Do you think that all the people who pity you now would pity you so much if they knew what you'd done? You think Doug feels sorry for you? He despises you –'

'You don't know that!'

'I know it,' Freda retorted with certainty. 'Every time he sees you he remembers who started the rot. Then he sees Stella and remembers that he no longer has his Billy. He watches you push your baby out in the pram and feed her. And I know – *I know* – that he's thinking of Billy.' She stood up and faced Vicky. 'I cheated him, yes. But I gave him a child to love. You killed that child –'

Vicky was distraught. 'Duncan killed Billy!'

'Because of you. Because you exposed us –'

'No! You did that, Freda!' Vicky snapped. 'I never said a word about you two, although I had enough cause. *You* told your husband what you'd done. I'll take some guilt, but not all of it. And not that.' She moved to the door, turning back for a final plea. 'If this family is going to survive, we have to work this out between us. I want to, Freda. Please, please, for everyone's sake, help me.'

Her sister's face was expressionless as she stooped and then suddenly picked up some of Billy's clothes. Determinedly she walked over to Vicky and shook them in front of her face.

'Why don't you take some of these, sister? Alter them

346

for Stella – go on, use Billy's blankets, his cot. His bed. Go on! You've taken him and his father away, now take the rest!' She threw the articles at Vicky with contempt. 'Dress your child in my dead child's things. Push your child out in my dead child's pram and feed her with my dead child's spoon –'

'Stop it!' Vicky shrieked, catching hold of her sister's hands. 'Jesus, stop it!'

'But I *want* you to have everything, Vicky. You deserve it for being such a good daughter, wife, mother. You deserve Billy's belongings. I don't. Go on, take it all. There are his shoes too, and his school bag –'

Reaching out, Vicky caught hold of Freda. With all her strength she clung on to her sister and held her tight to her. Freda struck out, but Vicky held on grimly, Freda kicking and screaming until, finally, she stopped. Exhausted, her head fell against her sister's shoulder, her body shaking with sobs.

'What did we do to one another?' Vicky asked, her voice little more than a whisper. '*Christ, what did we do?*'

Day by day the bomb sites were cleared, new buildings creeping up like spring shoots from the wreckage. The mood was lifting too, optimism slowly shaking off the sombre gloom of war. In the shops in town there were new fashions, rationing over. Women flocked to get the material and try on the fuller skirts. Ada and her daughters would have looked good in them – but none of them were interested. The world might be at peace outside, but inside The Sixpenny Winner the family was now at war amongst themselves.

There were few arguments, but a simmering hostility marked every day. Vicky and Freda had come to some kind of uncomfortable understanding, but it wasn't enough. Ada was working all the hours God sent in order not to think. And as for Doug, he was now a silent man, keeping to the background, no longer lucky, no longer in love.

And yet he would not move out of the bedroom he shared with Freda. It was her punishment to suffer his constant rejection and silence. It was his punishment to endure her, knowing what she had done. He would not talk to her either, addressing any enquiry through Ada. But Freda had been wrong about one thing: Doug didn't blame Vicky for the death of Billy. The pity was, he never told her that.

So the year limped on. Business at The Sixpenny Winner was good, scandal helped that. People were always hoping to catch a glimpse of Doug or Freda. Perhaps they longed for a public showdown, or merely liked to gawk, but although they were always disappointed, they kept coming.

'She's lost a lot of weight,' Lizzie whispered to Mac as they sipped their half-pints. She had thought she would have run her sweetheart to ground by now, but Mac was proving elusive. 'I saw Freda only the other day – with Ada, of course – and she looked awful.'

'Time heals,' Mac replied philosophically.

'Oh, I don't know about that. People have long memories. I don't think Freda will ever live this one down,' Lizzie replied. Catching Ada's eye she nodded to her and then turned back to Mac. 'Ada's coping.'

'Ada would. She's strong.'

Miffed, Lizzie continued. 'I wonder she can put such a brave face on – what with all that's happened.'

'What d'you want her to do? Fall apart?'

'I never said that, Mac!' Lizzie retorted, wondering

if her companion's admiration for the landlady was entirely innocent. 'I just thought that having lost a grandson, she would be more upset.'

'Ada's the kind that cries alone,' Mac replied, unaware of the jealousy he was provoking. 'Fine woman, that.'

'Well, I have to be off!' Lizzie said, getting to her feet and surprised that Mac didn't stand up with her. 'Aren't you coming?'

He shook his head. 'Nah, I'll just stay here a bit, luv. You get on with whatever you have to do.'

Minutes later, an infuriated Lizzie relayed the whole conversation back to Bessie Cork – leaving out only the fact that she and Mac had been in the pub. Smiling to herself, Bessie commiserated, wondering how Lizzie could think she didn't know about her visits to The Sixpenny Winner. Still, better not to tell her, Bessie decided, it was more fun to play along. For years Lizzie had come from the pub reeking of peppermint, sometimes a little the worst for wear, her hat tipped over to one side. Just as it was now.

'He *defended* Ada Hargreaves,' Lizzie went on, blowing her nose loudly as she watched Bessie stack some tins on the shelf. 'Is that Spam?'

Bessie nodded. 'That's what it says on the tin.'

'I don't like Spam,' Lizzie replied, her eyes brilliant with annoyance.

'You should have a brandy to calm your nerves, Lizzie. You're upset.'

She looked shocked. 'Oh, you know I don't drink, Bessie –'

'But it's only medicinal,' she replied, laughing inside. 'I know you're not one to drink normally.'

Lizzie nodded her head vigorously, her hat sliding further over to one side. 'I don't hold with it –'

'But Mac likes a drink.'

'Mac likes The Sixpenny Winner,' Lizzie replied sourly. 'I think he's a bit taken with Ada Hargreaves too, if you ask me: a widow, with more than a bob or two to her name. And to think where she came from, Portswood! Slums, that's what they are up there.'

Fascinated by the vitriol coming from the usually placid Lizzie, Bessie sat down to enjoy the conversation.

'Her father were common – an Irishman.'

'You don't say,' Bessie replied.

'And her mother, she was a terror. Milly Gantry was a right bitch. Everyone said so. Hanged herself.' The story was old news. 'So how Ada Hargreaves can go about giving herself airs, I don't know. She came from a bad family and look how her own turned out.'

'Bad.'

'I'll say!' Lizzie agreed eagerly.

She would show Mac Potter that she didn't need him. Who was he to keep her hanging on? They'd been seeing each other for years; the whole town thought they had an understanding. But he was pulling away now, letting his eye rove. All the way over the bar of The Sixpenny Winner.

'So what are you going to do about Mac?' Bessie asked, knowing her shot would hit the bull's-eye.

'Mac. He's fine,' Lizzie said unconvincingly. 'Why shouldn't he be?'

She was suddenly sorry that she had confided so much. Bessie would be sure to tell every one of her customers and it would be all over town by nightfall. Damn, Lizzie thought, why hadn't she kept her mouth shut?

'I thought you said that Mac was taken with Ada –'

'No,' Lizzie replied, trying on a laugh. 'He was just

being a gentleman, that's all. You know Mac,' she stood up, her expression forced, 'always on the side of the underdog.'

'Oh, yeah,' Bessie agreed mischievously, 'especially if she happens to be a widow with a pub.'

The furthest thing from Ada's mind at that moment was Mac Potter. Closing up for the afternoon, she locked the double doors of The Sixpenny Winner and then moved over to the till to count the takings. She had hoped that in time she could retire and pass The Sixpenny Winner over to her daughters, letting Duncan and Douglas run it; keep it a family affair.

Well, they'd had the affair, she thought grimly, but it hadn't been a business one . . . Money, Ada thought, staring at the cash in her hands. What was the point of it? Oh, it was good to have enough for once, but it didn't matter to her. She would have given every penny to have Clem and Billy back.

Her future, Ada thought dimly, wasn't looking too good. She wasn't old, full of life yet, but circumstances – as they had before – had hobbled her. If only Clem had lived . . . If only she could be normal, look forward to the small things other women took for granted. Like those Wolsey nylon stockings she had seen advertised the other day. They looked wonderful, so fine, glamorous . . . But even thinking such thoughts made Ada feel guilty.

And angry too. Why shouldn't she want to feel like a woman instead of this practical martinet, who spent all her time keeping the family together. She wanted the bloody stockings, wanted to feel a man next to her in bed. Oh yes, I do! Ada thought defiantly. I'm not an old mare yet. I've got life in me. But how likely was it that she would find happiness now? She had had it for a time, seen her two girls marry and have children, been the matriarch and enjoyed watching over a houseful. Then it had all gone sour.

But not for ever, surely? she thought. Time had moved on; even a tragedy could be overcome. Even Billy . . . Or could it? Her vigil over Freda had paid off and punished her daughter. But how? By turning her into a dull ghost. As for Vicky, she was sick with guilt. Both sisters were trying to find some real communication between them, but failing, always failing.

And then there was Douglas . . . Ada sighed. She missed him, missed that good-natured, big, tough man by her side in the bar. If the truth be known, she had come to love him like a son, had liked him around, laughed with him. Trusted him. But now Douglas was nothing more than a melancholic shadow.

And I miss you, Billy, Ada thought to herself. God knows, I miss you, luv. But life goes on – it has to – and this has gone on long enough . . . She was tired of the atmosphere, of the months of silences, guilty looks, half-finished sentences, because someone was always afraid of reminding someone else about what had happened. But why? It *had* bloody happened, Ada thought grimly. And nothing could make it otherwise. Their lives had been shattered by events.

But did they have to *remain* shattered? No, she thought. If Clem had been alive he would have been angry, but he would have moved on. He would have said his piece and then told everyone to settle their differences, and remember that there was a little one in the house, a baby. He was big enough to do that, Ada thought, but she hadn't managed it.

She should have got Vicky and Freda together in one

room and made them fight and shout until they sorted it all out. She should have knocked Freda and Douglas's heads together, told them to make up, or split up. But she hadn't. She had let the rancour, guilt and bitterness corrode every member of the family, let them become a peep show for the public.

And for what? They were further apart now than they had been when Billy died, and the longer it went on the more distant they would become. In the end – Ada dreaded the thought – the house would end up divided into camps: people not speaking to each other, avoiding each other, the simmer of unspoken resentment and pain coming to a boiling mass of hatred.

Oh no, Ada thought. She had been brought up in a family like that, she didn't want the same for Stella, or for her daughters. Both had been at fault, but nothing could change that. It was time to move on. She was ready.

But they weren't.

'So you see how it goes? Yes, I know what you're thinking, it's a hell of a do and no mistake. Little Billy dead, the whole family driven apart, as separate as lepers from common folk.

'But Ada were right, things had to move on, trouble were, how? Well, I'll tell you. This were the bit my grandfather liked. After so much trouble, it were time they had a bit of luck, he'd say.

'But before I go on, a word about Duncan. Well, he'd disappeared as quick as a snowball in an oven. No one saw sight nor sound of him. He was just there one minute, and gone the next. Hopped it, left everyone else to explain. But still, you know that part of the story. It's time to go on now.

'Time to talk about someone new coming. Someone not a bit like Duncan or Douglas. Someone whose coming to The Sixpenny Winner would change everyone's life.

'Did I say for the better? Well, that would be telling, wouldn't it? And jumping our story.

'Better to stick to telling it like it happened.

'And it happened like this . . .'

Part Four

Why do I love thee?
Why do I breathe?
Or curl my fingers nightly, to assume
Some cradle for their praying –
Why indeed?

Anon.

Chapter Thirty-Seven

Head down against the biting wind, Duncan hurried along the main street in the centre of Leeds. He was shuddering with cold, his face ashen, his lips almost bloodless. At the end of the street, he turned to the left and ran the last few yards to the men's hostel. Inside it smelled of unwashed clothes and sweat, a room beyond teeming with men. Over his head a weak light bulb gave miserable illumination to the walls plastered with posters for health, welfare and cigarettes.

Stamping his feet, Duncan stood by the reception table. A weary man with a ragged moustache studied him.

'It's freezing out there,' Duncan said, his teeth chattering.

'You're not dressed for the weather.'

'I left my coat on a bus,' he explained, the man giving him a disbelieving look. 'Have you got a room?'

'You'll have to share.'

'No singles?'

'This isn't a hotel.'

'I can see that,' Duncan replied, shelling out the fee and taking the old blanket offered him.

'Go down the bottom of the corridor, turn right, then left and you'll come to the dormitory. No smoking in bed, no betting and no fighting.' The man paused. 'You got that?'

'I've got it,' Duncan agreed.

'Oh, and you have to be out by nine in the morning. No later, or you pay for another night.'

'Well, who wouldn't want to stay here as long as they could?' Duncan replied bitterly, walking off.

There were two other men in the room when he arrived, one already asleep. The other – old and emaciated – was unwilling to talk. He just lay in his bunk and watched Duncan as he pulled the blanket round him and then swung his feet onto the bed without undressing. Then he coughed several times, phlegm thick in his throat, before finally settling. Moments later, Duncan was asleep.

Freda was waiting for him behind the bathroom door, naked. She was smiling, the moonlight making her white, her eyes closed. Then she turned into Vicky, then into a small broken child, blood coming from Billy's mouth. In his dream Duncan could feel the soft thud of his fist against his son's flesh, a noise which reverberated over and over again in his head. In the day, in the night. Constantly. Thud, thud, thud.

Duncan jerked into consciousness. On the next bed, the old man was still watching him.

'Bad dream?'

'Are there any others?' Duncan asked, wiping the sweat off his top lip.

'You look sick.'

'I was. I'm better now.'

'Because if you're sick, they won't let you stay.'

'I said I *was* sick, but I'm better now,' Duncan repeated shortly, although he could feel the cold sweat under his arms and soaking into his shirt.

He *would* get back on his feet, he told himself as he turned away from the old man. He had been unlucky, that was all. And as for Billy, that had been a horrible accident. He hadn't meant it. Everyone knew that. From the pub he had run off to Nora . . . Who would have thought that she would have nothing to do with him? Her rejection had come hard to Duncan. Suddenly there was nowhere to turn, no pair of soft arms to keep his mind occupied.

So he left Lancashire, using what money he had to buy some rudimentary clothes and a suitcase – which he pawned a month later when he couldn't find a job. What good was a suitcase if you had no clothes to put in it, and nowhere to go? Returning to Yorkshire he finally found work as a labourer, only to be fired a week later for fighting. He couldn't keep his temper, kept picking arguments, often with men big enough to flatten him. 'Stupid bugger must have a death wish,' someone said incredulously. 'If he doesn't watch it, Duncan Oldenshaw will end up in some alleyway. And he won't be singing.'

Two months after that incident, Duncan was living rough, walking from town to town trying to find a job, or a woman. His glossy good looks were fading with weariness, his health buffeted by spending too much time outdoors. Clothes he would have turned his nose up at before, Duncan now accepted gratefully from the Salvation Army. He shuffled with guilt and ill health, his fingers in mittens, his face half covered by a heavy growth of beard. He had no home, no family. He was on the skids.

In the end, he took to begging, but the police moved him on with contempt. He would be fined next time, so watch it, they warned.

It was then that Duncan lost control.

'So arrest me!' he screamed. 'I'm a bloody murderer anyway. Arrest me!'

They obliged, taking him to the local police station and

getting in touch with Stockport police. When they told them what had happened, Duncan was released. Oddly enough, he was reluctant to leave the jail, blabbering like a lunatic about justice.

From then on, Duncan existed on chance. And bitterness. When he could find labouring work, he took it, but as his health grew worse he was forced into unemployment. And no wage meant no food. At one o'clock one morning, on a freezing dawn in March, an unconscious Duncan Oldenshaw was taken by ambulance to the local hospital in Leeds. He was suffering from hypothermia and bronchitis, they said. If he'd stayed on the street one night longer it would have turned to pneumonia.

It was the end of the road for Duncan. He had nowhere left to fall. So, slowly, he coughed and puked his way back to some kind of strength, and then got a job as a porter in the X-ray department of the hospital. Stage by stage he grew back into himself, put on weight, shaved off his beard and began to take care of his appearance again.

The nurses could hardly miss the spectacular metamorphosis that was taking place before their eyes. The sordid porter who had never got so much as a second glance before was suddenly recognised as a handsome man. Within weeks they were flirting with Duncan, and a few weeks after that he had enough confidence to reciprocate.

But he kept his distance. He was still below par, and tired easily. He would have to pace himself. The guilt that had dogged Duncan since he had left Stockport was undergoing its own metamorphosis. Billy's death was his fault, Duncan knew, but he wasn't the only one to blame. Someone else had set the whole sorry business in motion.

His wife, Vicky. His docile, stupid, loving wife had outwitted him. She had plotted to get rid of him and she would have done so with the minimum of damage – if Freda had kept her mouth shut. But between the two of them they had ruined everything. His marriage, his job, his relationship with his brother – and indirectly they had taken Billy away from him too. That wasn't all. The bitch Ada had thrown him out without so much as a look back, cutting him off from everything he had worked for – and from his daughter, Stella.

They had ganged up on him, all of them. They had sacrificed him for their own guilts, thrown him out like the scapegoat into the wilderness. *Put it all on Duncan's back, then we can forget about it.* They had almost destroyed him – but not quite.

He was on the way back. And he wanted what was his. More than that, he wanted revenge, just as his wife had wanted. Only he wanted revenge on all of them – Vicky, Freda, Ada, *and* Douglas – his own brother, who had turned his back on him.

'Are you sure you aren't sick?' the old man asked again, cutting into Duncan's thoughts.

'No, not any more.'

'You're a bad colour.'

'Yeah.'

'A cold winter don't help any.'

Duncan nodded. 'No it doesn't.'

'You got family?'

'Yeah. You?'

'Nah, no family.' The old man paused, thinking. 'Gives a man something to live for, having a family.'

Duncan smiled at the irony of the words and then nodded again.

'You're right there, old man,' he said finally.

Oh yes, he had something to live for again, but it would take a while for him to get his own back, maybe a long while. Still, what did that matter? He had all the time in the world.

Back in the reception area of the hostel, a burly, bald-headed man had just walked in. Lighting a cigarette Al Weeks sat down and looked round. Carefully he read the posters and then glanced through the internal window at the huddle of men beyond.

'Oi, no smoking!' the porter said, walking out from the back.

Al stood up, making his bulk apparent, then took a long lazy drag on his cigarette.

The porter wilted. 'No rooms tonight.'

'Do I look like I need a room?'

'I dunno.'

'I'm looking for someone,' Al went on blithely.

'I don't know him.'

'I haven't told you who I'm looking for yet,' Al replied. 'A man called Duncan Oldenshaw.'

'No one gives names here.'

'He's about six foot, dark-haired, good-looking. With a cleft in his chin.'

'Try the local cinema. Cary Grant's playing there.'

Al smiled. 'Very good,' he said with mock admiration. 'Maybe I should just have a look around –'

'No!' the porter snapped, then softened his tone. 'The guests don't like being disturbed.'

'Oh, well then, we can't disturb the *guests*, can we?' Al retorted, inhaling again. 'Just have a think again about that description I gave you.'

'Is there money in it?'

'If you guess right?'

'Nah,' the porter replied sourly, 'if I *tell* you. Is there money *if I tell you*?'

Al felt in his pocket. 'Go on then, tell me.'

'I think the man you're looking for is in tonight, in the far room at the back.' The porter put out his hand, and Al dropped a half-crown in it. 'What the hell! Is that it?'

'D'you want to argue about it?' Al countered, seeing the man back down. 'How often does he come here?'

'On and off.' The porter paused, his eyes curious. 'What's he done?'

'Why should he have done anything?'

'Why you looking for him?'

'He might be my long-lost brother.'

'Yeah, I can see the resemblance.'

Smiling, Al tapped the old man on the arm. 'Don't tell him I've been asking after him, will you? If you keep quiet, there might be something else in it for you.'

'Like a black eye?'

Al laughed. 'I told you, keep quiet and there'll be no trouble.'

Chapter Thirty-Eight

It was taking Karl Straub a while to get used to Stockport. He had been the deputy head of a school in Cheadle, but after war broke out his German name made people nervous. But he was only *half* German, Karl had explained laughing. His mother had come from London. *You all know me, you've known me for years. Do I look like a spy?*

Joking about it did no good. Neither did trying to reason with people. They were afraid of anyone with a German name, and quite a few who had been jealous of Karl for a while saw their opportunity to strike. So his colleagues at the school whispered behind his back, stirring up the jealousy his early promotion had caused. Bit by bit they ostracised him. Bit by bit they forced him out. And then – suddenly – Karl was fired on some trumped-up charge of theft.

That was the worst blow. That Karl Straub would ever take anything! He was an honest man, but mud sticks. Karl knew that only too well; knew his reputation would precede him wherever he went to look for work as a teacher. It was on his record, after all. So, effectively, Karl Straub was pushed out of the teaching profession because of prejudice and a lie.

It would have been bad enough if Karl had been on his own, but he had his daughter, Elise, with him. He had looked after her since her mother died when Elise was five. It had been hard at first, but soon

Karl had adjusted and now the thought of sharing his daughter with anyone was unwelcome. In return she adored him, adored the brilliant deputy headmaster that people looked up to.

And – despite Karl's worst fears – she adored the exile just as much. Touched by her devotion, Karl struggled to find employment. At over forty years of age he was not called up to fight, but he had volunteered to assist the war work in any way he could. Trouble was, no one had wanted to have a man called Straub on their side. He's a bloody foreigner, they had said. A German, to boot. Probably a spy . . . But he looks after his daughter, some replied. He can't be all bad . . . Ah, that's just to fool you. She's probably a spy as well . . .

Finally Karl found a job in Manchester, working his way through the war in a munitions factory by the River Irwell. His work had been checked thoroughly and no one had ever asked his opinion on anything, or trusted him.

His time away from work had been spent with his daughter, Elise growing up during the war with just her father for company. A more outgoing child might have made some friends, but Elise had been timid, keeping to the flat whilst her father had been out, working diligently on the school books he had set her.

It was fortunate that Karl had been a teacher, so her education never suffered. The only trouble was that Karl had tutored in the Arts, his knowledge far advanced from the usual education for a ten-year-old. But her father had a skill, and that skill was being able to empathise with his only child.

So together they stayed in Manchester from 1943 to 1948, and then they moved when Karl heard about a job going for a teacher in Salford. He had arrived for the interview with high hopes, only to have them dashed immediately when they received his records. But I never stole the money! Karl protested vehemently. They never proved the charge ... They had never *disproved* it either, the School Board had replied, summarily rejecting him.

When that job fell through Karl had taken on anything which brought in money. For a normally gregarious man, he found life hard. His status had gone, as had his friends and his wage. All that was left was his child.

Then one morning in May 1949, Karl had been told by his landlord that he and his daughter had to move on. No explanation had been given. It wasn't the first time. So they had packed up their belongings, Karl had taken Elise's hand and together they walked to the train station.

There he directed her to a map on the wall.

'Well, what do you think?' he asked her.

Elise looked up at her father, baffled. She saw an elegant, bearded man with a suitcase in one hand, the other pointing to the railway map. Anything he said was all right with her; it always had been. But this time she had known it was different. There was a hint of weariness in her father's voice, something his good nature couldn't disguise.

'What d'you mean?'

'I say we close our eyes and jab our finger on the map. Where it lands, we go.'

She smiled. Why not? As long as she was with her father she would be safe.

'You do it.'

'No,' Karl replied, putting down the suitcase and taking his daughter's hand. 'You do it.'

So Elise closed her eyes, twirled her finger round in

the cool morning air and then jabbed her index finger on the map.

'Stockport!' Karl said happily, as though it was the one place he had always longed to go.

'Stockport?' Elise echoed.

'Our new home.'

Smiling, he looked at his daughter. Elise had matured now, he thought, from the quiet frightened little girl into a serene young woman. Too serene, perhaps, but then what could you expect if a girl grew up without peers of her own age? He had wanted so much for her – a happy childhood, a good career – but what had come of it? Oh, she was probably better educated than most girls of her age, but remote, in a way children are who grow up with adults.

'Now all we need to do is to find a train to take us there,' Karl said, picking up his suitcase again and looking round. 'We're going to the Promised Land, Elise, to a new adventure.'

And so Karl and Elise Straub came to Stockport, catching a midday train. The sun was shining when they arrived, Karl taking it as a good omen, Elise staring expressionless at the hilly little town. Together they then walked over the railway bridge, out onto Underbank and into the town beyond.

As they did so Elise stopped, her head cocked over to one side. 'Listen.'

Karl stopped too – and there it was, the sound of chimes coming over the sunny street. In the distance, on that still day, Winter's Clock welcomed them.

His spirits high, Karl took Elise's hand and then stopped outside the newsagent, looking at the cards in the window, advertising work and cheap rooms to rent. Quickly he made a note of several, and then walked in.

A red-faced woman was struggling with a small boy, the child crying loudly and trying to escape her grip.

Karl raised his eyebrows. 'Good morning.'

'What's good about it?' the woman snapped back, grabbing hold of the boy's shoulders and shaking them. 'What the 'ell 'ave you gone and done now! You daft little bugger!'

Amazed, Karl leaned over the counter. 'Can I help?'

'It's his nose,' she replied, exasperated. 'He shoves things up his nose all the time. If I didn't watch him he'd have the piano up there.'

The child's eyes were fixed, his mother pinching the bridge of his nose sharply.

'I can feel it!'

'Feel what?' Karl asked, transfixed.

'My rubber! The one I use to mark the papers. He were playing with it all morning. And then – as soon as my back were turned – up his bloody nose it went!' She shook the child again vigorously. 'I want . . .' another shake, 'that bloody rubber . . .' another shake, 'back!'

'If I could help . . .' Karl said, interrupting.

She glowered at him, her son's eyes glassy, his nose running.

'What the 'ell do you know about it?'

'I was a teacher. And some of my pupils used to put things up their noses too. It's a way of getting attention.'

The woman pushed her son over to him. 'Well, it looks like he's got yours,' she said, folding her arms and watching Karl. 'Go on! Let's see if an *educated* man like yourself can get that rubber back.'

Kneeling down, Karl looked the boy in the face. He then took a pen out of his inside pocket and hurriedly drew something on the palm of his hand.

Then he showed the drawing to the boy.

'Hey, that's summit!'

His mother leaned over and stared at Karl's hand. There was a clever drawing of a frog on his palm.

'Want me to do another one?' Karl asked the boy.

He nodded vigorously.

'OK. But first we get that thing out of your nose.'

'I can't,' the child wailed. 'It's stuck.'

'Silly little bugger,' his mother murmured behind him.

Karl carried on patiently. 'You just put one finger on this side of your nose,' he pressed the boy's finger against the left side of his nose, 'and now blow down the other side hard. HARD!'

'It was impressive,' the woman said later to a friend. 'That rubber came down our lad's nose faster than a rat down a drainpipe.'

'And there,' Karl said, pointing to the sticky article in her son's hand, 'is your rubber.' He then scribbled a cat onto his other palm and showed it to the boy. 'And here's your reward.'

Impressed, the woman looked Karl up and down.

'Well now, what can I do for you?'

'I'm looking for some rooms to rent for myself and my daughter.'

'You foreign?'

'Does that matter?' Karl countered pleasantly.

She seemed amused. 'Not up in Portswood, luv. Have a word with Mrs Driver, number a hundred and forty-two. She often has rooms.' She glanced at the sombre young girl by his side. 'You at school?'

'My father teaches me.'

The woman nodded. 'You probably get better learning that way.' She paused, before asking, 'Looking for work too?'

Karl nodded. 'I can do most things. I can teach –'

'I didn't mean as a teacher.'

'I can do odd jobs,' Karl went on hurriedly. 'You name it, I can probably turn my hand to it.'

'You work cheap?'

He smiled wryly. 'Is there any other way?'

Returning the smile, the woman continued, 'There's the brewers – they've got some vacancies, I think. Oh, and there's a pub up in Churchgate. I heard they were looking for someone to help out on a part-time basis. Nothing fancy, mind you, but it might tide you over.'

He was touched by the offer of help. Stockport was going to be the Promised Land, after all.

'What's the pub called?'

'The Sixpenny Winner. Cross town, go up to Churchgate and then ask, everyone knows it.' She looked at Elise. 'And you could get a job in one of the factories up there –'

Karl stepped in at once. 'Not Elise, she's not going out to work.'

'Suit yourself,' the woman replied, not unkindly. 'But if times get hard, they're always looking for workers at Henessey's or the brewers.'

The woman had been right, Mrs Driver did have rooms available, but they were grim, in one of the terraced squares in Portswood. The two rooms on the top floor of an old house looked out over the backyard privies and a rough patch of dry earth.

'I won't 'ave any trouble,' Mrs Driver said, a fat woman in curlers. 'You and your daughter are lucky I don't mind foreigners –'

'I'm only half German,' Karl interrupted her.

'Aye, but which half? The bad half, I'll be bound.' She sighed expansively as though she was doing them a favour talking. 'There's many round these parts who aren't so open-minded.' She paused, fiddled with one of her cheap hooped earrings. 'No wife?'

'She's dead,' Karl replied, his tone even.

'Well, that's not going to set you out from the crowd round 'ere. Plenty people lost relatives in the war.' She studied Elise with curious eyes. 'How old's yer daughter?'

'Sixteen.'

'I can see she's the quiet type. And that's good. I don't want girls running wild with the local boys. I won't 'ave that in my house. No mucky business.'

'You'll have no trouble that way,' Karl replied emphatically. 'Elise will be at home most of the time, studying.'

'Fer what?'

'I'm educating my daughter in the hopes she might be a teacher someday,' Karl replied proudly. 'I was a tutor myself once. Elise speaks German, French and English and she knows a lot about history and culture.'

'Not much use when you work in a factory, though, is it?'

Karl looked mortified, but his voice was even. 'My daughter is not working in any factory, madam.'

The word 'madam' effected a sudden change in Mrs Driver. Smiling, she drew herself up to her full height and smoothed down the creases of her blouse. She had a gentleman lodger, she thought. That would shut everyone up around these parts. Fancy, a gentleman *and* an intellectual. Elegant too. The clothes might be worn, but they had been good once.

'Well, yer welcome. Just pay your rent on time and keep out of trouble and you and your daughter'll do all right.'

When she left the room Karl turned and walked over

to Elise, who was looking out of the window. The sun had gone in, the grim row of the terraces now seeming foul and low, the door of one water closet hanging open from a broken lock.

'We won't stay long,' he promised her. 'I'll get a job and we'll go somewhere better.'

She turned and rested her head on his shoulder. 'I don't mind, Dad. Honestly I don't.'

Stroking her hair, he was thoughtful for a while before answering her. When would he manage to give her a good life? It was all right educating Elise's brain, but what good was that when she was surrounded by such squalor? He would get her out, Karl thought grimly. She deserved better. She deserved more.

'You may not mind, my love. But I mind. *I mind.*'

'Bloody hell, Doug!' Ada snapped. 'I've told you, get back to bed. You're no good to me in pain. Rest that back of yours.'

He was leaning against the doorframe, his face ashen.

'I can cope –'

'And I'm Winston Churchill,' Ada retorted. 'Get back to bed. I've told you, I can cope. There's a man coming this afternoon to help out – if he's any bloody good, that is.' She fumbled around for the piece of paper on which she had written his name when he had phoned earlier. 'He's called Straub –'

Doug's eyebrows rose. 'German?'

'I don't care if he's Himmler, if he gets the work done. I'll send some food up for you. Freda's cooking some pies.'

He flinched.

'Oh, come on, Doug! This can't go on for ever, you know. You can't live the rest of your lives this way.

The two of you have to split – or learn to get on somehow.'

'Never,' he replied coldly, turning and painfully making his way upstairs.

In the middle of cooking, Ada had just dropped a bag of flour on the floor when she heard a knock at the back door. Cursing, she tried to rub off the white mess on her apron, and called for Vicky. Then she realised her daughter was out with Stella and hurriedly wrenched open the door herself.

'Yes?'

'Mrs Hargreaves?'

'Who wants to know?' Ada replied, wiping her hands and staring at the tall figure who was silhouetted against the light.

'My name is Straub. Karl Straub.'

Nodding, she stood back and watched him walk in. Good God, she thought, he looks like a damn count or something. And the accent made him even more unusual. It was, she said to Douglas later, like having Bela Lugosi in the kitchen.

'I advertised for some help, Mr Straub. My son-in-law's hurt his back and we need someone to do the heavy work for a while.'

Karl nodded. 'I can do that.'

'I dare say you can, but can you do it well?' Ada countered, studying him. 'We've had a couple of workers here who were full of how good they were and turned out to be useless.'

'I won't let you down.'

'You don't look like a jobbing workman, Mr Straub, if you don't mind my saying so.'

He smiled. 'I was a teacher before the war.'

'So why don't you go back to teaching?'

Karl hesitated. 'I lost my job, and my reputation. Someone said I'd stolen some money –'

'Out!' Ada said at once.

Karl stood his ground. 'I stole nothing –'

'I'm not interested, Mr Straub.'

'Please, hear me out. For years, I kept in touch with the people who dismissed me. Only the other month they finally admitted that they had been wrong, and now knew that someone else was responsible for the theft. They admitted that I had been innocent all along.'

Ada was unconvinced. 'So why did they frame you?'

He shrugged. 'I'm half German. And I was living and working in England when this country was fighting the Germans. No one trusted me – even though my mother had been English. The name Straub damned me. There's more: I'd also been very successful in my profession and I'd gained a promotion over my colleagues, who were English.'

'Ah,' Ada said thoughtfully, 'but if you've got this proof of innocence, you could go back to teaching. Couldn't you?'

'I might. In time.' He paused, holding her gaze. 'But I need a job now. I'm not a criminal. I'm honest, reliable, and desperate.'

For a long moment Ada studied him, then said simply: 'It's long hours.'

'I can do that.'

'And we'd want you to live in. It's easier.'

'Oh.'

'That a problem, Mr Straub?'

'I have a daughter, madam.'

This was news. 'Doesn't her mother look after her?'

'Her mother's dead.'

'That's hard. War?'

'Before the war. She died of cancer, when Elise was a child. I've looked after my daughter ever since she was five. Elise is always with me . . . We have rooms in Portswood at Mrs Driver's.'

'Dear God! You've got your girl up there? The place is a dump, and I should know,' Ada said firmly. 'How old's your girl?'

'Sixteen.'

'Not a little one then?'

'No, she's quite grown up,' Karl replied, hoping against hope that the job wouldn't evaporate because he had responsibilities.

'Must be hard, bringing up a girl alone,' Ada replied sympathetically. 'We need help at the moment because of Douglas's being ill, like I said. But we are looking for someone permanent too.'

'Would you consider me, Mrs Hargreaves?'

'I don't know!' Ada replied honestly. 'That's jumping the gun. We have to see how things go. You prove yourself and maybe we'll take the matter further. Besides, you might miss your teachery ways.' She paused before continuing. 'How old are you?'

'Forty-two.'

'Too old to be silly any more, that's good. I have two daughters, and neither of them is looking to fool around. Do we understand each other?'

He smiled, warming to her.

'I understand. But you haven't asked me about my past.'

'Seems to me like you've volunteered enough to keep me occupied for a while,' Ada replied evenly. 'Look, I don't judge people any more, Mr Straub. Seems to me that it's a waste of time. You need a job. I need help. What's complicated about that? Besides, you have a daughter. Any man who can look after a child alone seems all right by me. I'll take your daughter as your reference.'

Karl nodded. 'Thank you.'

'Oh, don't thank me yet. Work hard and prove yourself and you can work here full time. There's two rooms at the top of the house which could be yours and your daughter's – get you out of that rat run at Myra Driver's.' Ada never had had the two second-floor rooms knocked through to one. 'But if you mess up, get lazy or greedy, you're out.' She brushed some of the flour off her apron again, a mist of white dust flying up into the air between them. 'Do well and you might end up with a permanent job and a decent home for yourself and your girl.'

He nodded eagerly. 'I won't let you down.'

'Oh, we'll see about that,' Ada replied pragmatically. 'I don't go on promises any more – just performance.'

Chapter Thirty-Nine

Pushing the pram down Churchgate, Vicky paused as she noticed the trap door open in the street outside the pub. Was Doug back up on his feet again? she wondered, walking over and peering down into the cellar. A tall, bearded man was heaving some beer barrels around, sweat pouring off his face and soaking into the shirt on his back.

Surprised, she walked round into the kitchen, Ada looking up as she came in.

'You were gone a long time.'

'We were in the park,' Vicky replied, lifting Stella and putting her on the rocking chair. 'Who's in the cellar?'

'Karl Straub, our temporary cellar man.'

'You found someone already? I thought Doug was getting better.'

'He will, if he rests up. Karl's going to fill in.' Ada paused, looked round at the pies she had made and counted them. 'Anyway, we need more help since your husband left.'

Vicky winced. 'I don't want to talk about Duncan –'

'No one does, but we have to admit things have been hard work without him. How d'you think Douglas did his back in? Doing the work of two men.' Ada stopped, listening. 'Hear that?' she asked, pointing to the cellar beneath their feet. 'That's the sound of a man working. Poetry, sheer poetry.'

'Straub's a foreign name –'

'German.'

'German!'

'Oh, come on, Vicky, he's only half German. And he's paid for that. His wife's dead and he's been bringing up his daughter alone for years. Now, if being German makes him the Antichrist, fine. But to me, he looks good.'

Frowning, Vicky picked a bit of pastry off the side of one of the pies. 'Is he living here?'

'Only if he proves himself and we take him on full time.'

'What about his daughter?'

'She'll come too.'

'Here!'

'No, the Manchester Ship Canal!' Ada retorted impatiently. 'Of course here. Where else? I'll move into the back bedroom on your floor and they can have the top two rooms.'

'It'd be cramped.'

'It'd be cheap,' Ada retorted. 'If we let them live here free, we don't have to pay him so big a wage.'

'How old's his daughter?'

'Sixteen –'

'Sixteen!'

'Is there a bloody parrot in here?' Ada countered, her hands on her hips. 'Why are you so against Karl Straub working for us?' She paused, shaking her head incredulously. 'Oh, I see. If they come here, there's no room for Duncan –'

'I never said that!'

'Good! Because I tell you here and now, if I thought you had any feelings left for that man I'd have you certified. And if I ever set eyes on Duncan Oldenshaw again, he'll leave here in a wheelchair.'

Thoughtfully, Vicky regarded her mother. 'Does Freda know?'

'About what?'

'Karl Straub.'

'Yes, she knows. And no, he isn't her type. Besides, your sister would never dare to fool around again, not now. She's learned her lesson once and for all. It was a hard lesson and, God knows, it hurt all of us.' She sighed. 'Anyway, Karl's not that kind of man. He's the old school, like your father and Douglas – respectable, the kind of man you should have married. An educated man.'

'Pushing around barrels of beer?'

Annoyed, Ada stared at her daughter. 'Hard work's nothing to be ashamed of! He used to be a teacher in Cheadle.'

'Really? What happened?'

For some reason Ada jumped to Karl's defence. 'Ask him to tell you the story himself. He told me in confidence. Anyway, he's taught his daughter three languages. So if pushing around beer barrels is good enough for him, it should be good enough for you.' She looked at her daughter, disappointment obvious. 'You've changed, Vicky. Not so long ago you would have admired someone with his qualities.'

Stung, Vicky looked away, her mother watching her. 'You know,' Ada continued, 'something came back to me the other day. Something you said that day. The day Billy died . . .'

Vicky tensed, waiting for her mother to continue.

'Just before Freda told Douglas about Billy, you told her to stop, to shut up.'

Her heart hammering, Vicky kept her head bowed.

'It made me think. Did you know about them all

along? Did you know your sister and husband were having an affair? Did you know that Billy wasn't Douglas's child? Because if you did, Vicky, why did you marry Duncan Oldenshaw? Why would you do that? Why would you *want* someone so low?' Again, Ada paused to let the words take effect. 'So I have to ask you, Vicky, although I won't ask you ever again, did you know about their affair? Did you know about Billy?'

Jesus, Vicky thought, it's finally come – the question she had dreaded for so long. Her startled, guilty reaction *had* been noted. It had taken a while, but finally her mother had remembered. And now she wanted the truth. And if she got the truth? Vicky wondered. If she told Ada – *yes, I knew everything* – what good would it do? It would just add to the distrust, her mother despising *her*, watching *her*, as she watched her sister.

And it would be worse than that. Ada would no longer think of her daughter in the same way, as the wronged wife, the good one. What she had done was bad enough, Vicky thought – and she was too much of a coward to add to it.

So she lied.

'No, I didn't know anything about Billy. Or that they had had an affair before we married.'

The lie bounced off the walls, Ada noting it.

'Subject closed now.' She turned, busied herself again. 'Be fair to Karl Straub, Vicky, give him a chance. We all need that in life. He might not be exciting or flashy, but he deserves some admiration.'

Still shaken, Vicky looked away. What her mother said was true. She *would* have admired Karl before, but now she saw him as a threat. The five of them had managed well enough alone: faced gossip, scandal, the exchanged looks and whispers that had become daily currency. And they had survived. Suddenly the thought of someone new coming in was unwelcome. Strangers brought trouble, Vicky thought. They filled up all the empty spaces where memories had lived, untouched, for so long. Soon there would be no place left for the past. The vacuum would all be filled as life moved on. Whether she liked it, or not.

The following day Doug staggered down into the pub, to find Karl polishing the brass work. He studied the tall man curiously, noted the dark hair and trimmed beard, and the wiry arms. A tutor, Ada had said – well, he didn't look much like a tutor now.

'Hello there,' Karl said, looking up and spotting him. His smile was welcoming. 'You must be Douglas?'

He nodded. Karl Straub – a foreigner, an outsider. Like they all were, in a way.

'I felt a bit better, the back's mending. But slow.'

'This is a nice pub,' Karl replied, turning the cloth over in his hands. 'You get a lot of trade here?'

'We do all right.'

The conversation was strained, leaving Karl non-plussed. He had been welcomed by Ada, although her daughters had given him a wide berth. At first he had put it down to being part German, but gradually Karl had overheard gossip and was beginning, slowly, to put two and two together. Now he was looking at Douglas Oldenshaw, the man who had been betrayed by his wife and made a laughing stock. The man who had turned in on himself.

'You'll be back serving again soon then?'

'No,' Doug said simply. 'I don't like people.' Karl hesitated, waiting for him to continue. 'I suppose my mother-in-law explained the situation to you?'

'Some of it.'

'I used to serve in the pub, but I don't now,' Doug explained, his voice a monotone. 'When my back's recovered, I'll be working in the cellar and helping out with the books. But not mixing.'

He looked white, puffy around the gills. Like someone who had held in tears too long, Karl thought. Jesus, he knew what that felt like.

'Ada needs help in the bar,' Doug went on after another long pause. 'If you turn out to her liking, she'll probably ask you to help her serving.'

'I'd like that.'

'Good.'

Standing awkwardly with the cloth still in his hand, Karl wondered what else to say. Douglas Oldenshaw wasn't the most forthcoming of men.

'You've got a daughter, I hear?'

'Elise, she's sixteen.'

'But no wife?'

'She's dead.'

A moment lingered between them before Doug answered: 'You're a lucky man.'

God, Karl thought as he watched him go, that was a hell of a thing to say. What kind of man wished his own wife dead? Then he thought of Freda, of what he had heard about her. Maybe she had been wild once, but she wasn't now. She seemed melancholic, her mother never letting her out of her sight for long. How could people live like that? Karl wondered. How could you eat and sleep with such unspoken hatred in the very air you breathed? And then he wondered if they did – in some uneasy way – actually need each other, bound together not by love, but by trauma.

'Karl,' a voice said suddenly behind him.

He jumped, surprised to see Vicky standing in the bar, Stella holding on to her hand.

'Ma wants you in the yard,' she said simply, turning away and then turning back. She was ashamed of the things she had said about him when he had first come and was now anxious to make amends. There was too much bad feeling in the house, without adding to it. 'You're doing a good job. Ma likes you.'

Relieved, Karl smiled, Vicky smiling back without thinking. He had a good smile, from the eyes.

'I'm glad. I'd like to stay here,' he said honestly. 'Your mother said that if it went well I could move in with my daughter. Elise would like that.'

'Nice name. Elise.'

'She was named after her mother.'

Vicky nodded, uncertain of how, or if, she should continue the conversation.

'Mrs Driver's place isn't so good, is it?'

He laughed from deep in his chest, Vicky warming to the sound.

'It's terrible! I worry about Elise being there so much of the time whilst I'm working, but she's a good girl. She stays in, studying most of the time.'

Interested, Vicky moved a little closer. 'Studying? What?'

'Languages, Art, English History. She wants to be a teacher some day.'

'A teacher . . . You must be very proud of her.'

'She's my reason to live,' he said simply, glancing at Stella. 'Your daughter's pretty. Very dark hair.'

'Like her father's,' Vicky replied, then stopped short.

The moment of comfortable conversation had ended. The oblique reference to Duncan had stepped into the room between them, breaking the peace.

'Forgive me, Karl, I have to go. Pop out and see Ma, will you, when you've got a minute?'

A little while later, Karl was in the yard, watching Ada chasing a large tomcat over the back wall. She was flicking a tea towel at it, the cat jumping out of her way and landing on the top of the outside privy, staring at her meanly.

'I can't believe my eyes!' Ada exclaimed when she saw Karl. 'Trudie Mossop had a cat that came in the pub and sprayed up the side of the dog's cabinet for years. Well, for nearly six months there's been no sign of the cat. Run over by the rag-and-bone man, someone said. Either way, it were dead. And that made me a happy woman. But now . . .' Ada stared at the cat on top of the privy, '. . . Trudie Mossop's gone and got herself *another* bloody cat! And judging from the look of this mean sod, it'll be peeing up the side of that case before you know it.'

Karl laughed, looking at the cat. 'Handsome animal.'

'It'd look better stuffed,' Ada replied, turning back to Karl. 'I wanted a word with you. You've not been here long, but I like the way you work and I like having you around. You've a nice way with you, Karl, a happy way, and God knows, we could do with some cheering up here.' She paused, wondering if she was jumping in too soon, and then went for it. 'You want to move in with your girl now? Get to work serving in the bar and helping me out?'

He was flushed with pleasure.

'Well, Karl, what d'you say?'

'Can't you tell from my face?'

'It's hard to tell anything under that foliage!'

They laughed together, Ada punching him lightly

on the arm. 'Get yourselves moved in over the week-end,' she went on. 'I'll have the rooms cleared upstairs. There's a bathroom up there too – a bit poky, it used to be a boxroom, but it'll have to do. Anyway, it's indoors, which is more than some can boast round here.'

He had stopped smiling, his head bowed.

Surprised, Ada looked at him: 'Have I said something wrong?'

He shook his head, mute.

'Oh, bugger it!' she snapped, 'I have, I've said something wrong. I'm always putting my foot in it.'

Blowing his nose loudly, Karl looked up. His dark eyes were teary. 'Thank you, thank you so much,' he stammered. 'I'll never forget your kindness and I'll never give you a moment's worry, I swear.'

Embarrassed by the show of emotion, Ada floundered, then, seeing the tomcat move back towards the pub, lunged after it.

'Head him off, Karl! That bugger's heading for the cabinet! HEAD HIM OFF!'

Upstairs, Freda was sitting by the bedroom window, looking out and seeing nothing. On the bed lay Doug, resting his back, pain making him even more withdrawn. Neither spoke. But both of them heard the laughter coming from the yard outside.

And it echoed, hollow, in their hearts.

Chapter Forty

Elise would always remember her first sight of The Six-penny Winner. Walking down Churchgate beside her father, she saw the large entrance doors of the pub, flanked by the windows with heavy, frosted glass. At the top of the windows were stained-glass panels, like a church, but from the outside no one could see in. Certainly not Elise, that chill June evening.

She was carrying a small suitcase with her clothes and books, Karl taking the larger case with his clothes and their few, shabby belongings. They walked with their heads held high – Karl had taught Elise that – but they were a poignant sight in hand-me-down clothes and shabby shoes.

It was threatening to rain when Karl entered the back gate, urging his daughter to follow him. In the kitchen, Ada was baking, Vicky helping her. The room smelled of warm bread and pastry, an immediate welcome to Elise, but sad at the same time. It had been years since she had been in a proper home.

'Well, hello there,' Ada said, wiping her hands and beckoning for the two of them to come in. She regarded Elise with interest: composed, pretty in a severe way, and shy. 'So you're Elise?'

She nodded, flushing.

Across the kitchen table, Vicky smiled at her. 'Welcome. We've been looking forward to your coming. That's Ma, I'm Vicky – and this is Stella.'

Relaxing, Elise walked over to the toddler and kneeled down. 'You're lovely.' Stella gurgled happily, while Elise stroked the baby's hair. 'What a pretty baby you are.'

'Oh, come on!' Ada urged Karl. 'Don't stand there with your coat on, looking like the rent man. Come in and take the weight off your feet.' She turned to Vicky. 'Put on the kettle, luv, will you? We could all do with cup.'

'I can do that –'

'Oh, *you will*, Karl,' Ada teased him, 'but for tonight, we'll treat you. Tomorrow it's all hands on deck again.'

Vicky watched in amazement as, far from it being a difficult situation, Karl chatted to Ada, and Elise played with the baby. A sudden, violent rainstorm bounced off the tin roof of the outside privy. Karl had taken their belongings upstairs and now sat relaxed in the kitchen, his sleeves rolled up. Elise's reserve was only apparent with the adults, Vicky noted. With Stella she was at ease, instinctively loving.

The evening drew on, Ada opening the back door to let the sweet smell of the rain come in. In the rocking chair in front of the grate, Vicky nursed Stella. The baby was fast asleep, Elise dozing off beside her, her head, slumped onto her arms, resting on top of the kitchen table.

'Don't disturb her,' Ada said in a whisper to Karl. 'Let her sleep.'

'I've never seen her do that before,' he replied. 'She finds it hard to relax normally.'

'The food was drugged,' Ada said, Karl laughing loudly.

'Shh!' she warned him, walking to the back door and sitting down on the step. A moment later, he joined her.

The rain had stopped, only occasional drops dripping loudly into the water bucket outside. A low, indigo sky pushed down onto the top of the terraces, the sound of Winter's Clock chiming far in the distance. Smoking a strong cigarette, Karl let the smoke trickle from his lips, his beard momentarily obliterated by a grey cloud. Surreptitiously, Ada sniffed the air. It had been a long time since she had smelled that same aroma, the old tobacco Clem had smoked.

'So, do you miss your old life?' she asked, keeping her voice low so as not to waken the sleepers behind them.

'Things change, and you can't stop it. You have to move on, or give up.'

Ada thought of Freda and Douglas upstairs. They hadn't come down and there wasn't a sound from above.

'We had a big house in Cheadle . . .' Karl began, Ada looking at him with surprise. He wasn't bragging, just remembering, '. . . with a cleaning woman and a gardener. My wife came from a rich family and I wasn't without my own funds. Sometimes – on summer nights like these – we would sit together for hours. Saying nothing. Just sitting, knowing everything and nothing. Heaven.'

Ada smiled, remembering her own past. 'Me and my husband were slum fodder, came from up Portswood way.' She glanced over to Karl. 'You know the place so I don't have to draw you a map. We were as poor as they come, but we thought we could do anything. He loved me, and I loved him. That was enough for us to take on the world. Not that he was ambitious, mind – I was always the one who wanted to get on. But he would have stood by me to the end – and back again.'

'What was he called?'

'Clem . . . What was your wife's name?'

'Arlene Elise.'

Ada nodded. 'Not many Arlenes in Portswood.'

They laughed again, softly, muffling the noise with their hands.

'I think Elise will be happy here,' Karl said after a moment. 'She's needed a stable home base for a long time.'

'Well, I don't know that it's so stable. There's many round here who would tell you different.'

Thoughtfully, Karl inhaled, then asked: 'What about your other daughter? Freda?'

'What about her?'

'Don't you worry? About her and her husband living like they do?'

Ada's voice hardened. 'She made her own bed, she can lie in it for as long as it takes.'

'To do what?' Karl asked, his sympathetic nature roused. 'What can she do to make up for the past? And Douglas – what will he do? None of it was his fault.' Ada hung her head, Karl misreading the gesture. 'Forgive me! I didn't mean to interfere.'

'You weren't. You were just voicing my own thoughts, Karl. I've been wondering about them for a while. It's hell up there, in their room. When I go in – and I don't much – there's an atmosphere which makes your flesh creep.' She looked towards the side entrance leading to the ginnel. 'I have the same feeling about that place. It's bad. Something hangs around there. I don't know what, but something that's bad luck.' She smiled, embarrassed. 'Listen to me going on! I never talk such rubbish usually.'

But he wasn't prepared to let her shrug it off so lightly.

'That's all we can expect from life, isn't it? To keep away from the dark spots, to listen to what we feel inside and keep to the light.'

Ada turned, surprised. 'You're a poet at heart, Karl Straub.'

'Everyone is,' he replied, as though surprised she didn't already know.

'I don't agree,' Ada said quietly. 'There are some right bastards out there. You never knew my son-in-law Duncan Oldenshaw. There was a bad sod.' She paused, wondering how much he knew. 'Just in case you haven't heard, he killed his son in an accident. Didn't mean it, I'll give you that, but it happened. I told him to clear off afterwards – and he did.' She shook her head at the memory. 'I didn't think he would, you know. Always thought he'd come back, that he'd feel *driven* to come back. But he never did.'

'Where is he now?'

'God knows,' Ada replied. 'In hell, if I had my way.'

'And he left Freda behind to face the music alone,' Karl said thoughtfully. 'She must feel bad about that.'

'She hates him. In fact she hates everyone,' Ada replied, sipping at her mug of tea and shivering as the night cooled. 'She hates her husband for not being Duncan, and Duncan for running off. And Vicky for setting the whole bloody awful mess in motion. She didn't mean it, but she wanted to get rid of Duncan and ended up . . . Oh, what the hell, life goes on. Oh, how it *does* go on.'

'And gets better.'

'If you say so, Karl.'

'I say so,' he repeated, smiling and getting to his feet. 'Now, you go up with Vicky and I'll tidy away.'

'But –'

'As a thank you, Ada,' he replied, 'please, let me. It's a hard lesson, I know, learning how to accept thanks.'

*　　*　　*

392

'You and Karl were having a good long chat last night,' Vicky said lightly to her mother as Ada brought in the ledgers.

With a bump she let them drop onto the kitchen table and then reached for her glasses.

'We were just nattering, like a couple of old women.'

Vicky studied her mother. 'You like him?'

Ada was staring at the ledger in front of her, and answered distantly. 'Karl? Yeah, I like him.'

'He's not much younger than you –'

'Have you seen my pen, Vicky? I had it with me first thing, but I'm damned if I can find it now.'

Smiling, Vicky pushed the pen over to her mother. 'It was on the floor, under the table . . . So, like I say, he's not much younger than you.'

Frowning, Ada peered over her glasses. 'Who?'

'Karl.'

'So what?'

'I just thought,' Vicky blundered on, 'that you two might . . . you know, you might . . . you know . . .'

'No!' Ada replied. 'I've no idea what you're talking about.'

Vicky took in a deep breath and then rushed on: 'I wondered if you and he might get to like each other.'

'But I *do* like him already!' Ada said impatiently, flipping open the ledger.

At once, Vicky put her hand over the page to obscure her mother's view.

'Ma, Karl Straub's a nice man. You could do a lot worse.'

There was a momentary pause before Ada burst out laughing. 'Well, now I've heard it all! My own daughter matchmaking! Me and Karl!' She laughed again. 'Oh, luv, it's not like that. A man and a woman can talk without falling in love.' She was still chuckling. 'You're a right romantic, Vicky. Honestly, *me and Karl!*'

Flushing, Vicky tried to make light of it. 'All right, all right! I just wondered –'

'Me and Karl!' Ada said again, shaking her head. 'Oh, Vicky, you really have no idea, do you, luv? No wonder you got in such a scrape with Duncan Oldenshaw.'

Vicky winced. 'I thought it might be nice for you to meet someone.'

Ada was on her feet in an instant, taking her daughter's shoulders and looking into her face kindly.

'It was a nice thought, pet, honest, it was, but your dad was the only man for me. And as for Karl, he's not my type –'

'But you said he was educated. You were singing his praises the other day.'

'As a man, not a husband!' Ada replied lightly. 'Besides, Karl Straub's not interested in me that way.'

'How on earth d'you know that?'

Ada tapped the side of her nose. 'Instinct, my love. Something *you* might do well to develop.'

She would run away, Freda thought. It was simple. That was the only option open to her. With loathing, she glanced over to the sleeping Doug – or was he feigning sleep? He did that often enough. But who cared any more? She wanted out, wanted to get away from this cursed pub and family, get away from memories and the thought of Billy. Billy, Billy, Billy, her son, Duncan's son. Gone. Both of them. Gone.

Only she remained here, in this damned place, with a man who looked at her as though he wanted her dead. But never said it, never shouted, hit her – never did anything which would break the malignant hold of their rage. So they could never move on, never forgive, forget, or even part. They were locked into a foul bondage, hate sealing them together like bricks in a wall.

She would have to get out, or go mad. And now this man had arrived, this Karl Straub. She had heard him laughing, talking to her mother, acting normally, bringing joy back into the house. And soon he was going to serve behind the bar, usurping her position, everyone of them relegating her further and further to the back of the queue. She was a mother no longer, a wife only in name, and she had no job left.

A foreigner had stolen that . . . Gulping at the night air as though drowning, Freda turned over in bed. *Was* Doug asleep? Her hand rested for a moment against his. At once he moved his hand away, Freda closing her eyes against the darkness. She would have to get away. It was true that Ada wasn't watching her as much now – she had no need, after all. There were no men in Freda's life. No chance of meeting any, no desire, if the truth be known. Besides, who would mix with Freda Oldenshaw? She was an outcast from the town's women, who had always mistrusted her, and too troublesome for the men. She would have to get away, she told herself again.

But there were the practicalities to think of. She had no money, no friends, no qualifications to get herself a job – nothing. Her whole life had been within the family, her job the pub, and then as a mother and wife.

She had nothing to equip her for the world outside. Besides, she was afraid . . . God, Freda thought, turning over and over repeatedly in bed, Doug silent beside her. She never thought Duncan would leave her like that, *never*. Never thought he would escape whilst she rotted in a prison of her own making.

One which she couldn't escape. One which she knew she deserved.

'Have you seen the way those two have moved in?' Bessie said to Lizzie when she called round later that week. 'Think they owned the place.'

'He's serving behind the bar now –' Lizzie skidded to a halt, flushing. 'Mac told me.'

'Oh, so you two are talking again, are you?'

'We never fell out,' Lizzie replied, a little too eagerly. 'Mac thinks the world of me.'

'Not enough to marry you.'

'Who said I wanted to get married, Bessie?'

'Sorry, my mistake,' she replied mischievously. 'It wasn't you I saw looking in the jeweller's shop window then?'

Lizzie flushed. 'I was looking at a watch.'

'For the third finger of your left hand? Funny watch,' Bessie said, pausing to greet a customer who came into the shop.

She served the woman hurriedly, overcharging her for some indifferent oranges. Amazing how she kept open, Lizzie thought. You gave better food to pigs.

'So,' Bessie said, when her customer had left. 'What about the German and his daughter?'

'He seems nice enough.'

'The girl's quiet.'

'That makes a change in that place,' Lizzie replied, still smarting from the ring comment. 'She wants to be a teacher.'

'She might *want* to be the King of Siam, but that doesn't mean she'll do it,' Bessie replied. *A teacher!* Who did she think she was? There weren't enough positions for English people, let alone foreigners.

'She's not really foreign. He's only half German –'

'Hah! That's what he says.'

'– and the girl spends a lot of time with little Stella,' Lizzie went on, taking off her hat and patting her hair.

Stunned, Bessie looked at her friend. 'What the hell have you done to yourself?'

'I went to the hairdresser's,' Lizzie said, flushing, 'had a change.'

'You're a blonde!' Bessie replied, laughing. 'Good God, Lizzie, you look like Harpo Marx!'

Annoyed, Lizzie touched her coiffed head. 'Mac likes it.'

'His wife had a poodle once, I'm not surprised.'

'Oh, Bessie, you've a wicked tongue and no mistake!' she retorted, hurt. 'Anyway, we're going on a day trip to Blackpool – Mac and I.'

The news wasn't welcome. Bessie hadn't been away for long enough – and not with a man.

Meanly, she leaned towards her friend. 'You know what they say about Blackpool, Lizzie?'

Her face was all innocence. '*What* do they say?'

'People go there for one thing and one thing only. And I don't mean the ice cream.'

Pleased to see her friend miffed, Lizzie got to her feet and moved to the door, smiling. 'Is that a fact, Bessie? Well, I never did.' She paused to deliver the final blow. 'They do say blondes have more fun, don't they?'

Bending over the pushchair, Elise looked down at Stella and winked. It was a hot day, the sun on the park lake reflecting back the sapphire sky. Together she and Vicky had walked Stella all morning, talking easily, Vicky glad of a friend, Elise revelling in female company.

Many topics had been covered over the weeks since

Elise had moved into The Sixpenny Winner. Vicky was bored, looking for company and so was Elise. It was the perfect setting for friendship. But until now Elise had never mentioned the past, the rumours she had overheard. There was no point asking her father about it; Karl never gossiped, so she had waited until the right moment arrived to ask Vicky.

Her curiosity had been heightened by the re-emergence of Freda. The shadowy figure of Elise's first weeks at the pub had now become substantial, Freda leaving her room more and more, coming down to help Ada out, or offer to walk Stella. To say that Elise found Freda fascinating was an understatement. She had never seen anyone like her before. Tall, blonde, oozing a kind of electric attraction, Freda was easing herself back into life. Everything she wore, Elise noted: the fine stockings, straight skirts, the shiny hair piled on top of her head. And the make-up, very subtle, but getting the most out of Freda's good looks.

Elise was also mesmerised by the effect she had on people. Walking down the street Freda attracted attention effortlessly. At first she seemed to dread it, but as time went on, she changed. Now the world could look and go hang itself, Freda's expression seemed to say. She was back in the land of the living.

Looking at the calm water of the lake, Elise turned her face up to the sun, Vicky's voice a soothing murmur in the deck chair next to her.

'D'you want to go to the cinema this week? There's a Bette Davis film on.'

The thought excited her. It would be a relief from books, from learning.

'I'd love to!'

'Good,' Vicky said simply, watching Stella as she ate an ice cream.

'I've never been to the cinema before. Dad never took me.'

'You'll like it,' Vicky replied, preoccupied. 'What was it like, being with him all the time?'

Elise opened her eyes and smiled. 'You know Dad, he was always good company. Even when people were cruel, he was always the same. Patient, kind. When he taught me at first, I was stupid, couldn't get the hang of things, but he was never angry. No one could have a better father.'

Studying Elise's profile, Vicky pressed her: 'Do you remember your mother?'

'Not really. I remember only that things were so hard when she died. Later, when Dad and I were on our own, all I seem to remember are the train stations, the buses, the walks to find rooms, lodgings.' She sighed to herself. 'Some people slammed the door on us when they heard our name. Others told us to get back to our own country. But this *is* our country. I saw my father cry once. He doesn't know this – he thought I was asleep. We had been moved on and had nowhere to go, so we slept the night in an air-raid shelter.'

'I suppose you hate this country?'

'No, my father taught me not to. He said we had been very happy here once. And one day we would be again. Hatred is pointless, he repeated over and over. Nothing is worth it – because hating takes more out of the person who hates than the hated.'

Vicky nodded. 'Sounds like him.'

'Sometimes I wonder how much he misses his old life, though. He was an important man, you know. People admired him, looked up to him. We lived in a big house with gardens and trees all around. We had a car . . . He was asked to give talks and my mother used to get all dressed up to go and listen to him.'

Surprised, Vicky thought of the man who now served in The Sixpenny Winner, a man with no anger, no resentment for the way his life had turned out.

'Was he never bitter, Elise?'

'About what?'

'Life. Losing his wife, his job, his home?'

'My father doesn't think like that,' she replied, turning to look at Vicky, her tone earnest. 'He's a good man.'

Yes, Vicky thought, he *was* a good man, and she hadn't appreciated that. Perhaps she couldn't recognise a good man any more. It was true that there was none of Duncan's flashy looks or sexuality about Karl, but when she was talking to him she felt relaxed and laughed a lot. She had never laughed with Duncan. Her time with him had been fraught with problems, deceit. She had been so blinded by infatuation that she would have done anything for him.

And in return, she would have got nothing – no love, no caring. He had never been in touch since running off, not a word to her or to their daughter. If he had simply left her, it would have been hard, but to turn his back on his own child – that showed him for what he was. And he was despicable.

'What about your husband?' Elise asked suddenly, cutting into Vicky's thoughts.

She jumped as though prodded with a branding iron. '*What* about him?'

'What was he like?'

'Think of your father and then imagine the opposite,' Vicky replied after a long moment.

'Do you miss him?'

If the question had been asked a few months earlier Vicky would have said no, but felt otherwise. Now she could honestly say that she seldom thought of him. Why was that? Had she come to her senses – or was someone else occupying her thoughts?

'No, I don't miss him. I don't miss his lying or his dishonesty.'

'But you must have loved him once?'

Vicky smiled. 'You know, for a girl of sixteen you're very wise, Elise. I never had a conversation like this with my mother or my sister. You're old for your years.'

Elise flushed. 'Is that bad?'

'No!' Vicky responded, laughing. 'It's fine, just fine. Don't lose that common sense of yours. Life takes some funny turns, you might need to keep a clear head.' She looked back over the lake. 'I was a bit like you once, wanted to get out and do things with my life. But I ruined my chances by being stupid, by loving the wrong man. Don't you do that, Elise. Don't ever forget what your father's taught you, or stop being yourself.'

Silence came between them.

Finally Elise spoke again. 'We'll always be friends, won't we? I don't ever want to move on again, go away, leave you and everyone else at The Sixpenny Winner. I couldn't bear it.' Her voice dropped, unexpected panic setting in. 'I couldn't bear it, honestly I couldn't.'

Without thinking, Vicky put her arm around Elise, then felt the girl rest her head on her shoulder. She said nothing else. The action was comfort enough. With one hand Vicky held on to Elise, with the other she grasped the handle of her own child's pram. The sun kept shining down, the water still, a swan gliding towards the little island in the middle of the lake.

For an instant Vicky's mind played a trick on her. Under the sun she could suddenly see a little boy, crying out excitedly and calling to her. Billy, the child who had died. Billy, whose death had changed everyone's life.

But now, finally, that pointless death might serve a purpose, bringing the hope of a new life in its wake.

Chapter Forty-One

Doug was only sure of one thing – he didn't like Karl
Straub. It grated on him to see how much he got on with his
mother-in-law, how he had so effortlessly been promoted
from handyman to bar keeper. What next? Perhaps Ada
would like to give the accounts over to him? Or maybe
there was a raise in the pipeline?

Having been so savagely duped, Doug no longer trusted
anyone. His days – mottled with the pain from his bad
back – were punctuated by stabs of resentment and
unease. If his own brother could betray him, surely a
stranger would? As for Karl Straub, who was he? Oh,
Doug knew what he told them, knew the hard luck story,
but was it true? Was anything true any more?

He had half expected Freda to make a play for Karl, and
when she didn't, Doug felt a strange sense of disappointment. Maybe he had wanted something else to blame her
for, something more to pile onto the heap of her sins. But
it never happened. Freda was polite with Karl, but remote,
just as she was with Elise.

The place was too small for so many people, Doug
thought angrily. In the past he would have thrown his
doors open to anyone, but that was the past, and look what
a fool he had been taken for then . . . Sighing, he got up off
the bed and stretched, his back easing momentarily.

He was still useful, talking with the suppliers, ordering
in, keeping the books with Ada, but his heyday had gone.
The pub seemed grim to him now, the sound of people's

laughter grating on his ears. Even when Ada played the piano – which he noted she did more and more – the sound brought him no comfort.

Raw from bitterness, he had let himself sour inside. At first he had thought he might grow to forgive his wife, but now he could hardly bear to look at Freda. For a man who was not, by nature, vicious, he was now a master in cruelty. He knew that she had wanted forgiveness, so he had withheld it – just as he withheld any physical affection.

Doug knew only too well how much that would affect Freda, with her high sex drive. As for himself he was too sick with bitterness to care. But how long would she hold out, he wondered. How long before she fell back into her old ways? Who would be the next conquest? The next Duncan? So when she touched him, he flinched, avoiding eye contact, the months passing in a welter of frustration.

Loneliness was Doug's punishment. His skin ached from the lack of tenderness. He longed for Billy, for the child he had thought of as his son, and still did. Billy might have been Duncan's child in reality, but it was Doug who had been the only father Billy recognised. Sometimes he would think back and try to remember if Duncan had ever shown any particular interest in Billy, ever tried to stake a claim, even subtly. But Doug could remember nothing like that. His deceit had been perfect, as had Freda's.

A sound overhead broke into Doug's thoughts. Elise was walking about. She was a quiet one, he thought, never got under the feet, and was obviously close to Vicky. And besotted by Freda . . . Doug sighed, stretched. He would have to pull himself together, have to start again. This inertia wasn't like him, it was alien and frightening. He had been a happy man before, a lucky man, making the most of whatever life had to offer. Surely he could get back that feeling? That optimism? Surely it was possible?

Then he saw his wife walk in and turned away, his spirits flagging.

'We have to talk,' she said firmly.

He ignored her.

'Doug! I said we have to talk –'

'What about?'

'Oh, so you *can* still speak then?'

Turning, he looked her in the face for the first time in months. 'Yes, I can speak, Freda. I just don't want to speak to you.'

She flinched, but held her ground. 'We can't change the past, Doug. We have to live in the future.'

'Very profound. Did you get that off the back of a box of matches?'

Stung by the retort, Freda hesitated for a moment before continuing. 'What are we going to do?'

'About what?'

'About us!'

'There is no us,' he said coldly, walking over to her. 'There hasn't been any *us* for months.'

'But, Doug –'

'I don't want to talk about it!' he said hurriedly, trying not to get into an argument. He had to keep his temper, he must never lose his temper again.

'You're my husband –'

'Oh, you remember. You forgot that for a while, though, didn't you?' His voice was controlled. 'Don't try to make things up with me, Freda. If my bloody brother had asked you, you would have gone off with him and left me without a second's look.'

They both knew it was true, and Freda had the courage not to deny it.

'But he didn't ask me, did he? And now there's just you and me left –'

'Without Billy.'

She swallowed, glass in her heart. 'It wasn't my fault that Billy died.'

'Indirectly it was.'

'Do you think I wanted it?' she snapped. Doug turned away from her. Infuriated, Freda caught hold of his arm and yanked him round. 'Do you think I wanted it?'

'Get off me!' he shouted, shaking off her grip. 'Don't touch me again.'

'So we're never going to touch each other? *Never?*' she countered desperately. 'We can't live like that! No one can. We can't share the same house, the same bed. For God's sake, Doug, punish me. Shout at me, hit me, but don't do this. Don't freeze me out, flinch when I touch you. It's too much to bear!'

'You feel bad now? Good! Because I feel like someone tore my heart out.' He caught hold of her hair and pulled her towards him. 'I loved you. I thought you were my world. And when Billy came along, I thought there wasn't a luckier man on earth. But it was all a lie, wasn't it?' He pushed her away, Freda falling back on the bed. 'You want me to make love to you again? Never! I would rather cut off my right hand.'

'You bastard!' she screamed as he moved to the door. 'Why don't you leave if you hate me so much?'

'Why should I? This is my home.'

'It wasn't before you married me.'

He turned, a chill in his voice. 'Look, I'm not moving out, Freda, not to please you. If you hate it here, why don't *you* leave? Find some man to support you. It should be easy enough.'

'I'm no whore!' she screamed, her fists clenched. 'And

I've had enough! You can wallow in your own mire, Douglas Oldenshaw, but I've taken all the humiliation I'm going to take. From this moment onwards, I'm getting on with my life. I'm getting some time away from here. A chance to breathe.' She moved to the door and then turned back to him. 'And the first thing I'm going to do is to get a job.'

It was at times like these that Ada missed Clem most. If he had still been alive she would have gone upstairs, laid down on the bed next to him and talked. But there was no Clem now, and she wasn't the kind of woman to pop off to the cemetery and talk to his headstone. Fat lot of advice you'd get from a slab of granite and a bunch of dead carnations.

Sighing, Ada pushed away the account books and stood at the window, looking out. Bessie Cork passed and waved, followed shortly afterwards by the Cooper family from the other end of Churchgate. Bet his wife doesn't know he's having a fling, Ada thought, remembering a conversation she had overheard in the pub.

The trouble was that men and women couldn't keep their hands in their pockets. They either thieved with them or fooled around with them. Suddenly Ada spotted a woman at the end of the street and leaned forward to get a better look. My God, she thought, Dulcie Granger, still on the game by the look of it. Avidly she watched Dulcie move by on the other side of the road, skirting the pub. Good thing, Ada thought, she and Clem had rid the place of her type long enough since.

Clem. Clem. Clem. Ada sighed again. Was she imagining things? After all, she was just going on a hunch. Oh yes, but her hunches were normally pretty accurate, she thought. If she had acted on a few before, she could have saved herself a lot of heartache.

So *was* Vicky interested in Karl? And *had* she seen Karl looking at Vicky in a way normally reserved for spotty fourteen-year-olds? No, she must be wrong, Ada told herself, Karl was reserved with women. But then Vicky did get on with his daughter very well . . . Bloody hell! Ada thought irritated, why didn't people just come out with things? If they liked each other, that was fine. They could go out together, maybe go dancing.

Yes, and she could buy a motorbike, Ada thought wryly. What the hell would Karl look like at the local Co-op dance? And as for Vicky – hadn't she had enough gossip in her life without adding to it? Karl was viewed with suspicion and had a daughter in tow. What kind of catch was that?

A good one actually, Ada realised to her own amazement. Karl might not be that young or that handsome, but he was sound, reliable, and a father. He knew about children; perhaps he would be one of the few men who would welcome a stepchild. But would he make a good father for Stella? Of that Ada had no doubt. She had seen Elise – that was advertisement enough. His daughter was sensible, pretty and caring. A little too serious perhaps, but that was no bad thing in this day and age. Besides, Karl had been a man of standing, once. It wasn't his fault that he had been reduced to such circumstances. And he was doing his level best to improve himself, working hard, serving in the pub with her.

Wickedly, Ada smiled to herself. She had done it deliberately, of course, making a virtue out of The Sixpenny Winner's notoriety. By putting Karl to serve at the bar she made sure that people came to gawk and talk about him – the foreigner at the pub in Churchgate. They wanted to hate him, but he won most over. Had a good ear, Ada thought, could listen to anyone. And offer advice, good advice too.

In fact he was becoming something of a local father confessor, she thought, smiling again. Oh Clem, you would have enjoyed this . . .

But were Vicky and Karl Straub suited? She didn't want another disappointment for her daughter, or for Stella. It could be a wonderful chance of happiness – or a recipe for calamity.

Either way, Karl Straub was a bloody sight better than Duncan Oldenshaw . . . Ada had asked around about her missing son-in-law, but no one knew anything. Or so they said. Lizzie once told her that someone she knew had told her that someone they knew had seen Duncan in Australia. But then, who could put faith in anything Lizzie said?

It hadn't mattered to Ada where the bastard Duncan was, but times were changing, and it might – *might* – become important. If Vicky and Karl got close, they might want to make things legal – and that would mean divorce. More scandal, but necessary scandal. Ada wasn't going to let anyone live in sin under her roof.

So for the first time in ages Ada wanted to know where her son-in-law was. She hoped that he was an *ex*-son-in-law, but felt sure she would have heard something if that had been the case. Duncan was alive, but where? Turning from the window, she frowned. Maybe she was taking things too quickly, but then again, Vicky was a fool when she was in love.

Ada knew her daughter couldn't think clearly for herself at such times, so she had to think for her, make sure that *if* she had another chance at happiness, no one buggered it up. And certainly not Duncan Oldenshaw.

So where are you, you sod? Ada wondered. Up to no good, I'll be bound. Thieving from some gullible fool or seducing some silly bitch who's fallen for the white teeth and the easy patter. I know you're alive, Duncan, I know you're breathing and living somewhere. And by God, I don't want you back, I just want to make sure there's nothing you can do to stop my girl having a second chance.

Still deep in thought, she turned – to see Doug watching her. For an instant she didn't recognise him, his figure darkly silhouetted against the back light of the kitchen.

'Sorry if I startled you, Ada.'

'I just didn't hear you come in. How's your back?'

'Better.' His voice seemed unnaturally controlled. 'I want to do more. Get busier.'

Ada knew she should be pleased, but there was something about Doug which unnerved her. Far from being the easy-going son-in-law, he now seemed like a person ready to explode.

'Don't rush it, Douglas,' she replied, 'just take your time. Backs don't heal overnight.'

He was still silhouetted against the light, a dark figure with a flat, emotionless voice. 'I've spent enough time lying around. You can think too much.'

Was he trying to tell her something?

'About what, Douglas?'

'You know.'

'No, tell me.'

'About what happened, Billy, Freda – and my brother.'

Strange they should both be thinking about Duncan at the same time, Ada thought.

'Have you heard anything about where he is?'

'No. Have you, Ada?'

'Nothing.'

'He could be dead.'

'We should be so lucky,' Ada said, wincing as the joke came out.

For a long instant Douglas stood still, a sinister silhouette. Ada couldn't see his face to read his expression, and then, finally, he spoke again.

'It's all my fault.'

'What!'

'I should never have let him in here,' Doug went on. 'I should have turned him away that night. You told me to. You knew all along, but I ignored you, begged you to give him a chance.'

'Douglas, this is not your fault.'

'It is!' he said, his voice hoarse. 'He ruined everything, took my wife, Billy – and I let him in.'

'Stop it!' Ada snapped, scared as she walked over to him. 'This has to stop! Enough is enough, Douglas –'

'Enough is never enough,' he replied, turning, his face coming into the light.

Oh God, Ada thought, noting the livid, red scratch marks on his neck.

'What the hell happened to you?'

'My *wife* . . .' he paused on the word, '. . . lost her patience with me. But I didn't strike back, Ada. I never would. I know how to keep control now, how to keep my emotions in check.' He touched the marks absentmindedly. 'They don't hurt.'

'Freda should never have done that –'

He cut her off. 'Oh, but she should. We punish each other, Ada. That's what our lives are for. I know that now. We live to remind each other of what we did. Of what we ruined. She looks at me and knows, I look at her, and know –'

Startled, Ada interrupted him: 'Jesus, Douglas, stop it! This is no way for anyone to live.'

'It's *our* way,' he said. 'Like they say – for ever and ever, until death do us part.'

Chapter Forty-Two

Since arriving at The Sixpenny Winner many months earlier, Elise's confidence had grown steadily. For the first time in her life she felt part of a family. It didn't seem as though Ada was her father's employer, but his mother. From being curt at first she had warmed to both Karl and Elise, and now included them in everything. They ate together, with Vicky, and Karl was often asked his opinion – although Ada just as often rejected it. Which was just like a real family behaved.

Only Douglas and Freda kept their distance. Elise wondered about that and was surprised by their obvious hatred of each other. No one told her about Billy – only that he had been Freda and Douglas's child, who had been killed in a terrible accident. Nothing more was said. Instinct told Elise that there was more to it, but she didn't dare ask anyone – even her father. Besides, if he knew, he would have told her. They had never had any secrets.

Which was how she knew that her father was in love with Vicky. He hadn't come out and said as much, but he had hinted that he was interested, almost feeling his way with his daughter, to see if she would approve. Approve! Elise thought, she would like nothing better. If her father and Vicky married she would have a real family, and a stepmother, a woman she liked and could talk to.

But then Vicky was still married, Elise thought, frowning.

Her father came in at that moment, walking over to the

window where she was sitting and looking down at her books. In one quick movement, he slammed them shut.

'Hey!'

'You need a change,' he said, smiling. 'You work too hard.'

'You never said that before,' Elise replied, certain that she knew who might have put the thought into his mind. 'I thought you wanted me to work hard.'

'I do. But you need some time off too.' He sat down beside her, looking cramped in the small wicker chair. 'Did I ever tell you how proud I am of you?'

'Every day.'

'Good,' he replied, smiling broadly. 'You've a clever brain, Elise, and you'll go far. You'll make a better teacher than I ever was.'

She shook her head. 'Never!'

'You will,' he insisted, 'I know that for a fact. You like learning – I do too – but you need to know more about life now.' He paused, picking his words carefully. 'I brought you up the only way I knew how. I wanted to keep you with me and teach you to give you the best chance I could, because you'd lost so much in other ways.' She tried to interrupt, but he hurried on. 'I know it was difficult growing up without a mother. I couldn't talk to you about the things girls need to talk about to another woman. I knew that sometimes you missed your mother, but I did what I could.'

'Dad, what's this all about?'

'I suppose I just want to know that I did a good job,' he admitted finally, Elise taking his hand and squeezing it hard.

'No one could have done better.'

'I don't know about that. When I think back to all the times you were alone, when I had to leave you to go to work ... You were so self-contained, so cut off.' He paused, remembering. 'It wasn't the best life for a child.'

She was surprised and showed it. 'I was happy with you! I never felt I missed anything.'

'You had no fun.'

'*You* were fun,' Elise replied, laughing. 'We had good times, Dad.'

'Hounded from pillar to post? Thrown out of places, insulted?' He shook his head. 'No, they weren't good times.'

'I don't see it like that,' she replied honestly. 'You looked after me. I was safe –'

'But you had had so much when you were little. We had had your mother, money, status – and then it all went. You and I became nomads, Elise. Maybe I was too busy worrying to notice what effect that was having on you.'

'What effect *did* it have on me?'

'It made you old before your time,' he replied. 'You look older, act older. You're nearly seventeen and you could be a woman in her twenties. That's my fault. I never let you be a child, did I? You never had friends because we were always on the move. You never went to kids' birthday parties, or a school with your own peers. You never talked to girls, or laughed with them. You were always with me. Always with me.'

'I never wanted to be anywhere else,' she replied, suddenly alarmed. 'I don't understand – do you want to send me away?'

Flinching at the suggestion, he kissed the back of his daughter's hand.

'I would never send you away! You're my life, you goose! I was just worrying, thinking you might feel that you'd missed out.' Reaching forward, he hugged her to him Elise's cheek resting against the rough cloth of his shirt. 'Are you happy here?'

'Very.'

'Me too,' he admitted.

She could hear his heart beating, the sound echoing in her ear.

'You like Vicky a lot, don't you?'

He tensed, then answered her. 'Well, she's a very nice woman.'

'More than that,' Elise replied, still leaning against her father's chest. 'I think you're a bit in love with her, Dad.'

'How would you know about such things?' he blustered, pulling away and looking into his daughter's face. 'I said you were old beyond your years.'

'And female,' Elise replied, teasing him. 'I see the way you look at her and the way Vicky looks at you. I think she likes you.'

He flushed, patently delighted with the thought. 'You two talk a lot. Has she said anything?'

'No.'

His face fell, Elise laughing. 'But she asks about you all the time.'

'She does?'

'Oh, yes, she asks about what you like to do, what you believe in, what you did before you came here.'

He was unconvinced. 'Anyone might ask those questions.'

'They might – but they wouldn't ask them the way she does.'

'Like how?' Karl said eagerly.

'Like she needs to know,' Elise replied. 'Oh, Dad, I like her too. A lot. I can talk to her and I really love Stella . . . Do you want to marry Vicky?'

'Marry her?' he repeated astonished. 'Good God, Elise, we hardly know each other.'

'So it's not serious?' she asked mischievously, watching her father's face.

'Well . . . I'm not sure if it is. It might be . . . I've never been interested in a woman since your mother died.'

'You never knew Vicky before.'

He nodded, then sighed. 'I shouldn't be talking to you about this! It's not fair.'

'Why isn't it fair? Who else cares about you the way I do?'

'I don't want you to feel left out.'

She laughed, punching him lightly on the arm. 'Oh, come on! I want to see you happy, Dad. You've done everything you could for me. For years I've come first. Now it's time you thought about yourself.'

He was touched, his voice faltering. 'You're a good girl, Elise.'

'Or I might be very devious.'

His eyebrows shot up. 'How so?'

'I might want to have Vicky in my life too. I might want her around just as much as you do,' Elise replied, her tone picking up. 'You're being too timid about this, Dad! I think Vicky likes you a lot – and I think you should say something to her. Or make a move – you know, ask her out, test the water.'

He was amazed, seeing his daughter in a whole new light. Who was this knowing young woman he had raised so wise?

'How do you know so much about courting?'

'I've told you – I'm female,' Elise said evenly. 'It comes naturally.'

'But I'm not Vicky's equal. I work here –'

'So?'

'I'm an employee; her mother pays my wages. Why would Vicky look at me as a catch? I'm not young, certainly not good-looking. I've no money, no home of my own, nothing to offer her.'

'Except honesty, love, affection, all the things you offered me.' Elise paused, then added, 'And if they make Vicky as happy as they made me she'll be a lucky woman.'

Douglas was fast asleep when Freda slipped out of bed and pulled on her dressing gown. Silently she moved down the stairs, pausing once when she thought she heard a noise. Then she moved on. The kitchen was in darkness, listless moonlight giving the only illumination as Freda walked to the back door. Noiselessly she opened it, then slid out to the ginnel exit, standing, looking out.

Her mind flicked up a series of memories and faces: lads from years earlier, even the late Mr Cork walking over to chat to her. She had been like a knowing angel, standing in her own grimy niche, the lamp overhead lighting her. Men had wanted her, come to look at her, talk to her, try to seduce her. But that wasn't really what Freda had wanted. Not so much sex, but power.

She had used that back exit like a picture frame, letting the dark brickwork act as a sordid backdrop to her own perfection. On show, she had acted the role she had made for herself – the teasing, unobtainable siren calling from the squalor of the ginnel. The local women might have thought she was easy, but she hadn't been. She had never given herself too easily away. And that – coupled with her heady sensuality – was why the men all wanted her. And how they had come to her, adored her. What power she had had to turn their heads, make them dream, long for her. Make their hearts bleed with aching.

But no one came any more . . . Freda stood in the exit, looking out. The ginnel was empty, the air cold as she drew her dressing gown tightly around her. Where had it all gone so wrong, she wondered. She could have had any man she wanted once. And who did she pick? The one who destroyed her.

Her eyes closed. She wanted to hate Duncan, but couldn't, could only remember the lovemaking, the times of total abandonment. Times when they were locked together and in some other existence where there was no pub, no Stockport, no greasy streets. Just them, the two of them. They had made love, laughed. Then, when they parted, they had caught at each other as they passed, too mad for each other to resist touching.

They had had a child too. And lost him . . . She looked down the ginnel and found no peace. She gulped in the night air and found no peace. She slammed her hands against the brickwork and dragged her knuckles along it until they bled, and still she found no peace. Then, suddenly and mercifully, the panic subsided.

Taking one last long look at the ginnel Freda closed the back door and locked it. Then she crept up the stairs and returned to her bed.

Only then did Ada move. She had been unable to sleep and had come down to think. In the darkness she had been startled by her daughter's emergence, thinking for an instant that Freda was back to her old tricks. But instead she had witnessed a despair she had not suspected. And wished she had not seen.

'*Hamlet!*' Vicky said, brushing her hair as Elise played with Stella on the bed. 'You want to see *Hamlet* at the Roxy?'

'Why not? They say that Olivier's wonderful in it.' She

tickled Stella as she wriggled on the coverlet. 'Oh, come on, Vicky, you like that kind of thing as much as we do.'

'*We?*'

Guileless, Elise looked up. 'Dad and me. We're going, and we want you to come with us.'

Vicky felt her heart racing. Oh God, she thought, she was getting involved. She was feeling something for a man again. Was it wise?

'Oh, I don't know, Elise –'

'Well, I do,' she replied firmly. 'Dad wants you there.'

'He said that?'

Elise looked away. Well, one little white lie didn't really matter, did it? Didn't Karl call them 'holy lies'?

'Yes – he said he wanted you to come, and would I ask you.'

Pleased, Vicky kept brushing her hair. She had found herself more and more interested in Karl, laughing at his jokes and trying to adjust to his emotional nature. Never before had she known a man who showed his feelings so readily. Karl could be moved to tears by listening to music on the radio, or by reading something which affected him. He didn't seem to care what people thought either, although Ada loathed such displays of emotion.

Only the other night they had been listening to Rachmaninov on the radio, when Ada had come in to find Karl's eyes moist.

'What's happened?'

'Nothing,' he had said simply. 'We were just listening to the music.'

'Jesus, I thought someone had died,' she had said, walking over to the radio and twiddling the knob. '*Much Binding in the Marsh* is on, that'll do you more good, Karl. It doesn't do for a man to cry, it's weakening.'

'What are you smiling at?' Elise asked, breaking into Vicky's thoughts.

'I was just thinking about my mother,' she replied, putting down the brush and getting to her feet. 'Tell your dad I'd love to go to the cinema.'

'Good. Tonight, at seven –'

Vicky raised her eyebrows. 'Tonight! What about Stella?'

'Ada said she'd look out for her.'

'You little sneak! You knew I'd say yes!' Vicky teased her.

'I hoped you would,' Elise replied, getting to her feet. 'We'll meet you at the Roxy –'

'But we all live in the same house,' Vicky said, baffled. 'Why don't we go together?'

Wrong-footed, Elise blustered on, 'Oh, Dad has an errand to run first. So we'll meet you there? At seven, don't forget. Seven o'clock.'

It was ten to seven when the rain started and drenched everyone in the cinema queue. Karl pulled his trilby further down; Elise ducked under the inadequate cover of a torn awning. Nervously she looked round for Vicky. God, please let her come, she thought. It had been hell getting her father to agree to the trip. Karl disliked the cinema – the seats were too cramped, he said. But in the end he had been persuaded because it was Shakespeare, little realising what surprise his daughter had in store for him.

'Here,' Karl said, taking off his trilby and putting it on Elise's head. Several sizes too big it fell down halfway over her eyes. 'It'll keep the rain off you.'

'Oh Dad!' she admonished him. 'I'm OK.'

Cold, he stamped his feet to warm them. 'It's bitter for October. And it's not even winter yet.'

Absent-mindedly, Vicky looked round, repeatedly pushing up the trilby as it slipped down her face. There was no sign of Vicky. Maybe she had guessed that she had been set up and had decided not to come, Elise thought. Maybe she had been wrong all along and Vicky wasn't interested in her father. Oh God . . . Still, if that was the case it was better that Karl hadn't known and been humiliated.

Anxiously, Elise looked around again.

'What *are* you looking for?' Karl asked, his dark hair plastered to his head with the rain.

'Just looking.'

'I never thought there would be a queue for *Hamlet*,' he went on, his hands deep in his pockets, his brow furrowed. 'I didn't think I would get soaked to the skin either. It had better be worth it, Elise.'

'Oh, it will,' she said, half-heartedly, her eyes still scanning the street.

There were only three people ahead of them in the queue when Elise finally saw Vicky. She was running down the High Street, a bright red headscarf covering her hair, her coat flapping in the cold and rain. Breathlessly she arrived, Karl turning and looking at her in amazement.

'I thought I might be too late,' Vicky gasped, smiling at Karl.

He didn't know what was going on, but was faint with pleasure.

'Too late – for what?'

'*Hamlet*!' she said, laughing. 'Elise said we should all meet up here at seven and I was running late. Stella wouldn't settle, I lost my bag and then I had to run all the way.'

Giving his daughter a knowing look, Karl smiled warmly at Vicky.

'You made it, though, and that's all that matters,' he said, pinching his daughter's arm. 'It wouldn't have been the same without you.'

Delighted that her ploy had worked so well, Elise made sure that Vicky sat on one side of her father and she the other. Satisfied, she then settled down to watch the film, taking off her father's trilby and putting it under the seat. Sandwiched between the two women Karl felt light-headed. His beloved daughter had organised this, he thought. His child had set him up on a date! He could have laughed out loud – nearly did, once, but controlled himself. As for *Hamlet*, there was nothing the Prince of Denmark could do that night to unsettle Karl Straub. As Olivier raged on the gigantic screen, Karl could only glow as he felt the warmth of Vicky's body only inches from his.

And yet he was so anxious not to make the wrong impression that he sat with his arms and legs tightly controlled. God, it wouldn't do for Vicky to think he was brushing himself against her . . . Karl flushed at the thought. Vicky was a lady; he would have to court her properly. He would take it slowly, get to know her, treat her well. It was imperative that he do this right. He knew now that she was the one he wanted, and he wasn't going to mess this up. Maybe he could take Vicky and Elise out for the day, to Southport perhaps. That was a good idea. Southport was classy, someone had told him, not like Blackpool. Yes, he would take them to Southport, that would be good . . .

He laughed suddenly, the sound just stopping short in his throat. Wedged in his too small seat he was locked like a mummy into immobility, Hamlet raging before his eyes, the two women he loved sitting on either side of him. He was a god, a pharaoh, a king. He was giddy, silly, young again.

He was in love.

Chapter Forty-Three

'I've got a job,' Freda said suddenly.

Surprised, Ada set down the cup of tea she was drinking. 'What kind of job?'

'Lennox Hats, in Hyde.'

'Not Alma Tomkins's place on Sutton Street?' Ada said, her eyebrows raised. 'That one's a right madam. Thinks she's everyone, and since her husband got that car –'

'I start Monday.'

Ada took in a deep breath. 'Well, it would have been nice to have talked about it a bit, but I think it's a good idea.'

Still on the defensive, Freda hurried on: 'Oh, and I don't need a chaperone.'

'No, you don't. I don't think you're going to do anything stupid now, Freda.'

'Think I've learned my lesson?'

'Haven't you?'

Warming her hands around the cup of tea she had poured herself, Freda stared into it. A single tea leaf was floating on the top.

'Gypsies say that's news.'

'Huh?'

'A tea leaf at the top of your cup is supposed to mean news,' Freda repeated. For a moment she stayed silent, then spoke again, her voice low. 'I'm sorry for what happened, Ma. I've meant to say that to you for a long time, but I couldn't. I was too . . . angry with everyone, especially myself.' She paused, still looking into the tea. 'I *did* care about what happened to Billy.'

'I know. I never doubted that, Freda.'

'Really?' she asked bitterly. 'I wonder. People round here think I was responsible. I suppose I was.' She looked at her mother, for once helpless. 'But I didn't know what would happen to Billy! Anyway, I've paid for it, over and over again – even if you don't think so. I *know* what you think of me, Ma, the way you look at me –'

Stung, Ada interrupted her. 'I don't hate you, Freda.'

'You did once.'

'I hated what you did. But I didn't hate you.'

'Well, if it's any consolation, I hate myself enough for you and Vicky.' She said the name as though it was sour on her tongue. 'Things are looking up for her again, aren't they? Seems like she's got an understanding with Karl. A romance is blossoming.'

The jealousy was there, Ada could hear it. In fact, she had expected it for a while. Which was why she wasn't against Freda getting a job. It *was* time for her to get out of the pub. She could imagine how it felt for Freda to see Vicky happy again, to know that her sister had a man who loved her, and a surrogate daughter.

From being the cocksure adulteress Freda had turned into a loveless, bitter loser. Ada studied her daughter, forgiveness finally coming.

'Will they marry?'

Ada shrugged. 'Vicky's already married, Freda.'

'She could get divorced.'

Carefully Ada studied her daughter. Was there some remnant of hope there? If Vicky divorced Duncan, did Freda *still* think she could make it work with him? Then

Freda looked at her mother, and Ada knew that was the last thing on her mind.

'Time will tell. Vicky might get a divorce.'

'She would have to find Duncan first, unless she's going on grounds of desertion. Then all she has to do is wait.' Freda's eyes narrowed. 'Of course she could accuse him of adultery – and cite me.'

'I don't think your sister would do that,' Ada said, flinching at the scandal it would cause.

'Then again, we could be really lucky. Maybe Duncan's dead. That way Vicky won't need the divorce at all, will she?'

Shaken by the venom in her tone, Ada shifted in her seat and changed the subject.

'D'you think you'll like working at the hat shop?'

'I dunno,' Freda admitted. 'That Tomkins woman thinks she's a fashion plate. Have you seen those hats? God, who wears things like that?'

Ada shifted in her seat. 'Actually I bought one there a long while ago. The ribbon came off the brim second time I wore it. Cheaply made – not that I didn't pay a good enough price for it. And when I asked for my money back from Alma Tomkins –'

'She looks a right tartar and no mistake. Still, it's a job. And a chance to get away from Doug for a while.'

'I know how bad things are between you two.'

'*Bad*. Yes, they're bad!' Freda agreed, her tone bitter. 'Guilt's kept me here for ages, Ma. But no longer. I've had enough. If Doug wants to wallow in misery, he can. But not with me. It's over between us.'

Alerted, Ada looked her daughter straight in the eyes. 'Is that why you want a job? Because you're looking for another man?'

To Ada's astonishment, Freda burst out laughing.

'A man! I want peace of mind, Ma, and that hasn't come with any man I've known.'

Looking through the window of her shop, Bessie Cork stared at Mac Potter as he stopped to tie his shoelace. What the hell was he wearing, she thought, and what had he done to his hair? It was parted down the middle, slicked back, his face shiny with scrubbing.

But Lizzie's away, Bessie thought, then smiled to herself. Oh, yes, Lizzie was away. And while that particular moggy was away, this particular rat will play. But where was he going? Putting down her duster, Bessie craned her neck to watch. Mac walked along, then hesitated. Immediately she ducked back so that he wouldn't see her. Then he moved on. Bessie came round the counter and walked to the door.

Well, fancy that! she thought. Mac Potter, all tutted up, going into The Sixpenny Winner. And not just for a pint, she thought, oh no, them were courting clothes. It must be catching, Bessie thought, first that German walking out with Vicky and now Mac trying his luck. But with who? Surely not Ada Hargreaves? Bessie tried not to laugh. The man was a bloody fool and no mistake.

Still, it would be interesting, almost worth going to the pub to watch. But then again, her being a tee-totaller, she would have to wait until Lizzie got back. Or Mac got thrown out of the pub. Whichever was soonest.

'How do?' Mac said as he walked in. Ada turned to greet him and then stopped short. Slowly she took in the parted hair, the shiny face and the best suit.

'By hell, Mac, you out to propose?'

425

God, he thought, she were quick off the mark and no mistake. 'Well, Ada –'

'All decked out, and looking grand,' she went on, eyeing him up and down and secretly thinking he looked like something that had fallen off a float. 'Quite the lady's man.'

'There's only one lady I'm interested in,' Mac said hopefully.

'Would I know her?' Ada countered, her sympathy going out to the long-suffering Lizzie. Mind you, she thought, Lizzie was bound to say yes. She would marry anyone for an army pension.

'You know her,' Mac said, twinkling.

'Does she come in here?' Ada teased back, Karl trying not to laugh behind her.

'You could say she's a regular,' Mac beamed.

Oh, she was a clever one, he thought. Teasing him, leading him on. Maybe it was going to be easier than he had hoped. Obviously Ada had had her eye on him for a while.

Meanwhile Ada was thinking of Lizzie and deciding that any woman desperate enough to marry Mac Potter deserved the bloody pension.

'A regular?' Ada repeated. 'Is she pretty?

'As a picture.'

'Of course, you're biased.'

'Others think she's a cracker too.'

Lizzie a cracker! The guy needed glasses, Ada thought, drawing Mac a pint and pushing it over the bar.

'You always know what I like, Ada.'

You've been coming here for years, I should do, she thought wryly.

'Well, I like to take care of my customers, Mac.'

'But some more than others?'

'I have my favourites,' she replied, hearing Karl snort behind her.

Carefully, Mac sipped his beer. A bit of Dutch courage never went amiss. 'Am I to take it that a certain lady has taken a shine to me?'

Lizzie's been stuck to you like a barnacle for years, Ada thought, baffled.

'I think you know well enough, Mac.'

He blushed, looked down at his pint. 'Perhaps that lady might like to take a walk with me?'

By God, Ada thought, Mac Potter certainly knew how to treat a girl.

'If you asked her nicely, I'm sure she would,' Ada replied, feeling almost sorry for Lizzie.

'Well then,' Mac said, leaning across the bar, his shiny face only inches away from Ada's. 'What d'you say?'

She frowned. 'What?'

'About that certain lady?' he went on, keeping up the subterfuge. 'Would she like a walk?'

Ada was losing patience fast. 'How the hell do I know? Ask her!'

Startled, he hesitated, then went in for the kill.

'Would you like to take a walk with me, Ada?' She blinked, momentarily losing the power of speech. 'Well, what d'you say?'

'I say that you haven't paid for that bloody beer, Mac Potter! And as for taking a walk with you, I would rather break the glass on this cabinet,' she waved towards the stuffed Sixpenny Winner, 'and take him for a run.'

Chapter Forty-Four

A good deal later that night, Ada went up to her bedroom and remembered what Mac Potter had said. She sat down on the bed, taking off her jacket. The room was cluttered and she would have to tidy it up, but housework had never been her strong suit. In fact, she hated it, only managing to keep the pub shipshape because she was afraid of losing trade, and face with her neighbours.

So for as long as she could remember, Freda had been doing the housework. She wasn't keen either, but although basically lazy, she liked the place tidy. Naturally Vicky looked after her own room and Elise looked after the rooms upstairs, hers and her father's. Now that was a careful girl, Ada thought approvingly. She kept home beautifully, dusted, cleaned, laid the fires, although Karl emptied the ashes, and generally made a little palace out of the rooms at the top of the pub. The rooms which had once been Clem's, then shared with Duncan, then, for a while, Ada's.

But now she was cramped into one room, which didn't bother Ada a jot as she spent so little time there. But she did miss Freda's housekeeping, Ada thought, ploughing through a stack of clothes on the bed as she searched for her reading glasses. She would tidy up, she would *really*. Tomorrow. Throwing off her shoes, Ada lay down, all thought of housework evaporating . . . She had never been a vain woman, even her enemies would admit that, but she had been pleased – God, how could she admit it? – at Mac's interest.

Not that she had any time for Mac Potter, or any other man. She had loved Clem and after him, well, no one else could come close. Ada sighed, fiddling with the belt on her skirt and undoing it. She was putting on weight, she thought. Still she was trim for her age, and hadn't got that many lines. Except for a few crow's-feet round her eyes. 'Laughter lines' they called them. Well, Ada thought wryly, she'd done plenty of bloody laughing over the years.

It wasn't her way to think too far ahead. Too many things in life altered at the last moment. There wasn't much point in planning. But she was pretty sure that Karl and Vicky would marry eventually. The thought pleased her. Vicky and Elise got on so well, indeed her daughter confided that she thought of Elise as her own child now. And it seemed as though Elise wanted to believe the same.

Elise had helped with Stella, and she and Vicky had become friends and confidantes. Ada knew how big a part Elise had played in her father's romance. The fact that she had succeeded had made the girl bloom. Feeling secure, she laughed more, was younger in her actions, her expressions. She was prettier too, her hair longer, loose around her shoulders, her clothes light-coloured. Far from being the serious little bookworm, she had now metamorphosed into a dazzling seventeen-year-old.

And Ada hadn't been the only one to notice. Over the past few months there had been more young men coming to The Sixpenny Winner, and it wasn't for the beer, Ada thought. They hung around, hoping to catch a glimpse of Elise and then rushed off, flushing, when they did. It was all so innocent, so sweet, so unlike the way the men had come sniffing around Freda years earlier.

Of course, if she had noticed, Ada knew that Freda had too. What did she feel, seeing Elise assume her previous role? She had said nothing, but Ada could sense her jealousy, or was it regret for the past? Whoever knew what Freda was really thinking?

Sighing, Ada sat up and looked at her reflection in the dressing-table glass. Beads and scarves hung from the mirror, an open pot of make-up on the top leaving a snail trail of white powder. At the back, an old perfume bottle stood to attention in the clutter. Clem had bought it for Ada almost twenty years earlier and although she had long since finished the scent, she couldn't part with the bottle.

Idly she touched her hair and smiled at herself. Mac Potter was an idiot, she thought. How could he really think she would be interested in him? As for Lizzie, she'd be hopping if she heard about it. It was always the same, Ada thought: if you ran after a man he wasn't interested; if you didn't give a damn, he came panting after you.

But he wasn't Clem. Not with that slicked-down hair and shiny suit. Not the way he slurped his beer and sang – out of tune – every time someone played the piano. Oh God, Ada thought, I might get lonely but I'll never be *that* lonely. Or maybe she would, years on. Maybe Vicky and Karl would move away and she would be left with Freda and Doug, the three of them rattling around the pub in grim hostility.

Bloody hell! Ada thought, getting to her feet. That was the trouble with thinking, your mind played tricks on you. Better to be busy. Hurriedly she picked up the clothes on the bed, ready to hang them all up and put them away. She would tidy the place, she thought nobly, get the room in order. The intention lasted all of five seconds. Then she stopped, chucked all the clothes onto the bed again, and headed back downstairs.

'No, don't look yet!' Vicky said, putting the finishing touches to the hemline of the dress Elise was wearing. 'Wait!'

The girl was giddy, dying to see what Vicky had done. Her first new dress, Elise thought, and not shop-bought, but made. For her. Just for her. Not a hand-me-down, not something off a second-hand stall at a market, but a new dress, in dark red wool with gold buttons. A dress any girl would be proud of, a dress she had never thought she would own.

Vicky had spent weeks working on it, her seamstress skills rusty. But she had been determined to see Elise in something young and attractive, not the dull clothes she normally wore. She's seventeen, she said to Karl, these are the best years of her life. I want to see her enjoy them.

If he was in love with her before, he was now besotted. Touched by the affection she showed his daughter, Karl looked upon the dress as a tangible display of love. Every stitch a thought, every hem a gesture of care. Vicky loved his child. And she loved him.

'Keep still!' Vicky commanded, Karl knocking on the door. 'No, not yet! You can't come in yet!'

'How long?' Karl asked, catching the excitement.

'A minute. Just wait outside!' Vicky repeated. 'I want you to see it as a surprise.'

Finally biting the cotton thread with her teeth, Vicky looked up at Elise standing on a stool. The girl was smiling, luminous in her red dress, her dark hair fanning her face. Full of youth, of hope.

'We're ready now. Come in, Karl.'

He walked in, saw his daughter and stopped dead, staring at her. Slowly he looked at the dress, then at Vicky, then back to Elise.

'Oh no!' Vicky said, laughing. 'You're not going to cry!'

Without answering, her hugged her, Elise getting off the stool and hurrying over to them. Hugging them both, Karl whispered in his daughter's ear, 'You're beautiful.'

'Does it suit me?'

'Does a crown suit a queen?' he countered, then looked at Vicky and kissed her cheek. His eyes were full of tears. 'I think I might die of happiness. I have the two women I love in my arms, and they're both beauties.'

Flushed with triumph, Vicky rested her head against Karl's shoulder, while Elise went to the mirror and looked at her reflection. She saw herself and then frowned, as though the image was disturbing. Slowly she turned one way and then another, the red dress flaring out at the skirt, her hair swinging in the still air.

'She knows,' Vicky told Karl, her voice low.

'Knows *what?*'

'That she's beautiful,' Vicky replied, feeling the girl's pride herself.

Karl was mesmerised, staring at Elise. 'You did that.'

Vicky nodded. 'It was a joint effort, Karl. You made her beautiful inside – I just finished the outside job.'

Resting against him, Vicky watched Elise run out of the room, calling for Ada. She was as dear to her as Stella, she realised, as much her daughter as the child she had with Duncan. She flinched at the memory of her husband, seeing the deceitful face and feral smile. Then realised that she needed something. More than that, she *craved* it. She wanted Karl Straub's child. She wanted to carry and give birth to Karl Straub's child.

'What is it?' Karl asked her, feeling Vicky tense in his arms.

'I can't say,' she replied, for once evasive.

He was suddenly alarmed. 'Vicky, what is it? It's not something bad, is it?'

'No. It's about us –'

'*What* about us?' his asked, alarm in his voice.

'You asked me something a while back,' Vicky went on carefully. 'Did you mean it?'

He frowned, then understood. 'I asked you to marry me.'

'What did I reply?'

'That you weren't ready to marry again.'

'Did I?' she replied, smiling. 'Did I really?'

His voice was hoarse with hope. 'You *want* to marry me?'

'Yes, Mr Straub, I rather think I do.' She felt his arms go around her, hugging her to him. This was a good man, Vicky realised; this was the safety of love. *This* was genuine.

'You mean it? You really mean it?' he asked her.

'Yes, I mean it,' she assured him, touching his cheek. 'I love you, Karl. And I love your child.'

'As much as I love Stella.'

She nodded. 'Yes. As much as you love Stella.'

'When can we marry?'

Tenderly Vicky touched his cheek. 'If I divorced Duncan on the grounds of adultery it wouldn't take long – but I couldn't do that, not to this family. You understand, don't you, Karl? There's been too much talk and finger-pointing; I'll not encourage more.' She

433

paused to pick her words with care. 'I think we have to wait, my love. After five years I can get a divorce on the grounds of desertion.'

'But that's so long –'

'Not too long. A year and a half have passed nearly, the rest will go quickly.' She kissed him urgently. 'We have each other, surely we can wait, Karl? Surely this is worth waiting for? I don't want to start our life together marred with bitterness and gossip. Let's do it this way, slowly. Quietly.'

Reluctantly he agreed. 'If that's what you want, that's what we'll do.'

'There *is* something else –'

He grinned. 'Oh yes?'

'I want *us* to have a child, Karl. One day, after the divorce, after we marry, when it's all sorted out, I want us to have a baby.'

Moved, Karl buried his head against her neck. He said nothing. Then, with infinite tenderness he took Vicky's left hand and kissed the palm, his lips resting for a long moment on her heart line.

Now into her third week working at the hat shop, Freda watched a regular customer trying on a hat. The woman turned her head from side to side, tipped it up and down, smiled at herself and then turned to Freda.

'What d'you think?'

'It's very nice, madam,' Freda replied, noticing Alma Tomkins watching her from across the shop.

The woman never seemed to let her out of her sight for long, the stout Mrs Tomkins wary of her new, good-looking employee. She didn't know much about Freda, only that when she first came she had been willing – and had grown less willing as the weeks passed.

'Are you sure it suits me?' the customer persisted.

Freda nodded, sliding the hat over to one side of the woman's head. 'There, that's better.'

'But it looks odd –'

'They're wearing them like that these days,' Freda continued, wanting to cram the hat down over the woman's head and shut her up. 'It's the fashion.'

The customer was not convinced. 'Maybe . . . but I don't know if my husband will like it. I'm going to a wedding with him, you see, and I want to look my best.'

They were all going somewhere, Freda thought – to weddings, christenings, or even to the shops. But it seemed all the women who came to Lennox Hats were living normal lives. They mentioned their husbands, their homes, their children, without realising how they scratched at Freda's fragile composure.

At first she had been so glad to get away from the pub, to be free, to be away from Doug. She had been cheerful, willing, trying to make friends. The women she worked with had responded, told her about themselves – and their lives. Their husbands, their children. Are you married? they'd asked. Have you got children? Every question chipped at the barrier Freda had built around herself. Every query resurrected Billy or reminded her of Douglas, waiting back home.

So she lied, made up stories. No, she wasn't married, she said and she didn't have children. At first she was terrified that she would be found out, but soon she didn't care. Anything was better than having to tell the truth. Besides, she was working in the nearby town of Hyde. No one knew about Freda Hargreaves – not Oldenshaw – in Hyde.

But the subterfuge didn't stop the questions. She was

so good-looking, the other women said, she *must* be courting. The implication was obvious – what was a woman of her age and looks doing on the shelf? God, it was almost a joke, Freda thought, wondering which was worse – to be thought a spinster, or be known as an adulteress?

'I think I'll try the other one on again,' the customer said, breaking into Freda's thoughts.

'Oh, for God's sake! Just buy the bloody hat!' she snapped, flinching as she saw Mrs Tomkins walking over.

'Miss Hargreaves, apologise to the lady!' she said hurriedly, the customer scarlet.

'Why?' Freda replied, sullen, her face set.

'Because you've been rude, that's why,' Alma Tomkins went on, red-faced. 'Apologise, or you lose your job.'

If she lost her job she would be back at the pub, would have to explain what had happened, or find other work. Which would bring up the same problems. Jesus, Freda thought, how did I get here? How did I end up here?

Reluctantly, she turned to the customer. 'Please forgive me. I have a terrible headache. I should never have spoken to you like that.'

'Well . . .' the customer said, hesitating, her face still crimson. 'I'm not sure –'

'You look wonderful in the hat, madam,' Freda went on, hating herself as she crawled. 'Your husband will love it and you'll turn heads. Please, buy it.'

When the customer finally left – with the hat – Alma Tomkins walked over to Freda, her florid face set hard. Here we go, Freda thought, here comes the telling-off. Having never worked outside the pub before she wasn't used to being told what to do. Instinctively rebellious, Freda wanted to shout at the woman, push her away, say – leave me alone, you don't know me, or what I'm like.

'Miss Hargreaves, I have to warn you that – headache or not – I will not tolerate such rudeness in my shop again. I took you on without a reference because you were new to shop work, and seemed enthusiastic. Please do not abuse my trust. This is a warning, Miss Hargreaves, mind your step.'

I want to step on *you*, Freda thought, her eyes blazing as she lowered her head. Humiliation was becoming second nature to her.

'Sorry.'

'You should be.'

'I am,' Freda replied, the woman's voice buzzing over her head as her thoughts ran on.

You don't know how sorry I am, lady. I'm sorry about this and so many other things that if I stood here for a year I couldn't apologise enough.

Finally Mrs Tomkins nodded. 'I'll let it go this time, Miss Hargreaves. But I'll be watching you,' she said, walking off.

You won't be the first, Freda thought.

For the remainder of the morning she worked diligently, charming to everyone, as only Freda could be. Inside she might be seething, but she was too good an actress to give herself away. When, around one o'clock, Mrs Tomkins told her she could take lunch, Freda grabbed her coat and hurried out.

Hungrily she gulped at the cold air, her coat flapping in the wind as the walked down the High Street. For a moment she was tempted to forget the milliner's and go to the cinema, where a Katharine Hepburn film was showing. But instead Freda kept walking, looking into the shop windows as she ate an apple.

437

She was just staring at a new television set when she noticed a familiar figure reflected in the glass of the shop window.

Surprised, she turned, Elise smiling broadly. 'Didn't you hear me calling you, Freda?' she asked. 'You walk so quickly I had to run to keep up.'

Her eyebrows raised, Freda looked at her curiously. 'What are you doing here?'

'Ada sent me with this,' Elise replied, passing Freda a brown bag. 'You forgot your lunch.'

'I know, that's why I'm eating an apple.' Taking the bag, Freda pulled out a sandwich, bit into it hungrily, then offered Elise one.

She was surprised by the gesture. 'No, thanks, I'm not hungry.'

'I am,' Freda admitted, eating quickly as she walked over to a bench and sat down. Crossing her slim legs, she beckoned for Elise to come over, the girl awkward in the presence of her idol.

'What's it like?'

'What?'

'The hat shop.'

Freda shrugged. 'Boring.'

'I've never been here before,' Elise said, looking round. 'Ada told me which bus to catch.'

'I forget you're a stranger round here. Mind you, not such a stranger now, are you?' Freda asked, finishing one sandwich and beginning another. 'These are awful. I can't believe Ma made them.'

'No, Vicky did.'

Freda paused in her chewing, then swallowed. 'She thinks I'm a lousy cook, but she's worse.' Carefully she glanced at Elise. 'You get on with my sister very well, don't you?'

'I like Vicky.'

'Everyone likes Vicky. They always did,' Freda replied, her tone even. 'When we were growing up, she was always the good one, always caring about people. I wasn't like that at all.' She winked, Elise delighted with the confidence. 'I was the black sheep. Still am.'

It was a fascinating thought, Elise willing Freda to continue.

'Mind you, you won't be seeing so much of Vicky, or your father, will you? I mean, now that they're so close, talking about the future all the time. They only have eyes for each other. That's love for you.' Freda recrossed her legs, not realising that she was unsettling her companion. 'I've felt pushed out of things for a long time. We have that in common, you and I.'

'I don't feel pushed out.'

'No, no, of course not,' Freda replied unconvincingly. 'Not pushed out, but you know how people are when they're wrapped up in each other. And your father's been alone for a long time.'

'He had me,' Elise said, her voice small.

'But you're his daughter, that's not the same. Besides, you're growing up now, quite a young lady. When they do marry, they'll have children of their own to think about.'

Freda lit a cigarette, Elise watching her. *Children* – no one had said anything about her father and Vicky having children. They had her and Stella, wasn't that enough? Besides, they weren't even married – why talk about children so soon?

'I don't think –'

'Love makes you selfish,' Freda went on, totally impervious to the effect her words were having. 'I was in love once . . . Oh well, that was a long time ago.' She looked

Elise up and down. 'You know, you should change your hair, it would make such a difference. I suppose the boys are all chasing you?'

Elise flushed, uneasy with her companion and yet flattered by Freda's attention. 'I don't know any boys.'

'That'll change.'

'I have to think about my work –'

Freda laughed. 'Work! Vicky used to be a blue stocking, always reading about politics and going to meetings. But where did it get her? She got married and had a baby, just like the rest.' Freda tapped Elise's knee. 'Why work all your life when you could marry and have a man look after you?'

'I like studying.'

'But studying's not working,' Freda said evenly. 'Working's dull, hard. You wouldn't like it in a shop.'

'Dad wants me to be a teacher.'

'What do *you* want?' Freda countered, looking into Elise's pale face. 'It's not your father's life. It's yours.'

'But he's been so good to me.'

'So?' Freda said. 'He'll want you to be happy, that's all anyone wants for their children. Anyway, when he and Vicky get married, he'll not be hanging over you all the time.'

Elise had never thought of her father's interest as something unwelcome, just as she had never thought of what his marriage might mean to her. Suddenly and unexpectedly, she was worried about the future. Her father had lived for her, they had been a team – would Vicky change that? *Would* she have another child, take Karl's attention away?

'Dad loves me a lot.'

'I know.'

'He wouldn't stop being interested in what I did.'

'No, course not,' Freda replied absent-mindedly.

'And Vicky's always made me feel welcome.'

'She's good at that,' Freda said bitterly. 'Vicky makes everyone feel special. Don't worry, you'll be fine. You might like having another brother or sister around.'

But Elise didn't like the idea one bit. Silent, she stared ahead, watching the housewives coming in and out of the shops, their baskets over their arms. Some were alone, others with small children clinging on to their skirts, crying for attention.

'I'll tell you what,' Freda said suddenly, 'I'll do your hair for you. Would you like that?'

Surprised, Elise nodded. 'If you don't mind.'

'No, I don't mind,' she said, getting to her feet. 'We outcasts have to stick together.'

Chapter Forty-Five

Dr Ellison was standing at the foot of Ada's bed, her clothes scattered around, a pair of stockings on the dressing table. Frowning, he looked at her.

'You've broken it.'

'Bloody hell!' Ada replied, exasperated. 'How long will it take my leg to heal?'

'Six weeks in plaster –'

'Six weeks!' she snapped, hauling herself up against the pillows. 'How can I lie here for six weeks? I've a pub to run.'

'Douglas is better now, and you've got Karl,' Dr Ellison replied evenly. 'They can run the place.'

'This is my pub!' Ada exploded. 'No one runs The Sixpenny Winner but the landlady. And that's me!'

'Ada, listen to me carefully. You've broken your leg and it has to mend. In plaster. You will have to let someone else look after this place for a while.' He put up his hands to stop her interrupting. 'No! It's no good arguing with me. You're going to have to rest for six weeks, and that's final.' The doctor walked to the door and called out for Doug, Ada watching as her son-in-law appeared a moment later.

'Mr Oldenshaw, your mother-in-law's broken her leg –'

'Broken it? Does it hurt?'

'Of course it bloody hurts!' Ada snapped, 'but what

hurts more is that I can't work for a while. You and Karl are going to have to run the pub.'

She was surprised to see that Douglas didn't seem to mind, in fact he seemed almost excited by the idea. Not that it was such a surprise, Ada thought; since Freda had been out working Douglas had mellowed. His back had improved, his melancholia restricted to the evenings, when Freda came home. And there was something else different about Douglas – he looked at Freda now. With interest. Warily, but with interest. The hatred was lifting.

Or was she just being hopeful? Ada wondered. Maybe there was some feeling left after all. Maybe . . .

'Karl and I can manage,' Doug said, breaking into her thoughts.

'Well, I'm glad to find myself replaced so soon,' Ada said shortly. 'Makes a woman feel good to know she's indispensable.'

'It's only for a while –'

'Six weeks,' Dr Ellison said flatly. 'Not a day less.'

'How did you do it?' Douglas asked Ada.

'Dumb luck,' she snapped. 'I fell.'

'How?'

'I tripped.'

'Over what?'

'Oh, for God's sake! I fell over my clothes, if you must know. I caught my leg getting out of bed and fell – smack – onto the ruddy floor!' She looked around. 'I never thought being a bad housekeeper was dangerous to health.'

Smiling, Dr Ellison moved to the door. 'We'll get that leg plastered for you today. Then you rest, d'you hear? It won't do you any harm, Ada. You've not stopped working for years. Time you had a break.'

'In Blackpool, not my bloody leg!'

After calling in to see Ada, Karl returned to the bar to find Doug getting ready to open up. Surprised, he watched him move around, setting out the tables and straightening the chairs, then polishing the bar surface. It was like watching a new man, Karl thought.

'Oh, 'lo there,' Doug said lightly, spotting Karl. 'We're all ready for business.'

Cheerful as he sounded, Doug was observing Karl carefully. There was no way he was going to allow Karl to take over now that Ada was out of the picture. He had put too much time and effort into The Sixpenny Winner to see his place taken over by an outsider.

'Pity about Ada,' Karl said sympathetically.

'She's not taking it well,' Doug replied, moving past him and bending down to open the trap door to the cellar. 'I'll be back in a minute to open up.'

Puzzled, Karl watched Doug move down into the vault, and then heard him whistling. Well, well, well, he thought. Certainly there had been a difference in Doug ever since his wife had gone out to work, but this was a transformation – now that Ada was laid up.

Karl wasn't a fool. He had had enough prejudice in his life to sense that Doug resented him. And here was proof. Doug had roused himself enough to make sure that Karl was not going to undermine him. And now they had to work together. No Ada for a while, no easy company and banter. Just him and Doug.

Sighing, Karl leaned over the trap door and peered into the cellar. 'You want a hand down there?'

'I can manage,' came back the reply.

'You sure? Your back's been bad.'

A moment passed before Doug's head popped up through the trap door.

'Let's get one thing straight, Karl. There's nothing wrong with me. My back's fine now. And I can pull my weight. You just worry about yourself, hey? I know what I'm doing.'

'Shame about Ada, isn't it?' Bessie said, when Lizzie came in for a half-pound of streaky bacon later that day.

'I heard she had a bad fall. Fell down three flights of stairs, someone said.'

'I heard she were drunk,' Bessie countered flatly.

'I thought it were her arm she broke. Not her leg. Still,' Lizzie said delightedly, 'serves her right for chasing my man.'

'Ada Hargreaves chased Mac Potter?' Bessie said, her voice amused. 'I saw him in his best clothes, with his hair slicked down, off to try and court her when you were away.'

'It's not true!' Lizzie chirped. 'He told me all about it when I got back. Said people would try and make it out to be something it weren't. It were Ada who asked him out for a walk with her –'

'A walk!' Bessie snorted. 'Don't make me laugh!'

'She were right put out when he said no,' Lizzie went on firmly, a little too firmly. 'No woman likes to be rejected. You know what they say – hell hath no fury like a woman mourned.'

'Scorned!' Bessie corrected her. 'Like a woman scorned.'

'Whatever,' Lizzie replied, her lips pursed, her hands folded over her bag. 'Whatever anyone says, I trust him. I trust my Mac.'

'You're doing a lot of "my-ing", Lizzie. Seems to me that Mac's not a man who takes too well to "my-ing" –'

'There's no point being bitter because you're a widow, Bessie Cork! You know as well as I do that you'd go after Mac soon enough if he gave you a second glance.'

Slamming her hand down on the shop counter, Bessie burst out laughing. Loudly. In fact she laughed so hard that tears poured from her eyes, Lizzie flushed with mortification.

'Oh, Lizzie,' Bessie said, when she could speak again. 'The only thing I could do with that funny little fella of yours is to use him as a doorstop.'

Making sure that Doug couldn't see her, Freda watched him at the bar. He was serving a regular, the man welcoming him back. He was smiling too, Freda thought, and holding a conversation. Admittedly he seemed a little out of practice, but it was obvious to her – and to everyone else – that Douglas Oldenshaw was very like his old self.

Like he had been before the tragedy, when he and his brother had worked the bar together. Freda had watched the two of them then, seen Doug's broad shoulders and watched as Duncan turned and winked at her; thinking of the sex they would have later. Wondering how long she would have to lie in bed before sneaking off to meet him.

She had loved Doug too then. In her own way. Not like Duncan, but she'd loved her husband's strength, the way he had worshipped her. No one worshipped her any more . . . Freda could see the two brothers in front of her, the memory tangible.

Blinking, she came back to the present. Now she could see only one brother, the same man who was suddenly rejuvenated. Freda knew her husband well enough to realise what had prompted Doug's resurrection – his desire to protect his own interests. But it still shook her to realise that it was only whilst she had been away that he had been restored to his former self. And now, busily guarding his empire, he was glowing in the absence of his wife. And yet only the other day she had caught him looking at her and felt – surprisingly – a jolt of excitement.

But then he had turned away and the moment had passed . . . Bitterly, Freda let the curtain drop from her hand and turned back to the kitchen. Everyone was moving on, making their new futures, all except her. Drawing some water, she set the kettle to boil and then automatically tidied the kitchen. Above her head she could hear Ada banging on the floor for attention, Elise's radio playing soft and sweet from the attic rooms. And then Freda heard something else – her sister laugh.

Frozen, she listened. It was a full laugh of genuine amusement. But then it would be, wouldn't it? she thought sourly. Vicky had a lot to be amused about. She had won. The quiet little bookworm had triumphed over her in the end. Freda was the one who was washed up. Freda was the one with no love in her life – no man, no child. Her sister had it all now, whilst she had *nothing*. Behind her, the kettle started to whistle faintly. Freda's gaze moved upwards and fixed on the ceiling as she heard her sister's footsteps move overhead.

Vicky had ruined her life. Forgetting the part she had played in her own downfall, Freda latched on to the relief of blaming someone else. It was Vicky's fault. Her sister had ruined her life.

Laughing again, Vicky turned up the volume on her radio in the room above, whilst below, Freda stood with her fists clenched, the kettle's soft whistle changing to a persistent and discordant screaming behind her.

It was past five when Stella toddled in to talk to Ada, Vicky following close behind her.

'What *are* you doing?' Vicky asked, staring in amazement as Ada leaned out of the window, her plastered leg stuck out at right angles as she perched on the edge of her chair.

Pulling a face, Ada looking over her shoulder – a home-made catapult in her hands. 'It's that bloody cat,' she said, jerking her head towards the window. 'I nearly got it a minute ago.'

Fascinated, Vicky peered over her mother's shoulder into the backyard. 'You're firing at the cat?'

'He's annoyed me long enough. One cat peeing all over the place was bad, but this bugger carrying on the tradition is too much,' Ada said, her tone perfectly reasonable. 'Anyway, I have to have something to do, stuck up here all day.'

'But it's dark,' Vicky replied. 'I can't believe I'm watching my mother firing a catapult at a tomcat in the dark.'

'Semidark,' Ada corrected her. 'There's enough light to see that bugger by. I bet Trudie Mossop trained him to come over here and pee everywhere just because I banned her son.' Suddenly Ada spotted the animal, frantically took aim and fired a paper pellet into the night.

The cat stopped and watched as the pellet sailed past him. Settling himself down on the pub wall, he then started to wash.

'Sodding thing!' Ada said, infuriated. 'Look at him! He's doing that to annoy me. Pass me my glasses, Vicky. I need all the help I can get.'

Patiently, Vicky handed her mother her glasses, then leaned against the windowframe and looked at Ada with amusement. Her mother's hair was dishevelled, her face flushed as she gripped the catapult, her arms leaning on the windowledge to give her better balance. Her plastered leg was decorated with an assortment of names, Stella blithely crayoning round her grandmother's ankle. As Vicky watched them, cold night air came into the room and made the net curtain flutter, a chill moon rising at the end of the ginnel.

'If I can just get a clear shot . . .'

'Why don't you wait until morning?' Vicky suggested, turning to see Freda walk in with a tray.

In silence, she laid it on the bed and tidied up the bedroom. The smell of hot soup made Ada turn.

'Tomato, good!' she said, waving for Freda to bring it over.

If she thought it was strange to see her mother firing pellets from her bedroom window, she said nothing. Always uncomfortable in her sister's presence, Vicky picked Stella up and moved to the door.

'I'll call in later again, Ma.'

'Good!' she said simply, adding over her shoulder: 'And bring me one of your knitting needles.'

'One knitting needle?' Vicky countered. 'What can you knit with *one* knitting needle?'

'Who said I wanted to knit? I need it to poke down this plaster cast and scratch my leg,' Ada replied, sipping at the soup. 'Damn thing's itching me to death.'

Waiting until the door closed, Freda then turned to her mother. The soup was hot, and Ada swore as she burned her lip. Her isolation had done nothing for her temper; idleness was not Ada's strong suit. Reading the newspaper lasted for only minutes, the radio was soon

declared boring, and as for sewing – who the bloody
hell sews for pleasure? Sewing was a punishment, Ada
had said firmly, any woman that *chooses* to do it is a
bit short.

'So, how's work?' Ada asked, turning to Freda.

'Same as usual.'

'A ball of fire?'

'Not quite,' Freda replied, sitting on the bed, her
blonde hair shining under the overhead light.

'You look tired, luv.'

'I am, Ma.'

'Not sleeping?'

'Not much.'

'Me neither,' Ada told her. 'This leg itches all night. I
just get off to sleep and then it starts. Come four in the
morning I could bite someone with fury.' Putting down
the soup she turned back to the window and looked out.
'If I can just get a clear shot at that cat.'

'He was in the cellar this morning,' Freda said. 'Karl
told me – said he's sprayed against the wall.'

Ada flushed at the news. 'Don't worry, before long
his spraying days are over! That cat has marked its last
spot.' Snatching up the catapult she glanced out of the
window and frowned, her attention caught by something below. 'Hey, the light's on at the back door.'

'So?'

'We haven't got money to burn, who left it on?'

'Vicky's just come in –'

'She should have turned it off,' Ada said impatiently.

A winter smog had started to form, masking the cat
on the wall and making a sulphur-coloured halo around
the lamp. Craning forward Ada strained to see if there
was anyone there, knowing full well that her view was
blocked by the stone lintel over the door.

'Maybe someone's there?'

'Like who?' Freda asked, disinterested. 'I tell you, Vicky must have left it on when she came in.'

Ada shivered, slamming the window shut. 'I hate that back door, always gives me the creeps. Go down and turn the light off, luv, will you? And lock up.'

Muttering under her breath, Freda moved downstairs again, crossing the kitchen and walking out to the back entrance. But just as she did so, the outside light went off. Startled, she stood in the doorway in the darkness. Then a hand went over her mouth, Freda struggling and trying to scream.

'Shut up!' a voice said. 'Ssh! Be quiet. It's me. Duncan.'

'I can see you're surprised but, like my grandfather said, people had always suspected Duncan Oldenshaw would turn up again sometime. Most hoped it would be in the morgue. But he was made of sterner stuff than that.

'You know, talking about all this brings it back. Like hearing my grandfather talk when I was young. He used to tell me the story of *The Sixpenny Winner* in snatches, like a serial you'd hear on the wireless. Only it was real. That's what made it so amazing.

'Fancy all that happening in one place, I used to say, and he'd wink and tell me I hadn't heard the half of it . . . So, you ready? Time to get on with it now, we're coming to the best bit. Time to tell you what happened next, though you'll never believe it. I didn't. But then later . . . Oh no, I'm not jumping the gun now.

'So there they are, at that grim back door opening on to the ginnel. Freda's little kingdom. And there's Duncan, smiling like a jackal in that murky, smoggy night.'

Part Five

Love many, trust few
And learn to paddle your own canoe.

Anon.

Chapter Forty-Six

Much as it annoyed him, Al Weeks had to admit that he had lost all trace of Duncan Oldenshaw. The thought irked him. He had watched out for Duncan for a year and a half, coming across gossip about him now and again as he worked on other jobs. Duncan Oldenshaw had hit rock bottom, on the skids, the rumour went. And no one deserved it more, Al thought.

Then later he heard that Duncan was working as a porter in a hospital, clawing his way back into some kind of life. But what kind of life could he expect? His behaviour had been loathsome and, indirectly, it had cost the life of his own son.

Then again, Al thought, maybe Duncan Oldenshaw had changed, maybe guilt had altered him, smacked him into respectability. But he doubted it. And always, always, Al remembered what he had heard in Yorkshire, about the time Duncan had helped his brother run the pub . . . That information Al had kept to himself, telling no one, not even Vicky. But maybe one day he would tell her. Maybe one day he *should* tell her. When he had proof – which was hard to find. But find it he would. In time.

Since she had sent him that note so long ago, Vicky had never asked for any more information and Al had never offered any. But the affection he felt for Ada and for Vicky made him keep an eye out for the man who had betrayed them. Al sighed to himself. Apparently Vicky was in love with someone else now, and would marry Karl Straub when she got her divorce from Duncan.

And just how would she go about that? Al wondered. On the grounds of adultery? He winced; Ada wouldn't like that. So would Vicky get a divorce based on Duncan's desertion? That was more like it, Al thought, unless Duncan conveniently died or topped himself. And although that had looked like a possibility a while back, the bastard was on the up again.

Sighing to himself, Al looked at The Sixpenny Winner. He had seen Ada on and off, coming and going. Handsome woman, with a sharp brain. Oh yes, if things had been different he could have gone for Ada Hargreaves in a big way. But there you were, he wasn't her type. But it couldn't stop Al from looking out for Ada's family and doing what he could – from a distance, and even though she would never know about it. A labour of love, he thought, embarrassed by his own fancy.

So it annoyed Al that he had temporarily lost tabs on Duncan Oldenshaw. He had never liked him and what he had learned over the last months had made him like him less. But perhaps it didn't matter any more. Apparently the only thing Vicky wanted from her husband was a divorce. Perhaps she just wanted Duncan to keep away, and *stay* away. Then she could marry Karl and never think of Duncan again.

Feeling the cold, Al turned and walked back towards the centre of town. He had business there. Someone wanted information. Didn't they always? And yet, much as he tried not to, he kept thinking of Duncan Oldenshaw.

And wondering why.

'Duncan,' Freda said simply, her mouth drying. 'Duncan, is it really you?'

Leaning across her, he flicked on the light, his face illuminated. His good looks were restored, the beard gone, his eyes bright with triumph. Then he turned the light off again, both of them plunged back into darkness.

She reached for him, then drew back, her voice hard. 'You left me! You left me –'

'I had to,' Duncan whispered. 'Your mother made me. She threw me out that night before I had chance to say anything to you –'

'But you never wrote, never tried to get in touch,' Freda grumbled, but her heart wasn't in it. Duncan was back, the man who had obsessed her for so long, the man she had tried to forget. And failed.

'I've never stopped thinking of you,' Duncan said, getting hold of her.

To his amazement, Freda pushed him away.

'It's not going to be that easy!' she snapped, excitement and fury fighting to get the upper hand. 'You can't just come back and think that nothing has changed.'

'You don't want me?'

She floundered. 'I don't . . . I don't know.'

The hesitation was all he needed. He grabbed hold of her, his mouth moving over Freda's, his tongue searching for hers. Moaning, she leaned against him, her hands moving inside his coat and grasping his back, pulling him to her. Their bodies moulded together, Duncan kissing her face, her neck, pulling aside the collar of her dress and running his tongue along her collar bone.

'Don't!' she said suddenly, trying to push him away. 'Don't!'

'I have to,' he went on, holding her more tightly. 'I've missed you so much.'

'Someone will hear us,' Freda warned him. 'Ma's in the bedroom above here and Doug could walk into the kitchen any time.'

In answer, Duncan pulled Freda out into the ginnel beyond. The smog swept around them, the cat's eyes shining greenly in the darkness as it watched from the wall.

'I've changed,' he told her, 'I have, honestly. I want to make things up to you.'

'What about Doug?' she asked, ducking out of his grasp again and leaning breathlessly against the wall. 'Have you seen him?'

'No, just you.'

'You have to talk to him,' she went on, 'explain.'

He frowned. 'Explain what?'

'That you've changed, that you want to come back here. It won't be easy. He's been murder to live with, Duncan. He's hated me since that day, won't look at me, talk to me, touch me –'

'I always said he was a fool,' Duncan replied, reaching out for her and stroking her cheek.

'Why didn't you take me with you?' she asked, her tone pleading as she fell back under his control. 'Why didn't you ask me to go with you? I would have done.'

This was the man who had made her feel wanted, who had made love to her, who had made her life exciting. The man with whom she had experienced the most pleasure – and the most pain. She was, at that moment, afraid of him and longing for him at the same time. They had been unlucky together, deceitful, betraying everyone for their own ends, and indirectly causing the death of their own child.

But she *still* wanted him.

'You never came to the funeral –'

'I couldn't,' Duncan assured her. 'I wanted to, but I couldn't. Billy was my child too, Freda – don't you think his death hurt me? I killed him. How d'you think a man lives with something like that?'

'How d'you think *I* did?' she countered, still pressed against the wall.

'You told them what we'd done –'

'So it's my fault!' she snapped, then dropped her voice as she glanced upwards. The light was on in Ada's room, but the window was closed.

'I never said that. We're both guilty. We were both wrong, but it was Vicky who caused all the trouble.'

'Yes, yes!' Freda agreed eagerly. 'It was Vicky. She's so smug now, Duncan. Got a new man, going to marry him.' She watched the effect the words had on Duncan, enjoying the pain she was inflicting. 'She wants a divorce so she can marry him.'

Stung, Duncan glanced at the door, almost as though he expected to see his hated wife walk out and catch them there. The idea of revenge that had hauled him back from the gutter burned in his stomach like a badly digested meal. Vicky was to blame. Vicky, the little bitch, the woman he thought he had fooled, had been the woman who had bested him in the end.

She had set him up, betrayed him to his brother, caused his banishment from The Sixpenny Winner and the cushy life he had enjoyed there. He could still see her face when she accused him of stealing from her, the disgusted looks on Ada and Doug's faces imprinted in his mind for ever.

They had all banded against him, even Freda, exposing their affair in a misguided attempt to force his hand. And what had happened? The death of Billy. A death for which he was to blame, a death for which he carried the stigma and guilt. Oh yes, he thought, holding Freda, none of you is innocent. But he reserved his deepest hatred for Vicky.

'You should see her,' Freda went on, her bitterness intense. 'She crows over me any way she can. And Doug lets her, lets her rub my nose in it.'

Duncan didn't really care. He was thinking of the way Doug had gone for him, struck out, losing control. He would have killed him, Duncan thought, if Billy hadn't got in the way. His son had saved him, he realised. Little Billy had actually saved him from his own brother.

He could still see the look in Doug's eyes as he had thrown the first punch at him. All the disappointment and anger had come to boiling point. Doug knew he had been cuckolded, fooled, manipulated into believing that Duncan had changed, when all the time he had been shitting on his own doorstep, and laughing at his brother behind his back.

'Duncan,' Freda hissed, 'listen to me!'

He looked back at her, smiling his winning smile. 'What, my love?'

'What are you going to do?'

Get back inside, Duncan thought, get back in amongst my enemies in order to tear them all apart once and for all.

'I have to make it up with Doug, Freda.'

'Hah!' she snapped dismissively. 'He'll never forgive you, Duncan, never. Not for what we did. Or for Billy's death –'

'It was an accident.'

'But he thought Billy was *his* child!' she went on, her tone impatient. 'He lost him twice, once when he was killed, and again when he realised Billy was never his.'

'I can make it up to him –'

'You can't! It's no good fooling yourself,' she told him, taking his hand and laying it against her cheek. 'We have to think of making a new life. Away from here.'

That was the last thing Duncan wanted. What revenge was there in running off with Freda? Besides, he wanted her, but he didn't love her. She was exciting, but impossible to live with. What he wanted was more complex – and would take time to achieve. Time, and cunning.

'Freda, darling, we can't go away yet. I have to make things right here,' he told her, stroking her face, soothing her. 'I have to make up for the past –'

'You can't. Nothing can change what happened.'

'I know. But I have to *look* as though that's all that matters to me. I have to be the prodigal, Freda, come back on my knees to take my punishment.'

Confused, she stared at him, trying to read Duncan's expression. The smoggy night wrapped like a winding sheet around them.

'What are you talking about?' she said at last. 'Why *did* you come back, Duncan?'

'For revenge,' he admitted, feeling her tense in his arms. 'And for you.'

She relaxed then, just as he knew she would.

'Revenge?'

He nodded. 'I want to get my own back on all of them.' Including you, he thought, but you'll be the last to know. 'Freda, darling, we have to be very clever –'

'Doug will never forgive you!' she repeated. 'As for Vicky –'

'Ah, Vicky,' Duncan repeated thoughtfully. 'Tell me, Freda, wouldn't you like to knock the smug smile off your sister's face?'

She nodded eagerly. 'Yes, yes.'

'So she wants to divorce me, does she?'

'She wants to marry Karl Straub –'

'A German?'

Freda shrugged. 'Thinks he's something special. Educated. An ex-teacher.'

'That's nice. They can lie in bed and read together . . .' Duncan murmured, 'whereas you and I never had time to *read* in bed.'

Reminded of their lovemaking, Freda realised that she would do anything to keep Duncan from leaving her again. It might not be to her liking, but she would play along with him, help him to achieve his revenge. After all, it would be good to see everyone suffer after all the suffering she had endured. Especially Vicky.

'What are you going to do, Duncan?'

'I have to see Doug, talk to him. You have to tell him I'm back, that I've changed, that I'm sorry –'

'He won't listen to me!'

'He has to,' Duncan insisted.

'But he won't, I tell you! He never talks to me and he'd never listen to me trying to defend you.'

Duncan smiled. 'I think you might be wrong, Freda. Doug is my brother and he sets great store by family. He might be more willing to see me than you think.'

Chapter Forty-Seven

Brooding, Freda sat on her bed and listened to the sounds coming from the pub below. Stan Foreshaw was on the piano again, she thought irritably, surprised to hear the sound of her husband laughing. *Doug laughing!* That was the first time in months. Flopping back against the pillows, she looked at her hands, the scarlet nails flashing in the lamplight. God, she felt good, real again. Her eyes closed, remembering the feel of Duncan's body and the smell of his skin as she nuzzled his neck.

How had she lived without him? She had existed, that was all. But now Duncan was back and she had to make sure that he stayed.

There was a sound from below – someone had dropped a glass, the shattering noise loud in Freda's ears. Ada wouldn't like that, another breakage coming off the profits ... I want to get out of here, Freda thought desperately. I want to go away with Duncan. But he wanted his revenge first. And how long would that take?

She would have to play along, be patient and concentrate. Perhaps in time things would be back to the way they were before, and then she and Duncan could pick up from where they left off.

Oh, who was she kidding? Freda thought angrily, her eyes opening. Everything had changed. The house was full, Karl and his daughter taking over Duncan's old rooms. There was no space for a prodigal.

'Oh, you're in here,' Doug said, walking in, surprised to see Freda. 'I thought you were downstairs.'

He seemed chirpy, almost happy.

'I have to talk to you, Doug.'

'What d'you want to talk to me about?'

Only weeks earlier he would have dismissed her at once, but he was mellowing. It was a good sign, Freda thought.

'About . . .' Oh God, how could she phrase it? How could she dare to face her husband and bring Duncan's name up? 'Do you still hate me?'

He hesitated, then sat down on the edge of the bed. It was the first time he had listened to her in a long while.

'I don't hate you, Freda.'

'I think you do.'

'It's in the past. Everything that's happened is over. We can't change it, so we have to go on.'

She was surprised by his reasonable mood. 'I'm sorry. You know that, don't you?'

He nodded. 'I know.'

'I would do anything to change things,' she went on, pausing to pick her next words. 'I was cruel to you.'

He turned, took her hand, the action so unexpected that she flinched.

'I never hated you, Freda. I loved you too much to hate you. But what you did broke my heart. But I can't – however much I try – stop loving you.' He searched her face. 'You should have told me about Billy.'

This was not what Freda had expected. Finally she had won back some affection and now she was about to blow it apart again by mentioning Duncan. Maybe, she thought, a more roundabout approach might be better.

'I wanted to tell you about Billy,' she said, her voice

466

low, her blonde hair falling over her shoulders as she looked down. 'But I was so ashamed.'

'But you carried on the affair after he was born.'

'Yes . . .' she admitted. 'I didn't see Duncan for what he was. I couldn't help myself. He was always after me, Doug, always pestering me.' Was that the right thing to say, she wondered? It would get her some sympathy, but how would it make Duncan look? 'We were both wrong. Me and your brother –'

'Don't mention him!' Doug snapped, gripping her hand tightly. 'Don't ever mention him to me.'

'But Duncan's your brother –'

'He *was* my brother,' Doug went on grimly, 'but he's dead to me now. As dead as Billy.'

Startled, Freda leaned down, resting her head on Doug's lap. She expected him to brush her away, but he didn't. He looked at her instead and some little longing came into his eyes.

'I want you to love me again, Doug.'

'I can't trust you. I want to, but I can't.'

'But I've been good. I've been so good for so long now.' Her voice took on a lilting quality. 'I haven't looked at another man, and never would again. I love you, I never realised how much before.'

He hesitated, then bent down and kissed her lightly on the forehead.

'I wish things could be like they were.'

'So do I!' Freda replied keenly. 'I wish things were like they used to be, when we were all together here – one big happy family.' She rolled over onto her back, taking Doug's hand and resting it on her left breast. 'Family is so important, more important than anything.'

He nodded, Freda waiting for him to speak again.

'I used to think that, but I know different now. My

brother taught me that. Duncan showed me how love and duty can make a fool out of a man. I took him in, thinking he had changed. I wanted him with me because he was my brother. My family. But he ruined everything. He corrupted everything he touched, and made me mad. He may have struck the blow which killed Billy, but I started the fight. I lost control – and in doing that I lost everything I cared about.'

It's the wrong time to tell me this, Freda thought angrily. Why didn't you speak up sooner, confide in me before? We had months to talk but you never did. And now you are talking, it's too late. I don't want you now, Doug. I don't need you. But I'll use you.

'It wasn't *all* Duncan's fault –'

'Stop it, Freda! Stop talking about him, or trying to make things better. It's over. I never want to see my brother again. I never want to hear his name come from your lips, or even think of him. He's dead to me.' Doug stared at his wife, then moved his hand inside Freda's blouse, feeling the soft flesh of her breast. 'Do you still want him? *Do you?*'

For a moment she hesitated and then reached up and pulled her husband towards her, her lips parted, her eyes half closed with what he thought was love.

'Where have you been?' Karl asked as Doug returned to the bar a while later.

'Upstairs.'

'I thought you'd been abducted.' He looked into Doug's face and smiled to himself knowingly. So a peace has been agreed at last, has it? Thank God for that. 'Mac Potter wants a top-up.'

'I'll see to it,' Doug said happily.

'Oh, and Ada said she wanted a word later,' Karl went

on, watching Doug with fascination. He was in another world, glowing with contentment.

'Fine.'

'Oh, and one more thing, Doug. There's a bomb in the cellar.'

'Fine.'

'Which is going to go off in ten minutes.'

'Fine.' Doug repeated distantly.

'It will probably kill everyone in Stockport.'

'Fine.'

Love, Karl Straub decided in that moment, was everything it was cracked up to be.

At two o'clock in the morning, Freda crept downstairs and moved out to the back entrance, without turning on the light. She was cold, shivering, as she waited for Duncan, the smog swirling round the ginnel like a restless ghoul. Finally she heard his footsteps in the distance and moved out in the alleyway to meet him.

'Hey!' he said, kissing her. 'Nice welcome.'

'He won't see you.'

Duncan frowned. 'What?'

'He was mad, really mad. He's not going to forgive you, Duncan. He said that you weren't his brother any more, that you were dead to him.'

This was not what Duncan had expected. For a long moment he stared ahead blindly, Freda holding on to his arm. So there was to be no return, no access to the warm belly of the pub where he could plot internally, in comfort. His brother didn't want to see him, didn't care if he was dead.

Surprised by the stunned look on Duncan's face, Freda tried to comfort him.

'It's OK, honestly. It doesn't matter now. It might all be for the best –'

'For the best?' he repeated contemptuously.

'Why not? You know where you stand now. There's nothing for you here, Duncan, so let's go away. Start fresh somewhere. Forget revenge –'

'Shut up!' Duncan hissed.

Freda backed away. She realised that he wanted her, but that she came a firm second to his need to wreak havoc. The thought was a bitter one, but Freda wasn't a woman who let go lightly. Duncan Oldenshaw was back, and by God, she was going to keep him this time – using whatever means it took.

Seeing Freda draw away, Duncan was immediately contrite. Don't blow it now, he told himself. There was more than one way to skin a cat.

'Sorry, sorry, luv,' he said, putting his arms around her. 'I'm just upset, that's all.'

'I know, Duncan. But why can't we go away together?'

'I want to get things sorted first.'

'But why?'

'Because I do!' he snapped back at her, adding slyly, 'And so do you, Freda. Think about how they've treated you. I was remembering what you told me – about Doug and Vicky – how they were with you. Think about it. You're not going to let them get away with it, are you?'

She knew it was a game, but played it anyway. 'Remember we have each other now.'

'I know. But even if you want to forgive them, I won't let them get away with it,' Duncan said hoarsely. 'Not after what they did to me – or to you.' He stared ahead down the dark ginnel. He had to get Freda on his side, kid her, lie to her, but get her on his side. 'Think of your sister. Think of Vicky.'

Freda's eyes flickered with fury. 'Smug cow!'

'Yes, smug, now that she has a new man –'

'He's not a patch on you, Duncan.'

'– a new man she wants to marry. But in order to marry him I have to give her a divorce. Which I don't intend to do.'

'You don't?'

'Why should I make things easy for my wife, when she made things so difficult for us?'

'She could sue you for adultery.'

'And let the whole story come out? People know about us, but not about Billy. Vicky won't risk that piece of dynamite being ignited. As for claiming desertion, she'll have to wait another three years for that. And a lot can happen in three years.' Divorce wasn't important to him, but revenge was. 'When I think back, our little Vicky was all over me once, said how much she loved me, how much she always had. God, it was so easy, like taking a dummy from a baby. She was desperate to marry me, to be with me. I could never stand her.'

'I know you couldn't!' Freda said eagerly. 'We duped her, didn't we? That marriage was a good cover-up for us.'

'It was, but she duped us in the end, and won.' He looked back to Freda, his insides curdled with bile. 'You don't want Vicky to win, do you, Freda? You don't want her to have a new man, a new life, and my child. She has everything, and you have *nothing*.'

Stung, Freda retorted swiftly, 'I have you.'

'Of course,' he lied, 'you have me. But for a while no one must know that. It must be a secret.'

'For how long?'

'Until we work out a way to get our own back on that little sister of yours. Until we make her pay for what she did.'

Freda nodded. 'Everyone thinks she was the wronged wife, the innocent one. If only they knew what she was really like. If only they realised how she lied and set you up.'

'She was sly – I never expected that of her,' Duncan agreed.

'She was angry when she knew you loved me, not her.'

Smiling slowly, Duncan ran his forefinger along Freda's bottom lip. 'What wicked women you both are. You *and* Vicky.'

'But I wouldn't hurt you, Duncan. Vicky did. And she would hurt you again if she could,' Freda went on, manipulating Duncan as he manipulated her. 'You should hear her talk, revelling in her luck. Nothing can be allowed to spoil her happy little family. She would fight like a tiger to protect it. You should see them together, going to the cinema, Karl always so caring, his daughter admiring Vicky like she was some kind of goddess –'

'Straub has a daughter?'

'Yes, Elise.'

'Go on.'

'They're so close. All four of them, counting Stella.'

Duncan winced. 'Stella's my child! That bastard's stolen my wife *and* my daughter.'

'Yes, yes, he has!' Freda said, egging him on. 'He's taken your job and your family. *He* could be Doug's brother now, not you.'

That was the final blow. Duncan's need for revenge had been strong enough before, but now Freda had massaged it, plumped it up to obscene proportions. A mist of anger floated in front of him. It shimmered in the smoggy night, and hung around Freda's eager, upturned face.

'You have to get your own back,' she hissed softly. If this was the only way to keep him, so be it. 'Don't let them win. An eye for an eye, Duncan. If you don't really want me, I'll walk off now, go back to your brother. Make love to him – oh yes, he's interested again. So tell me. Do you want thàt? Want Doug to have me whilst he slams the door in your face again?' She paused to deliver the next blow. 'Maybe you're not man enough for the fight. Well, don't worry about me, Duncan. I can manage without you. We all can. Vicky certainly. And Stella's growing up without even remembering you –'

'Shut up!'

She moved closer to him, her voice low, enticing. '*You* were the one who wanted revenge, Duncan. Don't give up now.'

He narrowed his eyes as he looked at her. 'You want it too.'

'Of course – but I have more patience than you. And I'm smarter.' She caught hold of his hair, jerked his head and then kissed him roughly on the lips. 'You're not the dirty fighter I thought you were.'

Provoked, Duncan pushed her against the wall, lifting up her chin as she smiled at him.

'You're a bitch, Freda, a conniving, hypocritical bitch.'

'And you, Duncan?' she replied smoothly, her voice thick with longing. 'Are you my match? Or can I beat you – just like all the others?'

In that instant she knew she had him.

Chapter Forty-Eight

Having sown the seed in Elise's mind, Freda watched it take root. From the girl being happy to see her father in love with Vicky, she was showing the first signs of resentment. It was obvious in the looks she gave them when they were joking together, or the way she flinched when they held hands.

Maybe she had been wrong, Elise thought, maybe it wouldn't be the right thing for her father to marry Vicky after all. And then she admitted to herself that she was jealous and the guilt set in. How could she deny Karl happiness when he sacrificed so much to bring her up? And as for Vicky, she was perfect for him. They were comfortable together, sharing jokes and intimacies, the way that lovers do.

And also the way that fathers and daughters do. It wasn't the same, Elise knew, but she had had all Karl's love and affection for years, and now – to see it slipping away, to see someone else receiving what she thought of as hers – was unexpected agony.

Deep in thought, Elise pushed away her books and stared out of the window. Mac Potter was coming down the street with Stan Foreshaw. Soon it would be opening time. She had wanted to stay at The Sixpenny Winner so much and had been so happy that she had been eager to matchmake Vicky and her father into a relationship. But now she wasn't so sure. What had Freda said – 'We outcasts have to stick together'?

Elise wasn't sure she liked the idea of being an outcast any more. She had had enough of it during the war. But then it had been bearable, because all the running and moving had been with her father. And there was something else Freda had said: Vicky and Karl might have children ... Confused, Vicky pulled her books back to her and tried to read, but her thoughts had nothing to do with French grammar; they were centred firmly on the idea of a child. A new child, who might usurp Elise's position. A baby who might take over her father's love, shut her out. She was almost grown up, she would be no rival to a beautiful infant.

Stop it! Elise told herself. Stop thinking about it. It might never happen. Vicky isn't even divorced, she thought. If they don't find her husband, she might never be free. And then there will be no marriage, no children. No rivals. Her father might even move on, with her, just the two of them again. She liked Vicky, but she wasn't – Elise paled at the thought – really willing to share her father with anyone.

The home life for which she had longed was within her grasp: A stepmother, a half-sister, a solid base at The Sixpenny Winner. The thought warmed her, and yet – deep in the corners of her heart – she was shocked by the price she might have to pay for it.

A family did not come cheap.

'If you keep poking that needle down your cast, you'll make your leg bleed,' Vicky said to her mother, taking the knitting needle out of her hand. 'When it itches, it's healing.'

'How would you know?'

'I worked at a hospital, remember?'

'I saw a ballet once, it didn't make me Anna Pavlova,'

Ada countered, looking round the room irritably. 'I can't stand sitting around like this!'

'What happened to the cat?'

Ada shrugged, looking away. 'I thought I had it. Got a direct hit on its arse and sent it off that wall like a sack of coal.' She paused, avoiding Vicky's gaze. 'Trouble was, it was the wrong cat. It was that tabby one from number a hundred and twelve. The woman played hell when she heard. I don't know what all the fuss was about – it was only a paper pellet.'

'You should have kept your glasses on. Then you wouldn't have hit the wrong cat.'

'He was sitting where that mucky bugger usually sits.'

'Well, maybe he's gone off now. You might have driven him away for good.'

'Where's Freda?'

'Gone to work.'

'Karl?'

'About to open up.'

'Douglas?'

'Helping him.'

Ada nodded. 'Have you noticed anything about Douglas? He looks . . . different. You know, happy. I haven't seen him like that for God knows how long. And as for Freda – well, I might be guessing, but I would say that even if those two aren't talking, they're doing something else.'

'I noticed that,' Vicky replied, 'and I thought the same. Maybe they'll work it out, after all.'

'Maybe seeing you and Karl together has reminded them of what they're missing.'

Smiling, Vicky leaned back against the bed head. She was, she had to admit, completely happy. Karl had proved his love repeatedly. He was attentive and caring – brought her presents, wrote her poetry, did all the silly, giddy things that some men did when they were in love. All the things she had never experienced before.

The days of her marriage to Duncan seemed so long ago – the uneasy, restless, sexy days when she had been blinded with infatuation. How stupid she had been, Vicky thought, how stupid to have been taken in by her sister and her husband. But the bitterness she had felt at first had faded. She had a new man now, a new life to look forward to; there was no point dredging up the past.

Karl was even considerate enough not to expect them to make love. He would never do that, he said, not under Ada's roof, not whilst Vicky was married. They would wait, he said, until things were legal, until they could stand up before the world as a couple.

And it hadn't been that difficult to resist, Vicky thought, not really. She had adored Duncan, longed for him, but her love for Karl was different. He wasn't exciting like that, she didn't burn wanting him, watching him, longing for him. Instead she looked at Karl and saw him as offering loving comfort. Lovemaking with him would be a part of their relationship, not the whole.

'I'd hoped that Freda would settle down,' Ada said suddenly, 'and I think she has. Finally. God, she was a problem and that's putting it mildly. I thought she'd go off the rails completely when Billy died.' Vicky winced, not wanting to be reminded of the past and the part she had played in it – some of which her mother still didn't know. 'But now I think Freda's seen which side her bread's buttered on.'

Vicky hoped her mother was right. 'She seems a lot

quieter. Different. She's a lot kinder too, taking Elise to the cinema, spending time with her.'

Thoughtfully, Ada regarded her daughter. 'And that doesn't worry you?'

'It would have done a while back. But not now. I think Freda's been lonely and needed a friend.'

'She had a sister.'

Vicky looked away. 'We were never friends. We never can be.'

'People change. Sometimes more than you can imagine,' Ada said magnanimously. 'Freda needs to be given a chance now. She lost her son, after all, and people weren't kind to her. I know I wasn't.'

'Neither was I,' Vicky admitted. 'But I hated her so much.'

'You had reason.'

'That doesn't make it right.'

Sighing, Ada shifted in her seat, her leg stretched out in front of her. 'You know, life's strange. If you didn't have Karl and the kids you might not be so forgiving, Vicky.'

The truth was unpalatable.

'Do you think I don't know that?'

'Good, I'm glad you do. Because no one was innocent in that sorry affair. I wasn't – I should have seen what was going on under my own nose, but I was too busy. I knew what Freda was like then – it should have been obvious. And I knew the kind of man Duncan Oldenshaw was. But I still let him in –'

'It wasn't your fault.'

Ada waved aside the objection. 'Oh, it was! I had his number the first time I laid eyes on him, but I let Douglas persuade me to give him a chance.' She paused, her voice hardening when she said, 'Well, I might have been stupid once, but if I ever cross paths with Duncan Oldenshaw again, he'll come off worse. I won't get caught a second time.'

Freezing December rain gave way to snow later, the streets spittled with white, ice forming on chimneypots and along the edges of the pavements. It was bitterly cold. In the Stockport streets, people hurried along, their heads bent to the wind, the shop lights patterning the cobbles. At six o'clock, Winter's Clock chimed the hour, Freda getting off the bus from Hyde and making her way towards Churchgate. She was just about to cross, when a car pulled up. Duncan leaned over and opened the passenger door.

'Get in.'

Looking round hurriedly, Freda did so. 'I didn't know you had a car.'

'Nice, isn't it?' he asked her.

'*Nice*. Must have cost you some.'

'I can afford it.'

She rubbed her hands together to warm them as Duncan pulled out into the road. 'What's your job now?'

'This and that.'

Grimly she smiled. 'I see.'

'I doubt it.'

'I don't suppose it's legal,' Freda went on, excited by the idea. This was more like it, something daring in her life again. Her hand ran across the dashboard longingly. 'Doug never got a car.'

Duncan said nothing. Freda didn't know that he had borrowed the vehicle for the evening. Best to let her think that he was doing well. That way she would be more likely to help him. A woman like her didn't want a loser in her life. And if she thought that he was doing something illegal, so what? She didn't have to know that he was earning a meagre living on the markets, selling cheap shirts and cotton remnants.

It hadn't been his choice, but what could you do? His job had been stolen from him by Karl Straub, the man who had taken over his place in the pub. And his wife.

'So where are we going?' Freda asked, leaning back against the seat and looking over to Duncan.

'A drive, I thought.'

'Oh, right.' She smiled to herself.

She knew where the drive would lead – to some quiet place where they could have sex. In fact, she longed for it, luxuriated in the suspense as Duncan drove out of the town centre to the countryside beyond Brinksway Banks. It had been a week since Duncan's re-emergence and she had seen him twice in Hyde. Their last meeting was hurried, Duncan preoccupied, Freda pressing him to stay with her longer.

He knew what she wanted and he played her like a fish. It was an old trick of Duncan's and one that had never failed him. Knowing she was longing for sex, he made her wait. Then when they made love again, she would be completely under his thumb.

'Miss me?' Freda asked suddenly, her hand resting on his shoulder.

'Every day. Did you miss me?'

'Life was hell without you,' she said honestly. 'You have no idea what it was like. I had –'

'It's the past, Freda,' Duncan interrupted her. 'We have to move on.'

Sighing, she let her hand move further up his thigh, Duncan's gaze fixed on the road ahead. It was lucky that she and Doug were talking again. He would never suspect her now, thinking he had punished her enough and that she would toe the line. If only he knew, Freda thought. If only he knew that I was with his brother, his hated brother.

Finding a dark, wooded area, Duncan pulled the car over and turned off the engine.

'So,' he said, looking at Freda. 'What do you want to talk about?'

She punched him lightly in the chest. 'Stop teasing! You know why we came here.'

'To look at the stars?'

'Duncan!'

'Or the night life? They say there are badgers up here.'

Sitting bolt upright, Freda folded her arms. He was teasing her, making her wait. And she didn't like it.

'Take me back home.'

'Home!' he echoed. 'Oh, I don't think you really want that, Freda. You have no home. You can't call that pub your home, not now. Just like you can't call Doug your husband, when you love me –'

'You're too sure of yourself by half!' she barked.

'I'm sure of you,' he replied, touching her cheek. 'And you're sure of me, Freda. You and I are a pair. We're alike, the two of us. We can't love anyone else. We were made for each other.'

'You still love me as much?' she asked, hoping for reassurance. 'I bet you had lots of women when you were away.'

'None was like you.'

'What *were* they like?' she asked, jealously. 'Richer, prettier . . . younger?'

'Come on, Freda, you're the one for me! We're a team. We both knew that the moment we set eyes on each other.'

She thought back to their first meeting: Doug introducing his brother, their eyes meeting, attraction instant and unnerving.

'So why don't we go away together? Just get away from here?' she pleaded, knowing that the words would irritate him and yet unable to stop herself.

'I told you! I have to settle an old score first. For both of us.'

'I *never* settled any old scores,' Freda said bitterly. 'I just took it all on the chin.'

He sighed. 'You know I'm doing this for both of us.'

'Whatever you say, Duncan,' she replied, knowing that he was lying and yet choosing to ignore it.

She *would* get him to do what she wanted, but in her own way. Gently she took his hand and placed it inside her blouse, his fingers closing over her nipple.

'Remember that?'

'I remember,' he said, his voice low as he began to kiss her eagerly.

In the distance the lights of Stockport shone out into the falling snow. Far away, Winter's Clock chimed; a bus changed gears on the slope of Underbank. All the birds were silent, the trees winter bare around the low dark hump of the car. No moon shone.

It was a bitter night. The night they plotted their revenge.

Chapter Forty-Nine

'You look happy,' Karl said to Doug as he came up out of the cellar, whistling.

'That's because I am,' he replied, struggling to find words. 'You know something? I don't know how to put this, but love makes things . . . Oh, you know.'

Karl nodded. 'I know.' He shook hands suddenly with Doug, smiling broadly. 'I'm so glad for you, so glad.'

Ashamed, Doug thought back to his earlier behaviour.

'I owe you an apology,' he began, his tone uncertain. 'I've been a sod with you, Karl. I'm sorry. I was a bit mad,' he touched his temple and pulled a face. 'I wasn't thinking straight.'

'I doesn't matter –'

'But it does. You've known me as a bitter man, but I wasn't always like that. And I'm not going to be like that again,' he said, his tone certain. 'I've got a second chance with my wife – and I'm going to take it.'

'Good for you,' Karl said sincerely. 'I wish you luck.'

'Thanks. You want to know something? I always thought I was a lucky man before – until things went bad. Now maybe it's time for me to be lucky again.' He nodded. 'Yeah, it's time to be lucky again.'

Elise knew that her father was delighted to hear that she had been successful in her application for a teacher training course. He hugged her, told her it was the start of her new life and generally made her feel special. Naturally, the news was shared with Vicky, the three of them taking Stella along on an outing to Southport. It was bitingly cold, the middle of winter, but Karl walked along Lord Street with *his girls* and felt like a sultan.

He then treated them to a tea at Marshall and Snelgrove, and if he was worried about money, he never let on. From time to time he would look at Elise and his eyes would fill with pride, Vicky watching them both.

She didn't know that Elise – for all her smiles – was vacant inside, couldn't possibly guess that the girl she loved as much as her own daughter was upset. And how could Elise tell her? Say – 'Southport is your special place. Yours and Dad's. It's the place you came when you first knew you were in love, walking hand in hand and looking at the shops, rationing coming to its slow end.'

I can't say it, Elise thought, watching Karl and Vicky. But inside she felt excluded, shifted to the sidelines. It was the same at The Sixpenny Winner now. Freda was cheerful again, apparently having made up with Doug. And even Ada was flirty – out of plaster – egging Mac Potter on just to annoy Lizzie.

Only she was alone, without a special person in her life. Elise sighed, glanced out of the shop window and watched the passers-by. Why was it that virtually everyone seemed to be in pairs, men and women, coupled off, the few solitary walkers seeming somehow sad, as though no one wanted them.

Annoyed at her own self-pity. Elise turned to say something to her father, but he was talking to Vicky, his bearded face turned to her, listening to her. *Loving her.* She might be sitting beside them but her father's attention was centred on one person alone. And it wasn't his daughter.

Stan Foreshaw's florid face leaned towards Ada.

'It's called *The Third Man*, with that bloke in it – oh, you know the one – big bloke with a funny name.'

Ada sighed. 'That narrows it down, Stan.'

'He's a bloody wonder boy. And there's another actor in it called something odd.'

Moving out from behind the bar, Ada banked up the fire in the pub and nodded to a couple of regulars. They had had a good New Year, the takings high. 1950, she thought, a whole new decade. Wonder what that'll bring.

'Orson –'

'Welles,' she finished neatly for Stan.

He nodded, some of his pint slopping onto his lap. 'That's the man! Well, it's a smasher someone said. Showing in London now, but not up here yet.'

Ada had little truck with the cinema. Since getting back on her feet she had spent as little time as possible sitting down, even though her leg ached much of the time. Her bedroom had become a prison and she had no intention of returning to it – except to sleep. Yet she had to admit that Doug and Karl had done a good job in her absence. There was nothing she could fault – and God knows she had tried hard enough. The two men had worked well together, even becoming friends.

Not that everyone was so pliable. Only the previous week some wit had scribbled 'NAZI BARRACKS' on the pub door and drawn a crude caricature of Karl wearing a German helmet. Amazing, Ada thought, you'd think people would want to forget the war. Mind you, before the war if someone had told her that Vicky would fall for Karl Straub she would never have believed it. After all, a Yorkshireman for a son-in-law was bad enough, but a man who was half German . . .

Thoughtful, Ada then considered Freda. *Freda and Douglas together again.* Maybe her daughter might have another child, a baby to make up for Billy. A child who really would be Douglas's. Ada liked the idea. The pub was full of life again with Karl and Vicky's ready-made family – so why couldn't Freda start again? Doug wanted it, Ada knew that. He hadn't said as much, but the way he looked at Stella was enough. And when he had heard about Elise being accepted for teacher training he had been delighted, as though the girl was part of his own family. Which she was, almost.

Maybe this new decade would bring new life, Ada thought, willing it with all her heart. Maybe the bad times were over, once and for all.

'Hey, you were miles away,' Karl said, watching her.

'I was thinking,' Ada replied, looking him up and down. 'You putting on weight?'

He flushed, his accent more apparent when he was embarrassed. 'I'm happy, I always put on weight when I'm happy.'

'I thought Vicky's cooking might have cured that.'

He smiled. 'I love her very much, you know.'

'Get away!' Ada teased him.

'I do, and I'll make her happy.'

Ada was watching him avidly. 'Oh God, Karl, don't start crying! You know I can't take that.'

He pulled himself together hurriedly. 'You know that I want to marry Vicky?'

'You've told me often enough. But first you have to get her *unmarried.*'

486

'I know. Vicky says we should wait for another three and a half years and then the divorce can go through automatically.'

Ada stared up at him. 'But?'

'But what?'

'Well, there's a *but*, I know there is.'

'Three and a half years is a long time.'

'It is that. But the only alternative would mean citing Duncan for adultery – and that would open up a can of worms for everyone.' Ada paused, regarding Karl thoughtfully. 'Go on, say it.'

'Say what?'

'Whatever it is you want to say!'

'I was just wondering if there *was* any other way, if it was worthwhile trying to get in touch with Duncan.'

Ada was surprised and showed it: 'What does Vicky think about that?'

'She won't even hear Duncan's name mentioned. But we have to talk about it.'

'Give her time,' Ada cautioned him. 'That man hurt her more than you know. He caused trouble for all of us. Maybe the wound's too deep to scratch open again just yet.'

'But –'

Ada put up her hands to stop him continuing. 'Let it be, Karl. Things have a way of working out in their own time. If you force matters, it could all blow up in your face.'

To Freda's utter amazement sex with Duncan was not as incredible as she had hoped. The disappointment made her savage. All her longing for him seemed slightly foolish now. He was good in bed, but her passion for him had waned. It was as though she had been starving for so long that finally the food had come and she no longer had the stomach for it.

The realisation made her bitter. What was there for her now? The scales dropped from her eyes in an instant. He was using her, Freda thought. Duncan Oldenshaw was relying on her obsession for him to manipulate her. He wanted revenge, but after he had got his own back, then what? Would he run away with her? Would he marry her? Take her away from her husband once and for all?

No, Freda thought, that was not Duncan's plan. The truth was bruising. After he had his revenge he would leave her again. With what? Nothing. Just her life at The Sixpenny Winner. And what would that consist of? The same old thing, day in and day out. Oh yes, it was true that Doug was beginning to love her again, but where would that lead? To her becoming pregnant? An unwilling mother, locked into a loveless marriage, always watching everyone else's good fortune.

Like Vicky's. Freda could hardly bear the thought of spending the rest of her life having Vicky's happiness crammed down her throat. She had got lucky, all right. Karl worshipped her, she had Stella – and the affection of Elise. Quite the little matriarch. But who knew what the real Vicky was like? Who knew that she had been so crazy about Duncan that she had married him knowing that he was Freda's lover and Billy's father? She wouldn't look so honourable if people found that out, Freda thought. But then again, if *she* exposed Vicky no one would believe her. They'd all think she was making it up to cause trouble. Because Vicky was the good daughter, wasn't she?

So good she had caused Billy's death, Freda thought grimly, her fury rising like a tidal wave. Her sister –

the caring Vicky – had robbed her of her son. Her son, and Duncan's, the one real hold she had over him. If Billy had lived, Duncan would never have left her, or his child. If Billy had lived she wouldn't be here now, putting up with her husband's calflike fawning, locked into the pub on a sentence which had no remand.

It was all Vicky's fault the way her life had turned out, Freda realised, bile in her mouth ... Her disappointment in Duncan suddenly found a place to fester. She was unfulfilled, cheated, and someone had to pay for it. And who better than her sister?

Oh yes, Freda thought, she would wipe that bloody smug smile off Vicky's face. She would see her sister miserable, just as she had been for so long ... Brooding, Freda chewed the edge of her fingernail. So Duncan thought he could use her, did he? Well, maybe she would use him as well. He wanted revenge, but so did she: revenge on her family, on fate, on him. But above all, on Vicky ... Silently Freda brooded. She thought of what she and Duncan had talked about in Brinksway Banks and decided that she would play along. But she wouldn't be doing it just for him, but for herself. In the end she would make sure that she got Duncan Oldenshaw – but it would be more an act of revenge, than longing.

Like he had said, they were two of kind.

Chapter Fifty

It was snowing when Freda finished at the hat shop. Hurrying out, she tied a scarf round her head and buttoned up her coat. Just as she reached the corner her bus came along. Freda put out her hand to hail it and a moment later she was sitting down, her bag on her lap, her gaze moving back to the snowy streets.

Better to let it happen naturally, she thought. Even Duncan had some morals.

'Sixpence.'

Freda passed the money over to the conductor and took her ticket without uttering a word. Beside her, an old man coughed wheezily.

Her job was a good cover. If she had been at the pub her hands would have been well and truly tied, Freda thought. Now she could come and go as she pleased, having been off Ada's leash for months. And Doug wasn't worried about what she got up to; he was convinced that Freda was committed to her marriage again. She had learned her lesson, their looks seemed to say. Freda had come to heel.

Like hell. Slowly the bus edged along, finally arriving in Stockport, outside the town hall. As Freda got off she could see a figure waiting for her, tucked under the stone pillars out of the worst of the weather.

'Sorry I was late. I got held up at work,' Freda said, linking arms with Elise and drawing her out on to the pavement. 'Ready to see the film?'

She was cold, shivering. 'I hope it's warm in there.'

'It will be,' Freda assured her, as they headed towards the Roxy and joined the queue. Nonchalantly, Freda looked round. 'Everyone likes Katharine Hepburn.'

Elise nodded, blowing on her hands. She was looking very pretty, the chill pinching some colour into her cheeks, her checked swing coat flapping around her trousered legs. Falling loose from its ponytail, her hair hung in tendrils around her face, her eyes brightly blue.

'I thought Doug wanted to see this film,' Elise said. 'I know Vicky did.'

'Well, they can see it some other time,' Freda answered her. 'I thought we'd have a girls' night out.'

Flattered, Elise fell silent. That the glamorous Freda should want to spend time with her was a revelation. She had thought that since Freda and Douglas had patched things up, she would see less of her idol. But Freda had been more, not less, attentive lately. They had had several such outings and gone to the shops together, Freda picking out some material for a dress and helping Elise with her make-up.

'You want to look your best,' she had said. 'Every woman should make the best of herself.'

'I'm not that interested –'

'But you must be!' Freda had chided her. 'You're a pretty young woman; you have to use that power.'

Well, it was one thing to talk about power, quite another to use it. If you were as lovely and confident as Freda you could turn heads anywhere, but Elise wasn't sure of herself in that way. She had never even had a boyfriend.

Looking round the cinema queue she suddenly spotted a man walking towards them. A handsome man, obviously recognising Freda.

'Well, hello,' he said, drawing level with them in the queue. 'I haven't seen you for a while, Freda.'

She smiled, their eyes meeting for an instant before Freda spoke. 'Hello, Morris.' She tried out the false name for size, Duncan watching her carefully. 'Good to see you again. This is my friend Elise.'

He turned, looked at the girl standing by Freda and noted how young she was. And how pretty. Flushing, Elise was achingly attractive, her naïvety making her all the more appealing.

'How do you do?' he said politely. 'Nice to meet you. Are you both going to see the film?'

What does it look like? Freda wanted to say. We're not in the queue to catch fish.

'We heard it was a good film,' Elise volunteered, her courage building. The man was so handsome, she thought, almost like a movie star himself. 'I like Katharine Hepburn.'

'Me too,' Duncan replied, 'although I've seen the film already. Pity that, we could have gone in together.' He paused, as though considering something. 'Actually, I wouldn't mind seeing it again. Would you let me join you, ladies?'

Later, in the darkness, Elise found herself trying not to think of the man sitting next to her. But she could sense him, smell the soap he had used, and felt almost giddy when he laughed. Furtively stealing a glance at him, Elise noticed how piercing his eyes were and how relaxed he looked, his legs stretched out in front of him.

Meanwhile Freda had caught the sizzle of electricity between the two. This was going to be so easy, she thought with pleasure. After all, how could a young inexperienced girl *not* be attracted to a man like Duncan? Elise would see him as thrilling, exciting – just as she had done at first. But the effect Duncan would have on Elise would be even more powerful, since she had never had a boyfriend. Never been kissed, or made love to.

Suddenly the intermission came, the house lights going on, Elise keeping her gaze averted as Duncan leaned over.

'Would you both like an ice cream?'

Freda nodded, nudging Elise. 'What about you?'

'That would be nice,' the girl replied, reaching for her bag.

'You don't need that,' Duncan told her. 'My treat.'

Both of them watched as he moved off and joined the queue for the usherette.

'Good-looking, isn't he?' Freda asked.

'Very,' Elise said shyly. 'How do you know him?'

'We go back a long way,' Freda replied evasively. 'I never thought I'd bump into him like this.' Suddenly she frowned, as though worried. 'Oh, Elise, we shouldn't mention this at home. You know Douglas would be so jealous, and Morris isn't the kind of man Ada likes.'

'But he's –'

'Listen to me, please,' Freda said kindly. 'Your father wouldn't like it either. Oh, we know it's innocent, but you know what fathers are like – overprotective. And I heard Vicky saying only the other day that she was worried about you joining the teacher training course in case you got involved with the boys.'

Elise opened her eyes wide in surprise. 'She said that? But I've never been interested in boys.'

'Oh, she didn't mean it badly. She's just worried, that's all. She wants to look after you, Elise – be like a mother to you.' Freda smiled wickedly. 'Trouble with mothers is that they don't want anyone to have any fun.'

'I wouldn't do anything wrong!' Elise hurried on. 'Vicky shouldn't worry.'

493

'She wants to do right by you, and to show your father that she cares,' Freda continued, supremely reasonable. 'Don't worry, Vicky doesn't mean to stop you having any boyfriends. It's just that she wants to make sure that she approves of anyone you go out with.'

Confused, Elise stared at her. 'But it's my choice who I go out with.'

'Of course it is! But she – Oh, it's nothing to worry about. I'm sure she'll ease off when she knows you're sensible. But that's why I wouldn't mention meeting Morris. Everyone would start reading things into it.' She dropped her voice, almost plaintive now. 'You know what my husband's like. You won't tell on me, Elise, will you? I mean, we're not doing anything bad, but Doug would be so angry with me. Worse, he might stop us from going out together again.'

That was the final straw.

'I won't say anything,' Elise promised her, glancing across to Duncan in the queue. 'He *is* very handsome, isn't he?'

'All the women like him. But he's very choosy.'

'Did you go out with him?'

'Once,' Freda said, making her tone wistful, 'but that's another story.'

'What does he do? I mean, for a living.'

'Oh, this and that,' Freda said evasively. 'But he's successful. He has a lovely car.'

'You'd think he had a girlfriend.'

Freda winced inwardly. 'No one special. He likes you, though.'

Elise flushed. 'No, he can't!'

'He can, and he does,' Freda insisted. 'I can tell from the way he looks at you. I've told you often enough, Elise, you're a very pretty girl.'

She felt dizzy at the compliment – and at the thought that this glamorous man might be interested in her. Her heart pounding, Elise moved her legs to let Duncan back into his seat.

Smiling, he passed her an ice cream. 'There you are,' he said, turning to Freda. 'And that's yours.'

With Elise turned the other way, only he could see the barely perceptible nod that Freda gave him. It was going the way they wanted, the gesture said. She's hooked.

Due to the freezing winter conditions, Stella had caught a bad cold. Worried, Vicky nursed her daughter, rubbing her chest with Vick and rocking her in the chair before the fire in the kitchen. Having never ailed a day in her life, Stella's illness worried Vicky. Anxious, Ada looked in repeatedly from the bar.

'She's asleep, that's good.'

'D'you think we should call the doctor?' Vicky asked her mother.

'For a cold? No. Kids always get colds and get over them.'

'But Stella's never had a cold before.'

'Vicky, stop worrying!' Ada said sternly. 'You can mollycoddle a child too much, you know.'

Rocking her sleeping daughter, Vicky glanced towards the door. 'Busy tonight.'

'Friday – what d'you expect?' Ada replied, putting the kettle on to boil. 'Where's Freda?'

'She was out with Elise earlier, but they're back now,' Vicky replied distantly, looking back to her child. 'Are you sure she's all right?'

'You worry too much. She's fine. Just a bit chesty.' Putting a blanket over the fireguard Ada felt it warm and then wrapped it around her daughter and granddaughter.

'Reminds me of when I was a child,' Vicky said, comforted. 'You used to do that to Dad too, before he moved upstairs.'

'He used to say that the warmth made his leg feel better,' Ada answered, thinking back. 'He suffered with that leg so much, and never grumbled. You should have seen it the day it happened, at Henessey's. God, the blood – all over the place it was. You wouldn't think a man could bleed so much and live.' She leaned towards Stella and touched her cheek. 'She's cooler now. Just keep nursing her, luv, that's all a child needs – to feel wanted.'

At two in the morning of that freezing day, Elise was lying awake in her bed. Through the partition she could just vaguely make out the sound of Karl snoring softly. Downstairs everything was in silence. She wouldn't think about Morris again, she decided. It was silly. After all, what would a man like that want with her? Freda was wrong, he wasn't interested in her. If there was anyone he liked the look of it was Freda.

It had been difficult for Elise to keep a secret. Nevertheless she had. As Freda had said, they weren't doing anything wrong, but the others might read something into it. And besides, Freda had been so good to her, the least she could do was to avoid any unpleasantness between her and Doug. As for Vicky . . . Elise turned over in bed, for once annoyed with her surrogate mother.

How *could* she worry about Elise and boys? Hadn't Elise been studious, always with her head in a book? When had she *ever* given Vicky or her father reason to be anxious? It wasn't fair, Elise decided. She wasn't a child. And besides it wasn't up to Vicky to tell her who she could or could not see. After all, Vicky wasn't her real mother.

She might have her father wrapped around her finger, but Elise wasn't going to be so malleable. Turning over again, she huddled under the covers, rubbing her hands together against the cold. She supposed that Morris was thirty at least, way too old for her . . . What was she thinking! Elise told herself sharply. She wasn't interested in him as a boyfriend.

Or was she? He was certainly handsome and she had little in common with lads of her own age, having never mixed with any of them. Morris was so easy to talk to, so relaxed – like her father, in fact. Uneasy, Elise pulled the covers over her head, the darkness complete. Soon she would be starting her teacher training course, meeting all kinds of people her own age . . .

The thought excited her and alarmed her at the same time. All her life she had been sheltered by Karl; now it was time to go out into the world. The difference was that this time her father wasn't going to take every step with her. He had other things on his mind: Vicky, Stella, the pub. Suddenly unsettled, Elise buried her face in her pillow. It was childish to resent Vicky, but she couldn't help it. Her father had other people in his life now, apart from her, whilst she had no one.

At the moment . . . Sighing, Elise lifted her head from under the pillow. It was just an infatuation, she thought, like falling in love with a movie star. She would never even see Morris again. Good thing too, she decided. Soon she would start teacher training and follow the goal she had set herself.

But had *she* set it, Elise wondered suddenly confused, or had her father? Whose idea had it been for her to be a teacher? Hers, or his? Just who was she trying to please? . . .

The cold early hours pressed down heavily on Elise as

she tried to sleep. Another hour passed, then another. Finally she dozed off, but woke only minutes later.

She had dreamed of Morris, bringing her an ice cream and kissing her cheek.

'Move over, Doug!' Freda said, jabbing her elbow into his ribs. 'You're snoring.'

He muttered in his sleep, rolling over, his right arm falling across her breasts. She would have liked to move it, but decided to leave it there. No point aggravating him. Besides, he might wake and want to talk. He had been silent for months and yet now he talked on and on. Trouble was, Freda didn't want to listen. There was nothing Doug could say that interested her any more.

She wondered then if Vicky and Karl had slept together, and decided that they must have done. Oh, they wouldn't admit it and they'd be sure to cover their tracks well, but that innocent lovey-dovey stuff couldn't be genuine. Freda wondered then how her mother would take it if she found Vicky and Karl making love – oh, there would be a ruckus then, and no mistake. Her wonderful daughter, behaving like a slut . . .

Wincing as Doug moved again, Freda stared upwards at the ceiling. There was a crack in it, running from the door to just over the bed. And above the crack lay Elise . . . Was she asleep? Freda wondered, guessing that she wasn't. If she was any judge Elise was lying awake thinking of Duncan.

The fact that she had a crush on him was obvious. With any luck it might become an infatuation. What a wonderful revenge that would be on her sister, Freda thought. Even better than sex. More thrilling, more dangerous. All she had to do was to make sure that things went according to plan. And how better could she get her own back than by using Duncan – not only to seduce Elise, but to betray Vicky. Again.

It was perfect, Freda decided, her toes curling with the pleasure of the thought, absolutely perfect. If she concentrated, she could almost imagine Vicky's face when she heard that her husband and Elise were having an affair.

'Freda,' Doug said suddenly, his voice low. 'Are you awake?'

She said nothing, just closed her eyes. Lovemaking with Duncan wasn't as thrilling as it had been, but sex with Doug was worse.

'Freda?' he repeated, leaning over her and studying her face. 'I love you, God knows, I love you.'

His voice plummeted, almost as though he regretted uttering the words. He was making himself a fool again, but he couldn't help it. In the past he had loved Freda passionately, and despite his better judgement that feeling was still rooted in his heart.

Her eyes closed, Freda lay still.

'I want us to be happy again,' Doug went on, touching her cheek, Freda unresponsive. 'I know we can work this out.'

She said nothing.

Sighing, Doug rolled onto his back. His heart was thumping and he had the sensation of drowning. He should have gone long ago, left Freda when Billy died. But he couldn't. The tie to her was too strong. So he had wanted to punish her, and had succeeded – for a time, until he had weakened. And then she had slid under his defences like a snake under a blanket. He was caught, and he knew it.

'Freda,' he whispered again, 'we have to make this work. We have to. Forget the past. I forgive you. Dear God, I forgive you.'

Forgive me? . . . For what I've done? Freda thought dully. Or for what I'm about to do?

Chapter Fifty-One

'He wants to see you again,' Freda said, her voice low as she caught Elise coming downstairs.

'Who?'

'D –, Morris,' Freda whispered, checking herself.

Flushing, Elise shook her head. 'He can't!'

'He told me yesterday. Said he'd been thinking of you all the time since you met. I think he's a bit smitten,' Freda went on, Elise listening, her eyes wide.

'Freda, give me a hand!' Ada said suddenly, as she arrived on the landing. 'What are you two whispering about?'

'Who's whispering?' Freda countered. 'We were talking about Bessie Cork. She's selling the shop –'

Unsettled by the ease with which Freda lied, Elise watched Ada take the bait.

'Bessie Cork selling up? Never! That shop's her life.'

'Well, I heard a rumour –'

'That's all it is, a rumour,' Ada concluded, drawing level with them. 'Now, give me a hand before you go to work, will you?'

Shooting Elise a regretful look, Freda walked off, leaving her standing on the stairs, her books clasped to her chest. Confused, Elise sat down, her head resting against the banister. Above she could hear Stella coughing and Vicky's voice soothing her, whilst below Doug was whistling in the backyard.

Morris was smitten by her. Never! She shook her head

and prepared to get up, but then changed her mind. It was all so thrilling, so incredible. To meet a man like that, good-looking, successful, charming – and he liked *her*. Her head swam with the romance of it all. Then another thought entered her head: her father and Vicky must not find out.

They wouldn't approve. And if Vicky was as interfering as Freda had suggested, any romance with Morris would be curtailed at the start. Disliking the idea of subterfuge, Elise did however comfort herself with the thought that she was sparing them worry – but knew she was kidding herself. She had been irritated by Vicky's presumption and suddenly wanted to show everyone she was grown up.

They had made their own lives. Well, it was time she made hers too.

That afternoon there was a problem in the cellar. Karl had gone down to get some port and found a leak coming from the far wall. Calling Doug, they had looked at it together, deciding that there was a crack in the cellar plastering which was letting in water from outside.

'. . . and that'll cost money to fix,' Doug concluded grimly, brushing the dust off his hands.

'We could have a go at repairing it ourselves first,' Karl replied, getting to his feet, his bulk making movement awkward in the confined space where the ceiling dipped.

'I suppose we *could* try replastering it,' Doug agreed, 'it's a hell of a job. But then again, I don't want to pay for someone to come in and do it.' He turned to Karl. 'Don't mention this to Ada, it'll only worry her.'

'She's limping. Did you notice that?' Karl asked him, leaning against the stone wall and folding his arms. 'I thought I was imagining it first, but I watched her again this morning and she's definitely walking with a limp.'

'I thought the same. She should see a doctor.'

'You try telling her.'

Worried, Doug shook his head. 'I think she rushed it, getting that cast off and running about like a two-year-old. She should have taken it easier, let it adjust. After all, that leg's weaker than the other one.'

'I suggested that she sit on a stool behind the bar.'

Doug laughed. 'I bet that went down well.'

'She said she'd rather be stuffed and put into the cabinet with The Sixpenny Winner!' Karl smiled, wiping the sweat off his forehead. 'So shall we have a go at the plastering ourselves?'

Doug thought for a moment before replying.

'It might do the trick. On the other hand, these cellars are so old, the damage might turn out to be a lot worse than it looks. God knows what's behind that wall. If we start chipping away, we could make it worse.'

'Then let's just plaster over it,' Karl suggested.

'And see what happens?' Doug queried. 'I'm not sure. Plastering over things sometimes only hides, not cures, the problem.'

Taking great pains with her hair, Elise put on her red dress and pulled her coat over the top. Finally she checked her reflection in the mirror, her mouth drying with excitement. Morris wanted to meet up with her. He had sent a message, via Freda, that he would be at the railway bridge at seven thirty. Would she come?

Of course she would . . . Hurriedly Elise snatched up her bag and moved to the back door. Vicky saw her and called out: 'Where are you off to?'

Elise froze on the spot. 'I'm going for a walk.'

'You're mad! It's snowing out there,' Vicky said cheerfully. 'Come and talk to me instead. Stella's asleep, I could do with the company.'

'Where's Dad?' Elise asked, her voice unusually truculent.

Vicky heard the tone and was surprised. This wasn't like Elise. 'He's busy with Doug. And besides, the pub's opening in a few minutes. I'd like your company, Elise. We haven't had one of our talks for a while.'

'That's not my fault.'

Stung, Vicky regarded the girl thoughtfully. 'Have I upset you in some way?'

'No.'

'It's just that Stella's been ill and there have been so many other things –'

'To do,' Elise finished for her. Then, ashamed, she moderated her tone. 'I didn't mean to be sharp, Vicky. I've missed our chats too, but I want some fresh air. I've been studying all day and I need a break.'

Unwilling to press her, Vicky nodded. 'Well then, you go and have a walk. But be careful –'

'I can look after myself!'

'I never said you couldn't!' Vicky countered, wondering what had possessed Elise all of a sudden. 'I was just worried about you –'

'Well, you worry about Dad and Stella. I'm old enough to take care of myself.'

One thing Vicky had been right about – it was cold. Her head down, Elise crossed Churchgate and headed for the centre of town and the railway bridge. The temperature was little above freezing, ice on the pavements, her shoes slipping so much that she struggled to keep her balance.

Then she saw him, standing at the end of the bridge,

wearing a trilby, his coat collar turned up. Slowing down she tried to collect her thoughts, but when Duncan saw her he threw away the cigarette he was smoking and hurried across the bridge.

Reaching her, he took Elise's hand. 'Thank you. Thank you so much for coming.' His tone was faltering, like a man unsure of himself. 'I wanted to see you again so much. I can't stop thinking about you –'

'I'm the same!' Elise replied eagerly. 'I can't stop thinking about you either, Morris.'

The false name jarred on Duncan, but he pressed on regardless. 'I've got a car, d'you want to come for a drive?'

It never occurred to Elise to question why he hadn't picked her up. Instead, she nodded. 'I can't be long, though, otherwise everyone will miss me.'

Sympathetically he looked at her. 'I understand. You're so young –'

'Not so young! I'm seventeen, eighteen later this year.'

'I'm a lot older,' Duncan replied, looking away. 'I shouldn't have asked you to come here tonight. It was wrong of me. I shouldn't have expected you to want to see an old man like me.'

She played straight into his hands. 'You're not old! Besides, you're much more interesting than boys of my age.'

'Freda said you were going to teacher training college soon. You'll meet someone your own age there.' He sighed. 'It's how it should be – but I couldn't help myself, Elise. I had to tell you how I felt about you. Nothing like this has ever happened to me before. I just fell for you.' He pulled her to him, Elise stiffening in his arms. 'Don't worry, I wouldn't hurt you, not for all the world. I just want to love you, that's all.'

Slowly he kissed her lips, Elise flushing and pulling away.

'I can't –'

'It's OK,' Duncan replied, soothing her. 'I don't want to rush anything. I just wanted to show you how much you mean to me.' He touched her cheek lightly, Elise fighting the temptation to kiss him. 'Have I scared you away, little one?'

He had chosen his paternal tone well, and Elise relaxed.

'No, you haven't scared me away ... I'm just so surprised.'

'About what?'

'That you want to see me again.' Elise admitted, flushing and cursing her naïvety. He would think she was a kid, a red-faced idiot.

'Of course I want to see you again! I want to take you out, spend time with you.' Duncan assumed a thoughtful look. 'Mind you, Freda warned me that your family might not like it much. Me being so much older –'

'It's nothing to do with them!' she snapped defiantly. 'My father's busy most of the time and as for his girlfriend – well, I like Vicky, but she's not my mother and she shouldn't expect me to do as she says. I'm not a baby. She has a child of her own anyway, so why bother me? Oh, I know, it's because she cares about me, but it's a ... nuisance.'

The outburst was better than Duncan could have hoped for. Freda's little well-placed comments had done the trick. Vicky was rapidly becoming the villain of the piece. The person against whom Elise would rebel. *Vicky* ... he thought of his wife, remembering her guileless expression the day she accused him of stealing from her, the way she had set him up and had him banished. Then he thought of living rough, without a home or a family. She had done that – exiled him from his brother and a comfortable life. She had done it and she would pay for it.

'What's she like, this Vicky?'

'Very kind,' Elise replied, 'she cares about me like a daughter.'

'But?'

'I think she wants to control me as much as she controls my father.'

'What's he like?' Duncan asked, lighting up a cigarette as he listened.

'Wonderful. He's always been there to look out for me. During the war, it was frightening at times. People could be cruel – but Dad was always there.'

'But not so much now? Not now he has this Vicky?'

The questions struck home, Elise wanting to confide in someone desperately. And who better than this man who liked her so much?

'I'm not jealous of her . . .' She paused, then added bluntly, 'Of course I am!'

'You need someone of your own,' Duncan replied, his voice gentle. 'I'd like to be that someone, Elise.'

She hesitated. 'But we would have to keep it a secret. Our meetings –'

'I can keep secrets.'

'But I can't,' Elise replied woefully. 'I've never needed to before. Dad and I shared everything.'

'But it's not just you and your father now, is it? There's Vicky too. I imagine that makes it hard, having to share your father.'

He understood! Elise thought. At last, someone understood.

'But I've never gone behind his back before. Never lied

to him.' Duncan looked away, as though annoyed, Elise panicking. 'But I could keep us a secret! I could, I know I could.'

His eyes were warm, understanding. 'You see, Elise, if they know about us, they'll try and separate us. You'll not be allowed to see me again. Ever.'

The thought was unpalatable to her. Even more than lying was. She was at the beginning of her first romance – no one had the right to scupper it.

'You must keep quiet.'

'I will,' she assured him. 'I will.'

'Can you meet up with me tomorrow night? Around eight?'

Elise hesitated, then nodded.

That was the beginning.

Three weeks passed, Elise meeting up with Duncan whenever she could, Freda often covering for her. She was at the library, Freda said, or she had gone for a walk. Too much studying gave her headaches. And when Freda met up with Duncan they would talk about Elise, checking on their progress.

'She's very shy.'

'You mean she's not let you go the whole way yet?' Freda countered.

'She's not cheap.'

'Meaning I am?' Freda replied sharply, looking out of the car window at the snowy streets. 'You should see Vicky's face. That Karl is all over her – *I love you, darling, we have a whole life ahead of us. You and me – and the children.*' She laughed hoarsely. 'The children! One of which happens to be sneaking around with your husband, Vicky. I want to tell her so much, but I can't. Yet.'

'Say nothing!' Duncan barked.

'Don't shout at me! I'm the one who set all this up. Am I likely to mess it up now?'

'Elise is a nice kid –'

'Oh, don't say you're getting cold feet, Duncan,' Freda replied, her tone deadly. 'Remember what's riding on this.'

'What exactly?'

'Your revenge! You want to get your own back on Vicky and so do I. When Vicky finds out what's happened she'll be floored. It might even break up her and Karl. After all, she wouldn't look like such a good stepmother-to-be, would she?' Freda paused, relishing the thought. 'Then after it's all over, we can start again. Somewhere new.'

He hesitated. Freda saw it and moved in for the kill.

'Just in case you're thinking of leaving me high and dry again, Duncan, remember this – I can get Doug on your back any time I like. I can tell him where you are, and what you're planning to do to that blushing virgin. You think he'd stand for that?'

Duncan paled. 'You wouldn't!'

'Try me.'

'Doug wouldn't believe you!' Duncan blustered, panicked. 'Anyway, I'd say we'd planned it together. He'd believe that.'

'Want to put a fiver on it, Duncan? Remember I'm the dutiful wife again now. And he'd never believe I'd have anything to do with you again. You killed Billy, remember? How could I forgive you for that?'

Duncan could see from Freda's face that she wasn't kidding. He was suddenly, unexpectedly, frightened of her.

'Think very carefully about crossing me, Duncan. When we've got our own back on Vicky we leave this town. *Together*. If I even suspect that you're going to dump me I'll tell Doug everything. And he'll come looking for you. You know that. Only this time you wouldn't get away so easily.'

He stared at her for a long moment. '*Why* do you want me?'

'Let's say I have my reasons.'

'You're a bitch, Freda,' Duncan said at last.

Smiling, she ran her finger along his bottom lip. 'That's what you like about me.'

'I'll say it again – Doug mustn't find out about us.'

'He won't,' she assured him. 'My lips are sealed, and Elise isn't going to say a word. This is her big romance – d'you think she's going to risk it? Doug will only know what we've done when we've gone.'

Duncan thought of his brother anxiously. 'I grew up with Doug, I know what he's like. He controls himself most of the time, but God help anyone who breaks his temper. He can I be a mean fighter.'

Freda raised her eyebrows, looking Duncan full in the face. 'So can I. Remember that.'

Chapter Fifty-Two

'Oh, I were so sorry I hear about your leg, Ada. I didn't think you could break the same bone twice. Unlucky that,' Lizzie said, leaning on the edge of Ada's bed in the Stockport Infirmary.

Ada had been admitted the previous night, having fallen down the cellar steps and twisted her hip badly. At first she had thought she had escaped with bruising – until she tried to move her leg.

'Did you bring a copy of the *Picture Post*?'

Lizzie shook her head. 'Couldn't get it. Bessie's stopped selling it. Says it's immoral.'

'Why didn't you try another shop?' Ada replied. 'Bessie Cork isn't the one person who sells newspapers. Anyway, I heard she was selling up.'

'Never!'

'That's what I said. But someone told our Freda about it.'

Lizzie frowned. 'Bessie would die rather than sell up. That shop's her life.' Curiously she eyed Ada's plaster cast. 'Does your leg hurt?'

'What do you think, Lizzie! That I broke it because I wanted something to do?'

'They say that it doesn't hurt when you first do it because of the shock,' Lizzie went on, 'but then the pain sets in later. Some people get gangrene too. I guess that's when their casts are too tight and it cuts off the blood.

Gangrene makes your leg go all black and green . . .
Want a grape?'

Ada sighed noisily. 'Lizzie, has anyone ever told you
that you make a bloody awful visitor?'

She flushed. 'I came to see you out of the goodness of
my heart!'

'You forgot the *Picture Post*!'

'You've a wicked tongue, Ada Hargreaves! God knows,
I'm not a person to call another, but –'

'Oh, dry up!' Ada hurled back, flinching as she moved
her leg. 'And give me some of those grapes, before you
eat the lot.'

In silence they finished the bunch, Lizzie spitting her
pips noisily into a brown bag. Then she screwed it
up into a twist of paper and flicked it into the tin
wastepaper bin.

Finally she looked back to Ada. 'How long d'you have
to stay here?'

'A week at least, so they can check it's all knitting
together all right.'

'A week . . . fancy,' Lizzie said, looking round her.

The ward was busy, nurses hurrying around, a radio
playing in the corner. And in the bed beside Ada's was
a young, narrow-faced woman knitting a blue baby
jacket. She kept looking over to Lizzie and smiling.

'Who's that?'

Ada glanced over and dropped her voice. 'She never
has any visitors. Says her husband's away but someone
told me he was in prison. She's six months gone, and
broke her leg last Sunday trying to move some furniture.'

'Fancy,' Lizzie said again.

'So, what's the gossip?' Ada asked, desperate for
something to take her mind off the fact that she was
in hospital and out of things.

'Nothing much. I saw Mac this morning. He sends his best.'

I bet he does, Ada thought drily. 'You two any nearer to getting married?'

'I'm not sure I want to,' Lizzie replied, her tone unconvincing. Hurriedly she changed the subject. 'I saw Elise the other day. Pretty girl, really growing up now. I bet she has the boys fluttering around her.'

'She's not the type,' Ada said shortly. 'Elise is interested in having a career.'

'So was Vicky once, but she changed her mind. A woman's never happy unless she's got a man and kids.'

'You don't have children, Lizzie,' Ada said patiently.

'I wasn't lucky, my man passing away like that. But there you go, I still say it's what makes a woman happy.' She paused, thinking. 'Freda and Douglas are getting on better, I see.'

Ada raised her eyebrows. 'How d'you *see* that, Lizzie? You got a hole in our wall I don't know about?'

'Oh, it's obvious! He's all attentive again, like he used to be. And she's looking well. Almost like she was in love.'

'You've love on the brain, Lizzie Antrim! Can't you think about anything else?' Ada replied, shifting her position again, the woman in the next bed smiling at her sympathetically.

'I was just thinking that it was nice the way things are working out,' Lizzie went on. 'You've had enough trouble, one way or another. It's good to see your family thriving.'

Well, for once she was right, Ada thought as Lizzie got to her feet.

'I'll call by again soon.'

'Bring me the *Picture Post*, Lizzie, will you?'

'I will,' she said, buttoning up her coat. 'And you take good care of yourself. Oh, and don't worry about the gangrene. You just keep moving that leg and you'll be fine.'

After all this time, Al Weeks thought. And now, if the gossip was to be believed, Duncan Oldenshaw was back in Stockport. But why? Thoughtfully Al sat in his car and turned on the heater, his bald head covered by a cap. Bloody cold, it was, and no mistake. And there was more snow coming . . . He stared out of the window at the street and thought about what he had heard.

Duncan Oldenshaw had been seen at the railway station in Stockport. And there was more to it. He had been seen with a young woman, hardly more than a girl. Well, Al thought, that wasn't surprising. Duncan was always with some female. His contact knew little else. Only that Duncan was back in town.

Why? Al thought again. Surely he wasn't trying to make things up with his brother, or Freda? No, he wasn't that stupid, Al decided. Besides, he'd have heard if he was fooling around with Freda. Or then again, would he? They were a sly couple, not likely to broadcast an affair . . . Al lit up a cigarette and inhaled deeply. Maybe Duncan had just come back for work, but then again, why would he return to a place he had been run out of? The uneasy rumour Al had kept secret for so long crept to the forefront of his mind and lodged there. Was it true? If so, Duncan was more of a bastard than even he imagined.

But he wasn't stupid, Al knew that. Duncan was crafty, immoral, but not stupid. So there had to be some reason he would risk returning, a reason so pressing that it outweighed the danger of his brother finding out about him coming back. But then again, Douglas Oldenshaw didn't know everything about his brother, did he?

Al didn't like to think of Duncan's chances if Douglas ever found out. Or maybe Duncan believed that no one knew what he had done so long ago. What a gamble, Al thought, what a hell of a gamble to take. He knew Douglas Oldenshaw's type – good men who tried to live their lives by the book. The trouble was that Duncan and his brother weren't reading from the same book.

'So much for plastering it over,' Doug said, up to his ankles in water.

Karl bent over to see the damage. The wall was crumbling in places, water flooding into the cellar, the barrels piled high in another corner out of the way.

'We'll have to get someone in to bank the whole wall up,' Karl replied, sweating as he struggled to shore up the brickwork. 'God, Doug, what a bloody mess.'

At the top of the cellar steps, Elise was standing, looking down. She had seen Duncan many times during the previous weeks, had fallen for him hard and finally they had made love. But it hadn't been as pleasant as she had thought. Instead she felt dirty, guilty – and like a child she wanted comfort.

A comfort she could only get from her father. Karl would be angry, but he would understand, she had thought that morning. She would just talk to him and explain. But when she came looking for him he was busy in the cellar and, besides, Doug was there.

'Hi, sweetheart!' Karl called out, when he spotted her. 'Don't come down, you'll get wet.'

'Dad, I wanted to talk to you,' she said plaintively. Surely she could get him alone for a few minutes? She had to talk to him, as she used to. If she had been able to talk before, none of this mess would have happened. 'Dad!'

He turned, waving to her. 'I can't come now, but I'll be with you soon.'

'I have to talk.'

'Have a word with Vicky,' he called back. 'She's upstairs with Stella.'

She didn't want Vicky! That was the last person she wanted. Vicky would be furious with her. After all, hadn't Freda warned her that Vicky was worried about her already, about her and boys? Well, what would she think about her and Morris? She would be angry, sure to tell her father rather than letting Elise tell him in her own way, and before you knew it the family would all know too. Elise didn't want that. She wanted it to be something between her and Karl, no one else.

'Dad, please –'

'Wait, love,' he replied, not unkindly. 'We're in a mess down here.'

'But –'

'Sweetheart,' he called back patiently, 'I'll be with you later.'

His attention was caught by a sudden crash as half of the wall came down, a flood of dirty water following. Swearing, Doug jumped back. Karl was soaked to the skin.

Alarmed, Elise called down the stairs. 'Dad! Are you all right?'

'I'm fine,' Karl replied, wiping the sweat off his forehead. 'We'll talk later, OK?'

Hesitating she stood at the top of the stairs. She felt like a child, out of her depth, longing for comfort. But it wasn't forthcoming. Anxiously she gripped the stair rail, her eyes fixed on her father, willing him to turn. But Karl was preoccupied, up to his calves in water, Doug trying to catch hold of a barrel as it floated past them.

'Jesus, I hope it's not sewage,' he said angrily.

'No smell,' Karl replied. 'Thank God for small mercies.'

'Dad!' Elise called out again.

But her voice was drowned out by the noise of the two men working below. And disappeared, unheard.

Silently Elise turned and walked back into the kitchen, lit by winter snow light, ice making faces on the windows. Outside the cat was sitting on the wall, watching her. It was true that she was besotted by Morris, and he by her, but she felt so shabby. What she had done was wrong. She had heard enough about girls who went all the way, how people gossiped about them, saying they had ruined their chances of getting a decent man.

Was that what she had done? Elise thought desperately. Shame filled her. Her father would be so disappointed, especially if he found out that all the work she had pretended to do had been a cover. She had skipped her studies to spend time with Morris, and now she was falling behind and probably wouldn't be ready to start her teacher training course in September.

She had wrecked everything she and her father had wanted. And for what? A man. But she *loved* him, she was sure about that. And he loved her. Only . . . Elise stared at the cold cup of tea on the table before her. Her stomach felt hollow, her mouth dry. All that clamouring, those hard kisses, the grasping and moaning in the back of his car . . . The memory made her burn with shame. And longing.

She had wanted him, had wanted to please him in order to keep him. But it was wrong.

'What's up?' Vicky said, walking in with Stella. The little girl was still chesty, her mother fussing over her.

'Nothing,' Elise replied, evasively.

'You look worried. Not fretting over your studies, are you?'

Elise shook her head, willing Vicky to leave the room. Lying was too difficult, too involved. It was turning her into someone she hardly recognised any more.

'Are you sure you're all right?' Vicky said, sitting down next to Elise and pulling Stella onto her lap. 'Tell me, luv, can I help in any way?'

For a moment Elise wavered. She wanted to cry, to put her head on Vicky's shoulder and confess. To be held and comforted.

'Elise, talk to me, please. I don't want you to be unhappy. That would make me unhappy too. You know that. Let me help.'

'I –'

She had been about to confide when Stella started to cough suddenly, her little face reddening Anxious, Vicky patted her on the back and rocked her, her attention concentrated on the sickly child. Elise knew that the moment for confession had come – and passed.

Chapter Fifty-Three

Walking past the central library, Al Weeks shivered in the cold and then headed towards the infirmary. His car had stalled and was parked almost a mile away, a fact that did little to improve his already bad temper. That morning he had heard about Duncan Oldenshaw again. Yes, the rumours were true: Duncan *was* back in Stockport. And he had a woman.

And that woman was Elise Straub, the daughter of Karl, the man Vicky wanted to marry. Which would make Elise, in time, Vicky's stepdaughter. The bastard! Al thought, disgusted by what he had heard. How low could a man get? He realised then what had brought Duncan back – revenge. But not a clean vengeance. This was sordid, squalid, using an innocent girl. Furious, Al clenched his fists in his pockets and lowered his head against the driving snow. The bugger had to be stopped. Yet Al had a nasty feeling that it was too late, that Elise Straub's life had already been upturned by Duncan Oldenshaw. Having an affair wouldn't matter for a hard piece like Freda, but for Elise it might prove devastating.

But if Al went to Douglas that would be fatal – to Duncan, at least. So he had decided on another plan of action. He would talk to Ada. She was the one with the coolest head, and she was the toughest. She was also the head of the family.

Arriving at the infirmary, Al shook the snow off his coat

and cap and asked for the ward where Ada Hargreaves was. A moment later he was confronted by a matron, pointing at the watch pinned to her bosom.

'What time does that say?'

'I learned to tell the time at school,' Al replied impatiently.

'It says twelve twenty-two,' the matron went on, 'which means that you have precisely eight minutes left of visiting time.' She eyed him like a piece of bad fish. 'Are you a relative?'

'A cousin,' Al lied.

'Really.'

'Yeah, really. On her late husband's side.'

The matron raised her eyebrows. 'I don't want Mrs Hargreaves upsetting. She hasn't settled well and wants to go home. Please try and keep her calm.'

'Oh, I will, Matron,' Al replied, walking into the ward and over to Ada's bed.

She was reading her *Picture Post*, her glasses sliding down her nose. As Al's shadow fell over the page she frowned and looked up.

'Al Weeks? Well, I'll be damned!'

'You can't ban me from the infirmary, Ada,' he said, teasing her.

'You still fighting?'

'You still being a pain in the neck?'

'Nothing changes,' Ada said, laughing and putting down her magazine.

To her surprise she was pleased to see Al, although the last time she had clapped eyes on him was the night when she had banished him from The Sixpenny Winner. But he had borne no grudge; had even sent her that kind note. Often Ada had wondered if he would show up at the pub. She would have lifted the ban, of course. After all, she'd forgiven him long ago. But Al had never showed up. Until now.

'So how's your leg?'

'Still attached to my hip.'

'Well, that's something,' Al said, putting his cap on the bed.

'Why the visit?'

'I could just want to call and see an old friend.'

Ada put her head on one side and looked at him quizzically.

'All right, I came to talk to you, Ada. I've got some bad news.'

She sighed. 'Go on.'

'You up to this?'

'My leg's weak, not my head! Get on with it.'

'Duncan's back.'

'Oh, bugger!'

'There's more.'

'There always is, with him.'

'He's calling himself Morris Broadbent. He's been back in Stockport for a while now. And he's been seeing someone.'

Ada's eyes widened. 'Poor cow – whoever she is.'

'That's putting it mildly.'

'Not Freda?'

'No, not Freda.'

'How many guesses do I have?' Ada asked drily.

Al hung his head. 'Think of the most unlikely person you could imagine.'

There was a long pause, Ada running names through her head. She thought of her daughters, of Duncan and why he would come back. For revenge. But by doing what, and using who?

'Bessie Cork.' Ada teased him.

'Very funny.'

'Lizzie Antrim?'

'Lizzie Antrim and Duncan Oldenshaw?' Al asked, his eyebrows raised. 'Are you joking?'

'Well, you said I should think of the most unlikely person.'

'Think of someone closer to home, Ada.'

A moment passed, a clammy sensation finally settling round her heart. 'Christ, no –'

'Ada –'

'Not Elise! Tell me it's not Elise.'

'Ada –'

She cut him off by throwing back the bedclothes and trying to rise.

'Sit still!' Al snapped. 'We have to talk this out. I could have gone to Doug, but you know what would have happened then. He'd kill Duncan for this.'

'*I'll* kill bloody Duncan for this!' she hissed. 'Elise is only a child. He's not . . . ? Oh no, he's not slept with her, has he?'

Al shook his head. 'I don't know.'

'I do,' Ada replied coldly. 'He makes a practice of seducing women. But not girls. I think that's a new low for Duncan Oldenshaw.'

'Apparently Elise is crazy about him.'

'Of course she is! All the women are. Freda was, Vicky was. He gets women under his thumb, doing things they would never believe they were capable of.' Ada paused, her tone bitter. 'Is Freda involved in any of this?'

'I doubt it,' Al replied. 'She'd hardly send her ex-lover into the arms of a young girl, would she?'

'Why not? She betrayed her sister.'

Al shook his head. 'Honestly, Ada, I haven't heard anything about Freda. Only Duncan and Elise.'

'I hoped that bastard had gone for ever.'

'We have to talk this out very carefully.'

She nodded. 'I know what you're thinking. If we go in all guns blazing Elise might up and run off with him. And that *would* be sweet revenge, wouldn't it? Vicky loves that girl like her own. To have her sleeping with Duncan, her own husband . . . God, the scandal.' Ada fought to keep her temper. 'Elise has a good future ahead of her, a good career. And he's not going to ruin that.'

'He already has.'

'No, not yet!' Ada said firmly, her gaze fixing on him. 'No one at home knows about this?'

'No one.'

'Good. I have to talk to Elise, get her to see reason. Although God knows if she will, even when she knows about Duncan.'

'There's more, Ada.'

She flinched, as though she had taken a blow. '*What?*'

'I heard something a long time ago, about Duncan. It's a rumour, but I've heard it a few times over the years and it's played on my mind. And now I know about Elise, I want her away from Duncan Oldenshaw – because I think he might be dangerous.'

'You're scaring me.'

'I know.'

'Go on,' Ada said finally. 'Tell me.'

'Douglas ran a pub in Leeds –'

'I know that.'

'– with his wife. It was a successful pub and they did well. By all accounts Douglas and Emma were very much in love. Then Duncan came on the scene. Douglas welcomed him and brought him into the pub to work with him.'

'I know this.'

'Bear with me,' Al cautioned her. 'Well, Duncan was

soon popular. Same old story, hey? But his interest was fixed on one woman, and one woman only: Doug's wife, Emma.' Al paused, but Ada said nothing, just kept her eyes on him, unblinking. 'So what, you might think? Duncan never had any morals. But there's more. Emma wasn't interested, she loved Douglas, was devoted to him. Then one night when Douglas was out Duncan tried it on. Emma rejected him. Someone overheard her playing merry hell with him. Then she said she was going to tell Douglas when he got back. Duncan was furious and stormed out.' Al paused, his voice steady. 'That night there was a fire at the pub. Emma died in the fire. Douglas tried to go in and save her – but Duncan stopped him.'

Ada flinched. 'Dear God . . .'

'Someone told me that they had seen Duncan leave the pub just before the fire started.'

'Oh God, no.'

'It could have been a coincidence,' Al said hurriedly. 'It could have been that Duncan was just leaving before anything happened. It could have been that the fire started accidentally after he'd gone. Or then again, it could have been that he started it.' Al rushed on, seeing Ada's face pinched with shock. 'Think about it. Duncan would really *have* kept Emma quiet then, wouldn't he? And it would explain why he was so keen to keep Douglas from going in to save her. If Duncan wanted Emma dead, he didn't want his brother to get her out.'

Ashen, Ada reached for the glass of water by her bedside. Her hand was shaking.

'How sure are you about this?'

'I told you, it's a rumour, but it's one that won't go away.'

'I can't believe Duncan Oldenshaw is capable of murder. Not murder.'

'I hope you're right,' Al replied. 'But can we risk it? Elise is very young, very vulnerable, she wouldn't believe any of this. She'd think everyone was just trying to break them up.'

Sipping the water, Ada felt her head swimming. It took her a while to reply. 'How did Elise meet up with Duncan?'

'I don't know.'

'Bit of a coincidence, isn't it? If it was just fate?' Ada ran her tongue over her dry lips. 'Freda wouldn't stoop so low, would she?'

'Never. Duncan killed her son.'

The child who was his son too, Ada wanted to say. But held her tongue.

'Besides,' Al went on, 'I heard that Freda and Douglas had settled their differences.'

'I thought so too,' Ada said quietly, 'but now I'm not so sure . . . I have to talk to Elise.'

'Will she listen to you?'

'How do I know?' she snapped back. 'But I have to try. Will you send her to me?'

'You know I will,' Al replied, getting to his feet as the matron approached. 'I know, I know,' he said shortly, 'I'm just going.'

'About time too,' the Matron said, standing by the foot of Ada's bed.

Thoughtful, Al moved away. Then he turned back and held Ada's gaze. 'Stop him, will you? And if you need help, just call.'

Carrying a basket of food stuffs, fruit and magazines, Elise was duly sent off to see Ada that evening. Al had called by at the pub, catching Elise in the backyard and telling her that Ada wanted her to visit. If Elise thought it was suspicious, she said nothing.

Arriving early, cowed by the intimidating matron, Elise finally made her way over to Ada's bed and sat down. She didn't want to be there, but she had no reason to avoid the visit.

'Hello there,' Ada said easily. 'What have you got for me?'

'Vicky sent some food, and Freda sent you the magazines,' Elise replied, putting the basket on the bedside table. She was aware of the woman in the next bed listening to their conversation. As was Ada.

'You have to keep your voice down,' she said, winking.

She had to be very careful, Ada realised. There was no point being heavy-handed – that would only make the girl wilful. And the last thing she wanted was to drive Elise further into Duncan's arms.

'How are things at the pub?'

'There was a flood in the cellar, but Dad and Douglas have just got someone in to fix it. They said it would be a big job.'

Ada nodded, for once uninterested in The Sixpenny Winner.

'And what about you? What have you been up to?'

'Studying,' Elise said vaguely.

She was so pretty, Ada thought, but obviously worried about something, and no wonder. Having a secret affair with a man old enough to be your father wasn't something a girl bragged about.

'How's Karl?'

'Fine. Busy.'

'And Vicky?'

'OK. She's tied up with Stella. She's got a real cough now. Vicky said she had her up all night.'

'And how's Freda?'

Was Ada imagining it, or had Elise winced at the name?

'Oh, she's busy at the shop. We went to the cinema the other day, saw a new Cary Grant film.'

'I like him,' Ada said easily. 'I like men with blue eyes. Makes them look so mysterious.'

Suspicious, Elise studied her. Did Ada know? Or was she just making a general remark?

'Do you like blue eyes, Elise?'

'They're OK.'

'What about dark hair? Do you like a boy with dark hair or fair hair?'

She knows, Elise thought, trying not to panic. 'I'm not sure.'

'Got a boyfriend yet?'

'No . . .'

Ada's tone cooled. 'Are you sure? Are you sure you don't have a boyfriend with dark hair and blue eyes?'

Flushing, Elise looked away. The woman in the next bed was talking to a nurse, her attention elsewhere.

'Well, Elise, *do* you have a boyfriend like that?'

'What business is it of yours?'

Stung by the tone, Ada countered the attack. 'It's very much my business, young lady! Now listen to me, only I know about this. Your father doesn't and neither does anyone else at the pub.'

'It's none of their business!' Elise said, close to tears. 'Everyone's so busy with their own lives, they wouldn't notice what I did anyway.'

So that was it, Ada thought. Elise had felt pushed out, and Duncan had struck at exactly the right time. But how would he know that – unless he had been tipped off?

'Elise, everyone cares about you. I care about you very much. You're like a granddaughter to me.'

'Huh!' the girl said suddenly, folding her arms across her chest.

'Don't "huh" me! I want to help you,' Ada snapped, then dropped her voice again. 'Who is this man you're seeing?'

'No one.'

'Elise, who is he?'

'I don't have to tell you that!'

'I'm not just asking to be nosy,' Ada countered. 'I need to know, Elise. It's important. I don't think you realise what you're dealing with.'

Elise could feel tears at the back of her throat. She knew this would happen, that she would be found out – and now here was Ada backing her into a corner. Why couldn't they just leave her alone?

'I knew everyone would try and split us up!' she blustered. 'Morris said you would –' She stopped short, her face paling.

'Is that Morris Broadbent you're talking about?'

Finally, Elise nodded. She was almost glad that Ada knew. The secret had been so hard to keep. She hadn't liked lying to everyone, and she hadn't liked avoiding her father's eyes either, or all the sneaking around she had had to do. Besides, after having sex with Duncan Elise had found herself floundering, the emotions he had manipulated so perfectly almost overwhelming her.

Ada's voice was low when she continued, 'Morris Broadbent isn't his real name. His real name is Duncan. Duncan Oldenshaw.'

Duncan Oldenshaw – Elise frowned. But that was the name of Vicky's husband! The man everyone despised. Her voice shrill, she jumped to her feet: 'You're a liar!'

At once the matron came over. 'Sit down, young lady! I will not have people screaming in my ward.'

'She's all right,' Ada said swiftly. 'She's just had some bad news. Leave her to me.'

As the matron walked off Elise sat trembling by Ada's bed. When she finally spoke again, her voice held pure hatred.

'It's a lie!'

'No, it's not. Morris Broadbent is Duncan Oldenshaw. And Duncan Oldenshaw is Vicky's husband.'

Shaking her head vigorously, Elise covered her ears with her hands. It was ridiculous, she thought. What was the woman talking about? How could Morris be Duncan Oldenshaw? How could he? Why would he lie to her, give himself a different name? Why? It was all rubbish. Ada was just lying, trying to break them up.

Exasperated, Ada leaned over and pulled Elise's hands away. 'Listen to me! I'm trying to help you. Duncan's fooled you, like he's fooled so many other women. He made my daughters into strangers, made them deceitful, convinced them to do things they would never have done before. They hate each other now because of him. Because he manipulated them –'

Elise's eyes were wide open, burning. She could hear the words, but couldn't take them in. It was all rubbish, stupid, obvious blatant lies, and yet ... And yet ... Again she shook her head; couldn't, *wouldn't* believe it.

'Morris loves me!'

'He's told so many others the same thing,' Ada replied sadly. 'He told Vicky he loved her, and all the time he was married to her he was having an affair with Freda.'

'No!' Elise whispered, her heart plummeting.

This was ridiculous! she thought, bewildered. This had nothing to do with Morris. Morris didn't know Freda ... Oh, but of course he did, Elise remembered suddenly. Freda had told her that they had once been close. Elise was incoherent with shock and confusion. 'No! I don't believe it! I don't believe it!'

'You have to!' Ada said, dropping her voice again. 'I'm going to tell you something now, Elise, which only the family knows –'

'I don't want to hear any more lies.'

'Are you so sure they're lies?' Ada countered.

'They are! They are!' Elise replied helplessly.

But Ada pressed on. 'Even your father doesn't know about this, so I'm going to have to trust you. Duncan killed Billy, Freda's son.'

Elise was beside herself, desperate to shut Ada up. 'I've told you, Morris is not Duncan Oldenshaw! He's called Morris, Morris Broadbent.'

Ada sighed. 'Listen to me, Elise. It was an accident. Duncan didn't do it deliberately. But nevertheless he killed Billy, and then he left Stockport. Only the family know that there's more to it. You see, Billy wasn't Douglas's son. He was Duncan's.'

Startled, Elise tried to shake off Ada's grip. 'I don't want to hear this!'

'Neither did I,' Ada replied, 'but I *had* to hear it, and live with it. Duncan Oldenshaw damn near broke up our family once and, by God, he's not going to do it again.'

'It's my life! I can do what I want –'

'With a man like that? Never! Listen, Elise, I know how attractive he is, how plausible, but he's a liar. Think about it – how could a decent man do what he's done? He's lied to you, pretended he was someone else. Why would he do that? *Why?* He's Vicky's husband – how would she feel if she knew?'

Breathing rapidly, Elise struggled to speak. All she wanted to do was to get away from Ada, from the words, the lies she was piling on top of her. She would go to Morris, Elise thought blindly, she would talk to him and he would tell her it was nonsense; that he loved her. And then it would all be all right again.

'I don't care what you say!' Elise said defiantly. 'He's not Duncan Oldenshaw, and even if he was, people can change.'

'No, they can't. They pretend to change, but what they are always comes out. And he's bad.'

'He's not, he's not!' Elise shouted, tears beginning to run down her cheeks.

Her eyes narrowing, Ada leaned towards the shaking girl. 'How did you meet him, Elise?'

She stopped short. 'What?'

'How did you meet Duncan?'

'It's not Duncan –'

'It is! How did you meet him?'

Trapped, Elise decided to tell the partial truth. She had to think clearly, but not give too much away, just answer the damn question and leave.

'I met him at the cinema.'

Ada could feel her throat tightening. 'Were you alone?'

'No . . . Freda was there.'

It was Ada's turn to flinch. 'And Duncan just came up to you?'

Elise hesitated. She didn't want to get Freda into trouble. She was her friend. Or *was* she? Realisation came thick as bile. Why would someone like the glamorous Freda make a friend out of her? That had always seemed so strange to Elise. Why would Freda seek her out . . . unless she needed her for some reason? But *why*?

Slowly, Elise answered. Her voice was flat. 'He just came over. He said hello to Freda –'

'Did she say hello back?'

The trap was closing in, Elise realised, feeling her palms moisten. 'She had to be pleasant to him! There were people all around us.'

'Then what happened?'

'He . . . he asked to see me again.'

Ada's voice was deadly. 'There and then?'

'No . . .'

'So how did he ask you?'

'He . . . he waited for me at the end of the street.'

Ada took in a breath. So Freda hadn't been involved, after all. Thank God for that. It had been all Duncan's doing.

'Which street?'

'The high street, by the library.'

'How did he know you would be there?'

Elise's voice was rising again. 'I don't have to answer to you! You're not my mother, or even a relative. You didn't give a damn about me before. I was just Karl's daughter, living upstairs, the good little girl, quiet with her books. No one gave a damn about me before – until now, now when I want a life of my own.'

Shocked, Ada tried to remonstrate with her. 'Elise, that's not true, we all care about you.'

'I haven't done anything wrong! He loves me and I love him –'

'How could you love him now you know who he is?' Ada countered. 'It would kill Vicky to find out –'

Scared, Elise felt her head buzzing. Was he really Duncan Oldenshaw? *Was he?* And if he was, what would everyone say when they found out? Dear God, what would her father say? Elise struggled to control her panic. It was lies, she told herself. She knew it wasn't the truth. But what *was* the truth? *That he was no good.* But he loved her! She knew that. He loved her and she loved him. Who cared what had happened in the past? This was now.

'Even if all this was true, Vicky didn't want him! She got rid of her husband. She has my father now,' Elise snapped, her eyes filling with frustration and confusion. 'Why does she have to know anyway?'

'God, Elise, listen to yourself! Why do you think Duncan came back?'

'I don't know!'

'For revenge,' Ada said firmly.

What was she talking about? Elise thought, Ada's face blurred through her tears.

'*Revenge?* Revenge on who?'

'His wife. Vicky. Your future stepmother. I don't want to hurt you, love, but you have to listen to the truth. Duncan wanted to injure Vicky – so he seduced you.'

'Shut up!' Elise shouted suddenly, shaking off Ada's hand. She had never felt so angry in her life. She wanted to hit out, to stop Ada talking, stop all the filth pouring out of her mouth. 'Shut up!'

'No, I won't!' Ada hissed. 'He knew that it would crucify Vicky when she found out. He did it because Vicky once exposed him for what he was – and I threw him out of The Sixpenny Winner because of it. Imagine it, Elise, imagine the deceit, the lies. And all the time Duncan was sleeping with one sister, whilst he was married to the other.'

Shaken, Elise stood up, her face reddening with rage and shame. 'I don't believe you! You have no proof anyway. How do you know for sure Morris is Duncan Oldenshaw?'

'I've been told by someone who knew Duncan well. There's no mistake, Elise. It's Duncan Oldenshaw all right.' Ada paused, her tone softening. 'I know how much this hurts, but you have to be warned. Duncan Oldenshaw is immoral and he may well be dangerous –'

'I don't believe you!' Elise hissed again. 'You just want me to be good and obedient, live a nice quiet life, be no trouble to anyone. That's what everyone wants, isn't it? Elise to be a spinster teacher. Well, I've never had any fun in my life and I've never fallen in love before. So now it's my turn.'

She was hoarse with pent-up rage. How dare this woman try to ruin her life? How dare she? No one could stop her from loving Morris; no one could tell lies about him and make her believe them. They just wanted to ruin it, that was all. Just as Morris had told her that they would – and he had been right.

'It's fine for my father and Vicky – they have each other – and Freda has Doug, but I have no one. I don't want to end up like you, on my own.' She backed away from the bed, her voice threatening hysteria. 'He loves me and I love him. He's the only person who really cares about me.'

'If you think Duncan Oldenshaw cares about you, you've never been so wrong in your life,' Ada replied shortly. '*He cares for himself.* No one else. He does everything for himself. He loves no one, thinks about no one, but himself. All he does is use people. I don't care if you hate me for ever –'

'I do hate you!' Elise said, the words almost spat out. 'I hate you –'

'So hate me!' Ada hurled back. 'But don't believe what the man tells you. He'll ruin your life, Elise. Keep away from him.'

'I'm not listening to another word!' Elise shouted, several of the other patients looking up, alarmed. 'I'm going to him and then we'll see who's right. Then we'll see that he wants me with him and that he loves me –'

'Elise!' Ada shouted, as the girl headed for the door. 'Keep away from him! Don't go near that man! Elise, stay away!'

But she had already left, the heavy swing doors of the ward closing noiselessly behind her.

Chapter Fifty-Four

Remembering the address Duncan had once mentioned, Elise was surprised to arrive at a squalid boarding house in Portswood. There was no sign of the nice car outside, only a couple of scruffy children playing with an old crate. Nervously she looked round, then shivered, feeling the cold as the snow kept falling. Night had set in, the white flakes landing on her hair and shoulders as she knocked on the door of number 18.

A thin woman in curling rags answered. 'What d'you want?'

'Is Mr . . . Broadbent in?'

'Nah,' she replied, looking Elise up and down. 'Who are you? His daughter?'

'I'm a . . . friend.'

The woman laughed, ushering Elise in. 'That's what they all say.'

In silence she then showed Elise up to Duncan's room, Elise hovering at the entrance. 'Can I wait inside?'

'Do what you like,' the woman replied. 'You look harmless enough.'

Inside the room there was an unmade bed, an unsteady chair beside it, a lamp with a torn shade giving scant illumination. A worn shirt and several pairs of dirty socks lay on the floor, an empty bottle of beer on the bedside table. It was a sordid place, stale with cigarette smoke and unwashed bedding. This can't be Morris's place, Elise thought. There was a mistake, there had to be. Admittedly he had said that he was just staying there for a while, but he hadn't mentioned how vile it was.

Slowly Elise walked round the confined room, then, having drawn the curtains, she flicked on the main light. The whole sleazy reality hit her hard. Ada's words came back like unwelcome visitors. *Morris Broadbent was Duncan Oldenshaw, Vicky's husband. He's a liar, he uses people. How could a decent man do what he's done?* How could a decent man live in a hole like this? Elise thought.

Shaking, she stood by the window, her arms wrapped round herself. He would explain, she thought. He would say there had been a mistake, that he *was* Morris Broadbent. As for this place, well, there was no shame in being needy, was there? When she and her father had fallen on hard times they had lived in some shabby places. Maybe Morris was just down on his luck, and ashamed to tell her.

But he had that nice car, Elise thought. Why would a man with a good car live here? She sat down suddenly in the battered chair. What if it *was* true? What if she *had* slept with Vicky's husband? The woman who would one day be her *stepmother*. The thought made her skin crawl. No, it couldn't be true! Why would he do that? Unless Ada was right – he had used her for revenge.

All the lies came back to her in the instant. He had asked about Vicky as though she were a stranger, asked about the pub, her life – whilst all along he knew everything. He had fooled her completely. Elise felt her mouth drying. She had given herself to a man who was a liar, a man who was just using her. A man as sordid as his room.

Another thought followed immediately. Freda had introduced them. Freda had said he was Morris Broadbent. So it had to be a lie! Elise thought, her hopes rising, because Freda wouldn't have betrayed her like that. Wouldn't have arranged the meetings, acted as a go-between – not if Morris was her sister's husband. *And her old lover . . .*

Elise closed her eyes, unexpectedly dizzy. She should leave, she thought, but couldn't move. No, she would stay now, stay until he came back, and then she would ask him for the truth, whatever that was. And then he would tell her that it was all a stupid mistake, that he *was* Morris Broadbent and that he loved her. Then he would face Ada and show her that she was wrong.

He would. *He would* . . . An hour passed, snow still falling, the temperature in the room dropping. Turning off the overhead light, Elise huddled into the uncomfortable chair and watched the door. She felt dirty and knew in her heart that Ada had been telling the truth. And as the minutes passed and all the lies came back to Elise, she became more and more certain that she had been exploited.

He had used her – and so had Freda. She had been so naive that she had never suspected either of them, just played into their hands. *But why?* That was what she had to know; that was what kept her in that room. She would look him in the face and ask him – why?

Another hour dragged its feet, then finally Elise heard footsteps on the stairs. One, two, three, up they came, coming closer and closer, whilst she sat still in the chair. After a long moment – as though someone was pausing outside the door – Duncan walked in.

He saw her and frowned, then quickly covered his reaction by walking over to her and pulling her to her feet.

'Hello, luv . . .' She turned her head away as he tried to kiss her. 'Hey, what's up? I didn't forget we were meeting, did I?'

'Is this where you live?' Elise asked, her voice low.

He shrugged, discomforted. 'It's temporary. I said I was just marking time. Things are looking up; I won't be here for long.'

He was uneasy. Why was she here? Why was she so brittle with him? Had someone told her the truth? God, Duncan thought with a jolt of fear, did his brother know?

'What's the matter, Elise? Are you angry with me?'

'Should I be, Morris?' She watched him, but he didn't flinch at the name. Maybe she was wrong, after all. Oh God, she willed, please let me be wrong.

'You look odd,' he said, hugging her to him and feeling her resistance. 'Has someone upset you?'

The words broke Elise's resolve. 'Someone said you weren't Morris Broadbent at all! That you were Duncan Oldenshaw, Vicky's husband. They said you were just using me for revenge.' She clung to him childishly. 'But they're wrong, aren't they? You *are* Morris, aren't you? Aren't you?'

The game was up. Duncan knew it and also knew that he had to get away. Fast.

'Elise, look I didn't mean for this to happen. I'm very fond of you –'

'What!' she said, bewildered. 'Don't tell me that you *are* Duncan Oldenshaw?'

'No, I'm Morris Broadbent,' he replied, but he was unconvincing, wanting to get rid of her and get out of town. 'Look, Elise, these things happen. We had a good time, I was very fond of you –'

'You *were*?' she countered, heartbroken. 'You *were* very fond of me? I gave myself to you –'

'If not me, it would have been someone else. That's life. We had a good time,' he countered, letting go of her as Elise began to cry. 'Oh, come on, don't get upset.'

'You are Duncan Oldenshaw, aren't you? But why did you lie to me?' she sobbed. 'Why would you do that? I thought you loved me. You told me you loved me.' She remembered what Ada had said and flared up at him. 'You told Vicky you loved her and you said the same to Freda.' She stopped short, her eyes blazing. 'She knew who you were! She knew all along. I trusted her as a friend and she betrayed me –'

'Look, Freda's OK –'

'She's still your girlfriend, isn't she!' Elise snapped, her humiliation crucifying. 'Oh God, I see it all now. You and she planned this together. You must have been laughing at me behind my back. I was so stupid, wasn't I? I fell for you, made it all so easy . . . But I never hurt you, either of you. Why did you do it? Why?'

'To get back at my wife,' Duncan admitted at last, flopping down on the bed and lighting a cigarette. 'You don't know what Vicky put me through. She had me thrown out of the pub, left me with nothing. You think this place is bad – Jesus, Elise, you should have seen where I ended up when that bloody lot finished with me.'

Blinking slowly, Elise tried to gather her thoughts. *There was no Morris Broadbent, only Duncan Oldenshaw.* And then slowly, reluctantly, she remembered what she had heard about him.

'You were sleeping with Freda, cheating on your own brother – and you killed Billy. That's why you were thrown out.'

Duncan looked at her, emotionless. 'You heard a lot about me.'

'I heard more,' Elise replied. 'I heard that you were Billy's father.'

Duncan winced, as though someone had punched him in the stomach. 'How d'you know that?'

'Someone told me.'

'But no one knows, except the family. Did Freda tell you?'

'No, Ada,' Elise replied, suddenly intimidated as Duncan stood up and towered over her. 'She told me all about you. Said I should keep away from you. Said you were no good.' Despite herself she suddenly reached up to him desperately. 'Please, tell me you love me. Say that and nothing matters. We could go away, the two of us. Start again.'

Irritated, Duncan felt her arms round him and wanted to push her away. But he wasn't cruel enough for that. She had been a sweet kid and hadn't deserved what had happened to her.

'Elise, come on, it's over –'

'No!' she said, crying and clinging to him. 'No! We could make it work, I know we could.'

'Stop it!' Duncan replied, suddenly annoyed. 'It's over.'

'But why? Why?'

He stared into Elise's upturned face. 'Does anyone know about us?'

'Ada does.'

'Shit!' Duncan said heatedly. 'Anyone else?'

'Freda.' Elise spat out the name.

'I thought Ada was in hospital. Does Doug know about us?'

'No, no one else.'

'Not your father?' Duncan asked, his tone wary.

'No! No one. How could I have told my father?' Suddenly her arms dropped away from him and she stepped back. 'You don't give a damn about me, do you? You're just worried about my father or Doug finding out. Well, you *should* be worried. My father would have something to say if he knew what you did.' She was ashamed, humiliated and desperate to strike back at him. So without thinking, she cornered Duncan. 'He'll get you for this. And as for your brother – I know all about what happened before – Doug won't let this go.'

Suddenly she stopped talking, alerted by the look on Duncan's face. He was angry, his eyes flat with fury. Startled, Elise moved hurriedly towards the door.

'I have to go –'

'Wait!' he snapped, reaching for her and catching her arm.

Panicked, she tried to shake him off, but Duncan held on. 'Listen to me –'

'I don't want to listen to you!' she screamed. 'Let me go!'

But he held on even more tightly. Remembering Ada's words, genuinely frightened in that grubby room Elise tried to break free, but Duncan held on to her as she struggled. Finally Elise kicked out, catching Duncan in the groin. He doubled up, gasping as she ran out, taking the stairs two at a time.

As she reached the hallway the landlady came out, but Elise didn't stop. Instead she ran away from Portswood, the snow falling heavily on her as she tried to keep her footing. Twice she slipped, but didn't stop, frightened of Duncan and ashamed of herself. Finally she reached Churchgate, Winter's Clock chiming the hour as she rounded the corner by Bessie Cork's shop.

'What the hell . . .' a voice said as she bumped into a man crossing the street. '*Elise?*' Doug said incredulously. 'What are you doing? What's the matter?'

She said nothing, just started crying, loud racking sobs echoing sadly in the snowbound night.

Chapter Fifty-Five

'Can't you drive any faster?' Ada asked, looking over to Al Weeks as he manoeuvred the treacherous streets.

'I'm going as fast as I can. I'm not sure you should have discharged yourself like that.'

'You think I could lie there, doing nothing?'

Al stared into the blizzard that was almost blocking the road ahead. 'We should be there any minute.'

'I've got a bad feeling about this,' Ada said, her hands clenched on her lap. 'Elise said she was going to see Duncan. There was nothing I could do to stop her.'

'Don't you know where he is?'

'If I did, we'd have gone there!' Ada snapped, staring ahead blindly. 'Duncan will have dumped her, poor silly kid. That's his way – especially if Elise puts pressure on him. God, Al, I'm so worried for her.'

He frowned, staring at the road ahead. 'So why are we going to the pub, Ada?'

'I'm just hoping she went back there. Please God, she went back home.'

'But Doug's there – and so is her father.'

'I know,' Ada said, her tone icy, 'and she might well have told them. And you know what that'll mean, Al. Oh, drive faster!'

'We'll get there, Ada. Just hang on.'

'It's not me that has to hang on,' she countered. 'This is a bloody business. And it's going to get worse before this night's out.'

*   *   *

Totally incoherent, Elise was lead back to The Sixpenny Winner by Doug. Supported by him, she walked in via the ginnel and the back door to avoid the customers in the pub. Worried, Doug settled her in the rocking chair and fixed her a brandy. Obediently she drank it, staring ahead, her eyes blank.

'What happened?'

'It's . . . it's . . .'

'You're scaring me, Elise. What is it? Are you hurt? Has someone hurt you?'

Sitting where she was Elise could see through the half-opened door that led to the bar. Her father was standing there, chatting to a customer she didn't recognise. The man was laughing, Karl passing him a pint of bitter. It was nearly closing time. Soon the pub would empty and her father would come into the kitchen. He would ask what was wrong. Then she would tell him and they would hear all about it. Elise flinched. Oh God, what would her father think of her? She had let him down so badly. She had shamed him.

'Elise,' Doug repeated, 'what's the matter?'

Turning to look at him, her eyes filled. She was just about to tell him – then Freda walked in. Her face was set, her eyes warning as she looked at Elise. In that instant Elise knew that Duncan had spoken to her.

Unsettled, she looked away.

Baffled, Doug turned to his wife. 'Freda, you talk to Elise, will you? She's upset.'

Freda was perfectly composed, dangerously so.

'Leave her to me, Doug,' Freda said simply. 'You go back and help Karl in the bar. It's nearly closing time.'

Waiting until the door had closed behind Doug, Freda then turned to Elise.

'What have you done?'

'What have *I* done?' she countered, baffled. 'You knew who he was, Freda, you knew it was Duncan. There *was* no Morris Broadbent. It was Duncan Oldenshaw all the time –'

'Keep your voice down, you fool!' Freda snapped. Elise was clearly stung by the tone in her voice: 'Why did you go running off to see him like that?'

'You knew who he was!' Elise repeated, staring incredulously at Freda. 'I thought you were my friend, but you both used me.'

'Elise, calm down!' Freda told her. 'You have to keep your voice low. We don't want people to overhear us, do we?'

'Why not?' Elise said heatedly. 'Why shouldn't everyone know? Duncan was very honest – in the end; told me he did it to get revenge on Vicky. I believe him too. You should have seen his face when he told me. He never loved me, he never gave a damn about me!' She shook off Freda's hand. 'Leave me alone! Haven't you done enough?'

'Elise –'

She cut her off at once. 'I liked you, I thought you were trying to help me. To help *us*. I thought he loved me –'

'Keep quiet!' Freda warned her as she saw Doug's shadow cross behind the glass door of the bar. 'I didn't know it would go this far.'

'How *far* did you want it to go, Freda? Duncan is Vicky's husband! And he's your lover too, isn't he?' Elise asked, her eyes brilliant with hatred. 'Go on, tell me! You've been seeing him all the time he was seeing me, haven't you? I suppose you were both laughing at me behind my back, sniggering about what a fool I was. You wanted to get your own back on Vicky too, didn't you? You were jealous, of her, because my father loved her. I knew you were, I used to see it in your face. But I let you fool me. And you both did. You and Duncan were lovers all the time, weren't you? All the time I was telling you how wonderful he was, how handsome, you were sleeping with him! You lied to me. You said he loved me, he cared about me. *He's smitten with you*, you said.' Memory came back, savage. 'You arranged for him to bump into us at the cinema, didn't you? It was no accident. You planned it all. And I hate you for it!'

'Elise, shut up!'

'No! No!' she shouted. 'I believed you liked me, that you wanted to help me. But now I know what you're really like. I know what you did in the past. You did the same to Vicky before me –'

Shaken, Freda grabbed her arm. 'Who told you that?'

'I did,' a voice said suddenly behind them.

Startled, Freda spun round to see Ada standing in the doorway, supporting herself on her crutches. Suddenly Freda was afraid, her mother's expression vicious. This time there was no way out, Freda realised. This time she couldn't fool anyone. Her mother knew. It was over.

'Ma –'

'Elise,' Ada said flatly, 'go upstairs.'

Obediently she shook off Freda's grip and hurried out. Ada watched her go and then locked the back door and pocketed the key. She had suspected her daughter of having some hand in the sordid affair, but until she had overheard their conversation Ada had hoped she was mistaken. Now there was no doubt. Freda had set it all up. Her daughter had ruined an innocent girl for her own revenge – and Duncan's. And she hated her for it.

'You're a bitch –'

'Ma.'

'Sit down!' Ada hissed. Then she walked to the door of the bar and called for Doug.

'No!' Freda said hurriedly. 'No, don't tell him. Ma, don't tell him.'

He came in, surprised to see his mother-in-law sitting at the table, her plastered leg stretched out in front of her. Slowly he studied her and then looked over to Freda. Her face was waxen.

'What are you doing out of hospital, Ada?' He turned to his wife. 'Freda, what is it? Will someone tell me what's going on?'

'Your *wife*,' Ada spat out the word, 'has been seeing Duncan again.' She could see Doug clench his fists but carried on. 'She and your brother wanted to get revenge on Vicky, so they hatched a little plot. Duncan seduced Elise to get his own back –'

He was across the room in a second, towering over Freda.

'You did what?'

'She's lying!' Freda pleaded. 'I love you, Doug, how could I do anything like that? She's guessing, lying.'

Her tone deadly, Ada continued, 'No, I'm not. Al Weeks told me all about it. He's good at finding out about people, Freda, and he knows everything. He came to tell me because he was afraid for Elise.'

Freda's eyes flickered. 'Afraid? Why afraid?'

'There are some things even you don't know about Duncan Oldenshaw,' Ada said grimly. 'Or you, Douglas. There are some things about your brother that he thought no one knew –'

'Tell me!' he snapped. 'Spit it out. I'm finished with playing games.'

'He was after your first wife, Emma.'

'No . . .' Doug said hoarsely.

'There's more.'

'Why tell him?' Freda shouted at her mother, panicking. 'Shut up! You're going to kill him.'

'Why do you care? Anyway, Freda, how do you *know* what I'm going to say?' Ada asked her daughter, surprised.

'I know that what you've already said is enough,' Freda replied, looking pleadingly at her husband. 'Doug, don't listen to what she says. It's lies, all lies.'

But he ignored her. 'Get on with it, Ada. Tell me everything.'

'Duncan wanted Emma, but she wasn't interested. I guess she didn't tell you because he was your brother; thought she could handle it on her own. Anyway, one night when you weren't around Duncan made a play for her. She chucked him out.'

'Go on,' Doug said dully. He was grey with shock.

'That was the night there was a fire at your pub . . . You tried to get Emma out, and Duncan stopped you.'

Unblinking, Doug stared at her. 'Go on!'

'Duncan was seen leaving the pub just before the fire broke out,' Ada said, Doug flinching at the words. 'No one knows if he was directly responsible, but he was there –'

'He stopped me going in to get her!' Doug said fiercely. 'He held me back. *He stopped me saving Emma.* He killed my wife?'

Ada swallowed. 'I can't tell you the answer to that, Douglas, not for sure. But he *could* have done – to keep her quiet.' She hurried on. 'You know your brother, he betrayed you once, when he had an affair with Freda. And now he's seduced Elise. With Freda's help.'

Shaken, Doug flinched. 'But Elise is only a kid . . . I don't believe it!' He turned on his wife. 'You wouldn't do that, Freda! Jesus, you couldn't. You *couldn't* do that –'

'She could, and she did.' Ada's voice was pure steel. 'Duncan could, and he did. And now your brother has to be stopped.'

Slowly Doug turned from his wife to his mother-in-law. His eyes were black with rage.

'Where is he?'

'I don't know –' Ada replied.

'He's gone,' Freda interrupted her. 'Like he did before. Gone off. Left town.'

'Is that true?'

Ada laughed, Freda turning on her mother savagely. 'What's so funny?'

'You are!' she said. 'How can you trust a word she says, Douglas? How can you even bear to look at her?'

'I want to know where my brother is!' he roared, frightening them both. 'Where is the bastard?'

'I've told you, Duncan's gone,' Freda repeated.

She had to make him believe it, and then somehow she would have to escape and go to him. Then they would get away. But if Doug found Duncan, it was all over – for both of them.

Hurriedly she tried to placate him. 'None of this was my idea. Duncan made me do it. And I didn't know about your first wife. I knew nothing about that.'

'Shut up!' Doug shouted, his fists clenched. 'Where's Duncan now?'

'I don't know! Honestly, I don't know –'

'Oh yes, you do,' he said, his tone terrifying. 'And I want the truth from you. For once, I want the whole truth. Tell me where he is! Now. Or, so help me God, I'll get it out of you somehow.'

* * *

Locking up the pub doors, Karl walked round to the back entrance and then looked up. He could hear, above his head, someone crying. Frowning he remembered that Vicky had taken Stella to visit a friend, and he knew that Elise was out. So who was it? Trying the back door he was further surprised to find it locked and walked round to the front again, skirting the kitchen and going upstairs to the rooms at the top of the house.

The crying got louder as he approached the door to his daughter's room. Worried, he knocked. The crying stopped. He knocked again. Finally Elise called out.

'Who is it?'

'It's Dad. Let me in, sweetheart.'

'I'm OK, Dad.'

'I heard you crying. Let me in.'

Sitting up on her bed, she wiped her eyes and stared at the door. Her father mustn't find out. It would destroy him. He would stop loving her.

'Dad, I'm OK.'

'Open up,' he repeated, hurrying in as Elise finally unlocked the door. Concerned, he sat down on the bed, Elise beside him.

'What's the matter?'

'Nothing.'

'Nothing doesn't make people cry,' he said kindly. 'You can tell me, love. You know you can tell me anything.'

'Oh, Dad,' she said, burying her head against his chest.

Karl's arms went round her protectively. 'God, love, what is it?'

'I can't tell you,' she murmured.

'You can. You can tell me anything,' he repeated.

What was it? Karl thought desperately, what was it? 'Talk to me, Elise, trust me.'

'I can't . . .'

'Are you ill? Upset? Is it your studies? If it is, it doesn't matter. It's not worth crying about.'

'It's not that.'

'Then what?' A thought struck him suddenly. Elise wasn't a baby, she was grown up now. He just hadn't wanted to admit it. 'Is it a boy?'

She nodded, her face still hidden.

'Did he upset you?'

'He . . . he didn't love me, Dad! He used me.' Her voice was breaking. 'He never loved me, he just lied to me. I feel so ashamed . . .'

With a shudder Karl realised that this was no innocent flirtation. His daughter had been used, and discarded. His baby had been hurt.

Karl's voice was quiet when he spoke again. 'Who is he?'

'Don't hate me! Please, don't hate me!' Elise begged him frantically. 'I couldn't bear you to be cross with me, Dad. I'm sorry, really I am. I didn't mean for it to happen –'

Gently he put his hand over her mouth. 'Elise, I would love you whatever you did. But you must tell me who this boy is.' He moved away his hand. 'Who is he?'

'Duncan.'

He didn't make the connection. 'Duncan who?'

'Duncan Oldenshaw.'

Chapter Fifty-Six

'He'll kill him!' Freda shrieked at her mother as Doug ran out of the front door of the pub and into the street beyond. He wasn't wearing a coat, just in his shirtsleeves, his head bare.

Only moments earlier they had seen Karl hurry into the kitchen and face Doug, his voice uncharacteristically raised.

'I'm going to get your bloody brother!' he had said, unbelievably angry. 'I'm going to make that bastard pay for what he's done.'

Try as she might to stop him, Doug had thrown off Freda and followed Karl. Desperate to protect her lover, Freda hadn't told Doug where Duncan was – but Elise had told Karl. And now both men were after him.

'Doug will kill Duncan!' Freda shrieked. 'We have to stop it.'

Unmoving, Ada sat watching her daughter. She was beyond disappointment. All she knew was that somehow her child had turned out bad. The daughter she and Clem had wanted and loved so much was immoral. There was no way Freda was going to change. What she had done to the family and now Elise was beyond understanding. She was a manipulative, deceitful liar with no feelings. If she had been half human, Ada thought, Freda would have sought to protect Elise from Duncan. But instead she had used her. It was inexcusable. So now Ada wanted her daughter punished, and the only way she could do that was to punish Duncan Oldenshaw.

'I said Doug will kill him!' Freda snapped again, rushing over to the door where Doug had left. Finding it locked, she moved back to her mother and put out her hand. 'Give me the key. Give me the back door key!'

Ada shook her head. 'Not yet.'

'What are you waiting for? Didn't you see Karl's face? Not so placid now, is he? And as for Doug – you know what he'll do to Duncan if he gets to him. I have to warn him . . .' She stopped short, loathing on her face. 'Of course! You *want* Doug to find his brother. You *want* me to be too late.'

'Sit down,' Ada said brutally.

'Give me the key –'

'Sit down!' Ada repeated, watching her daughter. 'It takes about twenty minutes to get to where Duncan lives. Al Weeks should have picked up Douglas on the street. As for Karl, he had a head start. But he's on foot.' She glanced at the clock above the range. 'Eleven o'clock. If the streets are quiet, they could be there very soon.'

Freda was panicking, her hands running through her hair.

'Let me phone Duncan at least –'

'No.'

'I have to warn him. Doug will kill him –'

'I don't care,' Ada said simply, looking back to the clock. 'Two minutes gone.'

'How can you sit there and count off the minutes! This is torture.'

'And you know all about torture, Freda, don't you? How many people have you tortured over the years? Your husband, your sister, Elise. And indirectly how

552

many others have suffered? Me for one. And Billy, poor little Billy, who never had a chance at life. But you've failed this time, Freda. Vicky's not going to suffer again –'

Freda turned on her mother bitterly. 'You think Vicky's so perfect, don't you? Well, let me tell you something about your favourite. She knew all about me and Duncan before she married him. She even knew that Billy wasn't Doug's son. But she wanted Duncan so badly she would have taken him whatever he'd done.'

She expected her mother to react, but Ada just looked at her.

'You underestimate me, Freda. I've known about Vicky all along. I guessed. But Vicky's never been bad, just stupid – infatuated, pathetically in love with Duncan Oldenshaw. You were the bad one, Freda, not her.'

Panicking, Freda started to beg. 'Just let me ring Duncan. Please –'

'Shut up and sit down!' Ada barked, watching as Freda grew more and more frantic. They both knew what would happen when Doug caught up with his brother. 'Another minute gone.'

Blank-eyed, Freda stared at her mother. 'Let me go to him. Please, let me go to him.'

'Oh, you can go to him, Freda, but not yet. You can go to your lover boy when his brother's seen to him. You can pick up the pieces of what's left. And remember, Freda, Karl's gone after Duncan too. He knows what happened to his child – how d'you think he's going to react if he gets to Duncan first?'

'But Karl's a reasonable man!' Freda blustered. 'He's against violence, always preaching about forgiveness.'

'That was before he knew about Elise,' Ada said icily.

'But you're right, Freda, Karl *is* a reasonable man. Let's hope he gets to Duncan first. Because Douglas isn't a reasonable man at all. Not now.'

'You can't *want* Doug to kill his brother!' Freda shouted hysterically. 'He'd be jailed for that.'

'If I had a mad dog, I wouldn't think twice about shooting it,' Ada replied bitterly.

'But Duncan's not a dog, he's a man.' Her tone hardened. 'Anything that happens tonight is your fault, Mother.'

'No, you started it, Freda! Now you can watch how your handiwork turns out.'

Freda was getting hoarse with fright. 'Why did you tell Douglas about Emma? How Duncan might have been responsible for the fire which killed her? *Why did you do that?* You might just as well have put a loaded gun in Doug's hand.'

Ada was unmoving. 'He had to know. He would have found out sooner or later.'

Freda was on her feet again, pacing restlessly. 'If you hadn't told him, he might never have found out! *I* didn't know about it –'

'And now you do, you still want to go to a man who might be a murderer?'

Stopping dead in her tracks, Freda looked at her mother. 'I don't believe Duncan did it. He couldn't have done.'

'Funny, until tonight there were a lot of things I wouldn't have thought *you* could have done,' Ada said flatly, looking at the blank face of the clock. 'Six minutes gone. They should be getting quite close.'

'Give me the key!'

'No!'

Breathing heavily, Freda sat down. Then she got up

and moved suddenly towards her mother, her hands outstretched.

He would explain to Stan Foreshaw later, Karl thought. He would tell him that he had had to borrow his van, that it had been an emergency. Luckily Karl knew Portswood well from the time he and Elise had once lodged there. It wasn't difficult for him to find the address his daughter had given him, the tyres scrunching on the thick snow as he drew up to the kerb.

Trying to steady himself, Karl took in several deep breaths, then got out of the van. A thin landlady answered his ringing the doorbell, Karl pushing past her and rushing upstairs to where Elise had directed him. Pushing open the door, he found Duncan packing, his grubby shirt-tail hanging out of the top of his trousers. Repelled, Karl looked round the sordid room, then glanced back to Duncan. This was Vicky's husband – and the man who had seduced his child.

Startled, Duncan turned to look at the stranger in his room. 'Who the hell are you?'

'Elise's father.'

Paling, Duncan reached for his jacket and pulled it on. 'I don't know what she told you, but it was all a mistake.'

'Which part of it?' Karl asked, his voice metallic with stress.

'She and me. We were close –'

'How close?'

Duncan studied the tall, bearded man standing before him. If it came to a fight, he might have a chance. Karl Straub didn't look the violent type.

'I cared about her.'

'You cared about her?' Karl repeated. 'As much as you care about your wife?'

Jesus, he knew who he was, Duncan thought, hurrying on lamely. 'Vicky and me, we're over. We can have a divorce anytime.'

'My child,' Karl said, his voice almost a whisper, 'you ruined my child.'

'I liked her a lot –'

'*You liked her!*' Karl repeated, outraged. 'She should have had a man who loved her, not *liked* her. She was worth that. Not worth someone like you.' He gestured to the room. 'Look at this, this is fetid. *You're* fetid –'

'Hey, watch it!'

Karl moved towards him, Duncan automatically stepping back.

'My daughter's heartbroken because of you. Not just because of a bad love affair, with a cruel man, but because you *planned* it. Because you're Vicky's husband, because you knew it would kill her to know what you had done to Elise. You slept with my child to get your revenge.' His voice wavered, his fists tight. 'What are you?'

Duncan frowned. 'Hey?'

'I want to know what *thing* does something like this.'

Turning away, Duncan flicked the locks on his suitcase and moved to the door. He was certain that Karl wasn't the rough type – a reasonable man, in fact, one more hurt than enraged.

'Elise won't ever see me again,' Duncan said, moving to the top of the stairs. 'I'm getting out of Lancashire. That's what you want, isn't it?'

'What about your mistress?'

'Freda? Oh, we go back a long way, but it's time to

call that quits too.' Duncan paused, thinking quickly. 'Maybe I should turn over a new leaf. Go straight.'

'How can you live with yourself?' Karl asked, baffled. He couldn't understand. 'How can you look at your reflection and live with what you've done?'

'She'll forget me in a few weeks –'

Flushing, Karl leaned towards Duncan. 'Elise will *never* forget you, and I will never forget you. And God will never forget you. Remember that, Duncan Oldenshaw, when you leave here tonight you leave with my curse in your ears and your soul damned.'

'I don't believe in God,' Duncan said blithely, walking off and heading towards the front door.

God, that had been a close shave, he thought, but he had got off lightly. All he had to do was leave town – and he wanted to do that anyway. Get away from Portswood, Stockport and Freda. He had come for his revenge, and had got it. What point was there staying on now?

Hurriedly he crossed the hall. If Karl Straub knew, that meant that Elise had told him. And that also meant that she might have told Doug too. A distraught father Duncan could cope with – but not his brother. Not after what he had done to him.

With his suitcase in one hand, Duncan opened the front door and was immediately pulled out onto the street. He fell clumsily to his knees, Doug raining blows down on his head, Duncan throwing up his hands to protect himself.

'Jesus!' the landlady screamed, lights going on in the other houses as people hurried out to watch the fight. 'Stop 'em!'

Duncan was trying to get up, but he kept losing his footing in the snow, his shoes slipping on the ice.

Uncontrollable with anger, Doug punched his brother's face, feeling his nose break and the wet warmth of blood on his knuckles. Berserk with rage, Doug couldn't see Duncan, only Emma's face and the black shell of the burned-out pub. Then he saw Freda's face – and Billy's, the night he died. All the images of the people Duncan had destroyed were imprinted on his brother's brain and fists until he was mad with fury, the snow falling on both of them as Doug kicked his brother into the gutter.

Around them people gathered to watch, Karl finally breaking through the huddle and trying to pull Doug off Duncan. But he was too strong, maddened, and out of control.

'Leave him! He's not worth it! He's an animal!' Karl shouted, moving between the two men. Douglas's eyes were unfocused as he tried to push Karl out of the way. 'Douglas, stop this! You can't kill your own brother! That would make you as bad as he is. That would make you his equal.'

Pushing Karl aside, Doug went after Duncan again. He was crawling on the cobbles, groaning, his jacket soaked with blood, his nose split open.

And still Doug laid into him. 'That's for Emma!' he said, kicking him in the stomach. 'That's for Vicky!' he said, kicking him in the kidneys. 'That's for Elise!' again he kicked him. 'And this is for Billy. For Billy!' As he said the child's name, Doug hauled his brother to his feet and then struck him full in the face, blood spraying everywhere as Duncan went down again.

'Enough!' Karl shouted. 'Enough!'

As though shaken from a trance Doug stopped. The crowd was silent as they looked at the bloodied figure in the snow and the big man standing over him. Blinking, Doug came back to reality, his arms hanging by his side.

He heard the whispers behind him – and then saw what he had done.

Turning to Karl, he said simply: 'Is he dead?'

Karl shook his head. 'No.'

'Then he should be,' Doug replied, breathing heavily. 'You should have let me finish him off.'

Slowly Karl walked over to Duncan, still lying in the gutter where he had fallen. Without emotion he looked down into his face and then studied his bloodied body. He would live, Karl thought. He would live and repeat his mistakes. Over and over. With someone else's wife, or someone else's daughter. His charm and good looks would lull them all in, and ruin them all. Even with a broken nose, Duncan would seduce any woman who took his fancy.

And then Karl Straub – gentle, kind, educated Karl – felt a rage he had never felt before. Not for Hitler, or for the bigots who had hounded him, but for the man who had abused his child. His Elise. The rage pumped up inside him like a black cancer; it choked him and made his stomach heave. And then he struck.

With the full force of his boot Karl kicked out at Duncan Oldenshaw's head. There was a whoosh as his foot moved through the snowy air. Then a strange sound followed. It echoed for an unhealthy moment like a child's scream as the steel toecap of Karl's boot shattered every one of Duncan's perfect white teeth.

Chapter Fifty-Seven

Knowing that Freda would snatch the key from her, Ada handed it over. Enough time had passed anyway, the deed would be done. Unmoving, Ada sat in the rocking chair and heard her daughter unlock the door and run out into the night. She didn't know how Freda would get to Portswood and she didn't care. She didn't care that Freda was dressed only in a suit, or that she wore no hat.

It was a cold night. But she felt nothing, no anxiety, no concern. Freda Hargreaves would never come back, Ada realised. Slowly she struggled to her feet and looked out of the back door. She had always hated that entrance and now she knew why.

Only a few yards away the ginnel beckoned. But there was no one there – no men come calling, no ghosts. Only the snow falling, covering the last footsteps her daughter would ever leave there.

Chapter Fifty-Eight

The scandal rocked Stockport, rumours circulating like dark moths. Duncan had been badly injured, the gossip went, his face disfigured. Freda had got her man in the end. But no one else would ever want Duncan Oldenshaw again. They were tied to each other by their own wickedness, locked into a relationship where every day they would look at each other and be reminded of what they had done.

There was to be no peace nor triumph for either of them. A story went round that Duncan had to wear false teeth after Karl had finished with him. Ada thought about that often; wondered how attractive Duncan would seem when he had to put his teeth in a glass at night. But she never felt any pity for Freda. She was simply glad that her daughter had gone.

That dreadful night Karl took Vicky aside and told her what had happened. He had expected her to overreact, but she didn't. Instead she had listened quietly. Then she had gone upstairs to see Elise. The girl had been sitting on her bed, her head bowed, flinching when Vicky walked in.

Without a word, Vicky had sat on the bed next to her. Gently she had taken her hand. Elise had never moved, too ashamed to speak. Then Vicky had put her arm around Elise, the girl rigid, Vicky holding her for a long moment before Elise finally began to cry. She cried and cried and clung on to the woman she had inadvertently betrayed, Vicky rocking and soothing her. Like a mother would.

Outside the bedroom door, Karl had listened and knew that from then onwards there was a bond between the two women he loved that would never be broken.

'Well, I'll be damned!' Bessie Cork said when she heard the news. 'I heard that Duncan Oldenshaw's neck were broken.'

'That would kill him, wouldn't it?' Lizzie replied, frowning.

'You *can't* kill that bugger!' Bessie retorted, looking out of the window of the shop. 'I saw Ada Hargreaves this morning –'

'How's she looking?'

'You'd think she'd be worn down, but not a bit of it! Looks like she'd had a bloody weekend in Blackpool.'

'Maybe she's glad that Freda's gone.' Lizzie paused, thinking. 'Perhaps Duncan and Freda will get married now –'

'You talk rubbish!' Bessie snapped. 'Marriage, marriage, marriage! That's the only thing on your mind, Lizzie Antrim. What about that Elise girl, hey? Ruined, that's what she is. *Ruined.* There's no man who'll have her now.' She continued to stare out of the window, dropping her voice. 'Not that I'm one to gossip, but if I've said it once, I've said it a hundred times – they're a rough lot at that pub.'

'Aye, Bessie –'

'Don't aye Bessie me!' she snorted back. 'Ada Hargreaves came from the slums and she can pretend all she likes, but in the end breeding will out.'

Time moved on and six months after Freda left The

Sixpenny Winner the atmosphere had changed completely. There were no more sly looks, whispers, no more undercurrents. In the pub, at least.

'Well, there's only one thing to be said for scandal,' Ada told Karl, 'it's good for business.'

That much was true. People loved to talk and they loved to gawk at the residents of The Sixpenny Winner. Luckily they also loved to drink. Daily the cash register tingled with money and although no one ever said it, the customers were almost disappointed that Duncan and Freda had gone, because now the days of calm had finally arrived.

Yet if it was easy for Ada to cope, Elise was not used to being gossiped about and only after she started her studies at teacher training college did she begin to regain her confidence.

Of all the people who had been involved, Ada expected Douglas to fare the worst. But oddly he didn't slip into depression. Freda had gone and, in her going, she freed him. Together he and Karl ran The Sixpenny Winner and Doug became an uncle to Elise and Stella, fussing them as though they were his own children. The devil had freed him at last, Ada thought wistfully. In time he would fall in love again. In time.

'Oi, Al Weeks!' Ada shouted one morning as she was preparing to open the pub.

Al stopped on the pavement and tipped his hat to her. ''Lo there, Ada.'

'You're a sight for sore eyes, Al! Where have you been hiding all these weeks?'

'I've been around.'

Ada put her head on one side. Al had been a good friend to her; she would never forget that.

'You busy?'

'Always busy.'

'Shame.'

He frowned. 'How come?'

'Well, I thought that if you weren't so busy, you might like to come in and have a drink.'

He raised his eyebrows. 'I'm barred.'

'Who barred you?' Ada asked, teasing him.

'Oh, some landlady a while back.'

'Sounds a right bitch.'

'She were a bit of a tartar all right,' Al replied, teasing her in return.

'So she barred you?'

'She did that.'

'What for?'

'Threw me out for fighting.'

'You still fight?'

'Too old.'

'You still drink?'

'I do that,' he replied, smiling as Ada held the door open to let him in.

The following winter the old cat died. In an act of revenge, Ada had it stuffed and put on top of The Sixpenny Winner's cabinet, where it stared out, unblinking, over the customers' heads. Mac Potter tried his luck once more, but Ada wasn't interested so he finally married Lizzie when he got tired of running. As for the corner shop, Bessie Cork never sold it and died there four years later.

Sometimes Ada would look out at night and think back, remembering, just as she would visit the rooms upstairs and think of Clem. She told anyone who asked that she had had a rum life, but a good one.

And when she died they put on her headstone the words:

ADA HARGREAVES,
Wife, Mother and Grandmother.
And dearly loved Landlady
of The Sixpenny Winner.

She thought God would laugh at that.

'So there you have it, the story of The Sixpenny Winner. I said it were a good tale, didn't I? The pub's still standing so you could go and have a look for yourself, and the dog's still there, with the stuffed cat sitting on top of it.

'Like I said at the beginning, my grandfather told me the early part of the story. Who was my grandfather? I thought you'd have guessed. It were Al Weeks. You look surprised, but there you go, it were Al Weeks and who better to know all about it?

'Of course, when I grew up I remembered things for myself – like Ada, when she were getting on, and the way Douglas Oldenshaw used to call time. People thought he'd been unlucky in love, but he didn't seem to mind. I think myself he found some widow over in Salford, but he kept it quiet. That were the rumour anyway.

'As for Elise, she distrusted men for a long time after Duncan Oldenshaw. Wanted someone ordinary, she said. With all her education she could have picked someone important, but that weren't her way. She wanted to love and be loved, and she was.

'The local lad she married thought she were a goddess. He were in awe of her and told her every day how much she meant to him. He were all right to look at, but he had no money to speak of, and little education. But he could give the one thing Elise Straub needed more than anything – he gave her love.

'We're at the end now, story over. Just one thing left to say. That local lad loved Elise until she died. Loved her a little more every day – and never so much as looked at another woman.

'How do I know? Because I wed Elise Straub. And that local lad were me.'